*Excellent story, compelli
book by Author Dennis C(
not too far-fetched. Mr. Calloway took a step into the future,
without inventing unbelievable technology to get the job
done. I was particularly drawn to the characters. I wanted
them to succeed. There are multiple parallel stories that come
together in the end. I look forward to what I hope is a sequel.*

G.S.

*I couldn't put the book down. The characters were excellent,
and the breakdown of civilized behavior was brilliant. It takes
talent to create a page turner, the research is just time
consuming.*

T.H.

*First book I have read from this author and it was great! I
found it very fast-paced and interesting. I confess that I love
post-apocalyptic literature and have read many books on this
theme. This book had a new twist to the theme. The only
problem I had with the book was that the characters were
almost too polarized - either good or bad - and people are
much more complex than this. Still, I enjoyed the book and
I'm looking forward to the sequel!*

K.U.

*"I found this book very entertaining and it kept my attention
from the first page to the last. I'm sure that the book could
have easily been 600+ pages or even longer had the author
'filled in all the details'. In some cases, the story didn't need
those extra details included. One of the story lines was
predictable based on the title alone, but the path the author
takes you on was interesting and entertaining. I found myself
rooting for the good guys and smiling when the bad guys got
what was coming to them. I can't wait to read the sequel.*

K.B.

*The book was filled with action, really showed the depth of
humanity's depravity as well as our capacity for great
magnanimity. Return to Earth was well written from a strong
woman's viewpoint. I thoroughly enjoyed the entire book.*

S.M.

The lucky ones who managed to escape to the moon could only watch helplessly as the rogue planet Lycos slammed into Earth. As fate would have it, they were the future of humankind, with visions of rebuilding the human race on Europa, a distant moon of Jupiter.

But in an attempt to mold this new world in his own image, the psychotic moon base leader, Soren, commandeers the ship for his select few and abandons those who might resist his unique vision of their future — condemning them to certain death.

Left behind on the moon with a handful of desperate survivors and dwindling resources, Tess Robinson, a rising star in NASA with a troubled past, is thrust into a position where she must make peace with her ghosts if they are to survive.

Now, in a frantic race against time and unimaginable odds, they must return to the broken earth if they hope to make the journey to Europa; but they must survive not only the final destructive forces unleashed on the planet, but the barbaric survivors they left behind.

RETURN
TO
EARTH

DENNIS CALLOWAY

10-6-2024

Faith —
I hope you enjoy the story!
— Dennis

First Edition Design Publishing
Sarasota, Florida

Return To Earth
Copyright ©2015 Dennis Calloway

ISBN 978-1622-878-14-7 PRINT HC
ISBN 978-1622-878-12-3 PRINT PBK
ISBN 978-1622-878-13-0 EBOOK

LCCN 2015930680

February 2015

Published and Distributed by
First Edition Design Publishing, Inc.
P.O. Box 20217, Sarasota, FL 34276-3217
www.firsteditiondesignpublishing.com

ALL RIGHTS RESERVED. No part of this book publication may be reproduced, stored in a retrieval system, or transmitted in any form or by any means — electronic, mechanical, photo-copy, recording, or any other — except brief quotation in reviews, without the prior permission of the author or publisher.

ACKNOWLEDGMENTS & THANKS

A debt of gratitude: to the team at First Edition Design Publishing (specifically Debi for her expertise, guidance, and patience in helping me through all the details of publishing my first novel and Michelle for her awesome editing and inspiring comments); to Beverly Herkommer for being my first reviewer and providing me with a wealth of meticulous and invaluable notes.

Many thanks to all of my relatives in Michigan, Mississippi, Texas and Maryland—their support has been uplifting! Thanks to my two daughters, Mariel and Nia, for their support, encouragement, and excitement! Thanks to all those who read and listened and contributed to the manuscript along the way; and very special thanks to my wife, MJ, for her enthusiasm, support and patience.

Table of Contents

I

THE MOON – SEPTEMBER 2053 1
  TESS 1

II

THE EARTH – AUGUST 2051 8
  STAN'S MAD DASH 8
  IN THE NICK OF TIME 16
  THELMA 25
  THE FLIGHT OF GALILEO2 33
  UNDERGROUND 55
  THELMA'S CRUISE 70
  LYCOS HITS 80

III

THE MOON – SEPTEMBER 2053 83
  STRANGE OBSERVATIONS 83
  NOLA AND SOREN 95
  THE BASE MEETING 103
  DAN STUMBLES ONTO THE TRUTH 109
  ABANDONED! 116
  THE COLD TRUTH 121
  HENRY'S DISCOVERY 128
  INTO THE VOID 136
  TROUBLE AT HOME BASE 152
  THE UNITED NATIONS' COMPOUND 166
  RETURN TO EARTH 179

IV

THE EARTH – OCTOBER 2053 192

    WRIGHT AIRFIELD 192
    MAN'S BEST FRIEND 196
    INSIDE THE FUEL CONTROL CENTER 201
    NO WHERE TO RUN 205
    THE SHELTER 214
    SHEILA 219
    THE BARBARIANS 224
    THELMA'S ANIMALS 239
    IMPRISONED 243
    ANIMAL CONVOY 251
    A WATERY GRAVE 255
    HARLAN PENITENTIARY 264
    THE FINAL PURIFICATION 284
    INTO THE LION'S DEN 300
    THE DYING PLANET 315

V

SPACE – JANUARY 2054 318

    THE CASSIOPEIA 318

VI

EUROPA - FEBRUARY 2054 344

I
THE MOON
SEPTEMBER 2053

TESS

1

"Tess! Wake up! Wake up! It's just a dream!"

Tess's eyes popped open at the sound of her name, but those eyes weren't the soft brown eyes she was complimented on as a young girl or swooned over as a young woman. They were dark haunted stones filled with fear, sadness, and something else: *unforgiving remorse*.

"I...uh...hey...okay. I'm o...kay. Oh God...sorry about that. I didn't mean to scare you," Tess said, the words sounding strange and distant to her ears.

"No problem, Tessy," said Reynald. "You have another nightmare?"

Tess thought about the fading dream and was amazed that it was already losing its sharp edges and hard reality. She knew that all but the worst part of the dream would be gone before she was even fully awake. But not the emptiness. Not the guilt. Those would stay. What always stayed in her conscious, awake mind was the sound of her husband Stan and their son Lenny, screaming hysterically as their bodies were shredded into hot strips of bloody skin and bones and hair.

She debated whether to tell him the truth this time. That she was having the same recurring nightmare. She used to think that her internal debate of whether or not to share with him was mostly because of her, because of her past. But the fog in her mind had been clearing lately, and she finally realized that the source of her struggle was because of *him* and a deeply intuitive sense that she couldn't trust him. Usually, when she had this dream or one similar, she just lied to him and said she didn't remember. Today, she was curious, "Yeah, same one. I don't know why I keep having it," she lied.

Reynald looked at her with a mixture of tired patience and barely hidden annoyance. "I know it takes time to get over things," he said patronizingly, "and it's not easy to lose someone you love, but you've got to get over this or you'll never be able to move forward with...your life."

With *me* was how he wanted to finish the sentence and Tess knew it. She also knew that Reynald was not an empathetic man and was extremely selfish. Why was she even with him? He wasn't half the man Stan was and never would be. The answer to that question was right in front of her. It was in her life now, in her work, in every goddamn thing she had to do these days. Rey was there because he was one way of coping with the shit that she and everyone else here had to deal with. He used her for sex. She used him for coping. It was a win-win solution, or at least she hoped it was. It was one way of being able to move forward one step at a time, one *day* at a time.

But today, she saw through his fake concern as easily as she could have seen through the innocently wagging tail of a dog, waiting to be petted and praised, while a steaming pile of shit sat simmering in the corner. "Rey," she said with a hint of bitterness on her tongue, and then she stopped. Did she really feel up to arguing with him today? Their arguments always ended the same way; he would tell her how much she clung to the past and she would tell him to go to hell. No, she decided. I'm done with him, and I'm done with his bullshit. "Forget it. I'm late for work."

Rey watched her as she slid off the bed (a bit unsteadily he noticed). He eyed the brown skin of her buttocks greedily as she threw on her jumper. He was tempted to ask her if she had time for a quickie, but he could sense that she wouldn't be interested even if she had time.

He remained in bed with his arms crooked under his neck. Ages ago it seemed, when their relationship was just starting out, he thought that he might be able to control her. But more and more, he began to realize that Soren was right; he couldn't control her, and if she began to get suspicious, she would fight them every step of the way.

Grabbing her boots and suit, she palmed open the door and stepped out, "Lock up when you leave," she announced. She didn't look back

2

Tess's gloved hand gripped the wheel of the Rover as her mind replayed bits and pieces of her nightmare. Despite how horrific it was, she was finding it hard to remember. Only general impressions and feelings remained; the things that would stay with her forever. Tangled within these thoughts and memories like poisonous vines in a field of dry crabgrass was Reynald and her general distrust (and dislike) of him. She had noticed that he was very secretive these days and seemed to always be running errands for Soren. She'd seen him hand-carrying reports from the astronomy lab, showing an active interest in maintenance bay activities, and even joining in on the weekly food count. He was really the *man about town* these days, and he did all of it in the name of Soren. *"Soren needs me to check on this"* or *"Soren needs to know the status of that"*. And speaking of Soren, where was he? The more Reynald seemed to be everywhere, the more Soren seemed to be missing in action. She thought about this and then laughed bitterly. Maybe Reynald is planning a coup?

She powered the Rover over a small gray dune. The floorboard vibrated as the underside scraped over several buried rocks in the dune. She took the Rover this morning, because she didn't feel like walking to the observation area even though it would have only been a 15-minute walk, which she usually enjoyed. And she purposely took the long route because it gave her a chance to clear her head and think, even while she put the Rover through its paces as she sped along the rutted road. Although she was familiar with the route and knew where the tricky turns were, she still forced herself to take it slow on the bumps, lest she have what they sometimes called an *out of body and off the surface experience*.

Her mind reluctantly turned to Rey again. His attitude toward her was getting uglier and uglier. If she had real feelings for him, she would have been worried he was about to break up with her, but she almost welcomed that prospect. He was becoming increasingly more difficult to talk to and when he *did* talk, he avoided answering any questions about his activities. At first, Tess simply thought that it was just one of his weird nuances, like answering a question with a question. But one day it dawned on her that he never, ever gave a direct answer to anything related to his meetings with Soren or why he was so interested in maintenance these days. When asked, he would spend a great deal of time talking in big, loopy circles. By the time he'd finished, you were either lost in the minutia, or you wanted him to shut up. One time, Tess let him drone on about nothing, and when he finished, she said, "So what? That still doesn't tell me what you've been doing."

The flash of dark anger that had crossed his face was brief, but it was there. He probably didn't even realize it had happened, but it did. In that brief instant, Tess knew that this was the real Rey; a carefully concealed monstrosity under the mask. A face that skirted the edges of insanity. The mean, hateful look was only there for a fraction of a second and then it was gone, replaced by the smiling and affable Rey. He squeezed her on the arm and then said he had to take care of some reports for Soren and was out the door. After that incident, she made it a point to never ask him about what he was doing. That had happened only a few days ago, and it was then that she told herself she was done with him.

His cold lack of sympathy this morning bothered her more than she wanted to admit. And the more she thought about it, the more she realized that her feelings of distrust were not just a symptom of this morning, but was how she felt *all the time*. They had been together for six months, and she was now starting to realize (maybe now finally accepting the fact) that she didn't really trust him.

She knew of course, that her current situation had initially blinded her to this realization. She couldn't blame herself though, not really. Everyone here went through some sort of an adjustment. You had to. The alternatives were either suicide or insanity, of which they already had a few of both. Some did quite well here. Others seemed to draw up inside themselves like turtles retreating from the outside world.

As she drew close to the huge silver radar bolted to the observation deck platform, she slowed down and prepared to pull the Rover into the Vehicle Recharging Station. She untethered the Rover's cable and plugged it into the power outlet. Through her gloved hands, she could feel the slight vibration of the electrical current flowing into the Rover. She turned her microphone on and heard the familiar beeps in her earpiece telling her that her microphone was now "live". "This is Tess at Observation Point Two. Checking in...over." There was a slight pause, and then a voice responded in her ear.

"Well hey Tess, you're out there early today, huh? I was wondering if you were going to check in or if you were just taking the Rover out for a spin."

At the sound of Henry's voice, Tess couldn't help but smile, despite how depressing the day started. Henry was not a very outgoing person. He was studious and always serious and prone to using extremely dry humor. Occasionally, he would make a statement during their meetings, and they wouldn't even know he was joking until he burst out laughing at his own joke. This little eccentricity made others feel uncomfortable towards him, but not Tess. She was a serious person too, and she knew enough about Henry to know that he was extremely reliable. She liked that about him and was always able to confide in him.

"If I had known it was you on duty Henry, I would have dressed for the occasion," Tess replied.

There was silence on the other end and then Henry guffawed. Tess raised her eyebrows and shook her head.

"So, what brings you out here so early Tess," he asked. "Your shift doesn't start for another two hours, give or take."

"I couldn't sleep," she admitted. "Old nightmares are still plaguing me, I guess. So, I thought I'd come out early and get some extra readings from this observation point. I don't come to this one much."

"Roger," Henry replied. "Actually, I'm glad you're up. Yesterday, I picked up some odd signals that I'd like to talk to you about."

"Sure Henry, no problem. Maybe we can talk later this evening, after tonight's meeting. I'll meet you at your station right after the meeting."

"Sounds good to me. Just ring me up when you're ready," Henry responded. There were a series of beeps and chimes and Henry spoke up again, this time a little more seriously. "I need to go Tess. It looks like one of the servers is acting up again. Call me if you need anything, I'll be right here."

"Thanks Henry." *Oddities? She thought. What kind of oddities?* Over the past two or three years, damn near everything you saw, heard, felt, and sensed out here were oddities. Well, she figured she'd find out soon enough when they met up this evening. She unpacked her equipment and connected them to the observation port outlets. After booting up the Navi-Computer, she typed in her location coordinates quickly, despite her bulky, gloved fingers. She watched the program on the screen run through its process of establishing its physical location.

The boot-up process finally ended. Next to the cursor a green line blinked on the dark screen, waiting for her to type her query. With a heavy heart, she typed in "E-A-R-T-H" and reluctantly aimed the receiver upwards towards the smashed remains that was the planet Earth.

3

Her breath always got caught in her throat whenever she gazed up at the place that used to be home to humankind. What remained of the earth couldn't really be called a planet in the real sense of the word. It was more like a planetary asteroid field in Tess's opinion. When *Lycos* smashed into Earth in the fall of 2051, the resulting impact left a gaping crater in the earth the size of Siberia. Over the past two years, Tess had observed that massive earthquakes, tidal floods, and increased volcanic activity had transformed the earth into a deformed and broken sphere that looked barely connected.

North and South America appeared to be loosely intact, but Tess could see that there was significant flooding. The European landmasses were reduced to a group of islands in an ill-formed archipelago and further southeast was nothing but a turbulent expanse of bright orange where Tess could see huge jets of lava being hurled miles high into the thin atmosphere.

Her weekly readings fluctuated wildly. It seemed to her that the entire planet was winding down. The earth itself seemed to be getting physically longer as if connected only by a *memory* of a gravitational field. Even the planetary rotation of the earth was erratic. The normal 24-hour rotation had increased from 24 hours to 30 hours and then from 30 to 40 hours. Over the past several weeks, it had crept up to 48 hours. Tess had a feeling that eventually, the entire mass would rotate at an increasingly infinitesimal rate or stop rotating altogether; perpetual daylight for one half of the world and perpetual night for the other side.

Held together by the weakened gravitational pull of the planet was a grotesque asteroid field that circled the planet. She hated seeing that field. It made her feel ill and somewhat disconnected from reality. She would always turn away quickly, breathing hard while trying to get her heart to slow down.

RETURN TO EARTH

As she looked through the high-powered telescope on this day, she could see that the North American continent still resembled what she remembered of the United States and Canada. But as she tracked east, it looked as if the entire east coast had been swallowed up by water. The rest of the planet had been so jumbled up, that sometimes she wasn't sure what landmass she was looking at.

She pushed away from the telescope and closed her eyes, certain that she was about to pass out. She came very close to calling Henry to let him know that she might need some help, but slowly she brought herself under control. Her mind was still going in a million different directions, and she was sweating profusely inside her suit, but she wasn't going to pass out—at least not *this* time.

Oh Stan, she thought. *Stan...Stan...*

II
THE EARTH
AUGUST 2051
(A STEP BACK)

STAN'S MAD DASH

1

They were running late...damn late! Stan thought for the third time that morning. He was part of a small convoy that consisted of only three vehicles; a military Humvee, his Jeep Wrangler, and some government-issued SUV, which followed closely behind him. He was driving white-knuckled behind the Humvee in front of him, constantly aware of his son's nervous chatter in the back seat and his mother-in-law's frantic, scared front-seat driving.

"Stan, don't take the curves so quickly! We're going to tip over!" She had one hand planted on the dashboard in front of her, and the other had a death grip on the passenger side hand rail.

"I know mom, but I'll be damned if I'm getting left behind!" Stan started calling Tess's mother "mom" barely a month after they got married. His parents had both died when he was young, so it took a while for him to say it without thinking about it. And it was a little weird at first, but he did it because Tess had asked him to, and he noticed that it made her feel good to hear him say it. At the moment, however, he was having an extremely difficult time trying not to *curse* at her, let alone call her "mom."

"Sorry for yelling at you mom, but those guys are really flooring it up there!" he motioned toward the lead vehicle. "I think I can get to the launch site on my own, but these men are armed, and we really need to stick with them." He glanced at his watch. "Plus, we don't have much time to get to the airfield." He swerved around a burning pickup truck. The engine was on fire, and a huge plume of black smoke poured out from underneath the hood. In back, Lenny stared at the burning truck with his mouth hanging open.

She's terrified, Stan thought, as he gripped the wheel tighter. If she only knew how screwed up his sense of direction was right now, she'd really lose it. He never realized how much he depended on the city buildings as landmarks and how heavily he relied on actual street signs to get him to where he needed to go. This place looked like a war zone. Store-front window displays were either missing or burned beyond recognition. Buildings on both sides of the street were damaged. Most of them showed fire damage, but occasionally, he would pass one with a huge gaping hole in it; the result of some very powerful explosives.

They had left the shelter some 20 minutes before in a flurry of confusion and mad panic, sprinting after the soldiers who were assigned to them. When they had returned to the shelter from the hospital that morning, they found that they were part of the last group scheduled to be taken by helicopter to the launch site. In addition to him, his mother-in-law Cora, and Lenny, there were only a handful of soldiers and a few civilians remaining. He didn't recognize any of the civilians, but he would have been willing to bet his last paycheck that they were politicians.

Stan wasn't too surprised to see that they were the last group to go. Mission Control had been quietly transporting small groups of people to the shuttles over the past month to avoid alerting the masses and quite a number of them had actually been *living* on the shuttles for weeks now.

During these last days, it was no longer a secret that the shuttles would be taking off from Wright Airfield in North San Antonio, Texas. And Mission Control desperately wanted activity on the base and near the shuttle to appear normal, so as not to incite a panic amongst the hundreds of people camped out in front of the electrical fences surrounding the airfield. There was a strong feeling that if the people outside the gates caught wind of an impending launch, they would riot. As callous as it seemed, when the time came to launch, Mission Control had hoped to do it quickly and without warning to the now peaceful people.

Before all hell broke loose, the plan had been for the remaining people to be transported to the shuttle by the two helicopters assigned to their shelter. When Stan and his family arrived from the hospital, a young army captain told them that the helicopters were returning from the airfield after dropping off a group of people. They had hustled up to the roof of the compound's main building and were waiting there when a huge explosion seemed to rock the building. They all ran to the edge of the roof and saw black smoke rising through the trees that bordered the compound, not more than half a mile away.

2

One of the security team members yanked his walkie-talkie off his hip and yelled into it, "Helo3-Alpha, Helo3-Alpha? What the hell happened?" When there was no answer, he tried the other helicopter, "Helo3-Bravo, Helo3-Bravo? I've lost communications with Helo3-Alpha. What's going on out there?"

The soldier was looking at them blankly when a frantic voice seemed to explode out of the talkie, *"Helo3-Alpha just got hit by a surface to air missile! Who the fuck has SAMs out here? Oh shit! We've been targeted! Evasive maneuvers! Evasive man..."*

Right before the helicopter pilot could finish his last comment, Stan caught a brief glimpse of a flash of light out in the woods, probably 100 or 200 yards away. An object flew straight from the flash and then angled up towards the sky and was gone, leaving a trail of white smoke behind it. *Missiles,* Stan thought, as the rocket quickly made its way to its target.

The helicopter went up in a ball of fire, sending huge shards of metal and shrapnel everywhere. The explosion knocked Stan off his feet and onto the tarred rooftop. As his head cleared, he looked around and saw that he wasn't the only one knocked to the ground. He helped Lenny up and went over to where Cora was lying and pulled her up. He was about to head back to the edge of the roof, when one of the soldiers urgently waved him back down. He froze in his tracks and dropped to one knee, motioning for his mother-in-law to do the same. Lenny copied what his father did. Stan couldn't hear anything at first, but then the unmistakable sound of men yelling drifted across the air. A minute later, they heard gunfire.

The soldiers were quick to respond. They motioned for everyone to follow them as they half crawled to the fire escape ladder at the back-end of the rooftop. They hustled down the ladder quickly, taking time to help Cora down without incident. Once down, they sprinted to the motor pool where they had only recently parked their vehicles. The lead soldier sprinted ahead of the group to get the motor pool doors open so they could roll out quickly.

As Stan, Cora, and Lenny got to the building, the wide silver doors of the motor pool slid open. The young soldier who had sprinted ahead tossed Stan the keys to his Jeep Wrangler. Two of the soldiers hopped into the only Humvee parked in the motor pool. The doors had been removed and Stan was thankful that he was driving his own vehicle. The other soldiers hustled the three politicians into a black SUV. Before hopping in the driver's seat, one of the soldiers looked at Stan solemnly and said, "Whatever you do, don't stop, and make sure you keep up with us. We're going to access the airfield on the other side of the river. That's our rendezvous plan, and other soldiers will meet us there, but we've got to do just one thing."

"What's that?" asked Stan

The young soldier grimaced and said, "We just have to *get* there!"

3

Now here they were, driving like mad men, trying to navigate the vehicle-choked streets. Debris was everywhere, and they were constantly swerving around stranded cars, trucks and buses...and bodies. They hadn't been driving long, but Stan kept nervously looking over his shoulders, thinking that they had been seen leaving the compound.

This was the first time he had been out of the compound and into the city proper since they had been evacuated. On one hand, Stan felt that they were lucky. The city was deserted since most people were either in shelters or at the airfield. On the other hand, there were a lot of dead bodies in the road. At first, Stan could not bring himself to purposefully drive over the bodies. It just seemed *wrong*. But each time he detoured around the bodies, he fell further and further behind the lead vehicle. The SUV behind him leaned on his horn each time Stan slowed down.

He tried to convince himself that it was just debris he was rolling over and not human bodies and he almost made himself believe this until he made the mistake of letting his window down to spit. As he prepared himself to spit, he heard the unmistakable crunch of bones under his wheels. He was so unnerved by this that he had no force to spit and ended up drooling on himself. It seemed every street they turned onto was littered with bodies. But they weren't just on the road. They were in cars, propped up against buildings, and they even passed a number of them hanging (apparent suicides) from upstairs windows. The vast majority of the dead, however, were the people caught up in the rioting and the apparent stand-off with the National Guard.

A few times, they came across people who seemed to appear out of nowhere, darting out of the shadows as their vehicles neared them. They either yelled for help or yelled for them to stop, but they all had the same crazed, murderous look in their eyes. Once, a group of men got close enough for one of them to actually break the rear-view mirror from the lead vehicle's right side. The man's momentum caused him to bump into the vehicle, which violently spun him around, momentarily disorienting him. Stan swerved quickly to miss him, but the vehicle behind him plowed into the man. Horror stricken; Stan looked into his rear-view mirror in time to see the man's compatriots laughing as they started stripping things from the dying man's pockets.

Stan could not tell how many times they had to detour from their planned route since he wasn't exactly sure what that route was. At one point, their speed dropped to a dangerous ten miles per hour because the street was jammed up with debris and burning vehicles. At this speed, they were like sitting ducks. Stan looked around nervously, unconsciously putting some distance between his vehicle and the lead vehicle, when all of a sudden, the lead vehicle appeared to rise off the ground as if it had rolled onto an invisible ramp. A fraction of a second later, an orange glow seemed to grow and swell underneath the vehicle, like a fiery whirlpool. The accompanying explosion catapulted the Humvee like a huge boulder being launched from a trebuchet. It landed on its hood, the front end collapsing beneath the Humvee's weight. Stan had only a second to wonder if the men were still alive, before another rocket smashed into the vehicle. The explosion jerked Stan to his senses, and he stamped down hard on the gas.

As he picked up speed, he could see people on the other side of the street, working furiously. He began to feel thick, smothering dread fill his senses, as he realized that they were probably reloading. He turned hard to the right to avoid the burned out remains of an armored truck and kept his foot glued to the floorboard. He was vaguely aware of his mother-in-law screaming. As he skidded past the burning military vehicle, he glanced into his rear-view mirror and could see a group of men and a few women firing into the third vehicle and at the rear of his vehicle. *"Get down!"* he yelled to Cora and Lenny.

Amazingly, they avoided getting shot, but one bullet ripped the driver's side rear view mirror completely off. Just before he turned at the next intersection, Stan saw the attackers firing into the last SUV at point blank range. Eyes wide and staring straight ahead, he floored the gas pedal again, his only thought being to get the hell out of this area as fast as possible.

He had driven wildly, blindly from the area, not paying attention to where he was going. He just wanted to be anywhere but there. When he finally slowed down after 20 minutes, he realized that he was nowhere near the river and this rendezvous location at the Wright Airfield. Behind him, Lenny spoke up, "Dad...are we almost there?"

"I'm not sure son," Stan said. He looked at Lenny and could see the strain in his face. He prayed that his son was handling this mess. "How are you feeling son?"

"I'm okay, just scared," his son replied. "Why were those people shooting at us?"

"They're scared too, but the only way they know how to show it is by hurting someone else." Stan believed most of what he told his son, but not all of it. He knew that in the face of certain death, the darkest parts of humanity seep out; the evil, despairing part of the soul that has no sympathy, no remorse, and no pity. They should consider themselves lucky if their demise came as quickly as the soldiers did.

4

As Stan drove, he continued to encounter homemade roadblocks that didn't make sense. One would force him in one direction, while another one would almost have him doubling back. Eventually, he was able to figure out where he was and using a map, they found at an abandoned gas station, he was able to map out the quickest route to the airfield. He had no idea what they would do once they got there, since the roads there were jammed with vehicles and people, but he had to try.

He glanced down at his watch and realized that it was gone. He looked out at the weirdly overcast sky and guessed that it was sometime past noon. *Lycos* was now so close to the earth that it was hard to tell if it was dusk or dawn.

"Is mom up there already?" his son asked. "On the moon?"

"No Lenny, not yet," Stan responded as he put the truck in drive and started forward. "At least I don't believe her shuttle took off yet." He silently prayed that he was right about that.

"Will she be there at the launching site when we get there?" he continued.

"Well Lenny, since she's the pilot, her job is to fly the shuttle, so she probably won't be able to come down and talk to us when we get there." He couldn't help keep the tremor out of his voice.

"And when we get on the spaceship, you and I will be sitting right next to each other," his grandmother added, hugging him now that she had moved to the back seat.

He smiled at his mother-in-law's reflection in the rear-view mirror. "Yes, that's right Lenny. They told me that—" he broke off immediately. In the middle of the road were several people: three men and a woman. The woman was apparently being attacked by two of the men, and the third man was running toward them waving frantically for them to stop. His voiced yelled for help, but his eyes said something else. After what had just happened to them, Stan was extremely reluctant to slow down, let alone stop. He moved to the other lane and started speeding up, when Cora yelled out.

"We have to stop and help them Stan! Those other men are attacking that girl. Maybe trying to rape her!" She blurted out. "You can't just drive past her like that. How can we call ourselves decent people if we just drive on by without helping?"

"Mom, we can't help *everyone!*" he retorted, a little too harshly. "We couldn't even help the people in our own convoy. The world's coming to an end, and people are getting desperate. I can't take on those guys by myself, and I don't even have a gun! Even if we were lucky enough to help the girl, she can't come with us because we only have three authorization passes. We can't do anything for her. I'm sorry. I just can't put you and Lenny in another potentially dangerous situation."

His mother-in-law, sensing his resoluteness, quieted down and looked nervously out the window. He felt terrible for saying the things he said, but he was afraid and worried that they were running out of time. He gritted his teeth and stepped down on the gas pedal, showing no intention of stopping, when something flashed to his left. *"Shit! Get down!"* he yelled automatically. *"Get on the floor now...get on...!"* All of sudden, he felt the SUV lurch forward and tilt sickeningly to the right. At the same time, the windows exploded and he felt sharp, stinging spikes engulf his body. Somewhere in the back of his mind, he heard his son screaming and felt his mother-in-law's hand grabbing at the back of his shirt.

Even while bracing himself for the impact, he tried turning in his seat to look at his son. He found he couldn't do it while the vehicle continued its slow somersault to the right. He involuntarily shut his eyes, while his hands continued turning the vibrating steering wheel. Although he couldn't see it, he could feel that the vehicle was now upside down because he could feel the blood rushing to his head. Time seemed to drag on with the vehicle hanging suspended in space—its wheels still spinning madly on air—when all of a sudden, he felt it crash to the ground. His seatbelt locked painfully across his chest as the airbag exploded into his face in a mixture of white powder and broken chips of glass and his last thought before the darkness swallowed him up was of his son.

IN THE NICK OF TIME

1

"Stan!" Tess yelled into the cockpit phone receiver. "His name is 'Stan Robinson'! He was the Director of the Aerospace Engineering group here at the base. He'll have a 10-year-old boy with him...our son. His name is 'Lenny'. And my mother is with them. Her name is 'Cora. Cora A. Colsen'." Tess paused for a minute while the Air Force Sergeant on the other end asked her questions. "Yes. That's correct. Thank you for checking again!"

She fidgeted in her seat while the Air Force Sergeant checked his roster again. On the other launch pad, about 200 yards away, sat the other shuttle, the *Galileo2*. They weren't scheduled to leave for another four hours, so if Stan didn't make it onto her shuttle, he would definitely make it to the *Galileo2*. Her shuttle was the *Galileo1*, which she thought was a stupid way of naming the shuttles, but that was done long before she came into the picture.

She could feel herself becoming more and more upset and was powerless to stop it. This wasn't like missing a soccer match or showing up late for church. This was their *life*. They *had* to make it. It amazed her how quickly things went from bad to shit. A year ago, she had noticed that Lenny seemed to always be out of breath, but she didn't think twice about it because he was an active kid. He participated in all types of sports, and he was *always* running. But when she started to get letters from Lenny's gym teacher expressing concern, she decided she'd better take him to the doctor. What she thought might be asthma, turned out to be cardiomyopathy. She and Stan were in great health and never suspected that their son may have inherited some hidden heart disease gene.

In a few short months, his condition worsened. It got so bad that he had to be hospitalized for at least a week. The doctor told Stan and Tess that Lenny's heart had deteriorated to the point where a heart transplant was the only option left if he was to see his 12th birthday. That night, they got his name on the heart transplant list. Sadly, there were more than a few hearts available as *Lycos* made its way to Earth. People started giving up after the national lottery and mass suicides were cropping up across the country like weeds.

Although Tess would not have turned down a perfectly healthy heart for her son, she made it clear that she preferred not to have the heart of a suicide if at all possible. In this respect, fate was on her side because two weeks after she put her son's name on the list, they received the heart of a little boy who perished along with his family while trying to get out of Houston. The child had died of head trauma in an automobile accident.

The surgery went well, but the doctors wanted to keep him in the hospital for at least two weeks while his heart adapted to its new body. They made it clear that to move him sooner than that would put significant strain on his new heart. Unfortunately, command was not on the same schedule as their son's recuperation efforts, and the launch was moved up by three weeks. The only problem was that they never anticipated just how quickly things would deteriorate after the lottery.

Many businesses had shut down and the streets became extremely dangerous, even with a curfew in place. Without a healthy number of police available, it became virtually impossible to do anything outside of your house after dark. With only weeks remaining before launch, Mission Control ordered Tess to stay on the airfield. In fact, she spent many nights actually *in* the shuttle performing system checks and electrical diagnostics. Stan and her mother had remained at the shelter hospital with Lenny, anxiously waiting to be cleared by one of the few remaining doctors at the shelter.

The doctors who had performed the surgery wanted Lenny to stay at the hospital up until the day of the launch, but had no true conception of how bad things were already starting to get. Lenny's primary doctor, however, was confident that Lenny was strong enough to make it to the shelter and the waiting helicopters. He had confided in Stan that things were getting progressively worse in the streets and that the helicopters wouldn't wait long. Stan knew the odds and didn't hesitate. He had contacted her via Mission Control to let her know that they would be at the shelter soon and then on their way to the shuttle, but that was the last time she had spoken to him.

She did the math again in her head. She had gotten confirmation that they had made it to the shelter and were waiting on the helicopters to return for them. The helicopters had left the airfield hours ago; still there was no word on their ETA. Where *were* they? She desperately wanted them on her shuttle, but in her heart of hearts, she knew that wasn't going to happen. Her shuttle was already 15 minutes behind schedule, and Mission Control was pushing her to start her countdown.

The *Galileo2* wouldn't be leaving for another four hours, and they would make space for her family; but she hated having to rely on that as an option. She groaned inwardly and leaned over to reach for the cockpit phone.

"They're going to start ignoring you if you keep calling them," said her co-pilot, Dan Melton, looking both anxious and old. His wife barely made it aboard. As he waited for confirmation that she was on board, he felt he'd aged 20 years in a matter of hours. He certainly understood Tess's concern. They were down to the last departure window of the day. They had to take off within the next 30 minutes, or they would both be forced out of the cockpit and replaced. Tess knew it too. Command allowed her some grace time, but if she delayed much longer, they would remove her...and him.

And there was no shortage of pilots either. Dan had a feeling that many of the pilots who were not selected were out there among the masses right now, rioting and fighting and possibly killing, to gain access to the ships. These were good pilots; good men and women, but that didn't matter. The closer *Lycos* got to Earth, the more imminent and real, death became. This stark realization seemed to burrow deeper and deeper into the psyche of every human being on the planet. It seemed to flip on some primeval survival switch that had been lying dormant under generations of civility and turn these good, normal people into mad animals, scurrying and killing in the face of annihilation.

Reluctantly, he muttered, "Stan and your family...they're Cat2. If they don't make this shuttle, they'll put them on the *Galileo2*. All Category 2 families have guaranteed space. You know that."

"Yes, I know that Dan," Tess snapped. "This is just too damn important for some moron to make an administrative error. Maybe there were some problems with the helicopters or..."

"*Galileo1*, this is Mission Control, over."

Tess yanked the mike from its holster, tearing the small metallic clasp from the control console, which rolled towards Dan's left boot. "*Yes?*" she said nervously, anxiously. "This is *Galileo1*. Has my family arrived yet?"

"Roger G1. Our pass authorization scanner shows that three '*T. Robinson CAT2*' scans were detected at Entry Point Delta Bravo 2 about three minutes ago; there was one female and two males. There's a note here that says they looked pretty roughed up like they were in an accident or something. I can't believe they made it in this mess. Looks like they'll be hitching a ride with Jack though, Tess."

"Thank God. Thank God!" Tess exclaimed, forgetting she still had the mike button depressed.

"Come again G1?" Control queried.

Tess thought she detected humor and ignored it. "Sorry Control. I guess we're ready for departure. Do we have greens across the board?"

"Roger G1. You're ready to go. Prepare your 10-minute countdown. We've moved G2's departure up by two hours, so we won't be very far behind you. It's getting crazy down here, and we still need to get ourselves onto Jack's shuttle. There are only three of us left to get you off the ground and Jack will depart with no Mission Control guidance."

Tess wasn't surprised to hear that most of the senior officers and Mission Control folks had already departed. She hoped the remaining three would have a chance to get to the other shuttle. She glanced out the cockpit window. The launch platform for *Galileo2* was still in Horizontal Mode. With her platform in the Vertical Takeoff Mode, she could see clearly past Jack's ship and onto the thousands of people just outside the electrified fence, about eight hundred to a thousand yards away. Although she was happy that Stan, Lenny and her mom made it to Jack's shuttle, she detested the fact that they were so close to the fence and the human menace barely half a mile away. A couple of weeks ago, there were maybe a few hundred. Today, she would have conservatively put the estimate at close to 5,000, maybe more. Outside of television, she had never seen that many people in person, and thought bitterly that the only thing keeping them out was the huge electric barrier fence that completely surrounded Wright Airfield.

2

Before the threat of annihilation, Wright Airfield was just a small, local airfield north of San Antonio, Texas on the eastern edge of the hill country. It was used primarily to house local training school planes, pesticide delivery planes, and a few personal planes. Periodically, the airport was used to transport some of the more dangerous criminals to Harlan Penitentiary. Harlan was built in the summer of 2035, some ten years after the old Huntsville, Texas prison burned to the ground. The hilly surroundings and the close proximity to the airport convinced Federal authorities to commission the building of the nation's first underground prison.

Oddly enough, the sturdiness of the underground prison was enough to convince NASA and the government to rebuild the Wright Airfield, complete with an electric-powered steel fence and an underground fuel depot. Many speculated that the new airfield, with its underground fuel depot, was built to house the nation's backup fuel supply in the event of a nuclear war. As things turned out, a nuclear Armageddon was the least of their problems.

As Tess peered out of her cockpit window, her thoughts turned dark. *This is it,* she thought. *This is the End of Days.* She saw thousands upon thousands of people out there, just outside the fence. They drove as far as they could go, and when they couldn't drive anymore, they walked. They were all coming *here*. Coming to Wright Airfield to...*to do what, exactly? Find a ride on the shuttle? Beg for a seat? Maybe even kill for a seat?* Tess had a strong feeling that when it was all said and done, Wright Airfield would be a place of death.

Her mind wandered as she went through the motions of preparing for the final five minutes of liftoff preparation. Memories of old church sermons and Hollywood-inspired apocalyptic movies swirled and beat at her consciousness. In her mind's eye, she saw the end of traffic jams and crowded airports, abandoned beauty parlors, and desolate gas stations. She saw empty playgrounds and empty schools, all the teachers and students huddled at home attempting to deal with the end of the world in their own, desperate way. Her mind floated back to the year she spent at West Point as an exchange student from the Air Force Academy. She remembered watching the plebes (and a few upperclassmen) walk back and forth on Central Area, trying to reduce their demerits for some long-forgotten offense. She thought of her cousin in Chicago and other more distant relatives in California, Michigan, and Mississippi. She closed her eyes in an attempt to block out the images that were swirling in her head. On and on the images assaulted her until she felt as if her brain would melt and dribble out of her ears and down the sides of her face.

And then she saw the face of her husband, Stan. She saw Lenny and her mother. It had been incredibly stressful waiting to hear that they had made it safely. Now that they were safely on board the *Galileo2*, she felt she could relax somewhat. Still...she felt uneasy. She knew that Jack was a great pilot and that he would get the *Galileo2* to the moon safely, but the same feeling she used to get when she put Lenny on the school bus in the mornings came rushing back to her now. She shivered violently and told herself that she needed to let it go. They made it. They *all* made it and would soon be off the planet and away from danger.

Her thoughts drifted back to the masses just outside the fence; those poor helpless souls who were not so lucky to be on a shuttle right now. She herself was lucky to get selected for this assignment and was thankful that her and her family would be able to leave. But her family almost got left behind because the launch schedules were moved up. Things were moving too fast, and when that happens, people get sloppy and careless.

And people, important people, told too much. What was the saying? *"Loose lips sink ships"*? It was a very true statement, and the main reason why the exact launch dates were to be kept secret. The lottery was supposed to have been kept secret too, but everyone seemed to know about it. All of this information was to be kept secret in order to avoid exactly what was happening on the ground at this moment. Tess imagined that a disgruntled and angry lottery-loser, who was privy to this key information, probably dropped a few hints on when and where the launch would happen, and the word spread like wildfire.

Tess's hands moved across the controls in front of her in expert fashion. She responded automatically to the tower's system-checks. One part of her was laser-focused on Mission Control, and another part of her couldn't stay away from thoughts of her future life on one of the moon bases. At this thought she looked up, but the first thing to catch her sight wasn't the moon. It was the planet-killer, *Lycos*.

3

Lycos was discovered quite by accident. In 2040, NASA engineered a powerful long-range satellite capable of leaving the solar system and equipped with powerful lasers to transmit pictures and information from great distances. The satellite, called *Pegasus1*, was designed to travel out of Earth's solar system and onward, towards the center of the Milky Way, in order to map as much of the galaxy as possible before losing the signal. It was to use Jupiter's massive gravity to slingshot it deeper into space.

But as it neared its rendezvous with Jupiter, it sent back pictures of a huge meteor seemingly headed straight for Earth. As the images improved, it was clear that this meteor was a partially destroyed planet that could have been traveling in space for millennia. Lyle Cannaster, an Australian astronomer at the Berkeley Institute, labeled the meteor after himself by giving it the designation 'LYC-05' and it did not take long for the nickname *Lycos* to stick.

Many of Lyle's colleagues were amazed that this meteor was able to get as far as it did, before being detected. And after months of astronomic calculations, the leading experts of the world predicted that *Lycos*' path would take it through the Kuiper Belt, a huge asteroid belt in the outer Solar System, and away from Earth. Unfortunately, it collided with a number of asteroids in the belt, ultimately putting it on a collision course with Earth.

As it were, *Lycos*' existence was kept secret for months in order to avoid mass panic and potential collapse of the economies of the world. But as hack astronomers began to identify the object, the story was that the meteor would miss the earth by miles. Eventually, a whistle-blower in the US administration shared a document online that basically told everything the government knew about the meteor and the shelters that were being built. Surprisingly, the world economies did not fall and after weeks of heated global debates and technical discussions, it was finally agreed and shared with the world, that *Lycos* was on a collision course with Earth.

It was then that Tess had seen unparalleled global sharing of information and technologies as the nations of the earth embarked on a massive effort to build underground shelters capable of surviving the impending catastrophe and subsequent nuclear winter. There were many failures, but scores of successes as countries around the world began to successfully build their shelters and populate them. India was reported to have the first operational shelter some three years later, but other countries quickly followed.

And throughout this feverish activity, almost as an afterthought, there was the *Pegasus1* still moving towards the edge of the solar system, preparing for its slingshot maneuver around Jupiter. But people were not interested in this story. CNN's focus was now on the shelters being built around the world, and the national lotteries that would determine who would live in the shelters and who would die in the conflagration above ground.

The general feeling in the United States was that the mission of the *Pegasus1* was an empty mission now. Once *Lycos* hit the earth, the equipment (and expertise) to retrieve and read the data that *Pegasus1* would send back would be nothing but bits of twisted and burned out circuits and metal. It was an unvoiced feeling that the *Pegasus1* was not important anymore, or so they thought then.

RETURN TO EARTH

A system failure on the *Pegasus1* satellite resulted in a bad entry approach and instead of accelerating, the satellite unexpectedly decelerated as it approached Jupiter. Its slingshot maneuver was compromised and Jupiter's massive gravity field pulled it off course and into a low orbit about the planet, thus ending its mission outside of the solar system.

There was a sort of collective national *sigh* at this, and then everyone promptly turned their attention back to the business of worrying about the shelters. Regardless of what was going on out in space, their primary concerns were more basic; *Would the shelters be completed in time? Who would be selected? Where in God's name would they hide if not selected?*

Months had passed and *Pegasus1* became a distant memory. If not for the studious efforts of a young satellite signal processing engineer, named Henry Wilhelm, the valuable data that *Pegasus1* was sending back would have gone unnoticed. Even though *Pegasus1* was now orbiting Jupiter, Henry had observed that every few months, the satellite and one of Jupiter's moons, *Europa*, would get just close enough to one another that the satellite would slip from Jupiter's hold and orbit *Europa* for several days to weeks at a time before being pulled back into a Jupiter-orbit.

This orbital-switching was rare, but held no significant importance considering what the world was currently going through; what was significant and ultimately extremely important was the valuable and timely information that *Pegasus1* sent back to Earth. As it turned out, *Europa* had been moving out of an ice age for years and close-up images received from the satellite showed huge landmasses on *Europa* that could possibly sustain human life. Whether *Europa's* atmosphere was breathable or not had yet to be determined; but for now, there was the possibility of long-term salvation, if only for a few.

Armed with this new information, the United States, in conjunction with the United Nations, created two bases on the moon capable of housing up to 100 people each. They sent up teams of engineers and space construction workers to build the moon bases and two generation ships capable of making the trip to *Europa*. Tess was one of a handful of pilots capable of piloting the huge, complex ships and ended up being on the short list of pilots.

As these old memories swirled in her mind's eye, she could hear Mission Control initiate their one-minute countdown. She turned her head and looked down at the crowd of people outside the fences. She couldn't be sure, but it looked as if the crowd had gotten bigger within the last 15 minutes! She looked over at the *Galileo2* and wished again that Stan, Lenny, and her mom were here on her shuttle. She exhaled sharply and resigned herself to seeing them on the moon in the next 18 to 24 hours. "Mission Control, pre-lift checks complete; ready for launch." She looked over at Dan and nodded. He nodded back and settled into his seat. At zero, she pressed the ignition switch and felt the ion rocket engines bellow into life, slowly lifting them from the launch pad and away from Earth.

THELMA

1

Thelma Branson was finally getting the hang of it.

Thelma and computers never really got along. In fact, Thelma and anything remotely resembling something that could contain electronics did not get along. As Thelma liked to tell her husband, "she and computers were mortal enemies." She would always get a good laugh out of that one, but her husband, Tom, always looked at her with one eyebrow raised.

During those days, he had called her *"Thelma the Thumb"* because to him, she was all thumbs. His all-time favorite comment was, "Thelma couldn't pour piss out of a boot if the instructions were printed on the heel!" He and his cronies would cackle loudly for the next ten minutes at this old joke before settling back to their card game.

Thelma was far from clumsy, but Tom labeled her with that many years ago simply because she couldn't bowl. But she would smile at them and continue about her chores or activities or whatever she was working on during those times. Now she thought about those times fondly, as she rapidly typed commands onto her small keyboard. One thing she remembered clearly though, was that after the incident on the cruise, he never called her clumsy again.

Yes, she had definitely gotten the hang of it. She was responsible for her shelter's camera monitoring, or at least one of four people responsible for the cameras. Right now, it was her shift, and her main responsibility was to monitor all of the access areas to their shelter. She was looking at Camera One which faced along the narrow underground pathway that ran parallel to their shelter. She punched in the long-remembered codes that instructed the camera to slowly swivel on its mount, giving her a clear view of this tunnel. This was the route they took to get to the main entrance of their shelter. Its length ran about a quarter of a mile and then disappeared around a jagged mass of rocks. The door to the entrance was five feet thick and well insulated. It was practically built into the rock wall and slightly hidden from view. Unless one knew exactly what to look for and where to look, it would have been almost impossible to find.

Thelma had gotten to the shelter several months ago which made it about a year after she last saw Jack Richards, her younger sister's husband, who was an Air Force Colonel working for NASA in Texas. She thought of their last conversation and how horrified she had been. She remembered Tom's look of incredulity when she told him what Jack had told her, and she remembered bitterly how he had laughed and laughed. "Good ole Jack...always the jokester" he would say. She couldn't tell if he ever believed her. When the cancer finally took him, she realized she had a decision to make. She settled their estate in Florida and moved to Houston, where she remained until she moved into the shelter.

Camera Three beeped and Thelma glanced over at it. It was the camera situated at the top level; the level closest to the street. All of the cameras were equipped with motion detectors and since Camera Three was the only camera located in an outdoor position, it was constantly beeping. Thelma stared at the screen closely but didn't see anything out of the ordinary. She thought absently that maybe a mouse had scurried by and was picked up by the motion detector.

So many people, she thought sadly. These days, she couldn't help but think of the massive loss of life that would happen soon. *God only knows if we'll even make it in this shelter,* she often thought. Sometimes, when it was late at night and all was quiet, she thought about her husband and her sister Mary and was bitterly glad that they were not around to witness this apocalypse. The memory of her sister reminded her of her sister's funeral and the last time she saw Jack just three months before Tom died of cancer.

2

"How's Tom doing these days Thelma," Jack inquired cautiously as he slowly pushed her away from the departing attendees at the funeral.

"The last few weeks have been wonderful for him Jack, thanks for asking. I debated long and hard on whether I should come here, but he was very insistent. I just wished he could have joined me." She grew somber and then added, "He really liked being around you and Mary, God rest her soul."

"I know Thelma, I know" said Jack. He was always cautious around her when he spoke of Tom. He liked Tom and despite Tom's crass jokes, he was pleasant to be around. He had been extremely active outdoors; if he wasn't fishing, then he was golfing or bowling, but this was all before his cancer came back with ferocious intensity. As much as Jack hated to accept it, in his heart he felt that Tom only had months to live, if not weeks. "Tom's a strong man and a fighter," he said to Thelma.

Jack parked Thelma's wheelchair next to a huge oak with a low cement bench squatting next to it. He sat down facing Thelma and took her hands into his. He held them for a long time before saying anything, his head cocked to one side as if listening for the right time to talk. Thelma noticed that he was gripping her hands tightly, but she bore it patiently and waited for him to get off his chest, whatever was apparently weighing him down. Just as she was about to break the silence, he leaned toward her and whispered in her ear, "Thelma, I'm shipping off for the moon first thing tomorrow morning. In fact, when I leave here, I'm going directly to the launch pad site. I'm taking additional supplies on this run. When I come back and leave again, I'll be ferrying—"

Thelma shrank back violently, interrupting his explanation, "The moon? You mean it's true? Are we actually taking people to the moon? But I thought this comet, or meteor, or whatever it is, was supposed to miss us by miles—by *thousands* of miles. That's what the news has been saying for months."

He looked up alarmed and wide-eyed, more surprised that she'd made the connection so quickly than worried whether they would be overheard. "Look Thelma," he said more urgently, "a decision was made some time ago regarding the moon, but I can't divulge the details to you; but what I *can* tell you is that I was not one of the original pilots selected to fly to the moon; Mary and I actually had slots for the North San Antonio shelter."

She stared at him uncomprehendingly, her mouth moving, but no words coming out. Jack opened his mouth to say more, but she found her voice before he could say anything, "A shelter? In North San Antonio? I thought the shelters were just a myth."

"It's no myth Thelma," Jack replied. "Very soon, the government will announce a national lottery to determine who will be selected to live in the shelters." He paused briefly and then continued in a strained voice, "Anyone 60 years of age or older will not be considered."

Thelma could only gape at him, a mixture of confusion and anger welling up inside her. "It just doesn't make any sense Jack! For months they've been saying the worst we'll see are meteor showers. Why in the world would we need underground shelters for meteor showers?"

She sat a minute, working it out in her head while Jack kept quiet. He could almost hear the pieces falling into place as comprehension slowly dawned on her face. "Oh my goodness, Jack! Is it more than just a meteor shower? I mean, will some of the pieces make it to Earth? It was supposed to pass us by completely. I mean—"

"It was a lie Thelma," Jack stated flatly.

"*What?*" Thelma whispered.

"It was all a lie. A cover up. A goddamn 'wool over the eyes' story," Jack said. "This thing is *not* going to pass us by Thelma. It's coming straight at us, and it's...huge. It's fucking *huge!* It...it'll destroy the earth." Jack was breathing heavily now; his eyes piercing hers like lasers. "It's called *Lycos*, and right now it just looks like a bright star up there, creeping along. But it's moving alright—very, very fast and on a collision course with us. Some of it will burn up in the atmosphere, but our best scientists estimate only a fraction will be burned off and..." Jack's voice trailed off.

"And what Jack?" Thelma asked.

Jack stared at his feet. Now that he was actually talking about this, he was starting to feel the enormity of what was happening. Without looking up at the sky, he could almost feel the weight of *Lycos* bearing down on him, crushing him where he sat. Of course, he knew it was guilt he was feeling, tremendous guilt. Only a handful of people in the entire country knew the truth about "the meteor". In the interest of "public safety", the decision was made to provide the public with misinformation regarding *Lycos*. An ingenious marketing campaign turned the onset of public fear into a "once in a lifetime Haley's Comet II viewing". He wasn't sure how the Heads of State in other countries were handling this, but from what he'd seen on CNN, they were passing on the lie as it was being fed to them.

Thelma touched Jack's arm gently. "And *what* Jack? What's going to happen?"

Jack felt as if his skin were crawling around on his bones. He hadn't realized until now *how much* wool had been pulled over the eyes of billions of people. He felt dirty and sneaky and incredibly guilty. Despite his open honesty with Thelma, he couldn't fight back the wave of nausea that was creeping up on him and slowly overtaking him. He looked up and saw Thelma watching him intently with worried eyes.

"It's not a meteor Thelma. It's a...it's a *planet*, or at least part of a planet. The theory is that this planet's sun went supernova some billions of years ago. The resulting cataclysm most likely destroyed the planets in its solar system. Unfortunately, for whatever reason, this rogue planet wasn't completely destroyed and was violently ejected from its dying solar system."

Thelma said nothing, but continued to stare at Jack; she stared *through* him.

"It's been traveling for a long time and when it gets here, some of the met...*planet* will burn up in the atmosphere, but its size and speed will enable it to make it through our atmosphere still pretty much intact." Jack hesitated briefly and then added, "Even after entering our atmosphere, this monster will still retain much of its mass, density, and speed. It's a planet-killer Thelma, and it will completely destabilize Earth's orbit. Earth can't withstand an impact of that nature. The scientists don't agree on the magnitude of the damage, but they *do* agree that if this thing doesn't destroy the earth on initial impact, then the ensuing earthquakes will cause the planet to eventually break up, creating deep fissures within the earth, and it will ultimately kick-start a massive chain reaction that will rip the planet apart. Nothing would be able to survive it. It could very well be the end of mankind on Earth."

"Oh, Dear God Jack. I...how...I...I don't understand..." Thelma's eyes had become very small in their sockets. The enormity of this information was unbearable. Jack waited until Thelma had mentally collected herself. "And these shelters—these *underground* shelters—will protect us?" asked Thelma hopefully.

Jack looked away and saw that another funeral party was arriving. Despite their distance, he could still hear the crunching gravel of the main funeral road as a dozen or so vehicles rolled slowly through the funeral grounds. *Your typical funeral scene,* Jack thought, with the exception of the bright red vehicle directly behind the hearse. It stood out as if in direct defiance to death itself. "Not all of us Thelma, only some of us, and it will depend on where *Lycos* physically strikes the earth. There's a group of scientists who believe that there is a small chance that the meteor or planet may not strike us head-on, but at an oblique angle. If that happens, maybe the earth will survive, but right now, God only knows." A sharp bark of a laughed escaped his mouth, startling Thelma. "Right now, our experts are saying that the projected impact area is somewhere in Russia, possibly Siberia."

He waited for Thelma to say something, but she just stared straight ahead. A voice drifted over to them from the group that had just arrived. Jack looked across at them and could see some of them crying as the speaker continued his eulogy. He glanced back at Thelma. "Only a handful of people know about this in the government, and they've known for a number of years. I'm sure you've seen the increased activity of shuttles to the moon. Thank God we were already half way finished with the American moon base facility because the UN facility would have been much too small for any significant number of people."

"For how many people Jack?" Thelma said quietly. "That's not what's important Thelma, what is—" "How many Jack?" she stated flatly.

"The US moon base will be able to sustain about 100 people for several years. The UN compound maybe a little less. If the food and supplies were rationed well, then that same number could survive a little longer. But of course, all this depends on how well the equipment is maintained."

"Two hundred people Jack? Oh my God. That's all?" Thelma grabbed Jack's arm frantically.

Jack wiped his brow with the back of his free hand. "I know Thelma, we've taken supplies, medicine, and food on every trip and 200 people was the optimum number with the best chances of survival. We might end up with plus or minus that number, but nothing significantly more than that."

"This won't remain secret for long Jack. What happens then? Martial Law? Rioting? Mass suicides?" Thelma looked at him pointedly.

"Under no circumstances are people to know about this Thelma. You mustn't tell anyone. People will find out in due time, but not now. You're right; all hell would break loose, and we would have complete anarchy and not just here. Word would spread across the globe like an internet virus and overnight we would have a meltdown of the global financial system, possible religious wars, and maybe even nuclear attacks. It might even compromise completion of the final stages of some of the shelters."

She started to say something, but he overrode her, "The only reason I told you about this Thelma is because I've been selected as one of the Team Leaders for the people going to the moon. I was an alternate, but the primary couldn't keep his mouth shut about the moon operation and was removed from the position." Jack withheld the fact that this pilot had been shot in the head when walking home from the commissary one evening. The Military Police never caught the assailant, but indicated that it might have been a vagrant passing through the local town.

"Because of Mary's untimely death and my promotion to Team Lead, there are now two available slots in the North San Antonio shelter. I want you and Tom to take those slots."

Thelma felt like she was swimming in quicksand. She couldn't seem to wrap her mind around everything that Jack was telling her. Planets and shelters and millions of years. It made about as much sense to her as the internet did when Tom tried to explain it to her after they bought their new computer. "What does that mean Jack? Are you saying that Tom and I will be able to stay in one of those shelters when this meteor or planet hits the earth?" She had to stifle a wild, crazy laugh at that last statement. She would never have believed that she, Thelma, could have uttered something so frighteningly Orson Welles-ish. Or would that have been Asimov? She didn't know, and at the moment, she didn't care. "Will we be safe Jack? I mean, are these shelters safe enough from this…collision?"

Jack averted his eyes for an instant and then replied, "I honestly don't know Thelma, but you'll be safer than the people left on top."

Thelma was about to comment, but Jack interrupted her for the second time. "If you remember anything, please remember these two things: don't tell anyone, outside of Tom. As I stated earlier, things will get quite bad as *Lycos* gets closer. At some point, even amateur astronomers will be able to tell that something is headed in our general direction, and it won't be long after that before they'll be able to tell that it's headed towards us—*directly* towards us. The other thing is that you and Tom need to get to the shelter as soon as possible. You will receive a text message stating location and arrival time. When you get that text, you and Tom need to haul ass to that pickup location immediately. As I said, the shelter is in North San Antonio, Texas, and I would suggest that you and Tom sell your house and rent a place out there, very close to the shelter. I've already given the Shelter Commander your current mobile number. Keep the account current and don't change the number."

Thelma nodded dutifully, making mental notes of everything Jack said. She thought of something else to ask him when she caught movement out of the corner of her eye. A young Marine was making his way towards them, moving in that stiff, authoritative way Thelma used to see in the military shows Tom enjoyed watching. They watched in silence as the Marine made his way towards them across the well-manicured lawns.

"Sir!" he saluted sharply as he neared them and then moved close to Jack to whisper in his ear.

"Thelma, I need to go, but don't forget what I've told you. Remember those two important items. Are you sure I can't take you home?"

"Yes, I'm sure. My neighbor from down the street is attending the funeral that you see there," she pointed to the group of people off in the distance. "He's taking me to the pharmacy to pick up Tom's prescription. I'll sit here for a minute and then make my way over to the church."

Jack leaned over and hugged Thelma before she realized it and turned towards the military vehicle parked on the pathway. The young marine nodded curtly to Thelma, "Ma'am", and then turned to follow Jack.

That was the last time Thelma had seen or heard from Jack. She assumed that by now, he was already situated on the moon. She sighed and went back to checking her monitors, every now and then glancing at the countdown clock, which slowly counted backwards from 22 hours and 37 minutes.

THE FLIGHT OF GALILEO2

1

Clyde Anderson stared out his portside window. It was very small and was similar to the port windows on cruise ships if one were unfortunate enough to be stuck in one of the lower-level, closet-sized cruise ship rooms. Actually, he was never even that lucky. His one and only time being on a cruise was anything but glamorous. His room didn't have windows at all. He just happened to pass by a room while the door was open and saw the small port window.

Well, he had a window now and boy was it a good one. He craned his head toward the window to look outside, where tens of thousands of people now congregated. He couldn't hear anything, but what he saw told him everything he needed to know.

He and his partners had just gotten buckled into their seats when the other shuttle raised its platform and blasted off; no fanfare, no one-minute countdown—at least not one that he could hear—and no warning. They just left, and Clyde could almost sense the change in the atmosphere on the ground. It was getting dangerous.

While there were two ships on the ground, the people were still cordial, still neighborly. They made room for pass-holders to make it through security. There was even lighthearted joking as Clyde and his group walked through. Disembodied voices yelling out, *"Hey, save me a seat buddy!"* or *"I'll give you the deed to my five-million-dollar home for that slot!"* Quite a few folks laughed, but the laughs sounded forced. Clyde had laughed too as he headed up the ramp and into the security and comfort of the shuttle.

Looking out at the rambunctious and angry crowd now, he could tell that there would be no more parting of the masses to allow for late arrival "pass-holders" to hop on board. He had a feeling that anyone foolish enough to show up now demanding passage, waving their authorization in the air, would most likely lose that arm, right before losing their lives. Now that the other shuttle was gone, the reality of their doom was clearer than ever. And with the monstrous *Lycos* hanging over their heads like the *Sword of Damocles*, they now knew that there would be no more round trips from the moon. This was it, and here was the last shuttle. The last hope before the final horror.

Hundreds of camp sites littered the grounds on his side of the fence. They were situated on the concrete and on the grass as far out as the manmade lake that bordered the southeastern edge of the airfield. He didn't have to see out the other window to know that the other side was just as packed.

He saw a few pockets of people pushing and shoving, but most were waving signs: "GIVE US A CHANCE AT LIFE!" and "PLEASE TAKE OUR CHILDREN!" Some expressed a little more anger like: "U WILL BURN N HELL 4 LEAVING US!" or "NONE CAN ESCAPE JUDGMENT DAY!"

Every now and then, the fence would shoot off bright sparks of electricity, where someone fell or was pushed into the fence. The soldiers controlling the power to the fences had to increase the voltage because too many people were attempting to climb over by using insulated ladders and other insulated materials. They increased it up to the point that even the insulated ladders started smoking. Clyde could see that this stopped the attempts, but he wondered for how long.

There were only a handful of soldiers on the "ship-side" of the electrified fence. Clyde could see at least five on his side and wondered if they actually had slots on the shuttle. He didn't think so. They were probably told that once the countdown started, they would simply come aboard and take their seats. More likely than not, they would find themselves locked out like the folks outside the fences. He had looked around in the cabin when he first came aboard and saw only a few soldiers. He also saw that there weren't many seats left.

A curious thing had occurred to him when he had boarded several hours ago; even though there were quite a number of soldiers mixed in with the masses, only a few still had weapons. In fact, the civilians were more heavily armed than the soldiers, yet no one had made any attempts to shoot at the ship.

Considering the circumstances, he thought that surely there would be at least one person out there with the attitude that if he doesn't make it, no one will. This line of thinking made perfect sense to Clyde because that was how *he* thought. He got his answer though when he heard over the loudspeaker that there were still a lot of slots open on the shuttle. Announcements stating that they were still drawing names based on social security numbers blared out over the loudspeakers every 15 minutes. Added to that were more appeasing and soft-spoken statements such as *"You still have a chance to be selected so be ready to present some form of identification!"*

It was all horseshit and Clyde knew it, but to the desperate people outside, it was a chance—however remote—at salvation. Regardless of how slim the chances were, it was still a chance for some lucky person to be called, and it was enough to prevent the crowd from rioting and overwhelming the fences and the shuttle. More importantly, Clyde realized, it was enough to stop them from firing at the ship and possibly disabling it.

Clyde looked around inside the shuttle and did a quick count of the seats. There were only about 20 seats remaining, which he assumed were probably for shuttle crew members and maybe a few soldiers. He wished that they would get the hell on board so they could leave. *Lycos* was getting closer and closer, and he had a feeling that soon the crowd surging against the fences would stop singing *Kumbaya* and start doing some real damage. At that point, they won't care how many seats are left.

He looked down at his left hand and adjusted the bandage that covered it. A smile, not more than a sneer really, played on his lips. He laid his head back, closed his eyes, and drifted back to a conversation he had not so long ago.

2

"Look here Anderson, this situation will get a whole helluva lot worse before it gets better, and it *ain't* getting better. I'm going to need good people on the ground to ensure civility when the shit hits the fan."

Police Chief Clyde Anderson stood stiffly at *parade rest* while Mayor Rendell spelled out the impending doom of the country and of Earth itself. Clyde Anderson was not new to disasters, nor was he given to panic and surprise when situations turned sour with no warning. He was a native of Florida and was very familiar with how quickly hurricanes turned calm situations into shit storms in the blink of an eye.

Although the room was quite cool when he entered, Clyde could feel slow heat rising within his body as the weight of what the Mayor was telling him began to settle more firmly on his psyche. *A goddamn comet is headed this way on a one-way fucking mission to smash us into oblivion!* he thought. Whenever he saw previews of some new sci-fi, world-ending blockbuster, he would laugh mockingly at it, dismissing it as stupid and unbelievable. But if what the Mayor was telling him was true, then this was no laughing matter. This was real, and it was terrifying. He could feel a small bead of sweat form at the nape of his neck and go traipsing down his back, zigzagging left and right until disappearing into the waist band of his cotton underwear.

The Mayor was saying, "...so you can understand why it will be extremely important for us to have a significant presence in the streets. We will need to ensure stability and keep rioting down to a minimum. The closer this rock gets to Earth, the crazier people will get. All sense of responsibility and sanity will completely disappear. People will start taking the law into their own hands."

Clyde started to say something but cleared his throat first. He didn't quite trust his voice at that moment. "Sir, usually the government has some kind of plan tucked away for just such emergencies, right? Maybe try to shoot it down or break it up into chunks. And what about underground shelters? Have they been working on building large underground structures and storing away animals two-by-two?" Clyde realized, belatedly, that all of his solutions were ideas he'd gleaned from the movies he so despised.

"Chief, you've been watching too many of those damn *Comet from Outer Space* movies," Rendell said, not without some scorn. "This meteor or meteor-planet is huge and according to my sources, our efforts will be as effective as using an umbrella to keep from getting wet in a typhoon. This thing will *destroy* the earth—completely. No huge crater in some God-forsaken place in South America or out in the middle of the Atlantic. No opportunity for us to crawl out of our underground caves and start a *Brave New World* two or three years later. This thing is on an extermination mission, and there is fuck-all we can do about it!"

This time, Clyde did speak and as he feared, his voice came out squeaky and high-pitched, "So what happens now?" He was totally lost. He could definitely see how things could, and would, get out of hand. "I don't understand why my men and I should be out there policing things up when this rock is just going to obliterate everything!" Anderson could feel deep despair sinking into his bones and hated it. He was never a weak man (or so he believed anyway), and this uncontrollable feeling was overpowering him minute by minute. "My guys will just want to be with their families during these last days...sir."

Rendell looked squarely at the chief, measuring him. He seemed to consider something, thought better of it, and then waved it away with his hand. "Here's the deal Chief," he whispered secretly and motioned the chief to step closer. "Remember the big to-do in the news a few years ago when Congress commissioned the building of three new TX

Class Space Shuttles? Something in the news about the Russians renewing their efforts to be the first men on Mars?"

Clyde nodded, not really knowing any specific details, but he remembered how frustrated he used to get whenever he turned on the TV to watch a game or the local news and every channel seemed to be doing specials on how the United States could not let the Russians get to Mars first. It seemed he could not escape it.

"Anderson! Are you hearing me? Listen up man! Once Congress got the appropriations to build the shuttles, everything quieted down. In fact, you would have been hard-pressed to find *anything* in the news about the shuttles." He waved his hand dismissively, and Clyde could see the soft fat underneath his arm jiggle. The toneless skin was pale like the belly of a dead fish. "Anyway, those shuttles were designed as *passenger* shuttles." He paused to reflect on something and added, "I think one was sold to the United Nations. Regardless though, the government has known about this disaster for quite some time and as we speak, are making plans to transport people to the moon."

For a fraction of a second, Clyde Anderson felt elated. The government, with its endless partisan bickering, nonsensical budget cuts and overspending, and miles and miles of red tape, was finally kicking into gear and doing something for the people. *Alright, goddammit, alright!* But his elation dissipated, almost as quickly as it came. There were close to what, 450 million people in the country? How in God's name could they transport that many people? It was impossible. And on the heels of this line of thinking followed a darker, more sinister train of thought: *No. They can't take all of them. So, who are they going to take?* Before he could verbalize this insight, Rendell preempted him.

"I see that the wheels are turning in there Chief," he smiled. "These shuttles will only be able to take anywhere from 60-80 people, maybe closer to 100, but I don't know the specifics. That's not the main problem though. It's the completion of the Moon Bases that's pushing the transportation effort to the last minute." Rendell continued, "You see Anderson, the government is building a couple of Moon Bases on the moon capable of housing at least 100 people each, with enough supplies to last them until they can confirm a breathable atmosphere on *Europa*."

The Mayor had not answered Clyde's question of *whom*, but instead provided him with information he would never have believed at any other time. *A Moon Base on the moon? Europa?* This was all new to him and very disorienting. He felt that if he didn't sit down soon, he would fall flat on his face.

"I can see that you're taking this very well, Clyde", Rendell crooned. He could see that Clyde Anderson was having a hard time, an extremely hard time, swallowing all this. And why shouldn't he? How many nights had he himself laid awake in a pool of his own sweat once he found out what was going on?

He turned his attention back to Clyde, who looked as if he'd just eaten something that the dog had spit out. "This is where you come in, my friend. According to my sources, the people who are going to the moon have already been selected. As we speak, they may already be secluded in undisclosed locations to make it easier to get them loaded when the time comes. Middle managers like us were never even considered," he lied.

His source had actually informed him that the government was planning a lottery, and those selected would be moved to secure shelters near the launch site, completely cut off from the outside world. What Rendell's source did not know was that the government had been secretly testing a cross-section of the American public within a certain age range.

This cross-section represented percentages of every ethnic background within the country. They were all healthy, and their psychological test results indicated that they would not only be the most likely to survive the physical and mental rigors of space life, but would be more willing to leave family and friends behind. Mayor Rendell never received the test, being outside of the age range, not to mention his unhealthy lifestyle. Clyde, unknowingly, rejected taking the psychological test. He had grumbled and balled up what he thought was "junk mail" and dropped it in the trash container.

"So, I need you and some of your best men. Men you can trust to help *rectify* this problem," Rendell continued smoothly. "You see, I happen to know where one of these compounds is located."

"Compounds?" Clyde stammered out.

"Yes, compounds. Shelters," Rendell replied. "As I said, the folks who are going to the moon have already been selected and have been living at these compounds for the past six months or so, and soon, very soon, they'll be secretly transported to the shuttles for liftoff."

Clyde was getting nervous and starting to sense some form of a conspiracy here that he didn't quite like. However, he liked the idea of being left behind on the planet even less. Dammit, he was a hardworking American who supported his country and paid his taxes. Why shouldn't *he* get a chance at life? How did those bozos get chosen anyway? Well, if there was something he could do about it, he was sure as hell going to try. And it was on the heels of that train of thought, that Clyde Anderson, Chief of Police, along with Mayor Rendell, outlined their plans to get themselves on a shuttle...or die trying.

3

Sitting in his seat on the shuttle, Clyde opened his eyes. *Well, that old fuck did die trying, and it was good that I was there to relieve him, and his friends of their authorization passes.* He looked over at two of his team members who were seated next to one another and nodded. They nodded back and looked over their shoulders for their compatriot. She was seated further back and gave a "thumbs up". Angie looked a bit roughed up, but they had to make the attempted rape scene look somewhat convincing or that Jeep would never have slowed down. Clyde looked out the port window again, and a worried look crossed his face. Someone down there must have been saying something really convincing, because a lot of people were moving up close to listen to him. Whatever he was saying to them was starting to get them riled up. Soon, they'll work themselves into a frenzy and nothing will be able to stop them.

4

"Charlie, get those goddamn doors closed now! I mean *NOW!*" Jack yelled into the voice mike attached to his headset. Nate looked nervously out of his side window again and rubbed at his face. He was staring out at the restless crowd below.

Jack was looking out of his own window and didn't like what he saw. Things had deteriorated more quickly than he had expected. They had already missed their launch window, and he sure as hell was not going to wait for the next window, some eight hours from now. Looking at the crowd, he wondered if even an hour was too long.

"Jack...Jack! They're starting to fight with the soldiers out there and some are starting to scale the fence where the power is out!" Nate's voice quavered on the edge of hysteria. He could see that the few soldiers guarding the shuttle and the fences would not be able to keep the horde of half-crazed and screaming people out. Many would be killed trying to get over and through the fence, but the overwhelming majority would easily crush the soldiers in their mad dash to the shuttle bay door entrance.

Jack was gripping the mike, but his voice had gone down a notch. "Okay...okay...calm down Charlie. You did good. If you hadn't gotten those doors closed, that crowd out there could have done some serious damage to the ship, and none of us would have been going anywhere. Now get yourself strapped in; we're getting the hell out of here!" He turned to Nate, "Tell Gil to get his team back in the shuttle, we're leaving!"

Nate whirled in his seat towards Jack, "What about the portside SRB?" He jabbed his finger at the small red diode blinking on the instrumentation panel. "I'm sure they haven't repaired it yet or at least looked at it to see if it really is a problem. You know as well as I do, the issues we've been having with these SRB's. If it malfunctions, we're dead! We *have* to get it fixed first Jack!"

"We're not 100% certain that it's going to malfunction Nate. One thing I *am* certain about though is if that crowd gets on this platform, there are a hundred different ways they could screw up this launch. Find out where they are, and tell them to get inside *now*."

Nate adjusted the mike on his headset and then yelled into it, "Gil, where are you guys? Have you verified the problem with the portside Solid Rocket Booster?"

After a few seconds of silence, a panicky voice came back over the speakers. "We're almost there! Ralph was snatched by the mob before security could lock the platform gates. They practically ripped him to pieces! You gotta let us in now...that gate won't hold them...they..."

Nate interrupted him, "Shut up Gil and listen! We can let you in through the portside umbilicus. How long before you can get there?"

Nate looked over at Jack. He was staring intently out of his side window. Nate could see him clenching his teeth.

"...there...ten min..." Gil's broken voice came back over the mike. "Say again Gil...you're breaking up!" yelled Nate.

"We'll be there...ten minutes. Just make...you're at...to let us in!"
"Roger, Gil, we'll be there, but you need to hurry!" Nate yelled, nervously looking at his watch.

Jack spoke without turning his head away from the window, "Nate, inform Gil that we're going to Vertical Takeoff Mode and start the countdown clock. Set it at 30 minutes."

Nate was about to say something when Jack held up his hand, "I know what you're going to say Nate, but we can't help that now. Midnight is upon us, and time is quickly slipping away. When I told Charlie to close the bay doors, I realized that some of our maintenance team was still out there. God forgive me, but I can't sacrifice the 50+ people in here for those few. I wish I could, but if we hadn't closed those bay doors when we did, we would have had hundreds in here in minutes."

"I know boss," Nate replied heavily.

"Either way," continued Jack, "we have to start the countdown now. The crowd out there has destabilized completely. They're killing each other out there Nate. They have nothing left to live for." His eyes were red and strained. Nate could see that he was stretched to the breaking point.

"Okay Jack, let's do it then," Nate looked out his window again. "And if that SRB decides to throw a fit, then it'll be a short trip, huh?" They strapped themselves into their seats as Nate started the countdown sequence.

5

Clyde was getting nervous. He, along with the other passengers on the ship, had their faces glued to the windows. A number of them were crying. They stared helplessly at the increasing violence outside. The soldiers were gone, and the only thing that kept the crowd out was the electrified fence. Clyde could see blackened and burnt bodies alongside the entire length of the fence; probably hundreds of them. The enormous weight of the crowd surging against the fence continued to push the helpless front line of people directly into the sizzling, unyielding fence, where they were hideously fried until they were nothing more than black bones covered with pieces of hanging flesh. It was a horrific scene and he couldn't imagine what the stench was like.

But the fence was losing its strength both in electrical power and stability. He strained to look further down the line and saw that the power there had already gone out and people were starting to scale the 20-foot fence. This was what was making Clyde nervous. Each time the crowd pushed, more people were fried, more people died, and more power was drained. The power surging through the fence seemed to wane after each surge, and the lights surrounding the launch site would waver each time.

He looked around anxiously for one of the crewmen to find out why the hell they hadn't taken off. Hell, the captain hadn't even spoken to them. He assumed that the bay doors were closed. If not, they would have been overrun by the people near the entrance, still hoping to get on.

Clyde gritted his teeth. He had worked too goddamn hard to get on this shuttle, and he wasn't going to sit here and watch his chance at life slip away. He looked around and spied one of the crewmen talking on the shuttle phone. He waved frantically for the crewman to come over, but the man ignored him and continued speaking on the phone. Cursing under his breath, Clyde unclipped himself and strode over to him.

"Sir, I'll be with you in a minute," the crewman said stiffly. "We're about to go to Vertical Takeoff Mode and you need to take your se—"

"*What the fuck are we waiting for man?*" Clyde spat into the man's face. "Can't you guys see that this crowd is losing it?" He waved his hand in the direction of the window. Several passengers seated nearby turned sharply at the sound of his raised voice. "The generators out there are dying, and when they go that fence will go, and this shuttle will be a goddamn sitting duck!"

The crewman's annoyed look dropped from his face like a rock. He stared uncertainly at Clyde, trying to figure out how to control this situation, knowing that he could not. The co-pilot had just given him an order and just that quickly, it flew out of his mind. He opened his mouth to say something, thought better of it, and then turned around quickly to head towards the cockpit.

Clyde stepped up behind him quickly, pushing the nose of the small automatic pistol into the tech's lower back. "I'll come help you!" he said in a loud, cheerily fake voice.

6

"Colonel Richards, sir, uh...we have a situation..." mumbled Tech Sergeant Jeffries. He stood helplessly at the cockpit door. He was sweating and wincing as Clyde's Glock pressed deeper into his lower back.

"No *shit* Sherlock!" Nate yelled without turning around. "I thought I told you to get to the umbilicus to let Gil in!" He was frantically checking readouts on the cockpit dash, whipping his head back and forth from the dash to the cockpit window out on the crowd below. The surrounding landscape looked completely alien to him. It was only four in the afternoon, but the skies were a dark, reddish color. The wind had picked up and seemed to blow non-stop. He could feel the ship slightly swaying.

"Yeah, that crowd out there looks nasty don't it?" Clyde pointed out.

Jack and Nate both snapped their heads around at this new voice. "Who the hell are you, and what the fuck are you doing in my cockpit?" Jack yelled. Then, without waiting for a reply, he ordered, "Jeffries, get him the hell back to his seat!" He then turned abruptly back to the controls.

"Sir…" Jeffries started, but never finished. Clyde brought the butt of his Glock squarely down on Jeffries's head. His eyes went wide for just a second, before his knees crumpled, and he dropped heavily to the floor.

Nate started to get up when Clyde motioned him back to his chair with the Glock. "No need for you to get yourself shot trying to be a hero, troop." Clyde said to Nate, whose eyes seemed glued to the gun. "Now sit the fuck back down, and let's get the hell out of here!"

"That's what we're trying to do buddy!" Jack snapped at him. "Look," Jack said, "we got a team out there, and they're on their way back in. As soon as they're in, we're leaving."

Clyde turned his gun toward Jack and said "I think we have serious problems *now*. Can't you see what's happening on the ground man? The electrified fences are dead and people are pouring through! And you may not know this, *El Capitan*, but I saw some of those National Guard tanks making their way here, and I can goddamn guarantee you that they're not coming here to make sure you take off safely. Misery loves company; the closer that rock gets here, the more those people are going to realize that they want to be on this ship. They don't care if there are enough seats or not. They want on…or they'll tear it to the ground."

7

Some thirty thousand miles away, Tess listened in horror to the drama being played out on Jack's ship. At some point, Jack flipped the communications switch that enabled her to hear what was going on. Whether he did it on purpose or not, she didn't know. All she knew was that her husband and son were on that ship, and there was a lunatic threatening the cockpit crew with a weapon.

"Dan, we gotta do something!" Tess blurted out, staring into the cockpit speaker. "Oh my God, Dan. Oh my God!" Tears started welling up in her eyes.

Dan stared at his hands, not wanting to face Tess. They were helpless. He knew it, and he felt that Tess did too. It would be impossible to turn around and go back, for a number of reasons, fuel being the main one. Even if they *were* able to go back, they would never be able to leave again. No, Jack's situation was bad and from what Dan heard over the radio, the maintenance team hadn't even confirmed whether they fixed the problem with the Solid Booster Rocket, which could explode during takeoff.

The other problem was the sheer number of people trying to get to the ship. Before he and Tess took off several hours earlier, there were thousands out there. By now, there must be tens of thousands all pushing their way towards the ship. He shut his eyes tight, as if to keep this ugly end-of-the-world image out of his mind. He was just about to open his eyes to see how Tess was doing when a loud crack rang out over the comms speaker, making him jump in his seat.

"Jack!" Tess screamed into the mike. *"Jack, what's going on?"*

"*You fuck!*" Jack screamed, ignoring Tess's screams over the intercom. "Are you trying to kill us before we even get into space?"

One of Clyde's men, Barton, had made his way to the cockpit after seeing one of the other crewmen rushing towards the cockpit. He came up behind the crewman and shot him from behind. The bullet entered the back of the man's neck and exploded out through his larynx, ricocheting off a far wall from the gaping exit wound. A few passengers started to get up, but changed their minds after Clyde's other compatriots started waving their weapons around, threatening to blow away anyone who moved from their seats.

Clyde scowled at Barton and moved close to him, whispering, "What the fuck are you trying to do Bart? Blow a hole in the side of the ship? I don't give a rat's ass about this lump of shit lying on the floor here, but you gotta be careful where you shoot. Do you understand me?"

"Yeah Clyde, sorry about that," Bart mumbled. He was high on dope and was just itching to waste someone...again. Earlier, he almost pulled out his revolver and shot the crying woman next to him when he saw Clyde head up to the cockpit with his gun in the other crewman's back. *This shit is getting interesting*, he had thought, as his bloodshot eyes followed the two toward the cockpit. All of them had expected something like this might happen, so they were ready.

"I was just trying to stop this dude here from getting the jump on ya," Bart droned on. "But you need to know too, that all them people outside are climbing the rails outside."

While Clyde was busy with Barton, Jack turned down the mike receiver, but left it on. He wanted Tess to hear what was going on here and didn't want to take a chance that Clyde would force them to turn it off. He was about to grab the heavy log binder on his side as a possible weapon to fling at Clyde when mention of the people outside on the platform, or "rails" as Barton put it, diverted his attention and forced him to look outside.

8

What he saw took his breath away. The electrified fence was completely dead and hundreds, no *thousands*, of people were pouring through into the area surrounding the launch pad. There were hundreds already scaling the two hundred-foot launch platform. He looked up at one of the external monitors and saw hundreds more climbing, falling, jumping, and kicking at the ship. No one had made it to the critical areas of the platform where the ship was connected to the Solid Rocket Boosters. They could cause some serious damage if they make it there. And to his disappointment, he saw a number of them carrying weapons, and a few carrying what looked like portable blow torches.

When he turned back to Clyde, he saw that Clyde was looking outside too. "You see what I mean?" Clyde said, turning back to Jack. "If we keep sitting here, this mob will do something to the ship that will either cause it to blow up in space or never even leave the ground. We need to be leaving *now!*"

"Look…uh…Clyde, we have a team out there, and they were trying to confirm a problem with one of the rocket boosters. They're on their way here now, but we need to get someone to the portside umbilicus to let them in. They're almost there, and we can send some—"

"*There's no time for that Captain!*" Clyde yelled through clenched teeth. He knew from the mayor that there would be a backup team on the ship, and he was within a hair's breadth of just shooting this jackass' face off and getting the backup pilot. He leveled the gun at

Jack's face, "I know you have a backup team who can fly this crate, and I'm sure they won't hesitate to take off after they see me put a 9mm bullet through that smartass hole in your face." Bart chuckled at this. "So, start this bucket of bolts, and let's go *now!*"

Jack looked at Nate, who had turned as pale as cottage cheese. He was beginning to realize that his options were rapidly diminishing. In an unsteady voice, he said to Nate, "Go to Vertical Takeoff Mode now and start the five-minute countdown on my mark. You bozos might want to sit down," he said to Clyde and Bart. He then faced his control panel, flipped the engine startup sequence switch, hesitated a second, and then said "MARK."

Nate grudgingly set the countdown switch to five minutes and started working his controls to start up the engine and booster rocket sequence. A low rumbling could be felt deep within the ship's belly, as steam began to billow through the tubes connecting the ship and booster rockets.

Ironically, there were a number of cheers from the passengers, despite the gravity of the situation. It turned Jack's stomach to hear it, knowing that the lift-off would kill his maintenance crew out there on the side of the ship, not to mention the hundreds already scaling the platform like ants. Somewhere deep inside, he felt a sliver of strained relief that they were going to Vertical Takeoff Mode, otherwise, those desperate human ants would be all over the ship. The thought of his maintenance crew dying, however, brought the realization that there were millions, billions of people who would be left behind to die.

They're all out there, somewhere, waiting to die, he thought. Thousands were here at the launch site, mad with fear; millions more were huddled in basements, packed in churches, and even hiding in underground parking garages. Some of the real crazies though, were sitting on building rooftops getting wasted—they were enjoying their primetime seats to the end of the world extravaganza. He thought of Thelma and the others in underground shelters throughout the country and wondered what their real chances of survival might be. *Slim,* he thought, *but better than sitting on the surface of the world when this rock comes knocking at the door.*

The loud squawk on the comms box interrupted his train of thought. "Captain! What's going on? Are you running a countdown *test*? We haven't made it to the top section yet. Ten minutes tops. You got someone at the umbilicus portal?"

Nate started to flip the reply switch to respond to Gil when Clyde stopped him. "Uh-uh, why don't you just leave it be? You have other things you need to be concentrating on. He'll know in short order what's going on."

"Man, that's just mean! He has a right to know that we're about to leave him and his team. At least we can give them a chance to get off the platform and away from the ship when it takes off!" Nate had found his voice and was angry.

Clyde simply smiled and said coldly, "They're dead already; they just don't know it yet. You know as well as I do, that they'll never make it down to the ground before lift-off. And even if they do, they'll never make it through the crowd to a safe distance. And let's say by some miracle, that they *are* able to get far enough away from the ship. Then what? They'll huddle together in some God-forsaken basement, scared out of their minds, waiting to be smashed to bits. No, Mister "Co-Pilot". No waiting, no stalling. We got two minutes before takeoff, and that's what's going to happen."

Nate turned shakily back to the control panels. Jack looked from him to Clyde. Although he sympathized with Nate, on some level, he understood what Clyde was saying. There was no chance for the maintenance team. He only hoped that their deaths would be quick and painless. He studied the control panel readouts, while Nate checked the crew reports on the main screen, showing everyone all buckled in and ready to go.

Bart had buckled himself into one of the two cockpit jump seats while Clyde saw to the removal of the crewman's body. He had motioned over two nearby crewmen to secure the body. Clyde was buckling himself in at the one-minute mark when Jack started the countdown. He opened the loudspeaker so that the people on the ground and on the scaffolding could hear and maybe get themselves out of harm's way.

9

The engines were running at full capacity as the ship initiated its liftoff sequence. Deep within the ship, the fuel line connectors started pumping fuel into the booster rocket sections as they started the ignition process.

"*Captain? Jack! Hey guys...what the fuck?*" squealed Gil from the mike. He was frantic now, and Jack could hear his team in the background. They were all yelling and cursing at the same time. Jack switched on the mike, ignoring Clyde and Bart's threats. The ship was within seconds of lifting off. He wagered that they wouldn't dare take a chance at shooting him now.

"Gil, I'm very, very sorry about this, but we've been commandeered by men with guns. And we've been forced to take off now. Forgive me, if you can, and God be with you and your team."

"Jack! No! We have families on board! You don't have to—" This time, Jack cut off the mike of his own accord. There was nothing more he could say to Gil that would make any difference at this point. He thought he heard shouting in the passenger section, and he had a pretty good idea where it was coming from.

On the other end of the mike and more than 30,000 miles away, Tess was frantic. She had been yelling for Jack, but had to accept the fact that he was too preoccupied with his current predicament to answer. All she could do now was wait until liftoff and pray that the booster rocket didn't malfunction.

Outside the *Galileo2*, the scene was complete chaos. The people on the ground were running in all directions. Some bolted towards the ship, but most struggled to run in the opposite direction. Because of the sheer mass of people, running was virtually impossible. Hundreds were crushed where they stood, while many tripped and fell to the ground, never to get back up.

Many of the ones who ran towards the ship were firing weapons; some stolen from the soldiers who were guarding the site. They fired wildly at the ship, occasionally hitting one of the climbers in the back or leg, causing them to plummet from the platform. There was a huge explosion in the crowd as someone tried to lob a hand grenade at the ship. The thrower's distance from the ship and poor throw resulted in the grenade hitting the back of someone's head. It fell to the ground and exploded, killing and maiming those nearest.

On the platform, near the ship entrances, a few men tried burning through the steel hatch with blow torches, while others banged on the sides with axes, hammers, and steel pipes. Their fervor, as well as their madness, seemed to increase in line with the building energy and rumbling of the ship's engines. Some continued banging on the ship even as the launch platform moved to its final vertical liftoff position.

Inside the shuttle, about a third of the way towards the back in the passenger section, Mikey Tomlin sat peacefully, but his eyes were wide as he stared out at the craziness happening outside. He wondered absently, if he should be more afraid than he was, but he wasn't. He was about to go into space for crying out loud! Before this, the most exciting thing he had ever done was ride the Space Mountain ride at Disney World two summers ago. At the time, he thought he was quite brave for doing that (for a ten-year old that is!).

His mother, seated next to him, hadn't stopped crying since they got on the ship. He guessed she was crying because Dad didn't make the flight. He tried making his way here from their home in Phoenix, Arizona and made it all the way to El Paso, but that was where he stopped. He had called and said that the roads were completely jam-packed and that he was going to purchase a motorcycle and try to take some back roads to see if he could make it here. That was the last time his mom had talked to him because the cell phone service just stopped working.

He and his mom came to Houston about a month before so she could take him to see an eye specialist. While playing dodge ball in gym class, he was momentarily caught off guard after tagging out the other team's best dodge ball thrower. His throw was a sizzling spinner that slammed into Rory Jenkins' back like a sledgehammer. His classmates were cheering and high-fiving each other when a red blur came smashing into the side of his head. That particular hit had barely wiped the smile from his face, when the real pisser hit him. The second thrown ball hit him square in the eye, causing bright sparks to flash in his brain. He only felt dazed and started walking to the side when one of the girls pointed and screamed, while frantically backing away from him.

Apparently, the ball hit him so hard, that it forced his eye out of the socket, giving him a grotesque, *"scared out of his mind!"* look. After the girl screamed, only then did he realize that his vision was screwy. Blurry kids directly in front of him and very blurry kids to the left of him. That was the last thing he remembered because his head seemed to explode, and he fainted on the spot.

As a result, he and his mom ended up driving to Houston to see an eye specialist, who operated on Mikey's eye and repaired the nerve damage. While he was recuperating at his Aunt's house, his mother received a mysterious phone call on her cell phone. Before he knew it, they were whisked away, just like that. Now, here he sat on a spaceship rocket, going to the moon. His eye felt much better, but his mother still wanted him to keep the bandage on it. So, with one eye, he surveyed the chaotic scene on the ground with suppressed fear and childlike fascination.

He was looking out his window when he heard the gunshot. Before he even had a chance to react, his mother was shoving his head down into his lap. But he heard something else right before she grabbed his head. Something much closer, but not as loud. He thought it must have been a ricochet, but the sound was gone immediately, lost amongst the screaming inside the ship. When things subsided inside and he was finally able to lift his head, he found very small bits of glass in his lap and on the floor in front of him. He picked up one of the pieces and stared at it curiously. He started to unbuckle his belt to examine the glass on the floor, when one of the bad people yelled at him to get back in his seat. He froze and slowly turned his head to look outside again.

10

As the platform made its slow ascent to vertical, the people who had climbed up on the front end of the platform begin losing their balance and falling to the ground. Jack was amazed that they'd hung on for as long as they did. He turned to look at Nate, who gave him an absent nod. He swiveled back to the controls and looked up at the countdown clock, which was unnecessary, because the countdown sequence was voice-delivered.

Jack and Nate hit the dual ignition switch at the same time, as the smooth, anonymous voice of a British woman said "zero".

Jack waited for what seemed like an endless second. The humming he heard a minute earlier went silent. He felt no air coming through the ventilation system. His eyes shifted right, and he could see the people outside. No one moved. They were frozen in time, a large mass of upturned faces. For a second, Jack was certain that something had gone wrong and that somehow, the main rockets were damaged in the gunfire. He almost shut down the sequence, fearing that the rockets would explode, when the roar of the powerful rockets filled the insides of the ship. Slowly, the ship began to rise.

The people clinging to the platform were jarred loose and tumbled to the ground, as the passengers inside stared on in horror. Gil and his team had been hustling down the platform to make their way to the ground ladders when the ship started rising. When they got to the level of the rocket exhaust ports, one of them tripped and fell over the side. The fiery ignition incinerated the rest, killing them instantly.

RETURN TO EARTH

The ship rose in a fiery ascent along the platform, picking up speed. The people on the ground closest to the rear of the ship drowned in the fiery deluge of explosions. The ones still standing, ran screaming in all directions, fire dripping from their bodies, as they stumbled and fell and rolled to their deaths.

There were a number of cheers inside the ship, but many screamed. Whether they were cheering or screaming, most of them were crying. Mikey was so focused on the window to his front that he did neither. He saw where the glass had come from on his lap, and this made him nervous. The strong rattling of the ship seemed to shake everything. He didn't know much about the inside of spaceships, but he had seen many movies where a broken airplane window always sucked the people out before breaking into a million pieces. He reached over and grabbed his mother's hand and closed his eyes.

Jack and Nate were furiously working the controls of the ship as it picked up speed and energy. "Nate, check the pressure dials. It looks like the pressure is stable, but it's less than optimal."

"Roger Jack, checking now," Nate replied.

Clyde sat in the jump seat with his eyes shut tightly. He hated flying...HATED it. He'd had a terrible experience many years ago when a flight he was on flew through terrible turbulence. The plane had rocked up and down and eventually hit an air pocket where it seemed to drop like a rock before the pilot and co-pilot regained control. Everything that he had eaten before that flight plopped into his lap in a steaming pile of vomit. He looked over at Bart and saw that he was nodding off. "Hey shithead!" he yelled at him, not without a hint of jealousy. "Wake up before you drop your gun, and it goes off and blasts a hole in the ship!"

Bart jerked fully awake and almost did drop his gun. "Sorry boss," he replied groggily. He glanced at Jack and Nate and looked back at Clyde. "Up, up and away, huh boss?" Clyde grunted and closed his eyes again, trying to control the rising bile in his stomach.

The ship rose slowly into the sky, the rockets nearing the second stage of their ascent. "Confirming stable pressure, Jack," Nate said. "Ten seconds to SRB separation." Jack nodded, keeping his eyes glued to the control panel. *Almost there,* he thought, as the countdown clock dropped closer to SRB separation. Once the propellant was used up, the onboard computer would automatically separate both SRB's, alleviating any concerns he had about the port-side SRB. He closed his eyes and waited for the inevitable.

For the second time that night, time seemed to stop in its tracks. Jack steeled his body for the explosion he knew was coming, but when the SRB's separated without incident, he felt himself shudder with relief. He didn't realize how tense he had been waiting for the rocket to explode. He thought absently, how sore his body would be later from the constant tension. He almost jumped when Clyde's voice from behind him shouted out, "See Captain, no problem, right?" Clyde was smiling, but the tension in his face betrayed the fact that he was terrified too.

Jack didn't reply. He was concentrating hard on the controls. Their speed had reached just over 3600 miles per hour. He estimated that they would be leaving Earth's atmosphere in less than five minutes. All gauges looked good, but he was slightly worried about the pressure gauge. It still showed within normal range, but at the low end of the range and wavering.

"Jack," Nate said, "are you reading the pressure gauges at—"

Jack interrupted him, "Yeah...I see it. Looks like it might be holding, but...I don't know."

11

Mikey opened his eyes again. He was terrified, yet exhilarated! His initial fright at the onset was over, replaced by complete fascination. They were high above the earth, making their way through the darkened skies. He stared out his window, straining to see stars. He had always like looking at the stars, but what made things different now was his *perspective*. In his backyard at home, he'd gazed up at the stars on quite a few occasions, craning his neck upward while trying not to lose his balance. Now, he was on the same *level* as the stars, in a matter of speaking.

As best he could, he looked toward the rear of the space craft and saw that they were far above the ground now. Texas slowly lost its uniqueness and began to blend into the surrounding landmasses. He looked further out and saw a huge shape in the distance. Despite the darkness, there was still enough light for him to see the jagged edges and irregular shapes that made up *Lycos*. He felt a shiver go down his spine, as he stared at the monstrosity.

Mikey turned his eyes away from the massive object and tried to look in the direction they were going, to see if he could see the moon, when he heard a small hiss. At first, he thought the pilots were pumping oxygen or something into the cabin because that's what they do once they got into space, right? He imagined he could actually feel himself lift a little from the seat.

He glanced at the window toward his front and was shocked to see that the glass was starting to crack. He thought that maybe the meteor had thrown some meteor rocks or something toward them. Then he realized that the bullet did in fact ricochet off the window. He stared in horror as the window seemed to grow tentacles right before his eyes.

12

"Continued decrease in cabin pressure Jack!" Nate called out over the loud engine noise. "We're hemorrhaging air somewhere and fast!" He started to unbuckle his harness when Jack ordered him to stay put. They had yet to jettison the External Tank and he didn't want to chance Nate getting hurt during this stage of the ascent.

"This can is bucking like a horse Nate; I need you here!" He flipped up one of the inter-cabin switches and snatched up the mike "Charlie, we're leaking air somewhere back there, and I need you to check it out!"

Clyde started to say something, but Jack cut him off rudely, "I don't want to hear it! Right now, I have bigger problems than your gun, so if you want to shoot me, then be my fucking guest!"

Clyde's mouth dropped open to say something, but the look in Jack's face told him that no amount of threats would work on this man. At least not now. In all honesty, he was getting scared. The ship was really shaking now and this threat of a leak was unnerving. He tightened his seat belt and closed his eyes.

Charlie scanned the interior of the cabin from where he was seated. People were crying and holding one another. He looked at his wife and saw fear so thick that he couldn't bear to look at her. He was afraid too, but he had to find out what the problem was or they would be in serious trouble.

As he looked, his eyes fell on a young kid only a few rows above him, pointing to one of the port windows. He followed the kid's finger to the fractured port window. His bowels seemed to go loose as he stared at the slowly spreading cracks. Picking up the mike on his seat, he called the captain. "Jack, this is bad! We got a starboard window that's cracking fast!" He yanked open the utility pouch nearest him and frantically dug around for sealant, praying that it would be enough to maintain the integrity of the window.

Jack wrestled with the increasingly unstable ship. The cabin pressure needle continued dropping. He could feel the pressure building up within the shuttle and it was becoming harder and harder to breathe. He was so busy fighting with the controls that he hadn't take the time to put his face mask on.

He couldn't see what was happening in the passenger compartment, but he knew it would be total chaos. With their face masks, they would be able to breathe, but the pressure would continue building unless Charlie could repair the hole before it exploded in on itself. He glanced over at Clyde and Bart. They both looked as if they were about to pass out.

With sealant in hand, Charlie tried to make his way up to the kid's row and over to the window when all of a sudden, it exploded inward. He felt as if he had been snatched by an invisible hand and thrown unceremoniously towards the small broken window. He made a herculean effort to grab the back of one of the seats and almost missed it. Two men grabbed at his outstretched arm and pulled him into their row. They hunkered there, holding firmly to their seats. Articles of clothing, books, and paper whipped around the passenger section before being sucked out the window. Whatever was not tied down was sucked through the widening window space.

Charlie could see the darkening void and knew that they would be in space very soon. Miraculously, he still had his headset on and he yelled into now. *"It's too late Captain! The starboard window is gone and I can see the entire side buckling. It won't hold for long. I'm sorry!"*

Everyone in the cockpit listened intently as Charlie spoke. Jack looked at Clyde dispassionately. "You've killed us all, you ass. You and your stupid partner there." Bart looked up dully. He had soiled himself and was mumbling. Nate hugged himself tightly, tears coursing down his cheeks. Clyde started to say something when there was a huge explosion in the cabin. The ship jerked violently, as smoke and screams drifted in from the cabin. And as the ship tore itself apart, the last thing Jack thought he heard, before white-hot fire tore through him, was Tess screaming desperately in his ear.

UNDERGROUND

1

Daddy, can we keep the fire truck? I like the noise it makes. Can you hear it Daddy? Daddy? Can you hear it? Can you? HEAR IT! Stan's eyes flew open. He could hear distant sirens and wondered somewhere if there was an auto accident or if a house was on fire. He tasted blood inside his mouth and when he moved to sit up, he screamed in agony. His hand flew to the small of his back and just as fast, he yanked it away. His back felt covered in spikes and when he looked at his hand, he could see that it was covered with blood. *Where am I,* he thought. *What hap...*and then the full weight of what happened hit him like a fast-moving freight train and he screamed again, this time not in pain, but despair.

The alarm he was hearing came from his vehicle, but as he listened, he could tell that it was already dying out. At some point, he must have come out of his seatbelt because he was lying on the inside roof of his SUV on his side. He could feel something pressing into his rib cage. He moved slightly and could see that he was lying on top of the inside dome light. He rolled onto his stomach and looked around the inside of the SUV, afraid of what he might see. He saw a lot of blood, and his stomach made a slight hitching sound.

He tried to rise to his knees, but the headrests of the passenger seat and driver seat prevented him from doing so. He resigned himself to just crawling on his elbows and tried to get to the back of the vehicle. Before he had moved a foot, he found himself staring into the open eyes of his mother-in-law. She had also become unbuckled from her seatbelt and was lying on the inside roof of the vehicle. He opened his mouth to speak to her when he noticed the impossible angle of her neck in relation to where her body was. Her neck was badly broken and surprisingly, there was no blood on her face, but there was no doubt that she was dead. He reached out with shaking hands to close her eyes. His first attempt poked her in the left eye and the yielding softness almost caused him to vomit. His second attempt was successful and he shuddered with relief.

He started his slow progress toward the back of the jeep to look for his son, afraid of what he would fine, when he heard very faint moaning. It was coming from above him. He rolled over on his back and saw that his son was still clasped tightly in his seat, his arms and feet dangling down past his head. *I've got to get him out of that seatbelt,* Stan thought. He peered closely at his son's face. The light was failing, but Stan didn't think it was nighttime just yet. *Lycos* must be closer now, blocking the light of the sun and casting a gigantic death shadow over the world. His son's face looked swollen and flush, but there appeared to be no cuts or scrapes on it. Stan reached up and around his son's waist and felt for the clasp which held the tightly buckled strap. He then braced himself under his son to catch him once the belt let use. Once in position under his son, he jammed his fingers into the red catch, but it wouldn't budge. It held tightly. He supported his son's weight so that he could lessen the pressure on the catch. This time, the red catch pushed in and his son fell into his arms.

It took Stan about an hour to extract his mother-in-law from the vehicle. He buried her under a pile of bricks he ferried from a partially destroyed office building across the street. He said a quick prayer and went back to the truck to salvage what he could from the back. He felt that the silent prayer was as much for him, as it was for his mother-in-law. When he had realized that their shuttle passes were gone, he felt an intense wave of despair, desolation, and guilt. Tess had expected them to be on her shuttle. If they missed her takeoff window, then they would be placed on Jack's shuttle, but she would be worried sick until she had confirmation that they were safely on board. With no confirmation, she would be waiting for them at the Moon Base when the shuttle arrived. This thought brought on another pang of sorrow, as he envisioned her wide scared eyes darting back and forth as the last few people disembarked from Jack's shuttle. *She's a strong girl,* he thought, *but this would practically unhinge her.* He stood there with his hands in his pockets and head hung low, trying without success to hold back the tears.

At some point, between the prayer and the first load of stuff from the truck, his son woke up. He started weeping when he saw the floral hat of his grandmother sitting at the top of the burial mound.

"Hey there son. It's okay", Stan said as he sat down next to his son. "Grandma is with Grandpa now, and I'm sure they're both happy to have each other again, don't you think?"

His son's wide eyes looked from his father's face back to where his grandmother lay. "Was she scared?" he asked.

"No, not at all," he lied. "She was just angry at all of this," he gestured around at the bleak and busted up buildings on the street. "I really think that she is in a better place, and I'm certain she'll be watching over us."

Lenny smiled a little and then looked around apprehensively. Stan looked around too. He thought he had heard some noises earlier, but he thought the noises were far away. They sounded much closer now.

He stood up stiffly and touched his son on the head, "Come on son. Why don't we find someplace that's a little safer, huh?" Lenny glanced over at his grandmother's burial site once more, wiped his face with the back of his hand, and then stood up next to his father.

Something crashed loudly in the alley behind a boutique shop, and it startled both of them. The first thing that came to Stan's mind was that the men who assaulted them and stole their passes had come back. But Stan knew this was not the case. The main entrance to the shuttle launch site was not very far, and the men would be foolish to come back here. Unless of course, they couldn't use the passes. After slipping on his backpack, Stan grabbed his son's hand and started making his way away from the overturned SUV and the burial site of his recently deceased mother-in-law. In his other hand, he carried his son's backpack.

They quickly moved down the trash-littered street, but like the other streets they had driven on, not all of the debris was trash. There were dead bodies everywhere. Now that they were moving away from the area where they were attacked, where the smell of the SUV's spilled gasoline was almost overpowering, he could now smell the fresh decay of the rotting bodies. The area looked like a war zone. He surmised that this area must have been blockaded by the military because of the DO NOT CROSS barricades that were lying on their sides. He didn't understand why this particular area had been blocked off. Across the street, one of the barricades had been thrust through the window of Sam's Fine Bakery. Moldy bread and other assorted discolored bakery items lay on the sidewalk in front of the store. They walked half a block further and found a pharmacy that was all but picked clean. After ten minutes of searching the store, Stan found a bottle of peroxide that had rolled under the shelving and surprisingly, a package of facemasks. He put one on, and then tied one on his son.

Many of the dead bodies that they came across had been shot. *This must have been horrible,* he thought, forcing his eyes away from the headless remains of a man's body. Just as they turned right at Fording Street, they heard crunching glass very close behind them. Stan whirled around; his lips pulled back in a vicious snarl as he yanked his son behind him. Earlier, he had found a policeman's baton, and he was now holding it like a medieval knight readying himself for battle.

In front of him, not more than 15 feet away, was a scraggly German Shepherd puppy, probably not even a year old yet. It looked at them with that odd, hopeful smile that only dogs know how to do. Lenny exclaimed excitedly and ran around his dad toward the dog.

"No Lenny! He...she...it might have rabies or something!" shouted Stan. His warning to his son was too late though. Before he realized it, the dog and his son had closed the distance between themselves. Stan looked down at them and tried to suppress a laugh. His son and the dog were rolling around on the ground; his son was laughing; the dog was licking.

"Alright, alright, that's enough. Come on Lenny, we need to get out of here," Stan told his son.

"Okay dad," his son said breathlessly. "Can we keep him? He's all alone and needs a family! Mom will love him when she sees..." he halted himself, his face contorting.

"Tell you what son, let's keep him, okay? You're right, he does need a family, and we're just the ones to be his family. Do you think you can take care of him?" Stan hoped this line of talk would help keep his son's mind off his mother and this whole crazy situation. Back at the safe house, he had told his son that they were going to ride in a space ship and go to the same place where his mother would be. Of course, that was before things went utterly and irrevocably wrong.

Lenny wiped a single tear from his face and nodded. "Sure dad, I'll take care of him. He'll be my best friend." He patted the dog's head and wiped at his face again.

Stan looked at the two of them, standing there amidst the backdrop of broken and burned out stores, abandoned cars, broken glass, and bodies. It was very surreal. From the time they left the SUV, he felt that his mind was swimming through mud. Everything seemed hazy. But as he stared at his son and the dog, a persistent thought finally broke through the fog of his mind. It occurred to him that they were the only ones in the immediate area. He had seen very small groups of people at a distance, but in a city this size, he felt that there should have been more people.

He began to wonder where they were, but realized that they would go to the place that offered any possibility of help. They would go to the airfield where the shuttles were. They were hoping against hope that they may somehow get a seat on the shuttle, or that maybe the shuttle could make roundtrips to the moon and back, scooping up hundreds of people at a time on each return trip. They would go to the airfield, and there they would stay until the very end. Stan hoped that the shuttles would be able to take off safely, but he knew human behavior and knew that in the end, the last thread of normal human behavior would dry up and snap and that desperate people would do anything to stay alive.

They walked for about a mile down Fording Street when he thought he heard voices. He froze and put his hand on Lenny's shoulder while raising his finger to his lips. The puppy looked up at them curiously and then proceeded to empty his bladder on the curb.

The voices seemed to be coming from down the street where a large pile up of cars blocked his view. He grabbed Lenny by the arm and was about to dive into one of the empty stores when he caught sight of the owners of the voices and almost burst out laughing. Coming around the five-car pileup were four sheep. A small baby lamb brought up the rear, tripping over the broken concrete in the road. They walked right past Stan, apparently not too worried about him and his small party.

At first, he wondered where the animals came from, but then remembered that there was a local petting zoo nearby. Once the animals trotted by, he grabbed Lenny's hand, and they headed across the street. He wanted to find a place they could rest overnight before it got too dark to see where they were going.

2

They crossed to the other side of the street and were walking past a huge underground parking garage when a man called out to them. Stan didn't see him initially when he looked down the alley because the man had been dumping trash in one of the several dumpsters lining the alley-side of the building. Stan yanked his head sharply towards the voice, immediately tightening his hand around the baton.

"Hello sir," the man said, a little more timid than the first time. He saw the anxious look in Stan's face, and his tightened grip on the baton.

"You don't have to worry about me sir. I'm just saying hello. There's a group of us down in the garage. Families, kids, a couple of pets. We've got food too. I saw you and your boy, and I figured I'd say hello. The way things are, I think it's better to be with others than out wandering all alone. Things have gotten very dangerous."

Stan slowed his pace and looked at the man. He seemed friendly enough, but things had indeed gotten dangerous. He thought he should just say hello and keep on walking, but exactly where was he walking *to*? To the shuttle launch site, where thousands were no doubt already amassing? He wouldn't get within a mile of that place. The people who stole his pass might be able to force their way through, but not him with an injured back and a young child. No, it was much too dangerous to go there now, and the chances of him getting on the shuttle without passes would be slim to none.

He looked at the sky and guessed that it was probably close to five o'clock in the afternoon. Tess's shuttle would be gone by now, and Jack would be leaving in less than two hours, if he hadn't already left. Even if he was still there, they probably had the shuttle doors closed. If they didn't, then they were fools.

"Hi," Stan said. He crossed the street toward the man and held out his hand. "Stan Robinson, and this is my son, Lenny—"

"Len!" Lenny blurted out.

Stan smiled, "Yes, that's right. This is Len, my son. And this furry fella is..." he stammered for a second. "What's his name son?"

Len thought for a second and then brightened. "His name is 'Buddy'!"

"Martinez. Nathan Martinez. Very nice to meet you Stan!" Nathan's strong grip gave Stan's hand two smart pumps and then let go. He extended his hand to Len and smiled. "Nice to meet you Len!" Len smiled uncertainly and looked up at his father. Stan nodded and said, "Go on son. You can shake his hand." Nathan gave Len a professional handshake with a mock serious look which made Len laugh.

"And how are you Buddy?" He briskly ruffled the dog's head, simultaneously scratching behind his ears. Buddy's leg started jumping, and they all laughed.

3

"We're at the bottom level of this parking garage," Nathan told Stan as they moved into the parking structure. "It goes down five levels, if you can believe that. There are signs everywhere down there identifying the bottom level as the building's fallout shelter. Surprisingly, there's only one person in our group who actually worked in the building. He told me there were several local and federal government agencies housed here, and this was their parking garage." They walked down the stairs even though there was still power in the garage. Stan had no objection to this. The last thing he needed was to get trapped in an elevator in an underground parking garage.

They descended deeper and deeper into the garage. Each level was more desolate than the ones before. Stan was not a claustrophobic man, but the deeper they went, the more he could feel the weight of the parking garage and the five-story building above them. Nathan didn't seem to notice. If he did, he didn't show it. He continued chatting amiably, as they made their way down to level five.

Nathan Martinez had been a successful entrepreneur. He owned his own construction company, which he built from a one-man handyman shop out of his garage. He attended college, but during his junior year, he got his girlfriend Angela, now his wife, pregnant. He dropped out to get married and took a job with a local construction company. After years of contract work, he decided that he could do a much better job and decided to branch out on his own. To his surprise, his small company grew quickly and before he knew it, he was the owner of a multi-million-dollar company.

Moving to the Tree Grove sub-division had been a dream-come-true. The houses were beautiful; each with cool glistening swimming pools and large inviting lawns. The secure sub-division was bordered by a man-made body of water and only accessible through the sub-division gates, manned by a 24-hour police security guard.

When the rioting started, they saw it on the news in neighborhoods they never heard of. Before long, it was happening right outside their windows. They had stocked up some time ago, and so they had no need to venture outside. Eventually, they lost power and had to consider the option of leaving their home.

"Many of us wanted to stay in our homes, but people were going crazy. Breaking into homes and killing others just for the hell of it! I had no significant weapons in the house, except for my handgun and shotgun that I purchased last year for home protection. I didn't think I would need it and wondered if I'd even be able to use it. As things turned out, I don't think we would be here if I didn't have them."

As they passed one of the sub-levels, Stan noticed a couple of expensive looking cars caked with dust and idly wondered where their owners were right now.

"Several families banded together, including Ralph Metzinger, the guy who worked in this building here. He told us about this place, and so we loaded what we could and made our way here. Luckily, we were the first ones here, but things were starting to get really bad then."

Nathan grew silent and Stan could see that he was trying to collect himself. He walked on in silence as they made their way down to level four, where Stan noticed only one car. All of its tires were flat and the windows were busted out. It looked as if someone had used it for target practice.

Nathan started talking again, his voice thick, "Sorry Stan, it was very scary when we first left. People everywhere in the streets; they were fighting and shooting one another. We came the back way, but when we got here, two guys jumped out of nowhere and demanded our stuff. We gave them everything they could carry, and they still shot at us. They killed Ralph's daughter with the first shot. They shot his wife too, but she died later from loss of blood and infection. They ran, but didn't get far. We caught up with them in less than ten minutes. You see, they couldn't go very fast with all of the stuff they were carrying. We got our stuff back and Ralph, well, Ralph took out his revenge on them. We didn't stop him though. We just kept our guns pointed at them while Ralph exorcised his demons on them."

As Stan listened to Nathan's recount of how Ralph had bludgeoned the men to death, he had expected to feel self-righteous or repulsed, but didn't. What he did feel was a smothering sense of grateful revenge. He considered his own situation and what had just happened to him, his mother-in-law, and Lenny. If they were all still conscious when their attackers stole their passes, he was certain that they would have been killed without hesitation. Could he do what Ralph did if he were in the same situation? Yes, without a doubt.

As they reached the bottom level, Stan realized that there was no longer a ramp to allow cars down here. Level 4 was the last level for vehicles. In fact, the only way in was through a door that resembled a bank vault door. In the middle at eye level, was a small peep hole.

Nathan picked up a rock sitting next to the foot of the door. He used it to rap on the door, but they were not random knocks. After about two to three minutes, someone rapped back. A series of long and short raps. Nathan listened attentively, and then rapped once. After a few seconds, Stan could hear bolts being drawn back and knobs turning, and then the door swung open.

Two men were standing in the entryway as Stan stepped in. They were both holding shotguns and were staring intently at Stan.

"Stan, this is Nick Wilton and this is Ralph Metzinger. Guys, this is Stan Robeson...no Stan *Robinson*." As soon as they realized that Stan was not a threat to Nathan, their demeanor changed. They lowered their shotguns and came forward.

Nick reached out to shake Stan's hand, "Sorry Stan, didn't mean to give you the cold shoulder. We just have to be very careful who gets in. We have families here. Children too, as you can see. We've had a lot of dangerous people show up and I'll be damned if we let just anybody in here."

Stan looked around. He had half-expected to see beaten down families and scared children huddled about one another, but instead, he saw several young children playing games and chasing one another. Some were even watching a movie! Stan looked stupidly at the screen and projector and wondered where the power was coming from when he saw long cords snaking along the back wall.

As if reading his mind, Nathan said, "We let the kids watch a movie or something once a day. It helps keep their minds off of...you know, what's going on out there." He jerked his thumb in the direction they had come.

Stan looked around and took in his surroundings. There were about 40-50 people in here and looking at the number of children, he assumed that most of them were families. There were a few older couples and some young couples, but most of the people looked to be anywhere from their early thirties to mid-fifties, putting him almost exactly in the middle at 41. He also saw a couple of dogs, several cats, and what looked to be a hamster in a cage.

"How long have you been down here?" Stan asked. "You look well-organized and almost comfortable."

"Yeah, I know," Nathan looked around, smiled and waved his hand at a little girl playing hopscotch. "That's my daughter there," he pointed, "Her name is Bonnie, and my wife Angela is over there with the other cooks preparing dinner. Yeah, we've been here for almost two weeks. Even before things had gotten bad in our neighborhood, we felt that we needed to be deep underground *somewhere*. This was the best place we could get to before the roads became congested with traffic. I'm sure you noticed that after level 4, this bottom level is completely blocked off to vehicle and foot traffic. The only way to this level is the way we came, and we always keep that security door locked and guarded."

Stan was impressed with the military-style security these folks had set up to secure themselves five levels underground. He could see now how these people could relax down here. Luckily, the late fall weather kept the air nice and cool. He could only imagine how hot it would get down here in the summer with no power to run the air conditioning units. But they wouldn't be here during the summer. No one would be here. Despite the sturdiness of this reinforced level, this place was designed to withstand natural disasters that originated on Earth. What was coming for them was not natural and where it originated, God only knew. This place will be so much rubble after *Lycos* smashes into the earth. Standing there in the artificial light, surrounded by laughing kids and socializing parents, he could almost feel the weight of the meteor as well as this place bearing down on him.

"You know," Nathan continued, "it was very scary here the first week we were here. There were only 20 of us then, mostly folks from my neighborhood. We could hear the crowds above yelling, screaming, and shooting. There were a number of explosions further away." He waved his arms around, "We didn't have anything here except what we carried from our homes, and we were too afraid to go out until the fighting died down. Occasionally, a group of people would try to get down here, but they couldn't get through the door and eventually gave up."

A few folks walked past them, nodding cordially. Stan couldn't help but notice a hint of uneasiness in their glances.

"About four or five days ago," Nathan continued, "the noise up there quieted down to a few shouts and sporadic gunfire – it's amazing how well sound travels down here! After a while, there was nothing. No vehicles, no voices, nothing. We started running out of food and supplies, so we organized scouting parties to search the surrounding areas above. Each time, they would return with one or two families in tow. Sometimes only half of the scouting parties would return; sometimes none at all. On occasion, we would have families or groups of people want to leave to see if they could get on one of the shuttles because they had heard there were slots available. They never returned either."

Len tugged on Stan's arm and asked, "Dad, can I go over and watch the movie?"

Stan looked over at the group watching the movie and then looked at Nathan, who nodded happily. "Sure, go ahead," said Stan, "but keep an eye on Buddy."

"Okay, dad," Len said over his shoulder. "Come on Buddy!" The puppy jumped up and ran awkwardly behind Len, trying to keep up.

"How do you think this place will hold out once *Lycos* hits?" Stan asked Nathan and Nick, once his son was out of earshot.

Nick took in a deep breath and shuddered as he let it out. "I don't know Stan. Honest to God, I don't know. There's a panel on one of the walls that describes how this fallout shelter was designed, and what it can reasonably withstand. It lists things like earthquakes and tornados, but for something like *this*, I haven't a clue how it will do. From the little bit of information the government actually put out, this thing is a planet killer. And if it's as large as they say it is, I don't think the earth will be in one piece when it's over."

"I tend to agree," said Stan. "I only hope it's quick." He glanced over at Len and the other children. They were laughing hysterically at the movie, totally oblivious to the world outside this microcosm.

Nick observed Stan watching the kids. "I sometimes envy their naiveté. Not a care in the world." He paused for a second and then looked at Nathan. "We finally got behind that wall, and you need to see it with your own eyes." He turned towards Stan, "I'm not sure Nathan mentioned this to you yet, but this is something you might want to see too."

4

As they moved deeper into the recesses of the fallout shelter, Stan couldn't help but be amazed at its expert design and functionality. From what he could see, he estimated that the shelter was anywhere from eight to ten thousand square feet. Where the kids were, would have been considered a common area. Just past that was a walled-in kitchen area with large entryways on each side. He could see part of a dirty gray exhaust vent coming out of the kitchen and up into the ceiling of the shelter.

Past the common area and the kitchen and built along the far wall to the right and along the wall to the rear of the shelter, were walled-off, independent rooms. Each room appeared to have its own door and looked large enough to easily sleep four to six people. Spaced evenly throughout the shelter were huge load bearing columns. Stan could see colorful scrawling and doodling on many of the nearby columns. They moved past the main area towards a narrow passageway flanked by a few storage closets. The passageway went on for another 15 feet before ending at a busted-up wall.

Nick looked at Stan curiously, "What line of business are you in Stan—or *were* in—before all this?"

Stan chuckled, "I'm an aerospace engineer with a specialty in Generation Engineering Design."

"Okay, I understand the 'aerospace engineer' part, but what the heck is 'generation engineering design'?" Nathan asked.

"I worked for NASA, and my team and I were responsible for designing self-sustaining generation starships capable of traveling extremely long distances in space over long periods of time. My team consisted of experts in the fields of biosphere systems, biological structures, psychologists, social engineers, and a number of lesser fields. Before the discovery of *Lycos*, we were working on a prototype generation starship that we hoped to test on a Mars expedition. It was designed to hold close to 500 people and house some 30 species of animals. It contained a biosphere ecosystem capable of growing crops, plants and trees and a water system containing over 25 species of freshwater marine life.

"But we never got the chance. After *Lycos* was sighted, we were seconded by the government and our project timeline got cut in half. We were directed to modify our generation starship design to one that could travel as far as Jupiter, or more specifically, to one of Jupiter's moons, *Europa*."

Nathan stared at Stan intently. They had all stopped just short of a narrow passageway and turned to look at Stan. "*Europa*? What the hell's on *Europa*?"

Stan explained to them the information they received from the satellite orbiting *Europa* and how it might be humankind's only real chance at long-term survival. When he had finished, Nick stated flatly, "It sounds like you need to be up there on the moon. What the hell are you doing down here?"

Stan looked at the ground and shook his head. When he looked up, his face was a mask of despair. "My wife Tess is the pilot for the *Galileo1*. We were headed to her shuttle when we were attacked. Because my son had to have open heart surgery, he couldn't be moved until damn near the 11th hour." His eyes started to cloud over, and he rubbed at them furiously. "I was knocked unconscious after we were attacked trying to get to the airfield and when I woke up, I was absolutely terrified that Lenny...that my son was dead."

Nathan put his arm around Stan's shoulders, and they stood that way for a few minutes until Stan recovered himself. "My mother-in-law didn't make it, and I found that our authorization passes were gone. So, we started walking and eventually ran into Nathan here. I considered trying to make it the airfield, but as you already know, the streets are extremely dangerous. Besides, the shuttles are probably halfway to the moon by now."

"Well Stan," Nathan said, "we're glad to have you here for as long as *Lycos* will let us. And since you're here now, we'd like to show you something that we just stumbled upon that you might find very interesting." Nathan turned towards the narrow passageway where several folks had congregated. As they neared the broken wall at the far end of the passageway, Nick added, "The entire underground structure is walled-in by standard drywall material and insulation. Beyond that is the actual solid brick wall of the shelter. Earlier today, we were loading some supplies back here because it's a little bit cooler as you can probably tell. We had some of the younger kids helping out, and they got a little sloppy." Nick pointed to the wall. "They stacked up too many boxes unevenly and they eventually ended up falling over into the wall here, knocking a hole into it. We felt a slight draft blowing through it and were just about to investigate it when you and your son showed up."

Stan looked closely at the wall. Sure enough, he could feel a cool breeze wafting through the small hole in the wall. "Do you guys have any crowbars or sledgehammers here? I have a feeling there is a manmade hole behind this wall."

"Our thoughts exactly," said Nathan smiling. "And yes, we do have crowbars and sledgehammers here. On our last run, we found a Home Depot that hadn't been picked over too badly and picked up some supplies and tools." Nathan stepped into one of the supply rooms and emerged with a pristine sledgehammer in his hands. He turned to Stan with a serious look on his face, "I guess now we'll see what's behind door number one."

5

Thelma had a raging headache, and she was pissed. She had been monitoring the fallout shelter and its inhabitants since they arrived. She tried in vain and without success to convince Bennett Watts, the shelter leader, to let the people in. Bennett was an ex-Marine, and although he was out of the Marines, he still wore his hair in the typical "high-n-tight" fashion.

Bennett was very strict about the rules, and Thelma respected that about the man, but the 45 or so people in the garage fallout shelter could have easily fit into their shelter since 39 of the 75 people who had slots never showed up. Thelma wasn't sure what had happened to them and didn't really want to know. Too much despair and death were happening everywhere, and she tried to isolate herself from that pain as much as possible.

Unfortunately, Bennett refused to even consider letting the garage folks in because he was afraid of running out of food and water. And it wasn't just Bennett who was afraid; it seemed everyone was infected with fear. She was afraid too, but she still had compassion for people. She could see that the people in the garage shelter were scared too, but they were peacefully coexisting despite the unspeakable horror hanging over their heads.

Bennett walked into the little alcove that was set up as one of the monitoring stations and stood behind her, looking at the people on the monitor. "Thelma, I understand how you feel, I really do, but—" he began.

"But nothing, Ben!" Thelma blurted out, as she whirled around in her chair. "You *know* we have the space *and* the resources to let those folks in here. When it's all said and done, our chances in here might be no better than their chances out there, but at least they would have *some* hope."

Bennett was stunned by Thelma's outburst and backed up a couple of steps. Being 6'4", he wasn't worried about being attacked by a woman Thelma's size—she was all of 130 pounds soaking wet. It was the fierceness in her face that caught him off-guard. "I, uh...we...it's not my call Thelma. We...er...have to vote on things like this, and the other team leaders just don't want to take any chances like this."

"What about the children?" Thelma pleaded. "We can just take the children. I'm sure the parents would be more than happy to see that their children are taken care of."

"Thelma, you know as well as I do, that we can't do that. Even if they agreed to that, some of them might still try to overtake us and force their way in. There are more of them than us and if we let them in, they could easily overtake us. Right now, they don't even know we're here, and I'd like to keep it that way. Remember, they have plastic explosives and there may be some in the group who would be crazy enough to use them to gain access here. No, we must remain resolute in this." He paused for a second and then added without much conviction, "It's the right decision." He turned around sharply and left the room, leaving Thelma to stare at the countdown clock and the helpless people in the garage.

6

Stan, Nathan, and Nick gaped at the empty space behind the brick wall. They were all at a loss for words.

"Now this is something you don't find every day in a parking garage," said Nick, shining his flashlight into the darkness in the hole.

"Well, being that this is a 'government-owned' garage, I wouldn't put anything past them," Nathan added.

Stan peered through the darkness, "Having been in the military most of my life, I've heard of a lot of crazy shit, so this is not too far off the scale. Plus, we knew that the government built a number of underground shelters around the country. Maybe they started on one here and decided to put it somewhere else."

Ralph walked up with the extra flashlights and handed them around. "I can tell you one thing; there was never a hint that anything was going on here except for..." he paused, seeming to remember something. "You know what? We had to move out of the building for almost a year because of a gas leak or something. I didn't think much of it at the time because we were temporarily housed in one of the oil company buildings downtown. The offices there were awesome, so none of us were too crazy to come back here when the building reopened."

"Hmm...it appears they reopened more than just your office," Stan added. "You know, this area might be a little stronger than the fallout shelter. I'd like to check it out. To use a military term loosely, this area might end up being our 'fall back' position when the shit hits the fan."

Nathan clapped him on the back. "Good idea my friend, I'm right behind you."

They laughed at this, and then the four men crawled through the hole into darkness.

THELMA'S CRUISE

1

"Come on, Thelma! The show starts in less than 15 minutes. I'm pretty damn sure that they'll give up our seats if we're not seated when the curtains go up!"

Thelma gave Tom a sidewise glance that told him he'd better shut up or have another drink. He opened his mouth to say something, thought better of it, and headed over to the bar.

Thelma continued putting on her make up. As she reloaded her powder puff, she thought once again about how much she was enjoying herself. Before this trip, she and Tom had only been on one cruise, and it turned out to be a disaster. On the second day out, the ship encountered mechanical problems and had to return to port in Miami. The cruise line was good enough to pay for another cruise for them, all expenses paid, with the exception of airfare. It would seem their good graces extended only so far.

Now here they were, making good on their second cruise opportunity and everything was going swimmingly. Other than Tom's occasional pestering, Thelma thought this was the best trip they had been on in a long time.

2

They walked hand in hand down the narrow corridor lined with brightly colored paintings of various ships. A cruise staffer squeezed alongside the wall and smiled broadly at them. Before he had a chance to ask if he could help, Tom reached out and grabbed his arm. "Hey young man, where can we find the..." he fumbled in his pocket for the two show tickets for that evening's performance. "Where can we find the *D.S. Littleton Amphitheater?*"

The young man politely disengaged himself from Tom's grasp and reached inside his jacket pocket. He produced a small brochure with a picture of two smiling men and a woman wearing what looked like tuxedos above the waist and leotards below. A huge white tiger lay before them, staring placidly ahead.

"You're almost there, sir. It's on the other side of the atrium just ahead." He pointed down the hall and Thelma saw a sign that read *D.S. Littleton Amphitheater.* A small black arrow pointed the way.

"I see it Tom! It's right there. Thank you, young man". Thelma was reaching into her purse for a tip, when the young man held up his hand, "That won't be necessary ma'am. It was my pleasure." And then he was off down the hall. He turned at the next corner and was gone.

3

The entrance to the theater didn't look like much to Thelma, but the moment she stepped inside, she was thunderstruck. They entered the theater from the top level of stairs, so she could see the other levels of seats circling the theater. But they didn't circle the theater entirely. It was more of a semi-circle going up three levels.

When she first found out where they were seated, she was disappointed and worried that they wouldn't be able to see the show. She hadn't complained though; to see Morash, Micah, and The Lady and her Cat in a live animal act on a *cruise ship* was unheard of! These guys had performed in Vegas, Atlantic City, New York, and even in Paris. Only few could be so lucky!

After a few stepped-on toes and banged knees, they finally made their way to their seats. As it turned out, they were only three rows down from where they entered the theater and Thelma was cautiously pleased to see that maybe their view wouldn't be too bad after all. Tom leaned over and kissed her on the cheek. As if on cue, the lights went out, save for the red orbs circling the stage. Thelma reached out and grabbed Tom's hand excitedly as the show started.

4

When the bright lights came back on, Morash and Micah Moriarty, who were not twins, but very similar in features and stature, were standing on a raised platform, while The Lady sat astride the "cat", a huge white Bengal tiger. They struck a pose of regal indifference, while the crowd cheered madly. Although The Lady stood barely an inch over five feet, she looked even smaller straddling the enormous animal. It had the same look that was captured in the advertisement; boredom and something else. *Restlessness.*

Despite Thelma's earlier misgivings, the view was excellent. Although the entire stage was surrounded by a wire mesh, Thelma found that the only way she could actually see the wire mesh was to strain her eyes to see it. Eventually, it just blended into the surrounding props.

One of the Moriarty brothers shouted out a command, and they all went into action. The tiger started off in a trot and then slowly picked up speed as he ran around the track circling the stage. The Lady rode him expertly as she waved to the audience. Thelma wondered if she was holding on to a lock of the tiger's hair, but after straining her eyes, she could see a white collar cleverly blended in with the animal's fur.

In a flash, the Moriartys raced up the ladder to the top of their respective trapeze stations and immediately started their high-flying trapeze dance, swinging back and forth, flipping, catching each other, twisting in mid-air, and then returning to station. Thelma was amazed (and a little scared) to see that they did all this without the benefit of a net. The only other people on the stage were the two trapeze hands managing the trapeze bars, ensuring that they returned to the correct spot every time.

A huge ramp, 40 to 50 feet above the stage floor was set up at each end of the stage and one particular act involved the tiger racing up the ramp at one end of the ring and jumping across a ten-foot span to the other side. What made the trick phenomenal was the fact that The Lady was riding the tiger like a horse, making him rear up on his hind legs and jump over obstacles.

After a few turns jumping the ramp, The Lady dismounted and walked the tiger over to one of the ramps, issued a command, and then proceeded to climb the trapeze staircase. Thelma stared intently, not really knowing what was coming next. She looked at Tom and could see that he was equally enthralled.

While The Lady climbed the trapeze ladder to the top, Thelma saw a small flame flickering within the area between the two ramps and trapeze ladders. In less than two minutes, the entire space was burning brightly; orange and yellow flames were reaching higher and higher.

Once The Lady reached the top of the trapeze, she positioned herself below Morash (Thelma thought Morash might be a hair taller than Micah) and grabbed his ankles. With only silence between them, Morash pushed off from his seated position with The Lady in tow. Morash and Micah proceeded to swing her back and forth, catching her, flipping her, releasing her. The tiger stared on impassively. At one point, he yawned hugely and licked his lips.

After a few "practice" runs, which was what it looked like to Thelma, The Lady called out a command, and the tiger jumped up obediently and quickly moved into position. She called out a slightly different command, and the tiger began running up the ramp. Without hesitation, he leaped to the other side, over the dancing flames, ran down to the other side, and waited there patiently.

The Lady started getting flipped again, but this time, she started doing multiple flips. At some point during the routine, she yelled out a command to the tiger and he immediately made his way to the ramp. Another command and he started his run towards the edge of the ramp. Morash had started his sequence and had just picked up The Lady.

Micah started his downward swing seated and deftly rotated his body so that his knees were hooked around the bar until he was hanging by his knees with his arms outstretched. Morash, holding The Lady by her wrists started his downward swing. Thelma could see the tiger sprinting and getting closer to the edge of the platform, strong back legs compressed for jumping. Morash released The Lady into an almost slow-motion somersault.

Thelma, like the vast majority of circus audiences, had never been on the flying trapeze, but she was astute enough to know if a swinging trapeze artist would be able to make his catch. It was simply a matter of timing. Thelma wasn't able to verbalize this initially, but she, like hundreds of the others in the audience, could see plainly that Micah had started his swing much too late. Each time Morash and The Lady reached the center point, the audience held its breath, hoping that she would not be released until Micah had corrected his swing timing to put him in the correct position.

Thelma could see them preparing for another downward swing. She silently cursed Micah for being behind in the rhythm, if there was one. She wondered deep down if Micah wanted The Lady dead. Maybe there was a sordid love triangle, where The Lady had been sleeping with them both and now one of them was planning revenge. Even as she thought this, she could see the white blur of the tiger rounding the last curve on the track; he was making his way to the edge of the platform where he would jump over the fire pit. But she didn't care about this. She wanted the Moriarty brothers to quit fucking around and synchronize their swings.

And as Morash and The Lady started their downward swing again, she saw him preparing to release her. She looked anxiously at Micah and could see that he had deliberately slowed himself. He would be *miles* from her when she was released. It wouldn't even look like an accident at that distance. It would look like murder.

In one smooth motion, Micah rotated himself into a standing position just as Morash released The Lady in a powerful somersault. Thelma screamed, along with close to 200 people, knowing intuitively that they were about to witness a real-life tragedy that would undoubtedly end in The Lady lying broken at the bottom of the fire pit, screaming and writhing in pain as the fire licked the skin from her body. Her spinning momentum slowed, and then stopped as she started falling toward the fire, her legs spread wide, arms reaching outward, face tense. Before Thelma's hands flew to her mouth, she fancied that she could see the lover's hate in Micah's face as he stared at The Lady while she plummeted to the floor.

As The Lady's downward descent increases, hundreds of pairs of hands move up to cover stricken faces and screaming mouths. She falls relentlessly towards the fire pit, her face a mask of grim expectation. As she falls, no one sees the white blur speeding off to the side of her. Their minds cannot imagine any other way this turn of events can play out and have already accepted her death—have already seen it in their minds' eye, when all of a sudden, her momentum is checked by the back of the leaping tiger. She lands squarely on his back, hands grasping for the collar as the tiger lands securely on the other side of the ramp.

The audience was completely silent, unable to believe what their eyes had just shown them. Thelma stared unblinkingly towards the stage, her breath finally forcing its way through her lungs. When the applause came, it came loud and long. Thelma could hear many people seated near her yelling, *"What happened? What happened? I didn't see it! I couldn't watch!"*

Maybe her morbid curiosity kept her from looking away, but she was incredibly glad that she didn't. That was the most amazing thing she had ever seen. She giggled weakly and felt a little stupid for thinking that Micah would plan to murder his lover in front of hundreds of people and in such a horrible way.

Tom stood up and stretched, rather shakily she saw, and suggested that they beat the crowd to the door and leave. He glanced towards the front of the amphitheater and saw two small kids running towards the stage. Thelma followed his gaze and saw with horror, one of the kids banging on the makeshift stage fence.

"Here kitty, kitty", the bigger kid said tentatively, holding out what looked like a licorice stick.

"You'd better stop JJ," the smaller kid, who could have been six or seven years old, said with wide eyes. "Mommy's lookin' for us." The fear on his face was as thick as jelly, but he wasn't staring at Jimmy anymore. His eyes were fixated on the huge face of the tiger moving slowly towards them.

RETURN TO EARTH

"Stop being a fraidy cat, Tommy, I know what I'm doing", Jimmy said, but in the back of his ten-year old mind, he began to doubt himself.

Tommy's little feet shuffled backward, but by mere inches. He was so fixated on the huge tiger approaching the fence, that all power of movement left him. He thought he could hear muffled yelling behind him, but that sound was very far off and uninteresting. Maybe those sounds were other kids coming to join the fun.

Jimmy, or "JJ" to his buddies at Goodson Elementary, licked his dry lips slowly. His idea of giving the tiger a piece of his licorice now seemed like a bad idea. A very bad idea. He wanted to drop the candy, turn around, and get as far away from this tiger as possible, but he couldn't make his body move. All he could feel was his body twitching as if trying to wake from a nightmare. He had extended his small arm through the spacing in the fence and could feel a dull pain in his elbow from being pressed up against the thin fence wire. As the tiger moved his large head towards the tiny piece of licorice in the equally tiny hand, JJ felt something deep inside let go as warm urine ran down the insides of his legs, filling his shoes. Just when he thought he was going to crap himself too, the tiger reached out with his tongue and licked the candy.

Jimmy continued to stare transfixed, as his bladder continued to empty itself. Apparently deciding that it liked the candy, the tiger extended his head to take a bite. Almost gingerly, the tiger bit down on the candy to retrieve it from Jimmy's hand. Jimmy, still transfixed, held his arm rigid, fist tight around the stub of licorice. The tiger went back to Jimmy's close-fisted hand for the remaining piece of licorice, but only a small sliver protruded from Jimmy's fist.

Jimmy's mind roared at him to drop the piece of licorice and yank his arm back through the fence, but his body seemed totally disconnected from him. Tommy's screaming finally pierced him, and he felt in control of his body once again. He turned his head towards Tommy, a slow, uncertain smile forming on his lips, thinking, *Yeah, this is so cool*, oblivious to the urine-soaked pants plastered to his legs. He started to withdraw his arm from the fence, but before his arm had moved an inch, the tiger's head, in one smooth motion, darted forward and sank his teeth into Jimmy's arm.

Jimmy stopped moving abruptly, thinking that his shirt had snagged on something. But as he was turning toward the fence again, he remembered that he had short sleeves on. He didn't feel any pain, only a weird itching sensation. The only coherent thing that penetrated the fog of his mind was that the tiger was now very close to the fence and that his arm, almost up to the elbow, was inside the tiger's mouth.

His mouth started forming the words "Hey, what's..." when he felt a tremendous force yank him towards the fence. The "itching" in his arm turned to immediate pain, and he could feel pressure on the right side of his face pressed up against the wire mesh fence as the tiger yanked on his arm.

Now he could hear others screaming. He looked up and saw the swinging people running towards him with long poles in their hands. He looked at the tiger again just before it pulled him violently into the fence again, pressing the side of his face tightly against the fence. This time, the tiger kept pulling and from far away, Jimmy thought he heard the sound his father made when he cracked his knuckles. He smiled languidly at the memory and as his arm was torn from his shoulder, the last thing he felt was the stub of licorice in his still closed fist.

5

Thelma stared in horror at the gruesome scene happening at the front of the stage. She made a move in that direction as if to help, when she felt a strong hand restrain her.

"There's nothing we can do Thelma!" Tom roared into her face. "You'll never get through the crowd to make it down there anyway. Look, everybody's running *this* way!"

Thelma could see that Tom was right. She could see a mass of people struggling to get up the stairs. They were climbing over the seats and over each other. She saw an elderly man get tripped up on the stairs and fall. And then he was gone, trampled under hundreds of shoes.

Tom grabbed her hand and trudged towards the door. The exit was jammed up with people, all trying to get out at the same time. Thelma looked to her left and could see that the exits there were jammed up too. Luckily, they were only a few rows down from the exit, and after a few short steps, Thelma could see the hallway outside. They were almost to the door when two men in front of them started fighting. The polite pushes immediately turned into an all-out donnybrook with spitting, scratching, hair-pulling, and the occasional cheap shot to the balls.

As Thelma stared at this spectacle, a piercing scream rang out behind her. She turned around towards the stage and saw...nothing. No one was moving on the stage. She saw the little boy that was near the stage lying in a dark puddle of what she assumed was blood. She looked at the stage and saw two bodies lying awkwardly on the worn mat. One of the bodies looked like one of the stage hands. The other could have been Morash or Micah, but she couldn't tell which. She didn't see The Lady anywhere but saw the other stage hand, and the other Moriarty brother climbing rapidly up the trapeze ladder. She also saw something else; the temporary, makeshift fence was leaning outward, almost touching the floor.

She heard another scream off to her right and turned just in time to see the white tiger (which was no longer white, but bloody red), jump on the back of a screaming woman. They both fell to the floor, and all Thelma could see was the tiger's muscular back working.

The crowd surged forward, desperately trying to get up the stairs and out the door. Thelma and Tom were pushed forward, and Tom had to hold onto Thelma to keep her from falling. To Thelma's dismay, the crowd surging from the back aisle pushed one of the doors shut, so now there was only one door to exit from.

Thelma could hear screaming noises directly behind her now, and something else. She heard growling, and that weird screaming noise that animals in the cat family tend to make. She turned her head slowly and could see panicked faces behind her. Some were turning their heads to see where the growling noise was coming from.

She faced forward again and saw that Tom was just getting through the door, crossing the threshold, when Thelma heard the tiger screaming along the back aisle to the left of her. The panicked crowd rushed forward, their combined mass forcing the door closed. Seeing the door rushing at her, she let Tom's hand go just before the other door slammed shut with the weight of 50 people behind it.

Right as she let Tom's hand go, she could feel the edge of the door slam against her side, pushing her off balance and causing her to fall. From the floor, she could see the door being pushed open, but the weight of the people on her side of the door, made this slow work. She started to get up on her knees when she felt someone, a woman most likely, step sharply on her leg, the heels of her high heel shoes (*stilettos*, Thelma thought madly) digging deeply in her calf. She opened her mouth to scream when she felt another heel dig into her leg, but closer to the knee. The pain was intense, and she could feel herself about to black out. *So, this is what it feels like to get trampled,* she thought languidly. It now felt like hundreds of heels digging into her calf, and she wondered how many women were trampling her at the same time. She craned her head towards her leg and saw the bloody, matted hair of the tiger digging ferociously into her leg. And this time she did scream, as many hands grabbed her and started shaking and pulling her...

6

"Thelma! Get up! It's starting! We need to get to our posts, now!"

Thelma's eyes popped wide open. She stared up at a dim fluorescent tube directly overhead. For a second, she didn't quite remember where she was. All she heard was shouting and someone screaming in her face. Thelma's roommate, Anne, had an iron grip on her arm.

"Thelma! The meteors are coming in! Communications is in contact with the other stations, and they're tracking a shitload of small ones coming in just ahead of the big one!"

Thelma sat bolt upright in her bunk and automatically scratched at her imaginary left calf. Each time she relived that horrific event in her dreams, she always woke up with a fiery itch in the leg that was no longer there. Anne, satisfied that Thelma was fully awake, threw on her jacket, and hustled out of the room, leaving Thelma wide eyed and breathing hard.

She reached over to the shelf built into the wall at the head of her bunk and grabbed her prosthetic limb and attached it, almost absent mindedly. She could hear the excited people yelling just outside her door. *This is it*, she thought anxiously, knowing that her anxiety would soon boil over into all out fear. She saw it in Anne's face and could feel it in her bones. Unfathomable fear, right on the surface of her skin and barely concealed behind her eyes. She got dressed quickly and went to her post.

7

"Estimated time to impact: Two minutes!" Bennett shouted. Thelma looked over her shoulders at Bennett and could see that he was drenched in sweat, despite the cool air blowing out from the cooling unit. A grim satisfaction came over her to see that he was just as

scared as she was. Each room in the shelter had its own self-contained heating and cooling units, in the event one area became uninhabitable. Thelma shuddered at the thought of anything down here becoming "uninhabitable".

From her training, she knew that they would continue to receive reports of meteor damage from one of the government's military shelter locations, but she wasn't sure how long that would last. The meteor shower would be a global event, showering the entire planet with meteoric debris, and all this would happen before the big one actually hit.

She turned back to her screen and looked at the people in the fallout shelter. Most of them were fast asleep. They had moved most of their gear and supplies into the space they called the "cave", but apparently had decided not to move in there until they absolutely had to.

She saw two men on guard duty walking around near the back of the shelter, smoking and talking casually; she spied one couple surreptitiously making love underneath their blanket. She looked at the group and could see that their numbers were dwindling. In the last 24 hours, more than half of them had left the garage and headed to the surface. There was an intense standoff as the ones who were leaving demanded their share of the food and weapons. It might have ended badly, had it not been for the man who came in a couple of days before with his son and little puppy.

From what Thelma could make out, most of them felt their chances would be better out in the open, then in the bottom level of a reinforced parking garage, five stories underground. The idea of being buried alive was not very appealing. She sympathized with them.

She counted about 30 people; a pregnant woman was among them. She wished she could help her. Help all of them. She accepted the fact that all of them, her group included, might perish when *Lycos* hit—sooner, if one of the smaller meteors hit them dead on. But at least her physical location offered some protection. If the people in the fallout shelter survived the initial collisions, they would still be in significant danger from the environmental changes, not to mention possible radiation effects. The thought made her sick to her stomach. Abruptly, she turned to Anne and had to shout to make herself heard, *"I'll be right back!"* Before Anne could protest, she was gone.

LYCOS HITS

1

Stan was having trouble sleeping. Just as he would start dozing off, he would jerk himself awake and then drift off uneasily again. He shifted around on his pallet and just when he began to feel sleep creeping up on him, a far-off explosion jolted him awake and he sat bolt upright. He glanced over at Lenny and was glad to see that he was sleeping soundly, despite the small jerks and twitches he made under his blanket.

He looked around the garage and most everyone was still asleep. He glanced to his left and saw Nathan standing up, stretching. *I guess I'm not the only one with insomnia,* he thought and rolled off his pallet to go chat with him.

"I see you can't sleep eith—" he started to say when all of a sudden, the air in the parking garage and in his *lungs*, seem to take on a solid, physical property that he could almost reach out and touch. It seemed he couldn't catch his breath, and it felt as if something were trying to squeeze out every ounce of air he had in his lungs.

He was standing right in front of Nathan and could see the same shock and fear in his eyes as well. The seconds seemed to crawl and just when he thought his lungs had squeezed out all the air he had, the heaviness disappeared and he could breathe again. But underneath his feet, deep underground, he could feel waves of strong vibrations, pulsing and moving, slowly picking up some kind of rhythmic speed.

"*Holy shit!*" shouted Nathan as he looked around the garage, eyes wide and arms held out in front of him. "That must have been one of the meteors that the government told us about. I remember them saying on the news that there would be hundreds of small to medium sized meteors that will make it through Earth's atmosphere."

Most everyone was awake now and many of the children were crying. Stan looked over at his son and saw that he was up too, wide eyed and scared. Buddy huddled next to him whimpering.

He turned toward Nathan and said, "I think we should start moving into the cave now. That was the first meteor of many. I think very soon now, the earth is going to be peppered with these meteors, and we don't have a clue where they're going to hit. This is it man. Whatever's going to happen is going to happen soon." Stan could still feel rumblings deep within the earth and wondered how much pounding a planet could take before enough was enough. The thought of what might happen made him queasy, and he pushed the thought out of his mind.

He went over to where his son sat and started grabbing their blankets and backpacks, taking a second to briskly rub Buddy's head. The frightened dog wagged his tail, but continued to whimper and moved closer to Lenny. Stan looked around and could see the rest of the group gathering their belongings. He looked at their faces and could see them mentally steeling themselves from the terror coming for them. Stan was afraid too. As he thought about it, he realized that he had never been this afraid in his life.

2

"Alright everyone," Nick yelled out. "Gather up your stuff. It's time we headed into the cave!" When Stan, Nick and Nathan broke through the brick wall and crawled inside the opening, their first thought was that it was indeed a cave. It was big enough for the entire group, but much smaller than the fallout shelter. The ceiling was about 20 feet high and tapered down to about eight feet at its lowest point.

Stan had a feeling that the rock down here was extremely strong. He had always enjoyed geology in school and was pretty sure that this rock was a form of hard granite rock—extremely strong and dense. He hoped that it would be strong enough to withstand the shock of the meteors, provided they don't land right on top of them. The only thing that seemed out of place was the rock wall at the far end of the cave. It looked odd and forced, and he made a mental note to check it out later when they got settled. As it turned out, he never got that opportunity.

The last couple of folks were coming through the entrance when they heard what sounded like military jets screaming overhead. Even this far down, it sounded terribly loud and made them all involuntarily duck their heads. This screaming was followed closely by several powerful impacts. Stan remembered from reports that this non-stop barrage would be devastating. The smaller chunks of rock accompanying the broken *Lycos*, would burn up in the atmosphere, but the ones that made it through would be capable of inflicting incredible damage.

The group huddled together inside the cave, an occasional flashlight beam stabbing out at the surrounding darkness. They all sat on the floor of the cave, tense and motionless, waiting to see what would happen.

They didn't wait long. A thunderous explosion, almost directly above them, seemed to shake the very foundation of the cave. Stan could feel the angry rumblings deep within the ground. He turned on his flashlight and could see dust drifting down from the cave ceiling. And then, in rapid succession, several huge explosions happened above them. This time, they could hear the fallout shelter fall in on itself.

Lenny was sitting between Stan's legs and had his head buried in his father's chest. He was shaking uncontrollably. They all were. Stan could feel himself smothering in a cloying blanket of fear and uncertainty. He had the strong taste of copper in his mouth and could feel his heart hammering in his chest. With all their technology and intelligence, here they were, huddled in a cave like Neanderthals hiding from a storm, waiting to be crushed like insects underfoot. Several more meteors pounded the earth above. The last one to hit was bone-jarring. It hit so hard that they were all bounced up into the air. The entire cave was shaking and small rocks and dirt showered them from the ceiling.

Stan felt nauseous. He didn't particularly like the idea of being buried alive in this cave. He bent over Lenny, covering him as best he could when something exploded in his head. He fell on his side, still trying to cover his son. He could feel himself slipping away as more and more debris fell from the top of the cave. From a distance, he could hear screaming. One of the screams sounded like barking. He lay on his side, wanting to help his son, but powerless to do so. His vision blurred, and he could feel himself drifting off or dying. Maybe it was the same. He started to pray, but got only as far as "Our Father" before a bright light filled his eyes as he sank towards darkness.

III
THE MOON
SEPTEMBER 2053

STRANGE OBSERVATIONS

1

"...read me? Tess...are you there? Come on...I can hear you breathing." The concern in Henry's voice started to come through.

"Yes, Henry. Yes, I can read you. I'm sorry. Whenever I see the earth like that, busted up and dying, I can't help but think of all those people who perished." This was mostly true, but it was also very personal for her; hell, it was personal for everyone, because everyone here lost someone there. She stifled the emotions welling up inside and stood up, her eyes still wet from crying. She had no desire to wipe them, even if she could.

"I'm almost done Henry. I just have to..." she paused as she glanced back up at the planet. Something up there had caught her eye, a reflection of light off her faceplate, but she wasn't sure what it was; it was probably another explosion. She stared intently at the broken mass, not focusing on any one piece. Henry started to say something, but she shushed him quickly. She was still staring almost ten minutes later and was just about to go back to the Navi-Computer when she caught the flash again.

She abruptly turned to the computer and started typing furiously, going back and forth between the mounted telescope and the keypad. Henry spoke up, "What's going on Tess? I can hear you punching in data. Did you see something?"

Tess answered him without taking her eyes off the scope, "I'm not sure Henry, but I'm picking up increased volcanic activity on Earth. I've recorded a number of flashes, indicating some serious explosions within the planet." She pondered this a moment. "Do you remember those scientists who came to our compound from the UN site not long after we got here? I remember them saying that if the earth's core was damaged enough, it would eventually destabilize and the planet would either self-destruct or simply break apart."

Henry was silent for a moment and then answered her, "Yeah, I remember them and I remember the discussion. It seemed farfetched at the time. Now...I don't know. What I do know is that we're not as smart as we think we are."

"Ain't that the truth?" Tess replied. She remembered how animated and passionate the scientists were during the discussions. She recalled how they argued about who identified the rogue planet first and who devised the best plan for humankind's survival.

At the time, she considered them self-absorbed and arrogant. Now, some two years later, she found herself thinking that these think-tank geeks were probably right, God rest their souls. And as she thought through this, a scary, intuitive connection slowly drifted up from the place where intuitive thought came from, and the thought caused her to sway on her feet. She grabbed the edge of the telescope panel to steady herself. She must have made a noise because Henry called her name over the mike again. "Tess! Hey...what *is* it? What's going on out there?"

"I'll tell you when I get in Henry. I think trouble has found us...again." She mounted the Rover and headed back to the compound, beads of sweat starting to form on her brow.

2

Rank certainly has its privileges, Soren thought, as he fingered the pink, almost delicate panties lying next to him on the bed. He heard the squeaky turn of the shower handles and realized that Sandra was only now getting into the shower. He wondered if that was why she was seeing him, so she could take a long hot shower. Everyone had access to hot water, but water was a scarce commodity these days and it was tightly monitored and controlled. Taking a "hop-n-pop" is what most of the residents called taking a shower these days. If you didn't get in, do your business and get out, you were liable to end up with soap all over you and no way to wash it off once the automated shower disconnected from the water flow-line.

Soren leaned over and grabbed Tess's morning report from the built-in nightstand. He had already read it twice, but was trying to envision how he would present it tonight at the council meeting. He wasn't sure how many people Tess had spoken with about this "new" development, but he knew it wasn't many. Despite her few friends, she was a loner. People liked her, but she was so damn depressing. And she was always challenging him.

Wilfred Soren had been the Director of the Space Habitat and Environment department years before *Lycos* hit the earth. The department languished for years due to overspending and late or incomplete projects. Many of his colleagues considered him an inept administrator, but for reasons unknown, he had "friends in high places" (there was a rumor that he was blackmailing one of the senior executives on the board, but this was never proven).

Through his government contacts, he had found out that this monster meteor planet was headed on a collision course with Earth, so he made it a point to be at the center of every discussion involving survival plans on Earth, as well as off. His main focus, however, was on the *off-planet* discussions because he was determined to make himself indispensable.

Any and all ideas concerning off-planet solutions were funneled through him. He convinced his staff that this was for their own good. That he had it on good information from his government contacts that people—smart people—were being kidnapped for their ideas. And that they wouldn't touch *him* because he had become too visible. He would be missed. So, he took their ideas and passed them off as his own. Eventually, as some of the better solutions began to gather popularity, these smart people did in fact start disappearing, but not by the government's hands. Soren wanted to ensure that he had no opposition or challenges when it came to the congratulations, not to mention "open slots".

3

One of the more practical off-planet solutions focused on revamping the current moon base. The existing moon base at the time was a two-room building large enough to house only four astronauts, so they started full scale operations to develop it into the UN compound that would hold upwards of 50 people. They didn't realize until they were almost finished and had almost lost an entire work crew, that they had built it on a fault line.

After this fiasco, the president's advisors brought government teams into Soren's domain to head up operations. They left Soren in place but ordered construction of a new compound, about five miles away. This compound would house the President and Vice President of the United States, their families, selected staff members, and various international leaders and their families.

Soren always knew that he would have a slot at the moon base, and he made sure that a few of his own people got selected as well. He wouldn't be at the UN compound, but as long as he was not on Earth, he was satisfied. He even *sold* a few slots. Although looking back, he realized that the money he got didn't go nearly as far as he had hoped. His primary responsibilities kept him on the moon, but periodically, he would have to return to earth for what he thought were political reasons. Eventually, he was able to pawn off his earthly duties to one of his lackeys, which just about eliminated his reasons for returning planet-side. This is allowed him to become an almost permanent fixture on the moon, eliminating any possibility of being left on earth when the final shuttles departed. He also hated the back and forth trips from the moon to Earth. It seemed he couldn't shit right for days after a trip from the moon.

As the operation matured and more and more people arrived, he took on a self-appointed leadership role in the compound even though there were a number of highly qualified leaders who would have been exceptional in the role.

One of those people was Tess Robinson. She was well-respected among her peers, was a rising military star, and a damn good pilot. She had only been in the space program for a few years when people started whispering how she should retire her commission and seek the SH&E chair role. In this position, she would have been *his* boss!

But to Soren, she didn't know shit about human nature and how when things got really bad, people transformed into monsters. Soren knew that once the meteors hit, they would lose contact with Earth and that they would need strong leadership here on the moon. Strong leadership, backed by an equally strong police force. He already had a number of his hand-picked people with him on the moon, but there were a few more still on Earth. He wasn't able to get them passes without taking a chance on someone catching on to him. Instead, he gave them the location of one of the safe houses transporting the last group of folks with passes.

He didn't find out until later that one of the last two space shuttles to leave the earth was overtaken by a group of men with stolen passes. Tess and her co-pilot Dan, relayed to him exactly what had happened on the other ship and why it exploded. Soren could see in his mind's eye, Clyde or one of his moronic men, shooting his gun on the shuttle like it was the O.K. Corral and causing the decompression in space. While he didn't mean for his men to kill Tess's husband and son for their passes, he couldn't have asked for a more effective solution to her rising popularity and constant questioning of his actions. Tess and her husband would have a made a formidable team here.

He turned his attention back to her report. She's a smart cookie, he had to give her that; but he would never be able to control her. *Too bad*, he thought, he could have used her skills. He re-read her timeline estimate and recommended actions, short and medium term. He looked up toward the ceiling, mentally calculating, his pudgy lips moving quickly, as if he were praying a silent prayer. *"We'll have to move up our timeline"*, he whispered to the room, and leaned over to punch in Reynald's room number.

4

"BANG, BANG! I got you alien!"

Startled, Tess snapped her head around to see two small boys playing under one of the lunchroom tables. A man and a woman, presumably their parents, spoke in hushed tones, their backs hunched over the table. The father gave one of the boys a stern look, and they immediately quieted down. *That won't last long,* Tess thought wryly. The man turned back to the woman, and they continued their quiet conversation while casting furtive glances around the cafeteria.

They were far enough away that Tess couldn't make out what they were saying, but it was apparent that they didn't want to be overheard. With the strict food rationing in place, the cafeteria was never really busy, and at this time of day it was practically a ghost town; these two wanted to ensure that they had some privacy by sitting in the most isolated part of the cafeteria.

To Tess, the last few days seemed like a blur. Everyone was on edge, and she would regularly see folks whispering to one another or clustered in small, secretive groups. She thought she was just being paranoid, but on her way down to the hangar one day, she came upon a group of shuttle mechanics quietly whispering to one another. They actually stopped talking and stared at her until she passed them. She looked back at them and saw that they were still staring until she turned the corner. She fought the urge to peek around the corner to see if they were still staring.

Now this couple. She wondered if Soren had leaked anything on Earth's situation and the potential ramifications. Frankly, she couldn't understand why he didn't keep everyone updated on a regular basis, instead of these infrequent council meetings. People needed to know what was going on, and it wouldn't be that difficult to keep people informed. For crying out loud, there were only about 100 adults here, give or take a few.

She looked toward the cafeteria entrance and saw Kyra speaking with Nola—having a heated argument seemed more accurate. Kyra Camacho, one of several computer engineering technicians at the base, was waving her arms this way and that, while Nola just stood there shrugging her shoulders and running her hands through her thick red hair. Exasperated, Kyra threw up her arms and stormed off. Nola stared at her with disdain, a small smile creasing the corners of her mouth. When she turned slightly, her icy blue eyes met Tess's eyes. She stared for a moment longer, turned on her heels abruptly and was gone. *That was odd,* Tess thought, as she looked around for Kyra. She saw her at the salad bar and waved to her. Kyra smiled an unhappy smile and walked towards her.

She sat down heavily at the table and before Tess could say anything, let out a huge disgusted sigh. "Nola is either incredibly stupid, or she's trying to sabotage me!"

"What happened K? What did she do?"

"I've been capturing data on Earth's orbit for over a year and now it's gone!" Kyra cried out.

"Are you serious? What did she do K…delete it?" Tess asked incredulously.

Kyra dropped her fork back onto her plate and stared at Tess, "Yes! That's exactly what she did! At least, I *think* that's what she did." Kyra took a deep breath, "Nola got transferred to our department about a month ago. I don't know if she requested it or was just reassigned, but we've been training her on some of the equipment. She actually caught on quickly and seemed genuinely interested in what we were doing. She's a private person, but seems friendly enough, especially with the guys." Tess smiled dryly at this. The ratio of women to men was almost two to one, not counting the few married couples. Only the very aggressive women seemed to catch the men.

"This week," Kyra continued, "she asked me about the orbital diagnostic work I was doing and whether I saw any anomalies in Earth's orbit. I was actually surprised that she was aware of what I was doing. I showed her the results of the data I was collecting and the increased destabilization of Earth's orbit. I told her that I would be presenting this information at the next council meeting because it was very important. She understood and asked if she could do some scenario-testing on the data, to determine worst-case and best-case scenarios. I thought this was a great idea, but told her we could take a look at it the next day, seeing that it was getting late and I was exhausted.

"I left, but she stayed late to finish up some other work and when I returned this morning, I couldn't log in. One of the techs finally helped me get logged-in, but all of the orbital data that I had collected over the past 14 months was gone. Even the data saved on the server was missing."

"What did you do?" asked Tess.

"I confronted her! She told me that I had not logged off and thought I had left my account open for her to run her scenario testing. She said things were going fine until the program hit a bug and began skipping whole blocks of data, so she ran a compiler scan and thought she was deleting bugs, when she was actually deleting compiler code and data packets. She said she tried to reinstall the data and the program from the server and ended up deleting the server files too."

Her eyes narrowed, and she leaned across the table towards Tess. "I'm *certain* that I signed out of my account when I left. One hundred percent certain. This project has been much too important for me to leave my account open. I'm not trying to hide anything. I just didn't want anyone to accidentally screw up my data. I can't shake the feeling that she hacked my login and did this on purpose."

Tess stared at Kyra, but didn't really see her. Her mind was furiously trying to add up the missing pieces. This unfortunate incident in Kyra's lab was but another piece of a dangerous cat and mouse puzzle.

In the interest of "public safety", Soren had required that all sensitive information come directly to him and forbade them to discuss any of their results with the others, lest they inadvertently cause a panic. He felt that people in general couldn't handle really bad news and that it was his job to keep things running smoothly until they departed for *Europa*.

And now that she thought about it, when was the last time they received *any* information on *Europa*? Henry was responsible for monitoring the *Pegasus1* satellite that was orbiting Jupiter and *Europa* and when she questioned him on updated photos of the planet, he became embarrassed and admitted that he didn't have anything because Soren had all satellite transmissions fed directly to the uplink in his unit.

Soren had told him, as he had told the others, that he would present all updated information on *Europa* at the council meetings. Unfortunately, he never presented anything of substance on the planet, and no one seemed to question him about it. Or maybe they were too afraid of him to do so. Puzzle pieces started falling into place in Tess's mind as she sat there listening to Kyra, but none of the pieces made any sense.

"Kyra, this can't be a coincidence," Tess whispered. "I submitted my final report to Soren this morning, and he hasn't mentioned it at all. I thought he would at least call me to ask questions, to make sure that my observations were accurate, but he never did. Normally, I don't expect him to contact me, but seeing that this is something he needs to bring up at the meeting tonight, I'm at a loss as to why he's ignoring me on this. He's not very technical, so I'm sure he didn't understand it fully."

"What observations were those?" Kyra replied shakily. Kyra was sitting on the edge of her seat. "What are you seeing out there Tess?"

Tess glanced around the cafeteria. The man and woman and the two boys were nowhere to be seen. Tess didn't recall seeing them leave. The only other people in the cafeteria was a couple sitting at the cafe bar, clearly into each other and too far away to hear anything. Nevertheless, Tess leaned closer to Kyra and said, "There is increased core activity on Earth. I've been monitoring this specifically for the past eight months now. I'm not sure what's happening on the planet, but it can't be good."

"Oh God Tess, this is what I feared would happen." Kyra said through clenched teeth.

"What? What do you mean Kyra?" Tess could feel her heart rate speeding up.

"About two months ago, before Nola came to our group, I ran some preliminary orbital simulations myself and the model predicted that Earth's orbit would eventually become highly elliptical. The only thing I couldn't define was the timeline, and its estimated distance at its furthest point *from* the sun, and its closest point *to* the sun.

"Before Nola erased my data, I had a pretty good hunch that at its furthest point the earth would be anywhere from 140 to 160 million miles from the sun – about 50 to 60 million miles more than it normally is. That estimate turned out to be fairly accurate, but now the earth is on its return trip from that orbit." She stopped talking and seemed to visibly prepare herself for what she had to say next.

"When *Lycos* hit the planet, Earth's structural integrity was severely compromised, and its mass drastically reduced. The first part of its highly elongated orbit has been proven true. The second part is what I'm worried about.

"The earth is now headed towards its closest point to the sun. Before *Lycos*, Earth's closest point to the sun was about 91 million miles. Now, if my model is correct, at perihelion the earth will come within 25 million miles of the sun. Tess...that's closer than *Mercury*! And the increased core activity that you've observing confirms that the earth is indeed moving closer to the sun as we speak." She sighed heavily. "In less than three months, the planet Earth will make Mercury look like a winter vacation spot."

"Jesus Christ Kyra, are you certain?" Tess asked quietly.

"Yes," Kyra replied, "but the worst part is that it won't take three months for *us* to feel the effects of the sun. Since Nola lost my data, I can't be certain, but I would be willing to bet that in about six to eight weeks, the temperature here will be so hot that everything will start to malfunction. The rising temperatures will eventually destroy our habitat and the ships. At three months, if the earth is still intact, it will be nothing more than a burnt rock in space, with a scoured and blackened moon still orbiting it. We won't survive a pass that close to the sun Tess. In less than a month, we need to be on our way to *Europa*."

Tess's initial despair turned into resolve as she mentally calculated what needed to be done. "Soren will need to present this at tonight's council meeting. I'll go talk to him first, but make sure you prepare your information. If he tries to push this off, let's make sure we're ready to share this with the group. I'm tired of his weak and self-serving guidance. This new information affects all of us and could mean the difference between life and death. Once those repairs on the *Cassiopeia* are completed, then we can get the hell off this moon."

"Well, since they've been loading all week, I imagine we should be able to get out of here within days, right?" Kyra asked tentatively.

Tess's eyebrows furrowed, and she looked at Kyra questioningly. *"Loading?* They've been working on the *guidance system* all week. If they're lucky, they'll be starting on connecting the Cargo Cabin in the next few days."

A frown creased Kyra's face. "Are you *sure*, Tess? I've been having a bad case of insomnia for the past couple of weeks, and when I can't sleep, I go jogging. A couple of times, my running routes have taken me past the shuttle bay, where they've been burning the midnight oil. Each time I peeked in there, I saw them moving stuff like supplies and medical gear. I even saw them carrying *luggage* on board!"

Tess could only stare at Kyra. As the Ship Commander, it was her responsibility to ensure that all ship repairs were being carried out correctly and timely. Based on her last meeting with Shelton Hayes, the shuttle maintenance chief, things were progressing according to schedule. *But whose schedule?* she now thought sourly.

For the past six months, Tess had made it a point to meet with the maintenance chief at least one a week in the shuttle bay. They would *"walk the ship"* while he discussed specific maintenance challenges or successes. Occasionally, she and Dan would meet there to go over some of the cockpit control diagnostics, but for the most part, she left the maintenance operations up to the very capable Shelton.

Until recently, she had never met with Shelton outside of the shuttle bay to discuss maintenance issues, so she was surprised (and somewhat relieved) when he had asked her if he could meet with her in the conference room for the last three weeks in a row. At any other time, she would have rejected this suggestion, but over the past month, she and Rey had been arguing almost incessantly. Her only peace of mind was when she was outside the compound taking her readings of Earth, or when she was in the shuttle bay observing the work being done on the *Cassiopeia*. She was starting to see Rey in the shuttle bay almost regularly. In an attempt to avoid the bitter and almost certain arguments, she gladly agreed to meet with Shelton in the conference room.

Now, as she sat here listening to the increasingly disconcerting news about what was happening in the shuttle bay, she wondered if she had made a wise decision allowing the venue of the maintenance update meetings to happen *outside* of the shuttle bay. In hindsight, it seemed ridiculous for her to avoid the area just because she was trying to avoid Rey, but he always seemed to be ready for an argument. At one point, Tess felt as if she were an actress in a play *(...and now comes Psychotic Rey, ready to instigate another pointless argument)*. He made it a point to always be there when she was there and from the moment she walked into the bay, he would harangue her endlessly until she departed. She wondered now if it had indeed been an act to keep her away. Her intuition hinted at this possibility.

"I don't know what to say, Kyra," Tess finally acknowledged. "I haven't actually been in the shuttle bay for the last two or three weeks, but I've spoken with Shelton many times." Her apologetic tone disgusted her, but she knew she had no one else to blame but herself. "I need to visit Mister Hayes and find out what's going on and why he's been feeding me these misleading, if not erroneous updates. Before I see him, I need to speak with Soren. There's something in the air, and I don't like it."

"I agree," Kyra said. "You and Henry are the only two people I really talk to. Everyone else either seems phony or is outright distant." She looked at Tess shrewdly, "I don't see you and Rey together much these days. Is everything okay?"

Tess sat back in her chair. Even though she had been expecting it, she still had to take a deep breath before diving into it. "Rey has been acting very weird lately and frankly, I don't trust him." Tess reflected for a moment and then added, "I guess I've *never* trusted him, come to think of it."

"Hmm...you know, I didn't think much of it at the time," Kyra said, "but I see Rey and Nola chatting quite a bit. I didn't think he was cheating on you though because they looked more like they were planning a coup than a midnight tryst."

Tess laughed and said, "I almost wish they *were* sleeping together. Then I would have broken up with him months ago." She paused for just a moment, and then added, "I actually broke up with him today anyway. I know I'm better than this, and I don't need his fake attention and questionable character."

"Good for you Tess! Even though men are in short supply here, we still have to have our standards!"

Both ladies burst out laughing again. After a few minutes, Kyra turned serious and asked, "How is all this going to work on *Europa* anyway Tess? We have the weight of the human race on our shoulders, and we're starting over, and on a new *planet* at that."

"I don't know Kyra, I honestly don't. First, we have to find out if the planet can even support us. From initial reports and findings, there's a good chance that *Europa* has very similar Earth qualities: breathable air, water, similar gravity, vegetation, and a whole host of other things.

But nothing has been confirmed and won't be confirmed until we can look at and analyze the data from the *Pegasus1* probe.

"After that, I don't know. Once we're secure and have shelters built and can feed ourselves, then I imagine all of the other pieces will fall into place." She thought for a moment and then added, "I'll tell you one thing though, I'm not interested in being part of an intergalactic harem!"

Kyra laughed and leaned close to Tess. "And it's not soon enough that we get off this rock, because I'm estimating that those birth control shots that we got when we first arrived here will expire in about six months; and I can guarantee nine months after that, we'll be having ourselves a little moon-based baby boom!"

Smiling, Tess said, "You may be right about that, but I won't be one of them! Anyway, the way things are going, we may be off this rock sooner than we think."

Shrouded in darkness in the cafeteria office, Reynald stepped back from the closed blinds and removed his earpiece. Apart from sporadic interference, Tess and Kyra's conversation had come through quite clearly. He packed up his equipment, peeked through the blinds again, and slipped out of the office quietly.

NOLA AND SOREN

1

Nola Sykes strode confidently down the slightly curving corridor; her fashionable high heels echoed with each step. The few people that she encountered looked first at her shoes, then at her breasts, before quickly looking away. She always knew that her confidence and icy stare made a lot of people uncomfortable, so during these brief encounters, she not only stared back but actually *glared* at them. They always looked away first, and this she found strangely pleasing.

She stopped at one of the small portal windows and looked out at the barren landscape of the moon. From this side of the compound, there was nothing but old craters and distant moon hills. Today, she had a staggering view of the earth. It looked bigger, as if it was actually getting closer, but she didn't really think that was the case. She stared at the misshapen planet and shuddered. Even though it had been almost two years since the impact, many people were still reluctant to look at it.

She turned away and continued on to Soren's unit. Up ahead, two men were replacing ceiling panels and chatting nonchalantly. They both turned at her approach and stared at her. She almost laughed out loud as both men tried to suck in their guts. The chubbier of the two was having a considerably harder time at it than his partner.

"Hello boys," she said, and ran her fingers through her luxurious red hair as she passed them, not waiting for a response.

The skinnier fellow only grunted, but his overweight cohort seemed more in control of his faculties and stammered out, "Uh...hi Miss Sy...uh...Nola. Hi Miss Nola."

She was fully past them by the time he got it all out. She waved her hand in the air without turning back, knowing that those two would continue staring at her until she rounded the curve up ahead.

As she neared Soren's place, she thought about her little spat with Kyra earlier today and felt herself getting angry all over again. *I hate playing the "dumb sexy chick" who doesn't know shit about computers. I have an advanced computer science degree, yet I have to sit there and let her lecture me on how to use a computer; and I think she suspects that I did it on purpose. Little bitch!*

She rounded the corner quickly, her mind still on her confrontation with Kyra and ran smack into one of Soren's bodyguards.

"Oww!" she said, "Watch it!" She shoved at the huge guard uselessly. Despite the force at which she bumped into him, he barely budged. He mumbled an apology to her and then turned to face the view plate just to the right of the door.

"Nola Sykes to see you sir," he said crisply into the mike and then resumed his position next to the other bodyguard. After a couple of minutes, the door slid open and Nola stepped into Soren's spacious unit.

2

Compared to the brightness of the hallways, the room was quite dark and as the door slid swiftly shut, Nola found herself cloaked in near darkness. She reached out, touching the wall to her left and guided herself down the hall to the main living quarters of the unit.

Gradually, the darkness faded as she made her way past the narrow kitchen and into the living quarters. On the stainless-steel counter sat several half empty liquor bottles and unwashed dinner trays—the aftermath of a big party, Nola thought as she walked past.

She walked into the living area and looked around for Soren. She had been here numerous times, but she was always amazed at how large the unit was. Only a handful of people actually had the pleasure of being inside Soren's unit, and the ones who did always wondered whether Soren had converted one of the five-person bays into one unit. The unit had two bathrooms and two kitchens, so Nola thought that it actually might be the truth, but she never asked Soren about it.

"What took you so long?" demanded Soren, stepping out from the bedroom, wearing only a robe. He pressed the contact on the wall, closing the door behind him. "You got off over an hour ago."

Nola cringed as she quickly walked over to where he stood. She didn't like to see him in these moods. She had an idea what his plans were and knew that it wouldn't do her any good to get on his bad side. She knew that there were a number of women here who could replace her, and she didn't want to take that chance. At least, not when they were this close.

She wrapped her arms around him, hugging him tightly. "I'm SOOO sorry baby; I got held up at the cafeteria. Kyra questioned me relentlessly about the loss of her data today. She forced me to go into excruciating detail on each step I used before the data-loss occurred. She didn't say so, but I *know* that she suspects that I did it on purpose." She paused a minute before adding the final piece. "And she was talking to Tess when I left to come here."

He pushed away from her, the half-smile on his face turning to a scowl, which looked more at home on his face. "Damn! *Damn!* That woman gets on my nerves! Kyra would have been mad for an hour or so, and then would have let it go, but that damn Tess...you would have thought she wrote the book on conspiracy theory."

"They *did* look animated as they spoke," Kyra acknowledged. "I hung around the cafeteria for a moment, just in case Kyra decided to go back to the computer room to retrace my steps. I don't want her to stir up anything at this point and since Tess is her best friend, I didn't know what would happen."

Nola had never gotten along with Tess, but it was evident that many people here actually liked her. She often heard people saying things like, *"She's very intelligent and has great ideas,"* or *"She's a great listener,"* or Soren's favorite, *"She should be in charge, not Soren."* Nola never saw what was so special about her. Sure, she was unique—black female astronauts had always been in short supply on Earth and now with the moon base population sitting at about one hundred people, even more so.

To Nola, Tess seemed depressed all the time and regularly admitted that she was racked with guilt for leaving her husband and son behind. Okay, so she left someone behind, *big deal!* When it came down to it, they all had someone back on Earth who didn't make it! Nola was all about making things work here and now, while Tess was a selfish independent who didn't matter at all. Not one single bit.

"Like I said," Soren added, "I'm not too worried about Kyra. On her own, she wouldn't pursue this, but Tess might get her riled up and start pointing fingers and throwing out accusations. We don't need any distractions or delays right now. And just so you know Nola, I've already initiated Operation REBOUND. After reading Tess's report and looking at Kyra's data, I'm convinced that we need to act now. But I'll need to quell any concerns or fears in the meeting tonight. I don't know who Tess has talked to about this, but I want to ensure that there is no spread of misinformation throughout the colony. There cannot be any unexpected delays or changes now."

Nola nodded. Things were getting very dangerous, more so now than when she left Earth. She had also seen Tess's report and knew that the meeting would get out of hand very quickly if the others knew about the information in her report. "What about Tess? She'll be at the meeting too. I don't think she'll sit quietly."

"I don't anticipate any problems with Tess. She understands our delicate situation here, and I expect her to cooperate 100% with us. Why would she want to cause a panic and stop the progress that could kill what's left of the human race? No, she'll be fine tonight. Just make sure *you* are ready when the time comes."

"I've *been* ready baby," Nola said as she closed the distance between her and Soren. She slowly untied his thick bathrobe and slid her hands around his waist. Not too long ago, he would have been seen as ruggedly handsome with an athletic build, but the lack of exercise (*and laziness*) gave him the appearance of ill health to which he added a seemingly permanent scowl.

He wasn't the best-looking man here, but she knew that once they arrived on *Europa*, he would be the one in charge. She knew that the old Earth social structure of one man to one woman would break down, since the ratio was now two women to every one man. She knew Soren and knew what he planned to do on *Europa*. He would consolidate resources for himself and his armed goons, and part of his "resources" would include the women. He often joked with her, saying, *"the women would almost be like my daughters, and the men would have to pay me to either date them or even marry them."* And then he would laugh so hard that tears would come streaming down his face, while she tried to hide the disgust in her eyes.

To Nola, it sounded a lot like plain old prostitution. These conversations nauseated her. She found herself comparing this "new world order" with the old world on Earth and wondered in amazement just how quickly educated people can revert to old feudal customs and barbaric actions. She would force her mind to accept it because all of the old ways and customs were gone. Barbeques and skyscrapers, swimming and IMAX theaters, airline business class upgrades and Sunday night TV, and the list went on and on. All of these things were gone, and in their place stood survival and black space, and the slow extinction of the human race.

Her mind briefly left her body as she responded to Soren standing there in his bathrobe. His open mouth found hers and one of his groping hands made its way to the small of her back and inside her pants. The other snaked its way through her thick mane of red hair where he wound his fist and pulled. Her head snapped back and she responded automatically, her breath coming in quick gasps. Her last clear thought before she succumbed entirely to nature, was that of walking into the darkness of a bear's den, with two greedy red eyes looking back at her.

3

Reynald waited patiently in the outer room of Soren's living quarters. It had its own separate entrance from the outer halls and was totally independent of the rest of the unit. There were no guards at this entrance, but as far as Reynald knew, he was the only one Soren had given access to. He knew Soren was meeting with Nola, so he let himself in and waited for them to be finished in the bedroom.

He didn't have to wait long. In typical Soren-fashion, he was up and out of the bed as soon as he was done, hurrying Nola along because he had another "meeting". Meeting or not, Soren was not one to cuddle afterwards. Soren shared this piece of unwanted trivia with Reynald not long after he started working for him. Nola knew this too and was quick to gather her belongings and leave.

Fifteen minutes later, Soren opened up the outer room, which was locked from the inside and invited Reynald in. "Come on in, Rey", Soren chirped, somewhat giddily. "You just missed Nola." He knew that Rey was in the outer room and knew that Rey was highly infatuated with Nola. But Rey gave no indication that the comment bothered him, except for the almost imperceptible twitch in his right eye.

"Oh, really?" Rey replied, not taking the bait. "Did she have any trouble at the lab?"

"No, nothing that we can't handle." He narrowed his eyes at Rey, "By any chance, have you seen Tess's recent report?"

"No, she changed the access code on her unit, so I guess that means we're not dating anymore."

"Oh well, such a relationship was not meant to last, right?" Soren laughed out loud and went on to add, "But this could be a fortuitous event for us when you think about it."

"What do you mean, Soren?

"You don't know? Then, I'll give it to you straight Rey; Tess is becoming a royal pain in the ass! Wait! I take that back...is *already* a royal pain in the ass!"

It was Rey's turn to laugh now, "Tell me what I *don't* know! She's a stone in my shoe, and I'm someone who cares for her."

Soren looked at Rey levelly and then broke out into laughter again. "Man, who are you kidding? You don't care for Tess any more than she cares for you! You've been sex'ing her, just like she's been sex'ing you, so don't even try to bullshit yourself into believing that you have anything more than that. Besides, I have plans for her, and you just might be the best person to do the job."

"Oh, really? Does it have anything to do with the report that I didn't see?" Rey inquired.

"It has *everything* to do with that report," Soren spat out. "And now that she's spoken with Kyra, she won't hold her tongue at the next council meeting. She's forcing our hand in this matter, and I don't quite like it."

Just that quickly, Rey could sense a change in Soren's demeanor. You never knew where you stood with Soren, Rey reflected. One minute, he was all smiles and clapping you on the back, and the next he was cutting your balls off. When it came to Soren, he always felt like a mouse playing tag with a cat.

"I guess I should have seen it coming," Soren said, walking over to the small desk in the corner of the room. He grabbed Tess's report and thumbed through a few pages until he got to a sheet with a green plastic paper clip. He handed this sheet to Rey and stood in silence as Rey read through the document.

After reading the report, Rey looked back at Soren. The man was eyeing him carefully, waiting for his response. "Do you think she'll bring this up at the meeting?" Rey asked carefully. He didn't want to come off as sounding too paranoid.

"You're goddamn right she will!" Soren shouted. "But one thing's for sure, we need to bury this before the meeting. If this report got out, people would panic and that would seriously jeopardize my plans. If Tess had her way, she would have made copies for the entire compound. Well, this is one report that they will not see or even hear about tonight; you can be sure of that."

"What report is that Soren? Are you talking about *my* report?"

Rey and Soren whirled at the sound of Tess's voice behind them. They were both shocked, but Soren found his voice first. "What the fuck are *you* doing here?" he demanded. "How did you get in here?"

Tess ignored Soren's indignation and stepped deeper into the room. "Don't get mad at me. Maybe you should tell your goons to do their jobs and that Nola is off limits. They seemed to be getting very friendly out there in the hallway." She continued coming towards Soren, almost within touching distance. "I came here to find out how you wanted to present my findings tonight, and instead I hear you say that you're not going to discuss it at all. *For God's sake, why not?* This report is very important Soren, and some very important decisions will need to be made very quickly."

Rey stood off to the side of them. He looked like a referee at a boxing match. Tess stood with her back to the open door. From Rey's vantage point, he could see the big bodyguard walking purposefully toward Tess and Soren.

Looking at Tess, Rey realized that she was probably the only one in the compound who was not afraid of Soren and his goons. She openly challenged him at the meetings which always ended in shouting and fist pounding. Even here in Soren's own quarters, she stood in front of him defiantly while the bodyguard slid past the kitchen.

"Soren, this is bullshit and you know it! We can't afford to keep quiet on this while we wait for more 'concrete' evidence. If we wait any longer, we won't have the power to pull out of the sun's gravitational pull. That is, if our equipment is still functioning by then. If *you* don't bring this up tonight at the meeting, I sure as hell will." She turned to leave, just as the bodyguard came up behind her.

In slow motion, Rey could see the guard's position change as he planted his feet and brought his huge arm back. Tess was very athletic, but she was caught completely off guard and had no time to register the punch, let alone block it. So, she stood there, watching the huge fist come toward her. In the last instant, her muscles responded, allowing her to turn her head slowly away from the punch.

The punch was hard and solid, but the fact that she turned her head away at the last minute, probably saved her from a fatal blow to the head. Even still, the punch connected with her head and for one second it looked as if it barely fazed her. She took a half step forward as if to run or maybe attack the guard, and then crumpled heavily to the floor.

Rey looked down at her. She twitched a couple of times, and then stopped moving. Rey leaned down to take her pulse. He looked up at Soren and nodded his head. She was out cold and would be that way for several hours.

Soren looked at the bodyguard with disgust. "The next time you fuck up like that boyo, you may find your ass floating in space without a helmet."

"Right boss!" the guard stammered. "I got a little distracted by Miss Nola and uh...it won't happen again, sir."

"Now take this bitch to the waste storage facility, and go help them at the hangar." Soren turned to Rey, finishing, "It's going to be a busy night."

The guard snatched up Tess's limp body easily and trundled off toward the entrance that Rey used earlier. In a moment, he was gone. "We should have just killed her and gotten it over with," Rey announced once the guard had left and the door slid silently back. "What if she wakes up and starts making accusations?"

Soren went to his closet and started selecting his clothes for the meeting. He had his back to Rey as he spoke. "It don't matter, Rey. By the time she comes to, her accusations won't mean shit. Now get the hell out so I can get dressed!"

At that, Rey turned smartly on his heels and headed out the way he had come. *Soren was indeed a loose cannon,* he thought. He would have to keep his eye on him and be ready to act if things got too far out of hand.

THE BASE MEETING

1

"Henry, have you seen Tess?" Kyra asked, touching Henry on the shoulder.

"No, I haven't Kyra. I went by her unit on my way here to chat with her about a few things, but she had already left. I assumed she was already here with you."

"She didn't come with me. I went by her unit too, and she was gone. I thought she might have been in the shower, so I let myself in. It looked like she hadn't been there all afternoon. When I saw her earlier in the day, she mentioned that she was going to talk to Soren."

Looking concerned, Henry said, "That's not like Tess. She's very punctual and was actually looking forward to this meeting. I wonder what's keeping her."

"I don't know, but I'll save a seat for her so she can sit with us closer to the front."

"Yeah, that sounds good Kyra," Henry replied as he followed her toward the front of the meeting hall. He felt a twinge of uneasiness stir deep down inside. He didn't really think anyone here could resort to foul play considering that they were only a fraction of what was left of the human race. But Henry was a very practical person, and as much as he'd like to believe that they were one big happy family here, he knew that some evils never went away.

He looked around the meeting hall as they sat down and frowned. "Is it my imagination or are there more empty seats than usual? When we first started having these meetings, I remember having to help bring in additional chairs. Now, there are chairs to spare." He scanned around again, "I don't see your buddy either," he smiled at Kyra.

"Who are you ta...oh! You're talking about Nola? No worries for me. I'd just as soon not see her anytime too soon." Kyra pantomimed a choking gesture, and they both laughed.

Off to the side, Rey kept a low profile. He didn't feel like fielding any questions about Tess. Even though they had just broken up, people would still assume that he knew her whereabouts. So, he stayed just out of noticeable range but kept his eyes on Kyra and Henry.

He looked towards the front of the room and saw Soren chatting amiably with Dr. Stone and some woman he had been dating. Frankly, he was surprised to see them here. Soren probably was too. Dr. Stone was the only full-fledged doctor in the compound, and Soren was not taking any chances.

As Rey watched, the conversation changed from serious to light hearted and all three of them started laughing at the same time, but

Soren seemed to laugh the longest and the loudest. He kissed the woman on the cheek, very close to her lips, Rey noticed, and heartily patted the doctor on his back. The kiss didn't go unnoticed by Dr. Stone and despite their joviality a moment ago, the man looked slightly embarrassed. Instead of coming into the hall for a seat, they both turned and walked abruptly away, almost at a run.

2

Soren made his way to the center of the stage and adjusted the microphone chip in his earpiece. "Hello friends and colleagues," he said warmly. "Thank you so much for coming. It takes a lot to run this place, and you guys are doing a helluva good job!" The attendees, numbering close to 40 people, applauded and looked around at one another. Henry looked around too, but to him, the room took on an unbalanced look that was more than simply empty seats. He looked up at Soren again, becoming more and more disturbed by the missing people.

Soren's tone took on a more somber note. "Still, every time I look up into the sky at what was once our beautiful home, I can't help but feel like something inside of me has died." The audience also took on a more somber attitude as they stared straight ahead, some started to tear up.

"We are survivors here, all of us," Soren continued. "We survived the devastation of the earth when that damn *Lycos* broke it to pieces. We all have our own stories of how we made it here. We survived the unfortunate accident of our last transport shuttle. Any one of us could have been on that shuttle when it blew up. Things on Earth were getting bad before those shuttles departed, but they were downright hellish when the *Galileo2* tried to take off. In those final days, people had nothing left to live for. Some became suicidal; many became homicidal. It was truly hell on Earth."

Kyra leaned over to Henry and whispered, "Is there a point to this? Why is he bringing all this up now?"

Henry could only shrug his shoulders; he was at a loss here too.

"I say all this, my friends, because we can't allow ourselves to descend to the level that our friends on Earth descended to. There have been rumors that we may have to leave for *Europa* a full six months before our planned departure date. There have been lies spread about how much food we have left and that we don't even have enough fuel to make it to *Europa*. People are worrying if *Europa* will even support life." He paused, looking around the room, allowing the weight of his words to sink in. "Well, I'll tell you this; we have nothing to fear, my friends! I've seen the reports, and I've closely monitored our fuel situation. We'll make it to *Europa* alright, and it will support us just fine!"

From the back of the room, Rey stepped forward and started clapping and cheering loudly. A few others joined in and soon, the entire hall was a chorus of cheers and shouts. Kyra looked at Henry, "Something's not right here, Henry. Soren said nothing about the deteriorating condition of the earth's orbit and that in less than three months, we'll be closer to the sun than Mercury. I know I put that in my report!"

Henry nodded back and said, "From my station, I've been monitoring the earth as well, and I've observed the explosions too. I actually thought Soren was going to use this meeting to start the mobilization process. It's evident from the work they're doing in the shuttle bays that they're preparing the *Cassiopeia* for departure." He thought for a moment and then added, "They've actually been stripping the *Galileo1* though, which is odd."

The clapping died down and Soren began speaking again, "I will admit however, that I have withheld certain information from you, my friends." The meeting hall grew very silent at this admission, as all eyes turned up to Soren. "As a good steward of our meager resources, I wanted to ensure that our food would last during our time here on the moon and once we arrived at *Europa*, so I instituted a strict rationing schedule. Well, about two months ago, we uncovered a cache of freeze-dried food rations and supplies, which will last during the trip to *Europa* and at least three months on the new planet. I thought it best to not share that information until now and for that, I'm sorry."

The audience, half expecting to hear of some scandalous story, let out a collective sigh of relief upon hearing Soren's "confession". A few faces looked skeptical, including Kyra's and Henry's, but most were willing to believe Soren and give him the benefit of the doubt.

"You probably have noticed that a lot of your colleagues are not here in the meeting. Well, some are preparing individual reports that they will present to you in just a few minutes. The others are helping in the kitchen." People exchanged confused looks with one another, while Soren continued on, "You'll be happy to know that because of my aggressive food rationing efforts, we actually have a *surplus* of food, and immediately following my presentation, I've directed our cooks to prepare a banquet of turkey, ham, spinach, apple pie, and the whole Thanksgiving cornucopia—*freeze-dried* mind you," (the audience chuckled at this) "to celebrate our continued survival and immense responsibility as the last peoples of Earth!"

At this, the audience was on their feet cheering and clapping. People were hugging one another; some were crying; some were talking excitedly amongst themselves. The dining facility personnel started bringing in mounds of food. Everything from the promised turkey and ham to several different types of meats and cheeses, a number of exotic-looking side dishes, and desserts of all types. The audience cheered even louder as more and more food was brought in.

Henry's mouth had fallen open. During his entire time here, he had never seen this much food prepared at one time. And from the look on Kyra's face, neither had she. He tapped her on the shoulder and had to almost yell in her ear, "I would really like to grab some of this food now, but I need to talk to Soren first. If he has other information that conflicts with Tess's and yours, I would really like to see it."

"Same here," Kyra replied, "This just sounds too good to be true. And where the hell is Tess? I can't believe she would miss this!" "Maybe she's in the kitchen helping out," Henry replied, "but we can give her an update when we see her; right now, let's see if we can make our way to the front to talk to Soren." His eyes scanned the front of the room, but he didn't see Soren. "Now where the hell did he go?"

As Kyra and Henry moved towards the front of the hall, Rey made his way towards the back and slipped out of one of the rear doors. A number of people rushed past him, eager to get to the food. No one even looked his way. He smiled and headed out into the hallway, eager to catch up with Soren at the shuttle bay.

3

"You're going to burn the burgers too!" Tess said to Stan for the second time. "Remember, the last time we had to wait until the coals cooled down before we started."

Stan looked up at Tess and said, "It's easy for you to give orders when you're floating in your hammock up there." His voice was loud, but held no hint of anger or frustration.

Tess put her hands behind her head and rocked gently back and forth in the hammock. She thought to herself how peaceful hammocks were, especially when your husband was doing all the cooking. But lately, she had been having these strange feelings that something was wrong. She tried turning her head to look at Stan, but it wouldn't move. She could see his vague outline from the periphery of her vision, but now, most of what she could see was black.

She tried to move her hands from the back of her head, but they were frozen in place. And even though she made no effort to make the hammock swing, she could feel it moving anyway. She tried calling out to Stan, but her voice sounded foreign to her ears. Her mouth felt stretched; grunting and gurgling was all she could manage through her vocal cords.

She felt herself rolling and knew that very soon, she would be rolling off the hammock onto the ground. She tensed her body as tightly as she could and felt herself fall from the hammock. When she hit the ground, her eyes flew open. She was half expecting to land on her face and break her nose and maybe a few teeth. But when she hit the floor, the only thing that happened was that she bounced up toward the low ceiling. It took her a long minute to gather her wits before she realized what was going on. Her hands and feet had been tied and she had a rag or something tied around her mouth, preventing her from speaking clearly. She had a bitter taste in her mouth that she initially thought was from the rag, but the more she explored the inside of her mouth, the more it began to taste like old blood.

As the fog in her head started to clear, she began to remember what had happened to her. She had gone to Soren's unit to confront him about her report. Rey was there, and then she blacked out. Was she hit? Her bewilderment turned to anger. Soren had gone too far this time. She didn't think he would have resorted to violence like this, but she never put it past him either. It didn't make any sense. *Was he trying to hide something?* she wondered as she struggled trying to get her hands untied.

Looking around, she could see that she was in one of the utility rooms, most likely the one in the East Wing. The West Wing utility room was very close to the conference room and was always in use. Chances are, they would not have put her there. When they first arrived here from Earth, they voted to shut down the artificial gravity in the East Wing in an effort to conserve power. They also reduced the heat in this section as well. Already, Tess could feel the cold seeping in through her jump suit.

Luckily, she was wearing her thermal suit. Oddly enough, she had been having problems with the heater in her room unit and was forced to sometimes wear her thermal suit when she went to bed. After she showered earlier, she put on her thermal suit out of habit and went to see Soren. It was blind luck that she was wearing it today because if she had been wearing a regular jumpsuit, then she'd probably be dead now from hypothermia.

First, she wanted to get that foul-tasting rag out of her mouth, so she tried to use her shoulder to push the gag away from her mouth and almost screamed in pain when her jaw rubbed up against her shoulder.

That one instant of pain seemed to bring a flood of memories with it. She was indeed hit. Someone had hit her in the mouth. It wasn't Rey, although he was in on it for certain. It was one of Soren's guards. Yes, she had come upon one of his guards trying to flirt with Nola. That's when she slipped into his unit.

Then she remembered having a conversation with Kyra about her data. About Nola too. She remembered that Nola lost or deleted some information on Earth or the moon. After she saw Kyra, she decided to confront Soren on her report to make sure he understood exactly what was going on. If he tried to weasel his way out of sharing this information, then she would be there to make sure everyone knew what was going on. Everyone needed to know that it was time to start preparing to leave for *Europa*.

But then she had overheard him talking to Reynald. He was saying something about destroying her report and not sharing it with everyone. She closed her eyes tightly. It didn't make sense. Why would he not share this news with everyone? If we do nothing, then we all die and even Soren has better sense than to wait until it's too late. He would never let that hap... At that thought, Tess's eyes popped wide open. *"Oh, my dear God, dear God"* she whispered in the darkness, as she began to frantically twist and squirm in an effort to loosen the ropes around her wrists and ankles.

DAN STUMBLES ONTO THE TRUTH

1

Dan was pissed. Of all the times to be sick!

He swung his legs over the side of the bed and sat there for a moment. His wife, Melissa, had called him on the unit intercom system to tell him about Soren's speech and the massive banquet of food. She couldn't stop talking about the food. His brain told him he was missing some good eating, but his stomach did flips each time he thought about it. Although his wife promised that she would bring some food back for him, he knew that it would spoil before he was well enough to even attempt to eat it.

Now here he was, burning up with a 102-degree fever and a touch of nausea to top it off. He was very hungry, but knew he wouldn't be able to keep any food down; however, water was a different matter. He hadn't realized how thirsty he was until he disconnected with Melissa. His throat felt as if it were lined with cotton. Unfortunately, the refrigerator in their unit was broken and so they had no cold water. He tried drinking the warm tap water, and the first swallow made his stomach lurch. *I can't drink this crap,* he thought, *I'll vomit for sure.* He thought for a moment what his options were and then remembered the cold water that the maintenance crews kept in the shuttle bay. Hell, they even had an ice machine in there. It was a short walk there and with him being on the flight team, there wouldn't be a problem with access.

He threw on his robe and donned his slippers. He considered combing his hair and maybe throwing on a jumpsuit, but all he could focus on was getting some cold water. He considered leaving a note for Melissa, but by the time it took to find a pen and paper, write a note, and post it where she'd find it, he could be halfway to the bay. So, with that in mind, he headed out of his unit towards the shuttle bay. As he shuffled along, he figured he would finally see why they were making so much noise over there.

2

Rey smiled as he looked around the shuttle bay. Considering how much time they had left, things were progressing just fine. All crucial supplies had already been moved on board over the past several weeks. Food, medicine, terrain vehicles, and much, much more had only taken a few days to load. Their only challenge earlier in the week was connecting the Cargo Cabin. It was a pre-loaded colony-starter unit, and it was heavy as hell.

The Cargo Cabin was positioned outside the ship and designed to be fastened to either the top rear of the ship or the bottom (it could only be connected to the bottom during a cargo-transfer maneuver in space). Contrary to how it sounded, the Cargo Cabin was a marvel of engineering. It was aerodynamically fitted to the top of the ship where it was connected by two powerful magnetic locking clamps. At first glance, it looked as if it were part of the ship, instead of an add-on. The top of the Cargo Cabin contained two female connectors for transferring the Cabin to another ship if that became necessary.

Things had been progressing well right up to the point where they had to place the Cargo Cabin into position on the *Cassiopeia*. The shuttle bay cranes groaned under the weight of the Cabin but held their ground. It wasn't until the Cabin hovered just mere feet from its connector that one of the cranes finally gave in and bent sharply over, dropping one end of the Cabin onto the top of the ship. They were lucky; only one of the quick release latches was damaged. The ship and the Cargo Cabin remained intact.

He looked up at the gleaming *Cassiopeia*. Although it was almost half the size of the United Nations' Generation Ship, the *Orion*, it was still a huge ship. At about 270 feet in length, it was bigger than any ship Rey had ever flown (and during his short stint in NASA, that number was a modest three and it was always from the co-pilot's chair).

He glanced over at the *Galileo1*, the shuttle that Tess flew on her last trip from Earth. The broken wheel struts stood out like an accusation. It reminded him of the huge argument between Soren and Skip Masterston; it was an argument that ended in Skip's death.

Skip was slated to be Tess's co-pilot in the *Cassiopeia* for the trip to *Europa* and during one of his inspections realized that the landing gear on the *Galileo1* had not been repaired as promised. He had gotten approval from the President's Chief of Staff to go back to Earth for at least 50 more people. Since the *Galileo2* was destroyed, there was plenty of space and more than enough supplies at both compounds to accommodate the additional people. And most importantly, they had time. *Lycos* was close, but it was still at least ten days away. They had received communication that the California air base and the passengers were secured and awaiting extraction.

Skip first brought the matter to Shelton, who did nothing but irritate him by telling him to take it up with Soren. Of course, Skip went to Soren and argued vehemently that he had approval from the

President's Chief of Staff, but Soren refused to budge on his position that he was under strict orders not to exceed personnel capacity. He declined to say whose orders those were.

Furious, Skip made a trip to the UN compound to meet with the President's Chief of Staff, who's new role in this new world order was population control and welfare. Unfortunately, rogue meteor showers from the approaching *Lycos* peppered the UN site for over an hour. By the time it was over, the life support systems had been destroyed, killing all but eight people (they were part of a survey team and had been out surveying the grounds north of the UN site). When the meteor shower hit, they found shelter underground and waited it out. If Henry's team hadn't gone out when they did to look for survivors, those eight would have been lost as well.

With Skip dead, Dan was the only one qualified to co-pilot the *Cassiopeia*. Rey was a qualified pilot and so was Chayton Dakota, but neither was rated to fly the huge TX1100 Generation Ships. There were a handful of other pilots in their group, but they were much further down on the food chain. As he watched the maintenance guys finish up their work, he could feel a nervous trickle of sweat coursing down the middle of his back. He hoped that flying the *Cassiopeia* would be as easy as the much smaller shuttles, but looking up at this behemoth he began to wonder.

3

He saw the last of the passengers mount the air-stairs to the shuttle. They were paired up like animals going into Noah's Ark. Rey chuckled to himself and thought how shocked they were going to be once they arrived at *Europa* and Soren unveiled his own version of monogamous relationships.

Soren's new world was to be a feudal society where he would set himself up as a king. He wouldn't have land to force servitude, but he would use their resources such as food and supplies from the starter kits. Things that the people would need to survive. And in his twisted world, women would represent the most valuable of all his resources. He hadn't been entirely clear with Rey about how he planned to structure this new system, but he was very clear how he would *enforce* it. He had a large number of *bodyguards* at his disposal, and he was quite sure that he would go unchallenged for quite some time.

He looked at his watch and saw that it was time to board the shuttle and initiate the launch sequence, when a hand grabbed him by the shoulders.

"Rey! Hey...what's going on here?" Rey turned to face the red face of Dan Melton, Tess's co-pilot. Dan was slightly out of breath and looked as if he would pass out any minute. He dropped his hand from Rey's shoulder and re-tied his bathrobe around his waist. "I came over to the bay to get some water because my fridge is on the blink. Seems like everything is breaking around here!" He chuckled at that and glanced around the shuttle bay. "What in the world are you guys doing here? I've been hearing a lot of racket over here lately, but I've been too sick to come see what was going on."

He saw people climbing the stairs to the rear of the shuttle. They were carrying luggage and personal belongings. He stared for a long time at several members of the shuttle maintenance team performing what looked like final launch preparations. "Are those guys doing pre-launch prep work? My wife spoke to Tess, and she told her that we might have to leave soon, but I thought that wouldn't be for another two to four weeks. This baby looks ready to go *now*." He glanced up at the Cargo Cabin at the top rear of the ship and his mouth dropped open.

"Wait a minute! This ship is leaving very soon! I mean, within hours, right?" He was starting to get another headache and wished he had a chair to sit in. "Am I right Rey? Are we leaving tonight? How could we have missed the announcement? Why wasn't I informed? Who's riding second seat? Is that you or Chayton? I'm too sick to fly. I can't believe Tess didn't contact me!"

Rey listened dutifully as he led Dan toward the shuttle bay offices, away from the activity on the main floor. He glanced at the clock on the wall as they stepped into the office. "No problem Dan. We're not leaving until tomorrow, so you guys have plenty of time. By the way, Tess left some notes for you, but I was planning to bring them by a little later."

He went over to the desk in the small bay office and started shuffling papers around on the top of the desk. "Where is that pad?" he said absentmindedly. He stepped behind the desk and sat down. He opened up one of the side drawers and started rummaging through the desk for an imaginary note. His fingers ran across the tips of a pair of scissors, and he slid them into one of the slim file folders in the drawer.

Dan plopped down in the chair facing the desk, water now forgotten. "I know I've been sick, but no one told me a damn thing!" He considered this a moment and then put his hand to his forehead. "Shit! I'll bet Tess decided to use Chayton as her co-pilot. He's probably her best choice after me..." he caught himself, and saw the twitch in Rey's eyes. "Sorry Rey, I don't mean it like that. I mean, she's always liked Chayton's flying, so I'm just assuming that he would be the one she would use. Hey...I've been out sick, so what would I know!" He tried to lighten the atmosphere, but the words or at least the thought was already out there; *Rey, you're a shit pilot, and you don't have the experience.*

"Anyway," he added, "whoever flies should have at least consulted me. We always plan our trips together, regardless of who's flying." He was starting to work himself up again and stood up, "This is bullshit Rey, and you know it! I should have been contacted at least." He angrily adjusted his robe, "Thanks for the update, but I need to go get my wife and let her know what's going on. Where's Tess? Is she on the ship now?"

"Hmm...*this* is interesting," Rey said, looking down at the papers in the folder, as if Dan had not said anything.

Dan stopped in his tracks and looked down at the folder in Rey's hands, "What is?" he asked.

"Okay, let's see here. It's a confidential memo to Soren from Tess. The subject is 'Non-essential Personnel'". He pretended to scan the paper. "It says *'The following names represent non-essential personnel and due to the scarcity of food and supplies, I must urge that you take into consideration my suggestion that the below-listed individuals be left here on the moon. So as not to jeopardize the chances of those selected to depart for Europa, these individuals should be left with only limited supplies.'*" He mentioned several names and then looked up at Dan earnestly and said, "'*Dan and Melissa Melton*'. Dan, I'm sorry, it says here that you and Melissa are staying here."

Dan stared at him dumbfounded. His mind couldn't comprehend what he was hearing. He stared hard into Rey's face, but Rey remained impassive. Dan stared a bit longer and then burst out laughing. When he was finally able to speak, he said, "God, that's funny as hell Rey! Who else is on that list? Let me see it."

He walked around the desk to look over Rey's shoulder at the open folder on the desk. At the top of the letter, he saw "Regularly Scheduled Maintenance Report". He quickly scanned the rest of the document, but it was nothing more than a routine maintenance report. The beginnings of a smile creased the corners of his mouth as he turned to look at Rey. He was thinking that Rey was finally loosening up and able to come up with an original joke.

Rey looked back at him and although he was smiling too, his eyes said something different. Dan must have seen this too, but it was too late. He only had time to see a flash of silver in Rey's hand before Rey jabbed the scissors deep into his abdomen. The scissors were not particularly sharp, but Rey was able to repeatedly stab Dan in the stomach. The only thing Dan was able to do was weakly grasp at Rey's shoulder, while wheezing in his face. He tried to scream, but the only thing that came out of his mouth were a few weak grunts. Each time he took a breath in, Rey would ram the scissors into his mid-section again. Eventually, his legs gave way and he crumpled to his knees, a mixture of blood and urine now streaming down his leg.

Rey, half-expecting Dan to scream caught him by his hair on the back of his head as he slid to the floor. With all the force he could muster, he slammed Dan's head into the hard desk and felt a sickening crunch as Dan's nose broke against the desk. Whatever fight Dan had in him melted away after that and Rey let him drop to the floor. He stole a quick glance out the small office window and didn't see anyone which was good, but was he really worried about it? Not in the least. The folks on the shuttle were privileged to be there. In Rey's mind, if anyone from the ship had seen what had happened, it would have been in their best interest to ignore it, close their eyes and dream of the new world, lest they find themselves stuck on the moon with the rest of the hapless masses.

He looked down at Dan and started when he saw Dan staring up at him accusingly, but the eyes were vacant. He put his fingers to Dan's neck and kept them there for a full minute. He felt no pulse. He pulled Dan's body behind the desk, went through a door in the back of the office, and emerged a few minutes later in a clean flight suit. He grabbed his flight folder, looked back once more at the desk, and then flipped the light off. He took two steps, turned around, and went back to lock the door. He trotted to the air-stairs and headed up to the shuttle. He noticed two maintenance people down below and yelled out to them, "Yo! If you two don't want to get left behind, I suggest you secure those bay doors now and get your asses up here. We're leaving!"

RETURN TO EARTH

The two men looked at each other and sprinted towards the interior bay doors. Rey laughed, ducked his head, and stepped inside.

Soren nodded at him as he made his way to the front of the ship towards the cockpit.

ABANDONED!

1

"Where in the hell is he?" Henry half shouted to Kyra. They had been looking for Soren in the meeting hall for the past hour, but were having no luck finding him. They asked several people who sat up close to the front, but no one seemed to know where he had gone.

"This is ridiculous!" Kyra yelled into Henry's ear. "He was just here! How could he have just disappeared? One minute he's talking to a few folks, the next he's gone. Let's just go to his unit; maybe he wasn't feeling well and headed back."

Henry looked around again exasperated. "Yeah, I think you're right. We're wasting our time here. If he went back, then we…" At that moment, out of the corner of his eye, he saw several people running towards the front of the hall. The fear and extreme anxiety in their faces made Henry's stomach turn. They were all yelling at the same time, making it difficult to understand what they were saying. Henry had a feeling that whatever the reason was, it was probably very bad.

"THEY'RE LEAVING!" the closer one said as he neared the middle of the hall. *"THEY'RE LEAVING US!"* he yelled out again as if no one heard him.

Albert Bueller, one of the facilities engineers, swiveled in his chair and yelled back through a mouth full of reconstituted mash potatoes, "What the hell you talking about Max? Are you crazy?"

Henry and Kyra ran over to where he was. To Henry, Max looked like he was about to have a heart attack right there on the spot. His face had a pale and unhealthy waxy look. He looked as if he would pass out any minute.

The man leaned over with both hands on the back of a chair. Others in the hall gathered around him, concerned that someone might be hurt. He lifted his face up to the others and still breathing hard he said very clearly, "The big ship, the *Cassiopeia*, is getting ready to leave! I went to the shuttle bay to borrow some tools, and the bay entrance doors were locked. I looked through the door window and saw the ship in the bay airlock and the exterior bay doors were opening up. Then, the ship's engines started, and the ship started moving towards the exit." He paused a minute, as if he himself didn't believe the next part and added, "I could see people *on* the ship. They were leaving…I'm sure of it."

Henry stared at the man. Stared *through* him. It didn't make sense what Max was saying. Even joking like this would be in terrible taste. Max's breathing had slowed, but now he was crying. "They're leaving us man! I could tell! All the supplies that used to be lined up alongside the hangar walls are gone. I can't even find some of the other engineers. I went by Torie's unit to tell her, and she was gone. It looked as if she had packed up her personal belongings and left. Does anybody here know what the hell is going on?"

Henry looked at Kyra, and they both turned toward the hall leading to the shuttle bay hangar. A number of onlookers had already gotten the same idea and were starting to run towards the shuttle bay. Soon, almost everyone in the hall had broken into an all-out run to see if what Max was saying was true.

2

Tess had finally wriggled out of the ties that held her wrists. A combination of blood and sweat finally helped her to squeeze her hands through the small loops. She imagined that if she were conscious when they put the ties on her, they probably would have made them a lot tighter. Hell, she's lucky they didn't kill her and dump her lifeless body out of one of the exterior hatches.

As she reached down to her ankles to undo the ties, she thought again about her last encounter with Soren. She had heard him say that he was not going to share her report with the others at the council meeting, and her initial thoughts were that he was being bull-headed as he sometimes was. But the more she thought about it, the more she came to realize that this was more than just simple jealously or an attempt to remain in his position. Soren was planning on leaving.

She undid her ankles and pulled herself towards the door, praying that it wasn't locked from the outside. This time, fate was on her side, and the door swung open easily. Jumping through the door, she half-bounced, half-pulled herself through the low gravity hallway towards the shuttle bay.

3

Most of the people in the council meeting were already at the shuttle bay entrance when Henry and Kyra arrived. They were pressed up against the hallway windows and looking through the small windows in the doors. Henry moved down to one of the hallway windows further down the hall and looked outside. The ship had made its way out of the bay and was turning toward the runway. Two men had donned space suits and were preparing to go through the airlock.

What were they going to do when they got inside, thought Henry, *stop the ship from moving?*

At that moment, Soren's voice boomed out over the interior intercom system, "Hello friends! Although, I would imagine that none of you see me as a friend now." Everyone froze in their tracks, not knowing what to expect from Soren, but fearing the worse.

"I know right now, most of you are wondering what's going on. You want to know why the ship is headed out to the runway. You want to know why you are being left behind." He paused for a moment as if waiting for the right moment. "That's right, you are being left behind." At that admission, some of the men started cursing; more than a few started crying. A number of them just stared in stunned silence, not willing to believe what they were hearing.

Ignorant of their curses and cries, Soren continued on, "Over the past year, I've often thought about how we, as the last of the human race, will survive this cataclysm. Billions of people on Earth lost their lives and only a handful of us survived. Even after we safely left the earth and made it here to the moon, over half our number was wiped out almost overnight by the errant meteorites that struck the UN compound. Let's face it people, the odds are stacked up against us, no matter what some may say.

"Our food supplies have been running low for the past six months. The water recycling unit has broken down at least twice this year. The compound is slowly wearing down. *We* are slowly wearing down. We were barely surviving here. I knew...I *knew*, that we could not successfully start life on the new planet with this many people. What if we got there and found that we couldn't live on the land? Then we would have to make our supplies last as long as possible, until we at least found a way to live."

He paused, looking out the window of the ship facing the compound. He could see the people pressed up against the windows. They looked very agitated. Behind him, he could hear crying. A few men spoke up demanding that he stop the ship and let the others on, but two of his guards put a stop to their little insurrection quickly.

He started up again, "I knew we couldn't take a chance and bring everyone, so I made an executive decision to bring just a handful of people. The *right* people. I've personally selected this team of 15 men and 34 women to be the progenitors of a strong and powerful new humanity. Of course, we have more women than men, because we have to replenish this new world quickly if we humans are to survive."

RETURN TO EARTH

He looked behind him and caught Dr. Stone's eyes. His eyes were smoldering as he held a wet cloth to his bruised face. "I bite my tongue as I say this, but if it's any consolation to you, not everyone was keen on leaving you folks behind. Yet, they were all given the opportunity to give up their seat for one of you and sad to say, no one volunteered. So you see, my friends, we all know what's important to humans when the rubber meets the road—survival. Survival in its most basic and primitive form.

"I know you all will make the best of what time you have remaining on the moon, but I would urge you to consider a few things. The earth is moving closer and closer to the sun. Not all of you would know that since you never saw the reports, but believe me, it *is* getting closer and it will pull the moon right along with it. In a matter of months, the moon will be so close to the sun, that if your machines don't break first, then the intense heat will kill you where you stand."

Tess had stumbled to the edge of the group and made her way to the shuttle bay windows, where Henry and Kyra were. They looked at her in shocked surprise. "Oh my God Tess! I thought you were on the shuttle. I thought you were *flying*." She broke down in tears, "I thought you left us…"

Tess and Kyra hugged, while Soren continued on, "We're lined up for our departure, so it's time for me to end my little soliloquy, but I leave you by saying, make it easy on yourselves. Kill yourselves. Don't suffer the indignities of either slowly starving to death while your world gets hotter and hotter, and your machines begin to die out. Don't end up like the earth in its final days. *Au revoir* my friends, *au revoir.*"

From her window seat inside the *Cassiopeia*, Nola could see many faces pressed up against the port windows looking out at them. Whatever sympathy she had for leaving them was drowned out by the overwhelming thought of being here and not there. When two of the ladies questioned the ethics of what they were doing, Soren came very close to throwing them off. Instead, he asked them if they would like to give up their seats and allow someone in the compound to come aboard. They exchanged horrified glances, shook their heads at Soren and sat down quickly. One of them, Torie she thought, started crying. Their generosity and love for their fellow man couldn't compete with the thought of being left behind.

Later, Soren came up to them and told them that had they gotten off, the doors would have locked behind them and there would have been two empty seats headed to *Europa*. They turned pale at that and didn't utter another word.

Nola had no such qualms. She pressed her face up against the window, knowing that Kyra was there amongst the crowd; she hoped that Kyra could see her on the ship. The thought made her smile.

The huge ship rolled out to the runway and moved into position. "Prepare for takeoff," Rey announced over the intercom system. A few people cheered, but for the most part, everyone else kept silent, lost in their own thoughts. Nola leaned her head back against the head rest in her seat and looked out the window again. The afterburners ignited, and she felt herself pressed back and down into her seat as the shuttle accelerated. The *Cassiopeia* lifted from the surface of the moon smoothly, banking left as it pulled away from the moon. With her head turned towards the window, she could still see the earth, looking alien and hostile. As she stared at the planet, she thought she could see very faint flashes of yellow-orange light. She closed her eyes tightly to fight off the rising bile in her throat.

THE COLD TRUTH

1

"I don't think everyone went voluntarily," Tess said to Kyra, who sat quietly brooding in the chair across from her.

Tess sat on the edge of the medical bed while the medical tech examined the cuts on her wrists. With Dr. Stone and Nurse Jackson gone, she was the only person remaining with any real medical training. She looked up at Tess. Other than the angry purplish bruise on the side of her face and a few minor scrapes and scratches, she was in pretty decent shape. Tess winced as the tech finished up the last bandage.

"Sorry, Tess," she said. She was a small, waifish girl who looked to be no more than 24 years old. "I just need to change the bandage over the bruise, apply some ointment, and then you'll be good to go."

"Thanks Julie," Tess said and winced again as she applied ointment to the bruise on her face.

Kyra eyed the ugly mark on Tess's face and shook her head, "You're lucky he didn't break your nose or worse. I can't believe he punched you like that! Hell...I still can't believe that those fuckers left us here to die."

"I know," Tess replied. Like everyone else in the compound, she was becoming more and more depressed about their situation. People walked around in a daze, lost in thought. Dan's wife, Melissa, killed herself, thinking that her husband had left her. Henry told Tess that she had run around screaming and scratching at her face, before locking herself in her unit. By the time they got to her, she was turning blue hanging from the ceiling fan in her unit. Two hours later, they found Dan in the shuttle bay office, lying in a coagulated pool of dried blood. His bulging eyes stared out at them from the darkness of the space underneath the desk. They imagined he came upon all the activity in the bay and was killed for being in the wrong place at the wrong time.

Tess let out a heavy sigh, "I still can't believe that they were able to connect the Cargo Cabin container without anyone noticing."

"What is that?" asked Julie.

"It's basically a heat-shielded cargo container that rides piggyback on the ship. It's designed to support long-term colonization efforts. You can't pack starter kits and long-term environment stabilization modules inside a shuttle, so those items are loaded into the cargo containers or Cargo Cabins. Once a ship enters orbit about a target colony planet, then the Cargo Cabin is released from the top or bottom of the ship, depending on how it was attached. There is a remote guidance unit built into each Cabin. Coordinates are fed into it and once it's released, small thruster jets maneuver it to the right location on the planet.

Julie looked at Tess with a blank look on her face, "Okay, if you say so."

Tess smiled and glanced over at Kyra. She seemed to consider something and her smile faded, "Like I was saying Kyra, I don't think everyone went willingly. Henry thinks that most of them went because it was either go or stay here and die. They've gone through all of the units and in quite a few of them, there are signs of a struggle. They found empty syringes in a few units, so some of them were probably unconscious when they were kidnapped. These were all women's quarters."

Kyra shook her head. The weight of this seemed to press her into the chair. Julie stopped working on Tess and dropped her hands to her side. "Oh my God," she breathed.

"What?" Kyra asked. "What's wrong Julie?"

Julie Dubois turned so she could face both women. "Over the past several months, I've been training with Doctor Stone in the operating room to improve my surgical skills. One day, while we were working on a patient, Mr. Soren came by and observed the entire procedure from the viewing room. He congratulated us afterwards and said to me that he was very impressed that someone my age was so competent in the OR. He hugged me and then left. I thought it was kind of weird, but I didn't think much about it. At least not until one of his guards contacted me a day before the council meeting.

"He said that Mr. Soren wanted to speak with me before the council meeting because he wanted to get more details on the work that I've been doing with Dr. Stone and present that to the rest of the compound. Sort of like praising me in front of everyone, I guess. The guard was on his way to come get me when I got a call that one of the cooks had burned himself badly. Apparently, I was the last person on the list, because they couldn't get a hold of Dr. Stone or Nurse Jackson. So, I left immediately to take care of the burn victim. I didn't get him stabilized until after the meeting started, so I just went to the meeting instead of going back to my unit."

"Well Julie," Tess said, "you're either the luckiest girl in the world or the *unluckiest*. They were probably going to take you with them, willingly or unwillingly. Lucky for us they couldn't find you, otherwise, we would have been without someone with any significant medical experience."

Julie looked uncertain for a moment and then sighed. She was terrified. In her heart of hearts, she wished she hadn't left her unit. She wished they would have taken her too, instead of leaving her here to die with everyone else. Another part of her realized though, that as the only person left behind with any medical training, she was going to be sorely needed. But she was going to need some help. "Tess," she asked tentatively, "is there any way to get inside the units for Doctor Stone and Nurse Jackson? I'm sure they have some medical books that I can use for training. I'm going to need a backup or something when the time comes, so I had better start training that person now. You're in charge now, right?"

Tess looked unsure for a moment and seemed to shrink from the question. With Soren gone, they were leaderless, weren't they? Despite the fact that not many people liked Soren, the fact that he was here represented some form of stability, regardless of whether it was positive or negative. Tess had never liked Soren and seemed to disagree with everything he said or did, but that didn't make her the leader. She didn't want the responsibility. She had her own problems and the idea of being responsible for a group of people whose future was uncertain, did not appeal to her at all.

"You know Julie, I, uh, I'm not in charge here. I mean, I don't know who's in charge now." She tried to keep the irritation out of her voice and barely succeeded. "Why would I be in charge anyway?"

Now it was Julie's turn to look uncomfortable. "I'm sorry Tess! I just thought that since you always had such great ideas that were different from Soren's, that you would be the right person to go to." She paused for a minute and then added, "People are asking what to do and all I hear is 'I don't know, go ask Tess.'"

Kyra joined the conversation, "She's right Tess. And you know as well as I do that the very reason Soren hated your guts was because you forced him to stay on his toes. You questioned a lot of his 'policies' not because you were being disagreeable, but because your ideas were not born of selfish reasons. They represented the relationships and conversations that you've had with so many of us. Right now, we need someone to bring us together or we'll surely tear ourselves apart. We do need you Tess."

Tess jumped up from the bed and backed away from Kyra and Julie. She didn't like the way this conversation was going, not one bit. "Look guys, I'll do all I can with helping devise a plan for rationing our remaining supplies, but I can't be responsible for this. Soren left us with nothing. *Nothing!* That little banquet he devised wiped out any hope we had of salvaging our food stores. I've heard people say we could make a trip over to the UN base, but we've done that once already since it was destroyed, and we plundered what little they had left. You're asking me to be the captain of a sinking ship, after the captain has already abandoned it!"

"What are we going to do then?" Julie asked. Her eyes were brimming with tears and her voice cracked when she spoke. "I mean, we only have about two or three months before we get too close to the sun, right?"

"I...I don't know," Tess said. "I'm sorry, but I just don't know what to do now." She jumped up and headed towards the door with thoughts of their uncertain future swirling in her head.

2

For Tess, the next couple of days went by in a haze of confusion and mixed emotions. Luckily, she had enough food to last her a week before she had to go to the commissary again, but she expected that there would not be any food remaining by then. Tensions were very high and someone always seemed to be knocking on her door. She met up with Kyra and Henry a couple of times and found out that people just stopped doing their work. People were falling apart already, and the compound was falling into disarray.

The last time she saw Henry and Kyra, she could see that they both had lost weight and more than a little sleep. Despite her initial reluctance, Tess was being drawn more and more into helping them find a solution to their dire circumstances. The idea of making a trip to the UN compound to scavenge for food and supplies came up again and again, but that would not be a very easy trip to make.

The United Nation's compound was about 15 miles away and without vehicles, it would take them at least a half a day to get there, provided there were no problems. Tess remembered that they had been very thorough during their last trip there. She didn't expect another trip would find much in the way of supplies if they went again. During that trip, they had searched for survivors. While Henry and his team were searching, Tess had taken some time to check out the other generation ship, the *Orion*. It was still intact, considering how many meteorites had smashed the compound. All but a small amount of the fuel reserves, however, had been completely destroyed.

"I say we take a team of four or five people and trek over to that UN station and see what we can find. There's got to be something over there that we can use." Henry stated adamantly the last time he and Kyra were with Tess.

"But Henry, you were there with us the last time," Tess replied back. "That place was gutted. Remember, we scoured the place for anything usable. What didn't float out into space with the wreckage was secured and brought back. The additional fuel we brought back the first time."

"I know Tess, but we've got to do something! There must be something we can do other than slowly starving to death or waiting until our life-support breaks down piece by piece when the sun starts baking everything. Take your pick!" He stood up and shoved his hands in his pockets and walked away. He turned around abruptly and said, "Do you guys know that we've had several more suicides this morning. It's only been 18 hours since Soren left, and already we've had four accidental deaths and seven suicides. Two of them went through the airlock and simply allowed themselves to be sucked out into space. Eventually, someone will get the bright idea that he or she needs to save us from our misery and despair by sabotaging the airlock—and that will kill us all for sure!"

"I heard about the suicides Henry," Tess said in a low voice. "Who knows, in the end, suicide may be the only way to go. Without Kyra's readings, we can't be sure how many weeks or days we have before Earth reaches a critical point in its orbit about the sun. I do know that the surface temperatures have been slowly rising. When the machinery starts to break, we'll feel like we're being cooked in an oven or microwave."

"*Don't say that Tess, ever!*" Kyra shouted at her. "Suicide is *not* the answer!" She crossed her arms and looked away. When she turned back to them, her face had taken on a more inquisitive look. "What about flying the UN ship? The *Orion*? Can it make it to *Europa*?"

Tess considered this for a moment. "Well, it appeared to be in good shape when I was last there, but I remember specifically that the rocket propellant levels were extremely low. Also," and a pained expression crossed her face, "I seem to remember that one of the engine power nodes were questionable, but I don't know if it had been replaced or not before the meteor storm. Without all six power nodes and enough rocket propellant, we could die floating in space, millions of miles from *Europa*."

"Oh *God*," was all that Kyra could say as she looked down at the floor. Tess put her arm around her and tried to comfort her. Their situation was bad, and it wouldn't be long before things turned dangerous.

As if he were reading her mind, Henry said, "We need to a have a meeting immediately. Everyone needs to be in attendance. By my count, there are a total of 44 adults and 19 kids. I'm not about to lose any more. If we keep to ourselves and stop interacting with one another, we'll become strangers to each other and when that happens, it'll become much easier for strangers to rob one another, even kill."

Tess looked at Henry and realized that he was right. The compound needed to stay together. They needed to act like a community again or things would surely fall apart. She could easily see them forming small gangs and terrorizing each other for food or water, until it got so hot that they all dropped dead where they stood.

"You're right Henry, we need to meet before things get out of hand and there's no turning back. People are still civilized and willing to get together to discuss how to survive this. This may not be possible in another two weeks. Maybe we *should* make a trek to the UN compound, if anything, to give some of us hope and to give others something to do. We can't fall into despair. If we do, then it's over for us." She walked over to Henry and hugged him tightly. "Thank you, Henry. Let's get everyone together in the next day or two so we can discuss this. Time is precious now."

Kyra jumped up, excited by the prospect of doing something. "Welcome back Tess! I'll start contacting the others!"

Tess turned to Henry, "Do you think you can get us some satellite photos of the UN compound from the space station uplink by the time we have our meeting? It would be good to show everyone what the plan is, and the images would make it real for them...and for us."

Henry thought a moment and said, "Yeah, I'm pretty sure I can get some downloads by tomorrow evening, as long as the uplink to the space station is still strong." He considered this and said, "I think it's behind the earth, relative to our position right now. I usually encounter a lot of interference when it's on the other side, but I'll try to boost the signal and see if I can connect to it."

"Okay, let me know if I can help," said Tess. To Kyra, she said, "Let's set the meeting time for 3pm tomorrow afternoon. That should give us time to do whatever research we need to do for the trip to the UN compound. Also, there are a couple of people who made the trip the last time who are still with us. Maybe I can talk them into making this journey again."

Kyra hugged them both and said, "I'll head to the cafeteria now and speak to some of the folks that are there. If anything changes before tomorrow afternoon, let me know."

"I'll head out with you," Henry said throwing on his jacket. "It's not as safe as it used to be. When hope begins to fade, the only thing people are left with are their unfiltered emotions. See you tomorrow Tess."

After they left, Tess had jotted down notes for the meeting the next day. Despite her earlier feelings, she was beginning to feel energized, but she knew there were a number of obstacles in their path. She looked down at her notes and hoped that she could be as convincingly positive as Henry was tonight.

HENRY'S DISCOVERY

1

Henry yawned, rubbed the heels of his palms against his eyes, and leaned forward to stare at the monitors again. He had gone to bed late and was up early to get the information he needed for the meeting. He looked down at his watch and realized he had only an hour before they had to meet everyone in the council hall. Kyra had done well getting people rounded up for the meeting, and they seemed just as excited as she was. At least it was better than the doom and gloom that had been hanging over everyone's head for the past several days.

During their first year on the moon, Henry and one of his colleagues, Larry Drucker, had been responsible for maintaining constant surveillance of the *Pegasus1* satellite that was orbiting Jupiter and *Europa*. They also monitored the live feed coming from the empty space station, which was still completely operational. Like clockwork, the station would send out images of the moon and of Earth every 12 hours, and would probably do so until its components wore out or its orbit became compromised.

Larry Drucker had worked as the Director of Astronomical studies at UCLA before being offered a position with the government. He lived and worked at the UN compound and was one of the survivors that Henry's team found after the UN site was destroyed. For months, Henry and Larry tried unsuccessfully to download the satellite feeds from the *Pegasus1* and the space station. It seemed they were always able to connect to both, but that was the extent of their luck.

As Henry stared at the computer equipment arranged along the wall, he found himself thinking of the men who went with Soren. Fifteen men were "selected" to join Soren and his folks, and Larry was one of them. He wondered why Larry had been selected and realized that Larry was probably the only person who could attempt to communicate with the *Pegasus1* satellite other than Henry. He was also the only other person here who could function as a navigator.

As he thought of Larry, he realized now that he never really trusted him. There was a sneakiness about him that Henry couldn't quite put his finger on. Late one evening, when Henry couldn't sleep, he had gone to his station to catch up on a few things and came upon Larry sitting at Henry's own workstation.

"Hey Larry, what's going on?" Henry had asked him.

Larry had whirled around so fast that Henry thought he would throw himself out of the chair. "What? Oh...hey Henry! I was uh, just uh, hey...what are *you* doing here this late in the evening?" He stood up and positioned himself between Henry and the monitor.

Henry remembered thinking that if Larry had just turned around and said something like, *'My workstation is compiling some data, so I hopped on yours for a minute',* then he would have believed him completely. But Larry's guilty look and shaky voice made him think that Larry was trying to snoop or something. *And how did he get my login?* Henry had thought later.

Henry looked past Larry toward his screen. It was just on the login screen, so Larry was either finished or hadn't started yet. Almost as if reading his mind, Larry said, "Sorry Henry, I was about to log on and copy the data from earlier today. I, uh, seem to have lost what you sent earlier." He gave a sheepish grin and tried to look innocent, but his eyes were guilty as hell.

Henry walked over to his workstation and nudged Larry out of the way. "Excuse me then," he said flatly. "I'll re-send it to you."

"Heh...okay Henry...thanks a lot!" And with that, Larry turned and headed out the door. After sending the data to Larry, Henry spent the next two hours trying to see if anything was different on his computer. He found nothing. Satisfied that maybe Larry didn't have a chance to do anything, he signed off and went back to his unit.

Sitting here now staring at his screen, he wondered why he didn't trust his instincts more back then. He always knew that Larry was one of Soren's guys. Someone that Soren relied on for information. But Henry could never prove that Larry was doing anything wrong. "I guess I just wasn't smart enough," he whispered to the dust motes in the tiny lab. "I'm here, and Larry is one of the 'chosen few.'"

He leaned back in his chair and stretched again. *This is fruitless,* he thought. *That damnable satellite and space station are nothing more than frozen junk out there.* He had been rolling a pencil between his fingers and out of anger, threw the pencil towards the wall, near Larry's old station. Exasperated, he got up to retrieve his pencil from the other side of the room.

The pencil had hit the wall, landed on the desk, rolled towards the back of the desk and then fell to the floor. Cursing, Henry got down on his knees to see if he could see where it went. He squinted at the darkness under the desk and thought he could barely see the pencil's eraser tip sticking out from behind the desk leg. He reached his arm under as far as he could go, but the desk was too big and he couldn't even get close to the pencil.

Cursing again, he was about to leave it there, when he caught site of a small rectangular-shaped piece of equipment plugged into the back of the computer. *"What the hell?"* he whispered to the darkness under the desk. All of the computers in the lab were the same, and Henry was curious why this one would have an additional connection in the back. He looked at the front of the computer, and there were three available ports there. *So why connect something back here, where it's hard to reach, when you have open ports in the front?*

He stood up and went to the side of the desk. It was a big desk and took him a minute to maneuver it enough to see what was plugged into the back of Larry's computer. From a small converter box connected to the back of Larry's computer, a black cable snaked its way along the back of the wall and ended at the main modem unit. He stared at the connection, trying to make an old memory click in his mind. He was about to turn away when he saw additional connections coming from the modem. He followed those connections and saw that they were connected to the main server farm for the space station satellite.

When it hit him, he almost tripped over Larry's chair behind him. Looking at the elaborate (and confusing) connections, Henry could see that Larry's computer was functioning as a server with a direct connection to the space station satellite. For the next hour, Henry checked all the connections for each of the other computers in the room. Every computer in the room was connected to a dummy server that was mirrored on Larry's computer. With this setup, Larry could feed them any information he wanted at any time. He could also block information from the other computers, as well as from the space station and the *Pegasus1*.

He sat down at Larry's console and booted it up, hoping he wouldn't have to override Larry's passwords. As luck would have it, the system only asked for the generic lab password. Apparently, Larry was so pre-occupied with leaving, he didn't think to password lock his computer. *Good enough for me,* Henry thought.

As Larry's computer was booting up, it dawned on Henry that it was quite possible that he never saw any data or images that hadn't been scrubbed by Larry. It was data that Larry *wanted* him to see. He would sit there day after day, month after month trying to capture data on Earth and on *Europa*; only to come away with relatively the same information. Henry became more and more agitated as he sat at the desk waiting for the computer to finish its boot-up sequence.

"That son of a bitch!" he said to the screen. "All this time! All this time looking for data that would never come!" He sat there smoldering

while the computer went through its routine of coming online. He checked the servers to make sure they were on and accurately connected. Finally, the menu screen popped up and Henry hastily maneuvered through the choices that would get him to the satellite downloads. He clicked on the download icon that was positioned at the top of the menu and held his breath.

The computer went through the process of connecting to the satellites. After almost a full minute, the computer beeped loudly. Henry was so deep in thought that he actually jumped when he heard the beep. The icon showed a basket with letters in it, indicating that something had been retrieved from the space station. He double-clicked on it and waited yet again for the system to go through the motions. Whatever the computer was trying to access was a big file. He tried not to let himself get too excited, but he was powerless to stop his anticipation.

When the folder finally opened, Henry's mouth dropped wide open. Had he been standing up, he probably would have fallen to the floor. Rows upon rows of images stared him in the face. He could tell instantly what most of the images were, but there were some that looked blurry and indistinct. Hundreds of images of the moon and Earth had been beamed back from the space station. The *Pegasus1* folder was empty however. Henry quickly scanned the images and found what he was looking for; the UN compound and the surrounding terrain from here to there. He sighed deeply. They had a map now, but it would not be a cake walk. Henry wondered if they would have trouble getting volunteers. He took out a notepad and leaned forward to examine the terrain images.

Fifteen minutes later, Henry was deep into the images. Printing out select photographs and furiously scribbling on his notepad. He was so focused that at first, he didn't hear the steady beep coming from the satellite server. He lifted his head and looked back at the servers. *Why is that thing beeping?* he wondered, especially since he downloaded all of the files already. He got up, ready to turn on the mute button when he realized that this was not the server for downloaded images. This was the server that they used to talk to Earth, before *Lycos* hit.

He stepped up to the server monitor and quickly typed in several commands on the keyboard. The server started the process of calculating the origination of the signal. As Henry waited, a thought struck him. Could this be the *Cassiopeia's* signature? What other signal *could* it be? The space station was empty, so it wouldn't have come from there. Maybe they've had a change of heart and are coming back for us! As humane as that would have been, he didn't think it was very likely. Soren and his group were gone for good. When the coordinates finally did arrive, Henry could only stare at them. He hastily double-checked them and then sprinted to the meeting, almost tripping over his chair in the process.

2

What is taking Henry so long? Tess wondered. She didn't know whether it would be easy or not to collect images of the UN compound, but he had convinced her that he should be able to get *something* that would help them. Tess doubted it though, because Soren and his folks had taken everything of value and that included the few images that they had collected during the early months here.

She and Kyra had started the meeting 30 minutes earlier and Tess had been peppered with questions the entire time. Her answers were brutally honest; she left nothing out. She wanted everyone to know exactly what was going on with Earth and what was going to happen to them here on the moon.

"Are you sure about how close we're going to get to the sun?" someone from the back of the room yelled out.

Tess looked at Kyra, who nodded back at her. "Based on our current orbit from the data Kyra was able to capture over the past 18 months; we are 90 percent certain that we'll come within 25 million miles of the sun. Just to help you put this in perspective, Mercury is just under 30 million miles away from the sun at its closest point."

"How hot will it get?" someone else asked?

"Too hot for us!" someone shouted. There were a few laughs at this, but not many.

"We estimate that the temps could range from 800 to 1000 degrees Fahrenheit, but we don't know for sure." She paused for a minute before plunging on. "One thing that I'm confident about is that we won't survive even the first orbit at this distance and these temperatures."

There was low murmuring as Tess watched the crowd. She could see the fear in their faces, but she had to press on. "Even if we manage to survive this first orbit, there is still the issue of diminishing food and supplies. As things stand right now, our food supplies will be depleted in less than a month."

No one uttered a word. She looked around the room and what she saw made her want to bury her head in a pillow and cry. Everyone had the look of death on their faces. Some were hugging one another; some had their eyes closed as if in prayer, but they were all in shock. And barely concealed beneath their emotional filters was another, more dangerous emotion that Tess could detect; that was anger. In the way they shifted from foot to foot. In the way they looked at each other. Their general body language revealed to Tess that the line between organized, rational behavior and chaos and was very thin and brittle. At the first real sign of starvation and impending death, their world would resemble Earth in its last days.

Marla Wilson, an English and history professor with short, cropped blonde hair, stood up and in a shaky voice asked, "Why are we talking about making this trip to the UN site? I heard that we collected everything there was to collect during the last trip. If there is no more food, what good would it do to risk our lives to go there?"

Tess groaned inwardly. She had been expecting this type of question, and now that it was here, she wasn't sure how to answer it. The woman was right. This could turn out to be a dangerous and fruitless trip. She knew they would not find any more food at the UN site.

And then there was the issue of transportation to the site. When they first travelled there, they had two rover vehicles and were able to cover the 15-mile distance in about 2-3 hours. They loaded up what they had found and travelled back to their compound. That venture took about 12 hours. Now, it would take them half a day, maybe longer, and whatever they found, they would have to carry back.

"That's a good question, Marla," Tess said. "We feel that there may be food that we overlooked the first time. Also, if there's any rocket propellant remaining in the other shuttle, we might be able to siphon it off and use it here. There will certainly be some challenges getting it here, but it's worth a try."

"Why can't we use the *Orion* to fly to *Europa*?" Andy Stratham, a California businessman yelled out. "When you guys returned the last time, you mentioned that it was in good working order and could still fly. I say we pack that thing up and fly ourselves to *Europa*." At this, there was clapping and a chorus of agreement. People were looking at one another and nodding their heads.

Tess looked around the room, hating herself for being the bearer of bad news. "As you folks already know, the meteorites that hit the UN site destroyed all of the backup fuel storage tanks and the fuel. The *Orion* still has fuel, but if I remember correctly, it wasn't a significant amount—at least not enough to make the trip to *Europa*. If we tried to take the *Orion* to *Europa* with its current level of fuel, we would die in space, still months from the planet."

She looked around and could feel the anger building up in the room. "There's one other thing people. The *Orion* requires six engine power nodes to make the trip to *Europa*. Before the UN compound was destroyed, I remember seeing a report that one of the nodes was damaged. I don't know if they had a chance to replace it before the compound was hit by the meteorites."

This seemed to be a bit more than they could bear. For a moment, it seemed as if they had an answer. A way to somehow fix the terrible wrong that had been done to them. They had dared to hope that there was still a chance for them. When Tess pointed out that this door might be closed to them as well, their optimism soured immediately and turned to frustration and anger. They were all talking at once, their voices rising in volume and intensity. Tess looked at Kyra. Her wide eyes reflected everything that Tess was feeling. She thought to herself that this was a room full of gas and soon, someone will strike a match that will start their downward spiral into chaos.

"Move! Let me through!" came a voice at the back of the room.

Tess looked out and could see Henry trying to force his way through the group of people. He was carrying several large envelopes as he squeezed through the increasingly agitated crowd. Everyone was now on their feet shouting.

Andy cried out, *"This is bullshit!* You guys don't know what the hell is going on. Come on Joe! Let's get the hell out of here. I knew we should have gone to the commissary to stock up. I'm sure by now, most of the food and supplies are gone." He didn't intentionally yell this out to the crowd, but his voice carried clearly over the din.

"That's a damn good idea Andy!" a burly man yelled out. Tess recognized him as one of Soren's ex-guards. "I saw some folks over there earlier today. If we're going to beat this thing, we need to get prepared!" A few other folks heard this and nodded their heads vigorously in agreement. Tess looked out at the crowd and could see that it was slowly degenerating into a very dangerous situation.

"Look people!" Tess shouted above the noise. "We have got to remain calm and be rational about this. We absolutely *must* ration our food fairly. If we start hording the remaining food and supplies, then a

lot of people will die very soon. Children too, for God's sake! We can't lose our humanity—not now. We must maintain our dignity, even in the face of certain death."

Again, Andy was the first to shout out, "Look Tess, there's a big difference here between being a gentleman and starving to death. This is Darwinism in its purest form. Some people are just not going to make it."

"*Look, you pompous ass!*" Tess spat out. "How in the hell did you get selected to be here? We can't travel to *Europa* and the earth is moving closer to the sun every day, pulling us along with it. When the heat starts frying everything and every*one*, none of us are going to make it, don't you understand that? We have nowhere to go."

Andy stood staring at Tess with his arms crossed. He was livid, mostly because she called him an ass and embarrassed him. He opened his mouth to speak just as Henry was making his way to the podium where Tess and Kyra stood. Henry was out of breath by the time he reached them. It was obvious to Tess that whatever he wanted to say was important. She handed him the mike and before he fully had it situated on his head, he blurted out, *"I'm picking up signals from Earth!"*

INTO THE VOID

1

As Henry stepped up on the podium, he handed Tess a printout of the coordinates where the signal originated from. She stared at it fascinated. How long had it been since they last received a signal from Earth? A year, maybe more? She couldn't remember. For two to three months after *Lycos* hit, they had received sporadic signals from Earth and for a time, brief voice contact. But the signals dropped off, week after week, until there was nothing but silence at the other end. She figured that there were a number of survivors on the planet, but those would mostly be the ones who were able to hide out in the underground bunkers.

From one of the observation posts, she had observed seemingly never-ending electrical storms and incredibly drastic changes on several landmasses. This was no doubt caused by the increasing number of powerful and destructive earthquakes. She felt that eventually, those earthquakes would destroy most of the man-made structures on the planet. The ash cloud that completely enveloped the planet days after *Lycos* hit, was now starting to breakup, replaced by a thin veil of gray-colored clouds. It made her shudder to think about the conditions that the survivors were dealing with on the planet.

She glanced again at the coordinates and the bird's-eye view of its physical location. Henry had written in the margin "South Texas". A memory pang as sharp as a knife went through her. The home that she shared with her husband and her son was somewhere here, undoubtedly destroyed by fire or earthquakes or both. Henry had circled a wide area, so she wasn't really sure where his signal was coming from, but a distant memory tugged at her from thousands of miles away. She looked away from the printout and then back again, hoping that something would shake loose in her memory. Something was there, but it was just past her reach, not quite formed in her mind yet.

The folks in the audience, not sure what they just heard, only looked at Henry. The others, who heard him clearly, stood there in silent confusion. None of them could quite come to terms with this discovery or whether it was significant or not.

Andy was the first to find his voice, "*So?* What the fuck good is a signal from Earth to us now? It's not going to help with this bullshit crap that Tess just filled our heads with. And hell, most of us barely got off the planet in the first place. Look, this changes nothing for me," he waved his arms around the room, "For *us*. We can't help those poor saps any more than they can help us." Several people had physically positioned themselves near him, as if to show their solidarity. To them, he said, "Come on you guys, let's go get that food."

Henry started arguing with Andy, but Tess barely heard them. Her mind was combing through months of meetings, lunches, images, dinners. There was something here, but she couldn't grasp it. The harder she tried, the more it seemed to slip through her consciousness and sit just outside her wall of recollection. Boredom, irritation, Stan, sunlight, boxes, Lenny, and other images and feelings seem to weave in and out of her stream of consciousness like smoke through a filter. Whenever she tried to force a connection, the feeling of understanding would cave in, and she would be left with nothing. She would then look away briefly and then look at the coordinates and physical location again and wait for the feeling to build back up.

Henry grabbed the mike out of the holder and yelled into it. *"You can't do this!* Andy, come on man, we've got to do this *together*! If you start stealing food, then you'll be no better than Soren when he left us!"

Andy and his group had been moving toward the door, but stopped suddenly and turned to face Henry. "Unless Earth is sending a ship here to take us to *Europa*, I don't give a shit about any signals. Anyone trying to stop us will be hurt badly. Take my word for it."

Tess had closed her eyes. Something Andy had said, 'Earth... ship... Europa' seemed to resonate in her mind. Those words were like glue for the other images floating in and out of her psyche. Standing there at the podium with her eyes closed, she didn't try to force any connections. She shut out the noise and the yelling and the threats. She had a sense that someone had started fighting, but she didn't allow herself to be dragged out of her semi-conscious state. Her mind drifted high above the clouds. These were white, billowy clouds, not the dirty gray nuclear-winter clouds slowly circling the earth now. She drifted through the clouds and could see far below her a large expanse of green trees and winding rivers.

She blinked in her mind, and she could hear voices. Not the angry voices of Andy and his potentially violent crew, but the voices of children and families. She opened her mind's eye and saw Stan running behind the bike that Lenny was just learning to ride. They had just taken the training wheels off and Stan was probably just as excited as Lenny was. But Tess had been a little upset that day. She and Stan had had a small disagreement. *"Stan, you have to make sure that he wears his helmet all the time; especially now with the training wheels off."*

"Yeah," Stan had replied. "I know, but we couldn't find his helmet, and he didn't want to be late. He wanted very badly to show you what he had learned. You know, you don't have that much time for your lunch break."

"I know," she replied tenderly, "I just don't want him to get hurt, that's all."

"We'll have it on for sure the next time hon; whenever that is!" he added mockingly.

A little guiltily, she replied, "My schedule for this rotation is pretty crappy, I must admit. I'm really sorry. I'll try to change it so that we can come out here more often. I wish we had a park like this near the house."

Stan looked around, "Yeah, I know. This is probably one of the better parks in the city. It's great for the families who live on base, but for those of us on the waiting list, we have to commute for our fun." He laughed a little too heartily at his own joke.

Tess smirked at him as he continued on, "Lenny and I have seen a lot of this park, and it's great once you get deeper into the interior. There are lots of bike trails and walking trails that go on for miles. There's even a man-made pond specifically for swimming. This little stretch here is probably the worst part of it though. I would give the park a ten out of ten, if it weren't for that!" he jerked his thumb over at the military facilities across the street from the park.

In her mind, Tess looked over at the tall barbed wire fence with the two tough looking Air Force MP's standing guard next to a small booth. Her eyes floated up to a sign above the reinforced gates with the wheels on the bottom. She re-read the sign that she'd seen hundreds of times when driving through these gates to head out to the shuttle field. 'Wright Airfield Air Force Fuel Depot and Underground Storage. Absolutely No Smoking Beyond This Point.'

She zoomed back to the present and bolted upright from her half slouch at the podium, as if she had been given a shot of adrenaline. *"OH MY GOD!"* she half screamed to no one in particular. Kyra started and almost stumbled from the podium. Tess still had her mouth piece plugged in and so the entire hall heard her when she yelled out. It was probably something about the look in her eyes, but everyone stopped talking and stared at her.

Despite the fierceness in her face, her voice this time came out very quietly, "I know what we need to do."

Many of them stopped talking to listen to what she had to say. Andy looked at her and then burst out laughing. He slapped Joe on the back and said, "Let's get the hell out of here."

Ignoring Andy, Tess remembered an aerial view of the shuttle launch site and several miles east, the large, almost rectangular shaped landmass of the fuel depot dome. She repeated a little louder, "I know what we need to do." This time, her mind went back to a meeting some two to three years before the public even knew about the meteor; when they discussed establishing an outpost on the moon as a base of operations for deeper space missions. There was an expectation that there would be an increased number of shuttle trips to the moon to transport building materials, supplies, and fuel.

She remembered the discussion that if they instituted a regular shuttle program to the moon, it would require the need for tons of fuel. And in an effort to cut down on transportation costs, it would be ideal to house the rocket propellant here, at Wright Airfield. With the increase in terroristic activities, it was an easy decision to develop an underground fuel depot at the airfield.

Andy and his crew had gotten everyone riled up again, and soon everyone was shouting and arguing once again. Tess walked away from the podium and in a loud and clear voice, yelled *"I know what we need to do! If you want to live, you all will shut the fuck up and listen to me!"*

At this, everyone turned to her, not uttering a sound. Even Andy turned toward her, arms crossed, waiting to hear what she had to say. It was probably the level of intensity and seriousness in her voice that shut them up, or maybe it was because she was offering them a sliver of hope in their increasingly dire situation. Whatever it was, they were totally focused on what she was about to say.

Tess lifted her arm and pointed, unerringly to Earth and said, almost reverently, "We need to return to Earth."

2

They had to reconvene the next morning to give Henry time to capture some additional images of earth and set up a workstation in the conference room. The only way Tess was going to sell the idea of them traveling back to Earth was to show them, all of them, exactly how it would be done. Deep inside, she knew that this was their only option. Maybe they knew it too, but the thought of going *back* to Earth after they struggled to leave it was too much for most of them to understand, let alone embrace.

She was confident it could be done, and there would be plenty of risks; but if it gave them a fighting chance at life, she would be willing to take that chance. There were some who felt differently and leading this voice of dissension was Andy Stratham.

"How do we know the *Orion* will even fly after all this time?" Andy levelled at Tess. He and his group were sitting towards the front of the hall, as if using their physical closeness as intimidation. Tess and Henry sat at the front of the room where Henry was trying to connect remotely to his computer (formerly Larry's old computer) in the lab. Tess had been looking over his shoulder. She was trying to ignore Andy's angry tone and derisive comments when Henry blurted out, "Alright! I'm connected!"

Tess patted him on the shoulder and looked out at the group, ignoring Andy's question... Everyone was there; 17 men and 24 women in the audience. There were 44 in all counting Henry, Kyra, and herself. They had lost 11 people since Soren's shuttle departed (two children to illness). Considering this new option, she was fairly certain that everyone would be here.

She adjusted her mike and began to address the group, "You all know me, and you know that I'm no good at lying, and I'm no good at sugar-coating things, so I'm going to let you know exactly what we're in for." A few heads nodded, and there was a low murmur of agreement in the audience. Andy crossed his arms and glanced around disgustedly.

"As I mentioned yesterday, Soren really messed us up. He leaves us and then makes the suggestion that we kill ourselves to avoid the agony of dying a slow death out here. Well, I say bollocks to that! I think we have a chance at life too, but our path will be a hell of a lot more dangerous than their path.

"The signal that Henry identified came from this location." She turned towards Henry and nodded. He clicked on the image and almost as if on cue, the entire audience reacted as if they were slapped in the face. They stared at what used to be San Antonio, Texas and tried to make sense of what they were seeing. This was the first time any of them had seen pictures of the earth after *Lycos*.

"I'm not sure if you guys knew this, but Soren ordered all satellite images to come to him first, so that he could review them before making them available to the rest of us, but he never sent them out or made them available for all to see. On numerous occasions, I heard him say that the colony needed to heal further before he would feel comfortable showing these images. Eventually, no one asked about the images of Earth anymore, including me."

Henry clicked through several more images. Most were of the Houston, San Antonio, and Austin areas. San Antonio North was where NASA Mission Control and Wright Airfield were located. Tess recalled how during those last days, people from all over the country had made their way to San Antonio North.

The first trip that she took in the *Galileo1* departed from the smallest of the shuttle sites just north of Tucson, Arizona (this trip transported most of the US government and UN folks). Despite the secrecy, the location still slipped out, but only a few thousand people were able to make their way to the site by the time the shuttle took off. The story was quite different at the Texas airfield. Wright Airfield was situated in the hill country just north of San Antonio, Texas. For several years, the airfield and the country's first underground maximum-security prison, Harlan Penitentiary, were the only major structures in the area. With the discovery of several major gas fields west of San Antonio, the city almost doubled in size in less than five years. By 2041, just ten years before *Lycos* hit, the city had grown close to 2.6 million people. Corporate and residential buildings pushed farther and farther north and west until only a few miles separated the airfield from the sprawling San Antonio North downtown district. Wright Airfield was selected as the final departure location for the

Galileo1 and *Galileo2* shuttles, but this information was leaked months before their departure dates. By the time Mission Control became aware of this, it was too late to change the departure site. Too many people were already aware and too many were actually tracking the shuttles, spreading their locations on social media like a virus.

This brought the city to a standstill, not that much work was happening during those times anyway, but it made vehicular transportation practically impossible. Tess felt a pang of guilt and loss sweep over her as she thought about her husband and son trying to drive through the throngs of people clogging the entrances to the shuttle field.

The pictures that Henry clicked through were nightmarish. What was once a sprawling city, whose stature almost rivalled Houston's, was now a broken and scattered landscape of twisted metal, blackened concrete chunks, and innumerable pieces of human livelihood. Vegetation was non-existent, but broken and rotted trees dotted the landscape like diseased tumors.

To Tess, this Texas city and God knew how many other cities, had been obliterated and wiped clean from the face of the earth. She felt she was looking at an alien planet and not a city where she once had a beautiful home. Everywhere, she could see huge caverns and uneven ground; the result of powerful global earthquakes. The satellite image was good, but not perfect. There was still a thin blanket of ash and cloud cover that obscured a great deal. The ash probably would not last long, but Tess had a feeling that the cloud cover would be a little more permanent.

She gave Henry a nod and a new image filled the screen. Using a laser pointer, she pointed to an area surrounded by rubble. From the amount of debris in the area, it was clear that this had been a fairly large building. To the right of the building were the unmistakable, evenly-spaced lines of a parking lot or parking garage. "This is the location of the signal that Henry picked up yesterday. Located about 150 feet underground is one of the three Texas shelters that the government put in place prior to *Lycos* hitting."

She motioned for Henry to move to the next picture. "As you can see, there aren't many buildings here, and the ones that *were* here had only two levels. This rectangular area here is Wright Airfield where the shuttles departed. Other than minor damage, the airfield looks intact and uncompromised". She looked around the room as if for effect. "I'm proposing that we fly to Earth, land at the airfield and refuel at the underground fuel depot."

At that, everyone started talking at once. Tess raised her hands, "Hey guys, come on, one at a time."

A woman from near the back spoke up. Tess thought her name was Rodella. Rodella Martin. She was a botanist from Florida. Tess remembered that Soren had complained about her once and realized that was probably why she hadn't been asked to join his group. "I was on your shuttle Tess, and I remember the chaos there and how bad it got right before takeoff. What if there are still a lot of people there? We might have trouble trying to get out of there, let alone refuel." There was a murmur of agreement as the woman sat down.

"That's an excellent point, Rodella."

Rodella called out, "I hate that name. Call me 'Della'." Several people laughed at that.

Tess continued, "Sorry, Della. As I was saying, that's an excellent point. It does us no good to land there if we can't take off again. But it's a chance we'll have to take. We can't stay here on the moon, and we don't have enough fuel to make it to *Europa*. We'll have to land at Wright Airfield, re-fuel as quickly as possible, and then take off. The entire refueling operation should take about three hours, but that starts once we have gained access to the depot and started the fuel pumps. We can only do this from *inside* the depot."

Andy spoke up and said bitterly, "It sounds like we might need to be able to defend ourselves and the ship. There are no weapons here, so what the hell are we supposed to use for weapons...harsh language?"

"There were two armories on the base, but I've never been to either of them. If we can find them, and if they still have weapons, then we'll be okay. Otherwise, our main focus will be to get refueled and off the ground as quickly as possible."

She hesitated a moment and took a deep breath, "As much as I would like to avoid any possible contact with survivors on the ground, we may have to go to the underground shelter." She could see the audience visibly stiffen when she said this, and she raised her hand to hold off their questions. "The *reason* we will need to go to the shelter is because we don't have enough food here to last the trip from Earth to *Europa*. We have plenty of water, but the food we have here will last one, maybe two months. It will take us at least 4 months to get to *Europa*, provided there are no setbacks."

Someone in back yelled out, "How do you know these guys in the shelter will even have food left? And come to think about it, how do we know they'll even share with us?"

"Well," Tess replied, "I know for a fact that this shelter was equipped to last for 4 years. The government estimated that the nuclear winter would only last 2 to 3 years. They get an 'F' for only building three in Texas and an 'A' for providing them with more than enough food. As far as them sharing with us, well, we'll just have to make them an offer they can't refuse. We'll bring them with us."

3

Tess sat in one of the large chairs next to the west wing airlock entrance. It didn't take her long to get suited up, and now she was alone with her thoughts, waiting for the others. Last night, she had expected significant resistance to the offer of taking the shelter survivors with them, but the group seemed to accept the decision as a necessary evil. She had no idea what to expect once they returned to Earth, so when the time came, they would have to determine how they would handle things at the shelter. Everything now was simply a wish list. It was quite possible that they could get to Earth and find that the depot was damaged and that the fuel storage areas were severely compromised, making the entire area a fuel-soaked sponge waiting to be spark-ignited by the landing ship.

For now, the shelter and the fuel depot were important, but distant objectives. Before they could start planning their Earth mission in earnest, they had a number of barriers to cross here first. They had to first make the trip to the United Nations' compound to examine the *Orion* to make sure it was fit for flying. Tess was fairly certain that there was enough fuel to leave the moon and make it to Earth, but that would be it. If the fuel depot at Wright Airfield was inaccessible, or if the fuel storage tanks were damaged, then they would be stranded on Earth to suffer the same fate as the others.

She glanced at her watch. *The others should be here soon,* she thought. After the long meeting earlier in the day, she would have enjoyed a good night's sleep, but their two weeks of night was coming to an end, and two weeks of sunlight was just a day away. So, the volunteers only had a couple of hours of grace time to get their suits and meet at the airlock.

She checked over her equipment once more, and by the time she had finished, Henry was coming towards her in his thermal jumpsuit, carrying his helmet. He waved to her and tried to smile, but it looked more like a scowl than anything. With his free hand, he kept adjusting the suit at the waist and in the crotch. "I must have put on a little weight since I've been here," he said to Tess, trying to sound casual. "This thing just doesn't fit like it used to."

Tess chuckled, "I think we all have Henry. I guess that's life in zero G, even with the artificial gravity turned all the way up!"

He grunted noncommittally and then adjusted himself again, silently cursing. Down the hall, Andy Stratham, Joe Ackerman, and

Marla Wilson, were headed in their direction. In a much too loud, much too jovial voice, Andy yelled out, *"Hey guys...are we gonna do this or what?"* His two compatriots looked too stricken to do anything but grunt and nod their heads. Joe looked sick and ready to pop at any minute.

When they arrived, Tess and Henry stood up and checked each person's helmet and suit carefully. Tess said, "You guys may not remember from orientation, but the EnviroTemp suits you're wearing are designed to maintain optimum body temperatures regardless of the outside temps. When the sun is on the surface, the temperatures could range as high as 300 degrees Fahrenheit. Once the sun is gone, the temperatures can plummet to as low as minus 300 degrees. The ET suits are rated for extreme high and extreme low temperatures, but unfortunately, the temperatures have started rising. Even now, during these two weeks of night, the temps outside are barely minus 100 degrees Fahrenheit. At this rate, it could be upwards of 500 degrees Fahrenheit when the sun hits us. These suits have not been tested at those temps, so I don't know what will happen if we're caught in the open during the day."

They all nodded their understanding. She pointed to the colored tubes in her helmet and their corresponding tubes coming through the suit from the backpack unit. "Your water and food receptacles have already been filled and you should have enough water and food to last at least three days. Granted, the food is tasteless, but the only concern here is getting nourishment in your body if needed."

She went through her mental checklist. "Let's see, we went over waste disposal and the oxygen tank. Oh, yes, the gravity settings. Essentially, the gravity settings within the boots work on the same technology as the gravity floors within the compound, except for the settings. You have three settings on your boots. If you put it on the first setting, 'GRAV-1', you'll be bouncing all over the place. Conversely, the 'GRAV-3' setting will make it very difficult for you to walk."

Andy interrupted her, "Why would anyone put the setting on three if you can barely move? It seems kind of stupid to even have that as an option."

"Since we've been here," Tess responded, "we've been lucky in that we haven't encountered any solar storms, but there have been reports of isolated solar storms closer to the mountains. If anyone gets caught out in one of these storms, it would be wise to make yourself as heavy as possible to avoid being blown across the surface. If the storm is really strong, you could be ejected too far from the surface and ultimately lose whatever gravitational hold you have on the moon."

Andy could only mutter a stunned, "I see".

"So," Tess continued, "we should all start out on the 'GRAV-2' setting and adjust as we travel. You saw from the map that it's pretty much a straight shot from here until we reach the foot of the Caucasus Mountain Range. There are a number of breaks in the mountain range that we'll have to go through." She pointed to the detailed survey map attached to the wall.

"If Soren hadn't taken the Rovers, we could have skirted around to the south of the range, but since we are very short on time, we'll have to go straight through." She paused for a minute and then added, "Unfortunately, this will force us to have to go through one of the craters that border this range. It's not very deep, but we just won't have time to detour around it."

Andy looked at the others, shaking his head, "How deep is 'not very deep' Tess?"

"The survey team estimated this crater to be close to 2600 feet at its deepest point."

"Hell Tess, that's almost half a mile!" Andy blurted out. "Do we have the gear for that?"

Tess pointed to Kyra rolling a large white container on wheels. "We have all we need right there. Henry and I will get everyone hooked up once we get to the crater. For now, everyone grab a climbing kit and let's get suited up."

4

Kyra checked each person from top to bottom, back to front, giving each one a thumbs-up when she finished. Tess looked at the four suited figures. She could clearly see each of their faces through the clear face plate of the helmet. "Radio check," she said into her mike. Henry, Joe, and Marla responded with a "check". She looked at Andy and tapped her own helmet and then pointed to him. A second later, he responded with a "check".

They stepped into the airlock and waited for Kyra to secure the hatch. Inside, the overhead airlock panel changed from red to green, indicating that they could now open the hatch leading out to the barren surface of the moon. Once all five were out, Henry turned to latch the door. He saw Kyra through the small port windows in the airlock and waved to her. She waved back and after a couple of seconds, blew a kiss to him. He pretended to catch it, and then proceeded to latch the outer airlock door. He turned towards the others, silhouetted by the far-off mountain range and a black, starless background.

5

Tess looked down at her direction finder and started out. This was only her second trip to the UN compound; the first had been by Rover. During that first trip, it had only taken them close to three hours to travel the 15 miles to the compound and that included a couple of stops. On foot, she estimated that it might take them anywhere from 10 to 12 hours, which should put them at the compound in plenty of time before the start of Lunar Day.

She was checking her reading again when Henry's voice crackled in her ear. "Tess, you might need to slow down a bit. Some of us are having a bit of trouble, er…walking."

Tess turned around and saw Andy and Joe stumbling around behind her. It was a comical sight, but she didn't feel much like laughing. They were on a tight schedule and didn't have time to waste. She saw Andy take two awkward steps and then trip over his own feet. Joe, barely able to walk himself, tried to stop Andy's fall and ended up falling himself. Marla deftly skirted around them to catch up with Tess. She sighed and glanced at her watch again. She knew immediately what the problem was. "Hey guys, did you set your boots to the GRAV-2 settings?"

Joe had gotten up first and started knocking the dust from his suit. He looked down at his boots and could see the small display reading on the instep: "GRAV-1". He looked over at Henry with an "oops" gesture and reached down to change the settings on both of his boots. Immediately, his stance became more solid and he gave a thumbs-up to Tess. Andy had gotten to his feet by then and began making the same adjustment to his boots. "Okay Tess, I think I'm ready to go now," he said a little sheepishly.

6

"How are they doing," Julie asked from the doorway of the radio control room. Kyra, who had been reading a book with her back to the door, swiveled around in her chair.

"Hey there Julie," she replied. "Their progress has been slow. I think they underestimated how difficult it would be to walk that distance in those ET suits. Joe and Andy had some walking problems earlier, but it looks like they're walking okay now. They're just not making time as quickly as they should." She reached over and pressed a key on her keyboard. Five small green dots glowed brightly on the monitor.

Julie came in and looked over Kyra's shoulder at the screen. The dots were all moving in a straight line and seemed to be traveling between two large objects. "Where are they?" Julie asked.

"They've entered one of the breaks in the Caucasus Mountain Range that leads to a crater just on the other side. It's one of the smaller craters in this part of the mountain range, and they should have made it there at least two hours ago. They don't have much time before Lunar Day hits."

Julie was still looking at the screen and saw that the green dots were now clustered together. "What's going on now?" she asked.

"It looks like they're about to descend into the crater. We'll lose contact with them once they start to descend and we won't hear back until they make it out."

"How long do you think they'll be in there?" Julie asked nervously. She stared at the glowing dots clustered at the edge of a dark irregular oval on the screen.

"I don't know Julie, but if they're not out of it in the next four hours, I think they'll be in serious trouble."

7

Tess checked the time again. They were cutting it way too close. Joe was just not keeping up. She almost sent him back, but the fearful look in his face told her that he would never make it back alive. No, they had to keep moving forward, all of them. Their slow pace now put them in very real danger of being out here during Lunar Day. She had built in some time for rest breaks, but Joe's inability to maintain the pace, slowly ate into her safety margin.

She faced the small group and pointed to the other side of the crater. "If you look across, you'll be able to see the top of some of the UN structures. Guys, we're almost there, but we have to deal with this crater first."

Joe inched forward to the crater's edge and peered cautiously into the darkness. The crater's bottom was cloaked in darkness; even the light from Joe's helmet was swallowed up by it. For Joe, the darkness conjured up images of movie-magic space ghouls; the ones that drain your spiritual energy, while sucking your body through a small crack in your face plate. Feeling resigned, he said, "Why don't we just go around Tess? It seems like it might be faster than going down into, into *that*."

Tess was about to respond, but Andy cut her off. "Are you scared, you little shit?" he said mockingly. "You couldn't wait to get out here, now you're afraid of the dark. Gimme a break!"

"Alright, that's enough!" said Tess. "Look Joe, first there's nothing down there. The moon has no indigenous life forms. If there were any non-indigenous life here, we would have found out ages ago. Also, as I pointed out when we left, we can't go around." She pointed to her left and right. "These mountain ranges extend much too far to either side of the crater, and we don't have the time to skirt around this range to the flat lands. It's just not practical Joe."

Joe nodded, but didn't look pleased about it. He was now wishing he had stayed back at the compound.

Tess faced the group and said, "Based on our survey information, the bottom of the crater in this area is about 200 feet deep. We should be able to rappel to the bottom fairly easily. It's coming up that will be a challenge. We'll be climbing out at the deeper end of the crater, and it's close to a 400-foot climb. Also, it's going to be cold down there. This mountain range tends to block much of the sun here, so this crater never gets much sunlight during Lunar Day."

While Tess checked each person's climbing harness, Henry worked on anchoring their ropes to a solid outcropping of rock about five feet from the edge of the crater. He worked quickly, pulling up the rope slack behind him. After double checking his work, he walked to the edge of the crater and fed the ropes over. One by one, he attached the ropes to each person's climbing harness.

Tess harnessed herself in and then faced the others. "Henry will go first, then Marla, Andy, and then Joe. I'll bring up the rear. Okay...let's go."

Henry sat at the edge of the crater and connected the rope to his own harness. He swung himself over and started lowering himself into the crater slowly, using the controlled descent device attached to the main rope. Tess peered over the edge until he reached what she estimated to be 20 feet and then turned to Marla, "Okay Marla, you're next."

She connected the descent device to Marla's rope and tapped her on the shoulder. Marla inched her body to the edge. "Well, here goes nothing!" Once she was fully over the edge, she started to winch herself downward into the darkness.

"Alright, my turn," Andy blurted out after ten minutes. He moved toward the edge of the crater.

"Hang on Andy," said Tess, "she's needs to go at least 20 feet. Give her a few more minutes." Andy stopped in his tracks and looked back at Joe, but Joe was staring intently at the space where Marla was just a moment before. He had the look of total concentration, but Andy could tell that he was scared to death.

"Alright Andy, let's go," said Tess, before Andy could say anything to Joe. He moved quickly to the edge and sat down. Tess hooked him up, and he slowly moved himself into position below the edge of the lip of the cavern.

8

Tess watched the slowly descending helmet lights make their way down the inside of the cavern wall. Henry communicated that he was already down and would be helping Marla get unhooked in a few minutes. She estimated that Andy still had another 30 feet to go. Joe was trying hard, but his progress was painstakingly slow. He had only moved about ten feet. She sat down at the edge and hooked herself up. *Oh God, this is taking too long!* she thought and looked at her watch again.

The cavern was only about a half mile wide and would take them about 20 minutes to traverse, but ascending the wall on the far end would take them two hours, at least. It was easily twice the height of the wall they were going down. Luckily, the reduced pull of gravity would not tire them out as quickly, but they would still have to be diligent in finding solid handholds and good footing. Tess realized that it was a mistake for Joe to come. He was a good technician, but it wasn't necessary for him to come. Tess only agreed because she wanted to break up Andy's group to prevent them from causing trouble while she was gone.

"Alright Joe, I'm on my way down. Let's get a move on." He was breathing heavily into his microphone. "Okay, okay! I'm going as fast as I can! I can't feel anything in these damned gloves!"

"Just use the lowering mechanism Joe," Tess said. "Don't try to actually climb down; just press the button like I showed you, and it will lower you only three feet at a time." Their individual lowering mechanisms helped tremendously in descending into the crater, but Tess grimaced at the thought that they would not be much help to them when they had to climb out.

After what seemed like hours, Henry's voice crackled in her ears, "Tess, we're all down. You've got about 30 feet to go to the bottom." Upon hearing this, she quickly lowered herself to the bottom, no longer worried about kicking Joe in the head. When her feet touched the bottom, she quickly unhooked herself. "Alright," she said, "let's get moving. Going up won't be so easy."

"That was easy?" Joe muttered under his breath. *"Oh man!"*

Tess took the lead again and moved off towards the far side of the crater, glancing at her watch as she went.

TROUBLE AT HOME BASE

1

Kyra sat back and looked over at Julie. Once the group reached the bottom of the crater, their signals disappeared from her screen. She was surprised that they lasted that long. She had expected the signals to weaken or drop off as soon as they started climbing down, but they remained brightly lit until they were about five to ten feet from the bottom. "Now we have to wait until they reach the top on the other side. They can talk to each other, but we are completely cut-off from them. Once they've started their ascent, we'll be able to re-establish communications."

Julie glanced at her watch and then looked at Kyra doubtfully. "When do you think that will be? They're really cutting it close. Will they have enough time to make it to the other ship?"

"You see this here?" Kyra pointed to a rectangular shaped marker on her screen. "This is the UN compound. It's about 200 yards away from the lip of the crater. Once they get out of the crater, it will only take them about 20-30 minutes to get to the UN compound. If I remember correctly, the *Orion* should be right…here." She pointed to another marker glowing near the edge of the compound. "Once they're inside the shuttle, they'll be safe." She looked up at the clock and added, "They just need to climb fast and get the hell out of that crater." Julie sat heavily in the chair across from Kyra and glanced nervously at the monitor. Kyra noticed earlier that she was wringing her hands as they spoke. Sitting there in the chair, she gripped the edges as if she might fall off. "Julie, is everything okay? I really do enjoy your company, but I can't help but wonder why you are up so early."

Julie looked at her and then looked at the floor between her feet.

Without raising her head, she uttered, "I'm pregnant Kyra."

Kyra's eyes widened in surprise, and then she burst into a huge grin. "Congratulations Julie!" she said, as she got up to hug her.

Julie was somewhat taken aback. She had expected a hundred reasons why this was wrong and a thousand reasons why she should abort the baby, considering the challenges that lay ahead. But Kyra was not judgmental and seemed genuinely happy for her. She found herself smiling—she couldn't help it. "Kyra, I thought you were going to say how wrong and irresponsible I was for allowing this to happen. And I didn't do this on purpose either. I just started getting sick from the birth inhibitor shots, so I stopped taking them for about a week. I was intimate a day after starting the regimen again, but I guess I needed to wait longer for the drug to be effective. Now, here I am, pregnant and the father is on his way to *Europa*. Talk about a long-distance relationship." She tried to laugh at this, but the laugh came out dry and chalky.

Kyra took Julie's hands in hers. "Our survival is going to be severely tested in the next few weeks. None of us know for sure if we will be able to make it to Earth, get what we need, and then make it to *Europa*. There are just too many variables with high degrees of risk. Whether we make it or not, at least you'll have something, or some*one* that you can focus on when things get difficult. Besides, you'll have the honor of being the first mother on *Europa*."

They hugged each other again and sat back down. Julie absently put her hand on her stomach and began to rub it. Something flashed within her peripheral vision, and she looked up at the monitor again. "What's going on with the screen?"

As they stared at it, the brightly lit images and contours first dimmed, and then flickered. After a few minutes, it stopped flickering, but stayed dim. Kyra moved over to one of the other computers and typed in a few commands. After a few minutes, a screen reading *Base Power Supply* centered at the top came into view. She logged in and made her way to a power layout grid, showing the energy and power layout for the entire facility. "Crap, looks like we're losing power or something, but it's not just here. It's all over the compound." She picked up the phone, dialed a three-digit number and waited. After quite a number of rings, the view screen lit up and a sleepy-looking face filled the screen, "Bob here."

"Bob, this is Kyra. I'm at the OPS center, and we've just had a power short. After looking at the compound power grid, it looks like there are isolated pockets of power-loss all over the compound. Would you please check it out for me? It may be nothing, but I want to be on the safe side."

Bob St. Pier was a power generator engineer at the compound and probably one of the sharpest guys there on the moon. A native of Louisiana, he typically didn't bite his tongue, and a run-in with Soren over supply usage the year before probably cost him a seat on the shuttle to *Europa*. He had no illusions about why he was left behind, but was speechless when he found out that his "girlfriend" had left him without ever uttering a single word about the departure.

He looked at the view screen and could see someone behind Kyra but couldn't tell who it was. "Sure Kyra, no problem. I can be there in...," he looked away from the screen for a second, "in about ten minutes. I'll be on channel four."

"That's great Bob. Thanks a million!" Kyra clicked off Bob's screen and reached over and turned on the internal communications microphone. She set one of the ten receivers to channel four, checking the volume to make sure it was high enough. She turned back to Julie, who was smiling at her. "What?" She said to Julie. "What's funny?"

"Just something you said to Bobby. You said *'thanks a million'* and I thought, *a million what?* I never thought I'd see the day when a million *dollars* meant absolutely nothing to me. If I had it, I'd trade it all in to be able to run through a field of grass, feel cool air on my skin, and the warm sun shining on my face." Her expression grew somber, and she rubbed her stomach again. "Do you think we'll really make it to *Europa*, Kyra? It seems like so much can go wrong, and what happens if we *do* make it to *Europa*? Will Soren and his people welcome us with open arms? They left us here to die, and they took everything that wasn't bolted down."

Kyra had wondered about that too. If they survived the odds and actually made it to *Europa*, what *would* Soren do? It saddened her to think that the last survivors of the human race would start warring with each other at the dawn of a new civilization. She looked at Julie and shrugged her shoulders, "I don't know. If we get that far, it may be in our best interest to land on another continent, as far away from the others as possible." She sighed and turned her attention back to the screen and was dismayed to see that the screen had gone completely blank.

2

Bob St. Pier trudged through the darkened hallway leading to the power generation station. He was getting increasingly worried about the flickering lights in the hallway. As he got closer to the station, he could hear a low humming noise and an intermittent thumping. The humming noise was the result of the power being fed throughout the compound. The thumping noise was what didn't belong. He looked up at the lights and waited. As he suspected, each time the thumping noise came, the power seemed to fluctuate. He listened carefully. The thumps were very erratic, sometimes 10 to 15 seconds in between, sometimes 30 seconds. At one point, almost three minutes went by before he heard the thump again.

He made his way to the huge fuel cell power generator and climbed up the attached narrow ladder. He walked carefully along the top of the generator, shining his flashlight down through the grill that covered the generator's inner workings. He hoped that whatever the problem was would be a straightforward, easy fix, but as he got closer to where the thumping was, he could see that the primary generator assembly was gone entirely. In its place, was the secondary assembly unit, which was only designed to act as a short-term backup to the primary. Someone had crudely (*or hurriedly?*) connected the secondary unit to the power outflow cables that fed the entire compound. Looking closely, Bob could see the haphazard way the cables were connected to the secondary unit. Leftover screws and bolts lay on the floor like discarded toys. He was disgusted to see that they had even used duct tape to secure some of the cables.

He moved directly above the secondary unit and immediately saw what the thumping noise was. He couldn't be sure, but he was willing to bet that the secondary backup unit had been functioning as a primary unit for quite some time before Soren's group left. They probably pulled the primary a couple of weeks before departing and hoped that the secondary unit would function adequately until they left.

The backup units were not designed to function as primaries and working at 100% capacity, Bob could see that the wear and tear was finally causing it to burn out. Light tendrils of smoke drifted out of the unit like a dying breath. Of the five small fans in the housing of the unit, only two were still moving smoothly; two were completely dead, and one seemed to be seizing up every few seconds. Bob stared at the assembly unit and wondered why Soren would take the primary generator with them. It was only good for providing electrical power and...

His eyes grew wide at the thought, and he jumped up and quickly ran to the ladder. He tripped on the loose grating and went stumbling towards the edge of the generator. Somehow, he managed to keep his balance and stopped his forward momentum only inches from the edge. He looked over at the narrow space between the generator and the wall and swallowed hard. He would have surely broken something, if not his neck, had he tumbled into the tight space. He turned shakily to the ladder and shimmied down, careful not to trip up on the last step. As soon as he hit the floor, he ran to an area separated from the generator by a waist-high short wall and went into the air converter room. He'd only gone two steps into the room when he stopped cold.

"*Oh my God*", was all he could whisper, as the erratic thumping continued behind him.

3

Almost there, Tess thought thankfully. Henry and Marla had made it to the top. To her surprise, Joe was doing quite well. He was only about 20 feet or so from the top, but Andy continued pushing him to hurry up.

"Andy," Tess said, "you're only making things worse by rushing him. He's almost to the top, so quit the heckling." She had switched the order going up because Marla was a better climber than Andy and Joe, and she wanted Joe to follow Marla's every move.

Andy hissed back at Tess, "We don't have a lot of time left, and I don't want to be stuck on this crater wall when Lunar Day hits. If you want to be stuck out here when that happens, then be my guest! Otherwise, Joe needs to get his ass in gear!"

Tess sighed and looked at her watch. They were still good on time. Closer than she liked, but they could still get to the shuttle and get buttoned down before the sun came out. There were higher-rated ET suits on the *Orion* that were probably better suited for the hotter temperatures. Once they got inside, they could change, and the others could go back out and check for supplies while she checked out the ship.

While Joe negotiated a place to wedge his foot in, she glanced down into the cavern. The bright lights of her helmet illuminated the depths of the crater, but only barely. She had never been afraid of heights, but looking down into the darkness of the cavern made her heart flutter and gave her a sense of vertigo. She found it hard to believe that they had just climbed out of that blackness.

The initial part of the climb wasn't too difficult. There were rock outcroppings everywhere, making it easy to find handholds and footholds. Unfortunately, as they got higher, their intended path got smoother and smoother forcing Henry to move laterally for better climbing.

Their continued lateral movement put them over a widening chasm where part of the ground was split away from the far wall. To Tess, it looked as if it was torn from the wall. Possibly the result of some long-ago smaller meteor, Tess imagined.

She tried using the infrared setting in her helmet to determine how deep that part of the crater was, but the readings were distorted. She estimated that it was at least another 150 feet down. She felt her heart fluttering again, but this time it was different, more pervasive; it seemed to go on too long. A terrible second later, she began to feel vibrations in her hands and feet and knew immediately what was happening. Just as she opened her mouth to say something, Henry yelled *"Moonquake! Hang on!"* and then all hell broke loose.

4

Henry had just disconnected Marla from the rope, when the moonquake hit them. He could feel the low vibration of the ground seeming to radiate all around them. They had learned early during their initial months on the moon that moonquakes were different than their counterparts on Earth. On Earth, the quakes rarely lasted more than 2-4 minutes, even the big ones; on the moon, the quakes seem to gather energy from surrounding quakes, until the entire area, sometimes as large as several hundred square miles, would shake and vibrate for 15, 20, even 30 minutes.

Henry looked at the vibrating anchor staked in the ground and snatched up his hammer to beat it in even further. He then lay flat on his stomach and inched his way to the edge of the crater to see how much further the other three had to go. To his dismay, Joe was still 20 feet below the edge, clinging to the rope, his helmeted head shaking back and forth. *"Come on Joe! Keep climbing! This quake could go on for 15 or 20 minutes. You can't stay there!"*

Joe pressed his head in even further into the rock, hoping that he would not break his face mask. Even though the earpiece was right there in his ear, Henry's voice sounded far away. He thought he heard him say, keep climbing, but he could barely hold on to the rope, let alone continue climbing.

More voices assailed his ears. He was now being bombarded by the constant chatter of voices, as well as the vibrating crater walls. He realized, fearfully, that Henry was right. He had to keep climbing. If he stayed here, he would eventually get jostled loose from the wall. He looked up and could see Henry leaning over the side of the lip of the crater, holding out his hand. *He's not that far,* Joe thought. *Maybe I can do this.* He lifted a tentative leg and placed it on one of the foot mounts Henry had nailed into the wall. "That's it, Joe!" Henry yelled. "You're doing great! Just keep those legs and arms moving. Make sure you maintain good footing. Yes, that's it."

While Henry had been speaking to Joe, Tess jammed in another cam. She wasn't the big climber that Henry was, but she had gotten into the practice of always putting in two cams. With Joe climbing above her, she put in three cams each time they got to a particularly challenging area. Now, with the wall vibrating through her gloved hands, she was relieved that she had three in now.

She looked up at Joe and was pleased to see that Henry's prodding was working. He was making good progress. He was only about five feet from the top and Henry's outstretched hand. Throughout the climb up though, she repeatedly had to tell Andy to slow down and not get too close to Joe's feet, and here he was again, right on Joe's heels.

"*Andy, back off! You're getting too close to his feet!*" Tess yelled up at Andy through her helmet mike, but she got no reply from him. She saw Joe lift a tentative foot to place on the next higher foot mount when the wall shuddered long and hard. If she hadn't had a good grip at that moment, she might have slipped and fell. Andy, in his haste, had already grasped the foot mount with his hand and had been preparing to pull himself up, when Joe's heavy boot slammed back down on the mount and onto his hand, hard.

Andy screamed out in pain and viciously yanked his hand out from underneath Joe's boot, which caused Joe's foot to be pulled away from the mount. At the same time, the sudden jarring of the crater wall caused Joe to lose his grip on the wall. With only one hand gripping one of the above mounts, Joe frantically tried to find his footing again, with no luck. He lost his remaining grip and went tumbling along the side of the crater wall.

Tess could see what was about to happen and hooked her hands as deep as possible into the crevices of the crater wall. She saw Joe tumble past Andy, his hands grabbing at empty space. The rope that Henry had staked down followed him like a long tail. Andy stared dumbly at this until he was yanked off his foot mount by the rope connecting the two of them. Tess clung tightly, waiting for the gigantic yank that she knew was coming. It seemed to take forever for that yank to happen and she almost relaxed her grip. Her initial thought was that maybe they had grabbed onto to something within the crevices, but she ignored the powerful urge to relax and tightened her grip even more. All of a sudden, she felt a powerful tug on her hips where the rope was connected.

The pull on her rope was tremendous and seemed to get stronger with each passing second. She screamed and leaned into the wall as tightly as she could go. She was hooked into the wall, but she was certain that if the force of their fall didn't dissipate soon, she would be pulled unceremoniously away from the wall, and they would all tumble down into yawning chasm below.

Just when she thought her hands were going to give out, she felt a slight lessening of the pull on her rope. It was still heavy, but the force of the fall had expended itself, and now she only had dead weight below her. But it wasn't entirely dead weight. Joe was in total panic mode. He was now hanging over the chasm and fought desperately to get to the wall. He looked as if he were having a seizure.

"Joe!" Tess yelled into her mike. "Stop twisting and moving! There are no hand or foot mounts near you. Once you stop moving, I'll try to get you and Andy anchored. *Joe! Answer me!*"

Joe could hear someone talking to him, but he couldn't make sense of what they were saying. Somehow, he had gotten twisted up in his rope so that his body was pointed straight down into the dark hole. He looked to his right and could see the wall clearly, but it was at least ten feet away from him. This part of the wall was angled inward and he saw no other way to get to it than to start swinging himself. But first, he had to get that goddamn rope from around his leg. He tightened his body again and tried to reach the rope around his leg. He tried again and again, each time getting more frustrated. The yelling in his ears came again, but he ignored it. All he could think about was getting that rope from around his leg and getting himself upright again.

Andy hung over the precipice in frozen horror. Like Joe, he couldn't reach the wall either, but he was not as far away from it as Joe. He still couldn't reach it though. Hanging there in open space, he couldn't remember ever having felt so helpless and vulnerable. He had to sit there and rely on Tess to pull them up, but even at their reduced weight, there was no way she could pull the both of them up together. If they had all the time in the world, then maybe, but they didn't have all the time in the world now did they? Plus, the moonquake was still rumbling and sending out rolling shock waves through the crater walls. Eventually, either the constant vibration of the wall would jar loose Tess's cams or Joe's spastic gyrations would put too much weight on the cams and yank them out of the wall.

Andy closed his eyes as Joe yanked on the rope below him; each time he expected to drop like a moon rock to the bottom of this crevice. If he could get one of his cams out and swing over to the wall, then maybe he could get it hooked. His hand went to his thigh belt to pull out one of the cams when his fingers brushed the hilt of another item connected to his thigh. *What is this?* he thought, as he tried to decipher the object through his gloved fingers. Just then, he remembered that he had exchanged one of the standard tools from the belt around his leg with a large field knife. He didn't remember why he brought the knife, but at that moment, he was certainly happy to have it.

Tess looked down from her position and saw Andy slide the knife out of his thigh holster. She screamed down at him, *"Andy! What are you doing? Put that knife away! You don't need that right now!"*

Andy felt as if he was disconnected from his body. He saw his righthand shift around the knife for a better grip. Then he reached down and grabbed the tightly vibrating rope that connected him and Joe. Thousands of voices filled his head at that moment, but he heard none of them. The only sound he thought he could hear was the sound of the rope being cut. After that, it was only Joe's screaming that filled his head as he fell head-first into the chasm.

5

Bob sprinted through the halls like a madman, only slowing down when the lights cut off. He noticed that they were staying off longer and longer. He sped up again when the lights came on and almost ran into someone coming out of one of the side hallways. He had just enough time to dart around them, catching a glimpse of their wide, shocked eyes.

He could hear Kyra's voice in his ear urgently trying to find out what was going on. She was becoming more and more frantic, he could tell, but he had no time to stop and talk. At the all-out pace he was keeping, he could barely catch his breath, let alone hold a conversation.

At last, he rounded the corner that lead to the ops room. He was terribly out of breath, but knew that it didn't have anything to do with him being out of shape. Through the dimming lights, Kyra saw him burst in and spoke up before he had a chance to catch his breath.

"What the heck is going on down there, Bob? The lights and the power have been acting crazy!"

"The...primary generator...is gone Kyra," Bobby said through heaving lungfuls of air.

She looked at him for a second and then asked, "How long do you think it will take to fix it?"

He looked at her blankly and then replied, "No...it's *gone*, Kyra. Soren and his people removed the *entire* generator...took it with them! To avoid shutting down the system completely, they connected everything to the secondary generator. But that's not even the kicker. Have you noticed how much more difficult it is to breathe? They've also taken the *air converter*. We've been living on borrowed time Kyra."

6

Julie jumped up from where she was sitting. "How could they do this to us? They took everything! Extra food, extra supplies, and now this! The fucking air converter?"

"I guess we shouldn't be surprised at this," Kyra said. "Soren's a psychopath, and this is probably what he sees as a humane death for us." She turned to Bob who had caught his breath, but still seemed to be struggling to get enough air. "What does this mean in real terms Bobby? How much time do we have before we run out of power and then out of air?"

"Since the air converter is gone, then the air we're breathing is what's left in the ballast tanks around the compound. Since there is no new air to pump into the system, then it will start recycling the old air. All of the ballast tanks will be used equally, so I will only need to check the level for one tank. That will tell us how much air we have left. If the power goes out first, though, then it won't matter how much air is left, because there won't be any power to get it to us. Based on when Soren left, I would say that the tanks have anywhere from 24 to 48 hours remaining, maybe less."

Kyra looked at him for a moment, her brow crinkled in thought, "Okay, this is what I want you to do. Grab two folks who know how to check the tanks, and get me those readings immediately. Julie, wake up Jeff and Lisa and have them get to the pantry to collect as much food as they can. Grab someone else to help you get the remaining medical supplies. I'll contact the supply team and have them grab the remaining supplies. Make sure everyone gets suited up and each person should have his helmet. We won't know for sure when the power will go completely, so we'll need to be ready. Our suits will sustain us for at least 12 hours, but after that, things will get really ugly. Take everything to the loading dock, so that we can get it on board the ship when Tess gets here." She handed Julie one of the radios and said, "Good luck Julie!"

7

"What the hell is wrong with you?" Tess had yelled at Andy as he reached the top of the crater. She had walked off fuming once Henry helped her to the top. When she turned around, Henry was just pulling Andy up over the lip of the crater. After Henry unhooked him, she marched directly over to him and confronted him. "You had no right to cut that rope! No right! I had three cams in, and they would have held all of us. All we had to do was talk to him and calm him down." Andy only shrugged his shoulders.

Marla was sitting on a large rock looking down at the ground. Her shoulders were slumped, and she was shaking her head. Henry stood next to Tess staring at Andy. He had relieved Andy of his knife before he pulled him completely over the edge of the crater and now stood protectively next to Tess in case Andy got any more stupid ideas in his head. Andy was expendable; Tess was not.

They spent the next ten minutes peering over the edge of the cavern and tried every channel, hoping Joe would respond, but there was nothing but silence. Henry looked at his watch and saw that they had just under an hour to make it to the UN compound. If Joe had survived the fall, they probably would not have had enough time to help him. He cursed to himself and looked over at Andy, who stood off to the side, not looking at anyone. He had expected Andy to look more shocked when he hauled him up, but he hadn't shown any emotions. When Tess confronted him, he looked more bored and impatient than upset or angry.

With a heavy heart, Tess started making her way towards the UN compound which lay just on the other side of some low hills. The moonquake had subsided to low rumblings as they headed off. Marla got up and started after her. Andy was about to follow suit when Henry stopped directly in front of him. Not caring whether anyone else heard him, he confronted Andy in a low and menacing tone of voice, "You try any more shit like that again, and I will leave your ass here. That's a promise."

Andy's face twitched, but before he could utter a sound, Henry turned and followed after Tess and Marla as they headed towards looming antenna towers of the UN compound.

8

Kyra swung her flashlight across the room and found her chair. She walked over to it, dropped her duffel bag on the floor, and plopped down in the chair. There were a few neon lights in the room, so she wasn't in total darkness, but it wasn't enough light to work to. And the computer was still down.

After Julie left, she went to her own unit to get suited up and to grab a few things. She looked down at the duffel and sighed. Everything that she wanted or felt she needed, fit into the medium sized duffel bag. It saddened her to think that all she owned in the world could be slung over her shoulders and hauled around like an airplane carry-on. She made sure to pack the items Henry had given her. The *Away Team*, as they called themselves, copying the old *Star Trek* movies, had already packed their duffels and stored them in the hangar—Tess's idea of being prepared for the worse.

She turned her attention to Tess and the others. She was desperate to contact her. They needed to know that their time here at the compound was limited. She knew that Tess would not waste time at the UN compound, but their power and air supply would be at extremely low levels in less than a day.

The lights flickered again, stopped, and then flickered once more. This time they stayed on, and Kyra breathed a huge sigh of relief. She turned to the computer and punched the power button. It quickly cycled through its initialization and setup programs. Kyra tapped her fingers, while the hard drive hummed and clicked. Within seconds, the main screen materialized into view. Kyra quickly clicked on the server connected to the satellite and hoped that it was still broadcasting the locations of Tess and the others. She was desperate to see if they had made it out of the crater yet. She had felt the moonquakes here too, but they were no more than rumbles deep underground. She hoped it was the same for the others.

The locator screen popped up, and she was ecstatic to see that they had made it to the UN station. But something was wrong. Someone's locator had stopped working. She clicked on the mike to speak and saw that Tess was actually trying to contact her.

"...is Tess, do you read, over," Tess's voice came through the speaker. Kyra pressed the talk button. "I'm here Tess! Our power has been going in and out. It just came back on. How are you guys doing? I see you made it to the UN site. One of you broke your locator or something. I only show four of you."

There was a second of silence that Kyra thought was too long. She was about to speak again when Tess responded. "Kyra, Joe didn't make it. We were climbing out of the crater when the quake hit. He...he lost his grip and fell."

"Oh God, Tess!" Kyra exclaimed. "I'm so sorry. The rest of you are okay?" Her voice came out tentatively, fearfully. If something had happened to Henry...

"The rest of us are fine, K," Tess said. "A little shaken up, but we're good. We're in the ship now, and so far, everything looks good. There were several higher-rated ET suits here and Henry, Marla, and Andy are changing into them as we speak. It will take me a few hours to complete a run-cycle of the engines and batteries before we can leave. While I'm doing that, the rest of the team will look for supplies and whatever other items they consider useful."

"Tess," Kyra said very clearly, "Soren and his folks took the generator and the air converters with them when they left. Our power has been ebbing steadily, and the backup generator is barely able to keep the power on consistently." She glanced down at the illuminated dials on her watch. "I estimate that we have anywhere from 9 to 12 hours before our power is gone completely. When that happens, no more electricity and no more air."

"*Goddammit!*" Tess's voice shot out of the speaker box. "That son of a bitch gave us no chance! No chance at all!" When they had made it to the *Orion*, she let herself feel that maybe they'd have a chance after all. A small one, but still a chance. Now she could see that slim margin eroding before her eyes. She looked over at the others. They all had the same look of grim desperation painted on their faces. "Okay Kyra, I understand. It'll be close, but I think we'll be able to get back to the compound before the power goes out completely." *Why do these things have to be so close all the time?* she thought sickeningly. She looked at her watch and said, "We will target our ETA at the compound for 1500 hours. I know I don't have to ask you, but please make sure everyone is ready to go. The quicker we get loaded and out of here, the better."

"We're already working towards that Tess. Good luck, and see you at 1500 hours." She clicked off and leaned back in her chair. She thought about her conversation with Julie earlier and wondered if any of them would ever see *Europa*.

THE UNITED NATIONS' COMPOUND

1

The UN compound was a ghost town if it could even be called a town. There were over 60 men, women, and children here when the asteroid hit. The United States leadership and their families, various United Nations' leaders and their families, and a number of academic and military personnel. All but the eight members of the survey team were killed when the meteorites destroyed the facilities.

Oddly enough, the actual impact only killed a handful of people. It was the gaping hole and freezing temperatures that did the rest. When the asteroids hit, they actually rolled through the compound, destroying walls and protective barriers. The people who didn't get sucked out through the holes, froze to death immediately. The rest asphyxiated. The only ones who survived were the ones working outside the compound in their suits. There were only eight. Henry and his team had found them and brought them back to the US compound.

After changing into the *Orion's* ET suits, Henry and Marla went to check out maintenance, while Andy checked out the south end of the compound, where the cafeteria supplies were. Tess had told them to look for an engine node for the shuttle. The shuttle required six nodes and number six was showing signs of degradation. Tess recalled bitterly that they had extra nodes at their own compound, but Soren made sure to relieve them of those as well.

2

Henry and Marla slipped into a wide opening in the compound's east wall. They moved slowly through the battered and twisted hallway, careful not to rip their suits on the many jagged metal edges that seemed to protrude from every wall. They stopped frequently, while Henry consulted the compound map. The last thing he wanted was to get lost in this dark maze of cold metal. They were headed to the maintenance bay, because Tess had told them it was probably the best place to start, but she admitted that the nodes could be anywhere in the compound.

He and Marla investigated every room they encountered on their way to the maintenance bay. They opened the door to what looked to be a machining shop and both screamed at the ghastly scene of bloated, floating bodies; their eyeless faces caught in a frozen rictus of pain and terror. Orbiting these swollen bodies like satellites were eyeballs. They drifted slowly across the room, frozen veins trailing behind each eye like the tails of comets. He and Marla looked at each other shakily and continued down the dark and battered hallway.

They finally made their way to the maintenance hangar bay and looked through the door portal windows. Henry groaned inside. The hangar bay was decimated. From what he could see, this must have been ground zero for at least one of the meteorites. The entire back half of the hangar was gone and only the ragged edges of the still standing sides were visible. What hadn't been blown out through the hole was damaged beyond usability. The few things that remained were physically connected to the still standing walls or the floors. It was practically scoured clean. *No nodes here,* he thought sourly.

He looked at his watch and saw that they would have to go back to the ship soon. Luckily for them, the ship had not been docked in the bay at the time the meteor hit. It actually sat on the runway as if they had been preparing to take off. He called Tess and reported in. "Tess, there's nothing here we can use. And we didn't find a node for the ship. We've been over the entire East Wing of the compound, and what hasn't been blown out into space is totally trashed. We're on our way back to the ship."

"I understand," said Tess. "Thanks, and hurry back. I've completed my run-up on the flight systems, and everything looks good. We can probably take off in about an hour. Andy, you need to wrap up your search and head on back, copy?"

Sitting in one of the few chairs that had not been sucked out into space, Andy looked at the devastation dispassionately. They all blamed him for what happened to Joe. Even though they didn't say anything else about it, they still blamed him. He could see it in their eyes. Especially that damn Henry. Before Soren departed, Andy could count on one hand how many times he had interacted with Henry. He couldn't remember what any of those discussions had been about; all he knew was that he had never warmed up to Henry before and knew now, that he never would.

Tess called back over the mike, "Andy, did you copy last transmission? Over." He thought about the trip they were planning to Earth. God, what a crock of shit! We'll never make it there; if we do, we'll never take off. He could only imagine in his mind's eye what the planet looked like now. Huge crevices dug deep into the earth, spread miles across the surface; never ending earthquakes and folks, let's not forget the radiation. No, he was not looking forward to going back to

Earth. He was convinced that they should find whatever fuel is left here and try to make it to *Europa*.

His mind turned to Joe. *That fucker should never have come with us,* he thought sourly. If he hadn't been so damned clumsy, he'd have been alright. *Well,* he thought, *what's done is done and can't be undone.* I'll always choose *me* before anyone else, and I'd do it again if it came to it. He stood up and slung the cloth bag over his shoulders and started walking towards the ship. He was wondering how he would hide his little find when Tess's voice started to come through the mike. He cut her off and flatly answered "Roger, on my way in now."

Tess clicked off the transmitter button. She was concerned about Andy. Not his wellbeing, but his state of mind and attitude. She didn't know what to do with him. She thought he was skirting the edge of some mental breakdown, the moon life finally getting the best of him. He had cut Joe away very quickly with seemingly no thought about it. She wondered just how far he would go if the right circumstances presented itself. She made a mental note to keep an eye on him and never put herself in a position to be dependent on him.

Without that other engine node, the chances of them making it to *Europa* would be slim to none. She was confident that the damaged node would get them to Earth, but leaving the planet would be a different story. By the time they landed on Earth, the damaged node might be completely unusable and without six fully-functioning engine nodes, they would not be able to take off from the planet. If, by some longshot miracle, the engine node held out, then they might be able to depart Earth, but it wouldn't last the 4-month trip to *Europa*. It would burn out and they would find themselves drifting in space, hundreds of thousands of miles from *Europa*.

If they had more time, they could really search the place to see if a usable node was here, but Tess didn't hold out any hope that they would find one. Plus, Kyra had said the power was failing and that they only had hours left before equipment started shutting down. The hand they were dealt was bad and getting worse all the time. She felt their existence was purely at the whim of fate and that at any time, Lady Luck could pull the rug out from under them and send them all sprawling into oblivion.

She completed her pre-flight check and looked out the window to see where Henry, Marla, and Andy were. In the rear camera, she saw Henry and Marla making their way to the rear ramp and towards the external door portals. She looked at one of the side cameras and saw

Andy making his way to the ship too. He was carrying a small sack, which he had slung over his shoulder. For a minute, she got excited, almost willing to erase all that Andy had done recently. But she got a better look at the sack and could see that it was much too small to be the engine node. She clicked on her transmitter, "What do you have there, Andy? It's too small to be the node." He looked directly at the camera mounted inside the ship and said, "Nothing, just some satellite maps. Maybe we can use them." He tightened his grip around the sack protectively.

3

Once Andy and Marla were on board, Henry informed Tess that she could close the ramp. As Andy passed him, he asked about the maps, but Andy just muttered something about showing him later. He let it pass, but he didn't ignore the fact that Andy couldn't look him in the eyes. *Shifty son of a bitch,* Henry thought. *He's got something in that bag alright, and I'm sure it's not some damn maps.* With that thought in mind, Henry made his way up the ramp just as the ramp locking mechanism clicked into place.

Tess walked into the passenger compartment and waved at Andy and Marla as they headed to their seats. "We're taking off as soon as Henry gets up here and buckled in." She glanced at Andy. His face was slick with sweat, and he looked on the verge of puking. "Andy…are you okay? You look sick."

He looked at her and gave her a barely perceptible nod and started moving to his seat. She shrugged and headed back into the cockpit when she thought she saw movement outside in the darkness. In a weird twist of events, Lunar Day was still a couple of hours away. Tess attributed this to the erratic rotation of the earth, which forced the moon into its own changing orbit.

She peered closely through the large front windshield, trying to focus on the darkness. Only the ship's ground lights were on, so she flipped the forward lights on to see if she actually saw something or not. She stared again and saw a large dust cloud about a mile southeast of the runway. It was moving fast, and it was coming in their direction.

Tess was leaning on the console and staring intently out the front window when Henry came up behind her. "Hey Tess, what's going…" Henry's voice caught in his throat as he looked out the window. "What the hell is that?" he said, pointing out at the billowing dust and dirt that seemed to be coming directly towards them. Andy and Marla exchanged glances and then got out of their seats to see what was going on outside. Andy stomped over to the window, pushing Marla out of the way. Ignoring her remonstrations, he looked out at the bleary landscape.

He saw the dust cloud which was about a mile away and immediately whirled on Tess. "We need to get the fuck out of here! That's probably another Earth...uh...moon...quake or whatever the hell they are. It's coming right towards the runway and could cause enough damage to it that we won't be able to take off at all!"

"Settle down Andy!" Tess yelled at him. "It's not a moonquake. It could be a dust storm, but its movement is not random. If it's a dust storm, then we're perfectly fine here." She turned back to the window.

"That's not good enough for me," Andy said, his voice dangerously low. She turned again to face him and saw the dull gray object in his hands. For a minute, she couldn't place what it was and then slow recognition dawned in her eyes. What Andy held in his fist was dangerous, but not just to her. It was dangerous on a much larger scale. It was a *hope-destroyer* and could obliterate any chance they would have at survival. Apparently, Andy had found a surgical laser tool. Some were more powerful than others, but all were capable of inflicting very serious harm. The one Andy was holding looked practically new.

In some part of her mind, she had expected something like this and wondered why they hadn't kept a closer watch on him. And as fate would have it, Andy would be the one to find something he could use as a weapon. She didn't know if it still worked or not, but she didn't want to find out.

"Andy," Tess said, trying to speak lightly and nonchalantly, "you need to put that laser away right now. If you discharge that in here, several things are going to happen. One, you might shoot me, and if you shoot me, then you hurt our chances to get out of here. The other thing is that if that laser has enough power, it'll cut through me and possibly into the control panel behind me. It might even be strong enough to breach the hull of the ship. I've seen those lasers in use and the concentrated beams are very powerful. If the hull is damaged, then none of us are going anywhere. Do you understand what I'm saying to you?"

Andy's mouth was working, but no words came out. He backed up so that he could have all three of them in his sights. "That's a chance I'm willing to take," he finally said. "You saw what I did to Joe, and I won't hesitate to kill any of you fuckers if you try anything." He looked over at Henry as he said that.

"Now start this fucker up right now. Right now, damn it! We need to get the hell out of here while we can. Can't you see what's happening out there?"

Tess was too nervous to turnaround completely to look out the window because she wanted to keep Andy in sight. He had gotten himself wound up, and she didn't want him to mistake her actions for anything more than just looking out the window. From her direction though, she was able to see that whatever was out there was gone now. As if reading her mind, Henry spoke up and said, "Andy, whatever it was is gone now. See." He pointed out the window, but Andy didn't follow his pointing finger. He only stared at Henry as if contemplating some big decision. "Come on Andy," he continued softly, "just put that thing down before someone gets hurt. You don't want any—"

"*Shut UP!*" Andy shouted at him. "And put your helmet on, we're going on a little walk outside. All of you! Get your helmets on! And Henry, whatever it is you're *thinking* about doing, I wouldn't. You might be thinking that this thing won't fire, but it will. I've already tried it in the compound. Just put your fucking helmet on and move to the ramp door." Tess and Marla donned their helmets as they all walked towards the door leading out to the ramp.

Once inside the rear storage area of the huge ship, Andy closed and secured the pressurized door and punched the button to open the rear ramp. He leaned back against the wall watching them while the ramp slowly lowered itself to the ground. By God, he was actually starting to feel pretty good. He felt in control. He was now making the decisions, instead of being an innocent bystander. He looked over at Marla and assessed her from head to toe. *Yeah,* he thought, *she will be quite pleasing when the time comes.* She looked around and saw him staring at her, and the look on his face told her what he was thinking. She turned away in disgust.

"Andy," Tess pleaded, "what are we doing here? We really need to get back to the compound. They're running out of power as we speak and when that goes, so will the air. The longer we stay here, the less chance we'll have to get to them before it's too late. Please, put that away, and let's go home."

"Well," Andy replied sardonically, "it would suck to be them, huh? Actually, we're not going back there. Our friend Henry here is getting off at this stop. And then you, me and Marla baby here are getting off this rock."

"*What?*" Tess said. "Why would you say something so crazy Andy? When we depart for Earth, there is no way in hell I'm leaving anybody here to die." She was starting to get angry, not wanting to believe that Andy could be serious. And it really was crazy talk. She was beginning to wonder if space dementia was really a true sickness or not. "You want to do exactly what Soren did to us? Just abandon our friends?"

Andy laughed, but there was no humor in it. He looked out at the slowly opening ramp. "Well, that's where you're mistaken *sugar*." The way he said *sugar*, reminded Tess of Reynald, and she felt her stomach clench. "We're not going to Earth," he continued. "We're going to catch up with Soren's ship. They can't be too far ahead of us, and I know we have enough fuel to catch up with them."

Henry started laughing. "You're fucking crazy man! Why would Soren allow you or any of us for that matter, to join his group? That's why he left us. That's why he left you. Why can't you get that through your thick monkey brain Andy? Soren left us here to die, plain and simple. They would never slow down and allow us to board their ship. We would be chasing their fumes until we ran out of fuel, hundreds of thousands of miles away from *Europa*. You're crazy; you're a coward, and you're a fucking murderer."

But Andy was not to be goaded. He had come this far and had not lost it. He had to admit though, that he was seething inside. He wanted to burn a hole right through Henry's skull at that moment, but he was worried that he might miss him and burn a hole in the wall. *Once he's off the ramp, with the black landscape of the moon at his back, then I'll slice his ass open,* Andy thought. He had considered leaving him alive, but now the arrogant prick needed to be taught a lesson.

Using the nose of the laser, he motioned for Henry to get off the ramp. He intended to show them he meant business. "Come on Tess. You and Marla get your asses down here too. I'm not taking a chance on one of you closing the ramp on me."

Tess and Marla moved down the ramp to join Henry on the ground at the foot of the ramp. Henry was looking off into the distance towards the front of the ship. Andy joined them on the ground, putting some distance between them. A thought occurred to him that he might have to have Marla tied up during the trip to avoid any chances of the women overpowering him. He felt a shiver of warmth in his groin at the thought. "Tess, Marla, move away from Henry."

"Andy, you can't do this!" Tess cried. "We need Henry. He's the only one who can figure out how to connect with the satellite orbiting *Europa*. And this is so *wrong*, can't you see that?"

Henry stepped away from the women. "Don't worry Tess. I'll be okay." He stepped away from the ramp and moved back. He raised his hands above his head dramatically, slowly walking back. He looked towards the front of the ship again and then sank to his knees. "Please Andy!" he pleaded. "Can we talk about this? I don't want to die out here. I don't want to be alone!" The pitch of his voice was a high, whining sound.

Andy stopped right at the edge of the lowered platform and smiled, *Now, that's more like it,* he thought. "There, there Henry," he said confidently, still smiling. "Let's not show our true colors in front of the ladies. This is just the way it has to be. It's almost like survival of the fittest." He chortled chummily, "In a way, you're almost like good ole Joe. His fear of heights and the fact that he was overweight is what led to his downfall. Your downfall is that you're too trusting. You don't like me, but you don't keep your guard up around me. Since I knew that you didn't like me, I promised myself that if the opportunity came, I would take advantage of the situation." The smarmy smile he had pasted on his face slowly transformed itself into a sneer, "You've always been the big, tough guy on campus Henry. Why don't you show us how tough you are now?"

Henry turned his face upward, his eyes widening somewhat. Was he praying, Andy wondered? He didn't know or care. He raised the laser to the level of Henry's face and placed his finger on the laser release button.

What happened next reminded Andy of the times he would be awakened in the middle of the night by a loud noise outside; maybe a fire truck siren or some late-night party animal coming home from the local joint in his piece of shit, backfiring car. When these things woke him up, he would be in such a state of confusion that he wouldn't know where he was, what time it was, or even who he was. Of course, his head would clear up within seconds and he'd be very aware of what was happening. This feeling was what was happening to him now. One minute, he was aiming the surgical laser at Henry's face and the next, he was lying on the ground after being hit from behind. The blow was hard too, right in the soft spot of the space suit.

He saw the laser on the ground, only inches away and made a move to grab it when a boot came down hard on his arm. It took a second for the pain to register as he snatched his arm back, cursing furiously. He attempted to raise himself from the ground when he realized that his arm would not support him. It gave away weakly as he fell back to the ground, the pain of his broken arm shooting lightning bolts of white-hot sparks through him.

"You broke my arm you fucking ape!" he yelled at Henry, but Henry had been on his knees. He looked up at them from the ground. "Tess, I need medical attention now! I need to..." he broke off. "What the hell are you smiling about?" He looked around the circle and could see that they weren't smiling at him. They were looking past him, just beyond his shoulder. In all of his blind fury, he hadn't had a chance to think about what had hit him from behind. It had all happened so quickly. He shifted himself around on his knees and stared into the eyes of what he first thought was a ghost or something his imagination had conjured up.

Joe stood just behind him, holding a huge wrench. His faceplate was scratched up and his suit looked as if he had been dragged over miles of rough, rocky road. Apart from the frayed and torn up appearance of his suit, his eyes were fiercely bright. "Oh God! I can't believe I caught up with you guys! I could see the lights on the ship and some tiny figures at the window and thought there was still time to get here." The look on his face changed immediately. "But when I saw the white exhaust smoke, I was worried that I might be left here, so I opened the throttle. I couldn't go too fast though, because I could barely see out there. If it hadn't been for the ship lights, I never would have made it here."

"Well," said Tess, "you're a lifesaver Joe". If you hadn't come when you did..." Her voice trailed off.

Joe looked down at Andy and involuntarily tightened his grip on the wrench. "My communications connection was gone when I woke up down in the hole. I tried contacting you guys, but I got back nothing. Only static."

"Tell you what guys," Henry interrupted. "Let's finish this story on the ship. We need to get the hell out of here and back to base." He was holding the laser in his hands.

"Henry's right you guys," Tess replied. "I've lost communications with the base right now, which means all of their power is probably gone. Joe, would you please pull that Rover up onto the ramp? We'll take it with us—you never know when it may come in handy." She looked over at the four-wheeler and smiled. *That bike saved Joe's life...and Henry's for that matter.*

"What about him?" Marla asked, looking down at Andy. "Maybe we should leave him here because I really don't trust him anymore."

"I don't trust him either, Marla, but I'm not ready to condemn him yet." She looked around the desolate UN compound, "Especially not here. Let's bring him, but he needs to be restrained. Can you take care of that Henry?"

"No problem Tess," he said, walking over to Andy. He handed the laser to Marla and then grabbed Andy roughly by his non-injured arm, "Get up you piece of shit!"

"Hey! Easy man! I'm hurt here!" Andy wailed.

Henry hauled Andy up the ramp while Marla walked behind them with the laser pointed towards Andy. Tess raised the ramp and re-pressurized the cargo bay before opening the cargo pressure door. As she headed for the cockpit, she could hear Andy complaining about his injury while Henry tied him tightly to his seat.

4

Joe's story of survival straddled the thin line between bad luck and blind luck. By the time they landed back at the US base, he was able to fill them in on what had happened to him after he had fallen into the crater.

"I don't remember much about the falling part." Joe said, "I remember the quake and looking up to see Henry holding out his hand to me. And I remember Andy cutting the rope. That was very clear in my head." His eyes were dark as he looked over at Andy sitting on the last row of seats. Marla was able to set his arm and gave him a mild sedative, which seemed to calm him a little, but not before he was able to throw a fusillade of curse words at her.

"When I woke up, I was lying on a pile of loosely packed dirt. There was a huge jagged boulder about a foot away that I miraculously missed. Judging from where I'm sore the most, the hole must have gotten narrower and narrower. I think bouncing from side to side is what actually slowed my descent.

"Luckily, I hadn't broken any bones, but I was sore as hell. I tried climbing back out, but the smooth walls extended quite far up. To be honest though, with no safety lines, I didn't want to take a chance and slip and fall. I didn't think I'd survive a second fall.

"I considered waiting it out, but I had the feeling that you guys wouldn't be at the UN location for long, and I was freezing. I sat there in the dark, trying to think and trying not to feel sorry for myself when I realized that we had lights *inside* our helmets. The outside light was busted for sure, but since I was still breathing air, I thought maybe the inside light would be working too. And it was! And that was when I saw the tunnel."

"There was a *tunnel* down in the hole?" Henry asked. "A *man-made* tunnel?"

"Yes!" Joe cried. "I couldn't believe it. I thought it was just another hole going deeper into the planet, but I couldn't go up, so I had no choice but to go down into it. Once I got into the hole, I actually had to lower myself down about five feet or so into the tunnel, and it was high enough that I could stand up.

"After about 15 minutes of walking, I came across a lot of abandoned equipment. Hole-digging stuff it looked like to me. I wasn't sure where the tunnel led to, but I hoped it led straight to the UN compound. My only concern was that it might be blocked because of the moonquake." He looked around uneasily at them. "And if it was blocked, then there might be dead bodies too.

"So, I walked. Just when I thought things couldn't get any worse, my helmet light started dimming, so I moved faster, not as cautiously, and ran smack into the back of that Rover out there." He hitched his thumb in the direction of the storage area. "I tried not to think about what would have happened if I hit that thing head on and broken my helmet." He grew reflective for a moment and then added, "I don't know why they left it, but thank God for small favors, huh? And that little mini-Rover is just like ours, so it didn't take long to get it going.

"I rode along for a few minutes when I came to a fork in the tunnel. Since one direction was completely blocked, I didn't have to worry about choosing the wrong tunnel. When it finally ended, I was probably a mile from the ship. It's so frigging dark out there that the shuttle light was the only thing I could see for miles around. By then, my helmet light had died completely."

"Lucky for you our timetable for Lunar Day has been thrown out of whack. Otherwise, you would have been caught out in the open," Henry stated.

"Yeah, you're right about that. As I got closer, I thought I could see you guys in the cockpit, so I floored it. The whole time I was thinking that you would take off just as I reached you, passing over me without ever knowing I was there.

"The next thing I know, I see someone at the back with their arms raised. I didn't think much of it at the time. I was just happy you weren't about to take off. But then I saw someone—I guess it was you Henry—get to their knees with their arms up. I sort of got the feeling that you saw me coming." He looked over at Andy strapped to his seat. "And I saw him pointing something at you. I'm not a genius, but I kind of figured this was a bad situation, so I dismounted on the other side of the ship and snuck around to the back. The wrench I found in the tunnel came in handy."

"You did great Joe," Marla said to him, smiling.

Henry was nodding, "Yeah, thanks Joe. I mean it. I'm not sure what's gotten into Andy, but we'll need to keep him restrained until, well, until we get to *Europa* I suppose. Things are going to hell at the base as we speak. The power is going, if not already gone, and they're probably breathing off suit air by now."

"What happened?" Joe asked.

"In a nutshell, Soren screwed us...again. He took most of the air processing equipment with him, as well as the extra power generators. As soon as we get to the base, we'll have to load up and take off for Earth."

As if on cue, Tess spoke over the intercom, "Alright guys, we're here. Prepare for landing." She circled over the darkened compound once and then brought the *Orion* in for a landing using the vertical landing jets. She taxied the huge ship as close to the hangar as possible. She could see people in the open door. They were waving and hugging one another. She spoke into the mike once more, "Helmets on everyone. Let's get out there and load up so we can get the hell out of here." She looked over at Marla and Joe. "Can you guys keep an eye on him? I don't trust him and I sure as hell am not going to untie him right now."

"No problem, Tess," Joe said, as he patted the huge wrench sitting beside him.

"I have stuff I need to get!" Andy yelled as he struggled in his seat. "You can't keep me tied up like some animal!"

Henry had reached the door, but turned back when he heard this. He walked back over to Andy and stared at him coldly. "You're lucky we're bringing you at all. We considered leaving you here. Your plan would have killed us all. You're dangerous and a liability, and you can't be trusted. I really don't give a fuck about your shit, but I'll send one of the guys to secure whatever you packed." He started to leave again and then turned back, "And you can bet we'll thoroughly search it too." To this, Andy had nothing to say. All he could do was look into Henry's unrelenting stare. He stared down at the floor, afraid that Henry would see the murderous revenge he felt at that moment. *Everything in its own sweet time,* he thought. He would wait and he would watch. And then he would act. He smiled at this comforting thought, while the others headed to the cargo bay.

RETURN TO EARTH

1

There was not much fanfare about the departure from the moon base, but a few people had to be talked into getting on the ship. They had given up hope and had consigned themselves to die there when their air ran out. Had it not been for Henry's efforts, they would have remained locked up in their units.

Leaving the gravity of the moon proved even less eventful. Tess and her young co-pilot, Chayton Dakota used a standard moon slingshot maneuver to help them maximize their speed and distance, while conserving what little fuel they had remaining. Chayton was a junior pilot who had just entered the space shuttle program with NASA. His experience came entirely from a shuttle simulator, yet he took to Tess's instructions well and was now at the controls while Tess addressed the others on board.

"To most of you, it must seem as if all of our options have been taken from us by forces out of our control. Well, I have to agree with you that things do look grim. I know some of you wanted to stay at the compound, but you would have faced certain death back there. Some of you even suggested that we go straight to *Europa* from here." A murmur of agreements arose from the group.

"As appealing as that sounds, it would have been a fatal trip for us. We simply don't have the fuel to make it all the way to *Europa*, and we would never have caught up to Soren's ship. We would have burned up all our fuel and never even seen a glimpse of them. Our momentum would have eventually got us to *Europa*, but we would have been months dead by the time we got there.

If by chance we *did* survive the trip, we wouldn't have the fuel to slow our rate of approach and land on the planet. And with no maneuvering ability, we would have most likely gotten pulled into *Jupiter's* orbit." She looked around at the pensive, frightened faces. She could almost see a cloud of uncertainty hanging over the group. They were nervous and so was she. And she still hadn't told them the bad news.

"I need to be perfectly clear with everyone on what we're doing now and what we hope we can do. There are a number of obstacles still facing us, but one major problem has been solved and that's where we need to land. We've tracked the shelter beacon and determined that this particular shelter is about two miles from Wright Airfield in North San Antonio, Texas. This is actually the airfield that I took off from; that most of *you* took off from. So, I know this area and I know how we will be able to refuel. There is an underground fuel storage facility and as long as it's intact, then we should be able to refuel. We won't know how bad the area is until we have visible contact."

Sheila Walker, a young drilling engineer from Tulsa, Oklahoma, raised her hand. "What about the shelter? Will we be going to look for survivors?"

"Unfortunately, Sheila, we're not on a rescue mission. We're barely surviving ourselves as it is. If there was enough food at the fuel depot, then I would gladly refuel, stock up on food and then take off. I don't want to be on the planet any longer than we have to. But since I know the depot doesn't have long-term food storage facilities, then we will need to go to the shelter to negotiate with them for their food. Basically, transportation for food.

"The underground shelter was designed to house people, food and supplies in this type of event. The air base was not. If we *do* go to the shelter and find people, we need to be very careful how we interact with them. We have plenty of room here on the ship, but we need to be able to trust these people." Her mind went back to the throngs of people massed outside the gate before she left Earth. It was a violent scene.

"During my last few days before we took-off, it was terrible at the airfield. We might be in very real danger if a large enough group of survivors see our ship and decide not to be friendly. If the group at the shelter is small, then we will certainly bring them with us." Her normally dark brown skin grew even darker, "We're working on a group of assumptions you guys. If any one of them turns out to be wrong, then we could very well find ourselves stuck on planet Earth."

Neal Marklewitz shifted in his seat and tentatively raised his hand. "So, once we refuel and stock up, then we should be able to get to *Europa* with no problems?" Neal used to work for NASA and although he wasn't familiar with the *Orion* specifically, he had a strong working knowledge of the basic shuttle components.

Tess looked over at Henry and sighed. "As usual Neal, you hit the nail on the head. The last assumption for us is a big one. We are in dire need of an engine power node. Six nodes are required for takeoff. Five of our nodes are in good condition. The sixth one is damaged. Five of them were enough to help us leave the gravity of the moon, but we will need all six of them in order to lift off from Earth. We hope to find one at the airfield."

Someone in the back said what everyone was probably thinking, "Tess, what are our chances of finding this node on Earth? I don't know about everyone else, but I'm thinking that things are pretty fucked up there. Fires, earthquakes, and God knows what else. How do we know if these nodes will even still be there?" There were murmurs of agreement throughout the group.

Although Tess had been expecting this line of questioning, she was still almost at a loss for words. Everything that he said was true. Their situation was desperate, and they were relying on luck more than Tess would have cared for. In a word, their situation was...tenuous. "You're right; we're taking a big chance going back to Earth. If we can't find the engine power node, then we will not have enough power to leave Earth's gravity and our fate will be the same as those on Earth now." She wiped at her forehead, wondering what it would take to convince them that this was the last resort.

"If we could make it to *Europa* right now, I would turn this ship around and head straight for it. But we can't make it. We don't even have enough fuel to get to Mars. We need fuel and we need one more engine node. Both of those items are on Earth. There's a strong chance that we can get both at the airfield."

"That's bullshit, and you know it!" Andy yelled from the back. He was the only one seated in his row, and he was still tied up. "How do you know that those nodes are there Tess?"

Tess glanced briefly at Andy, "As you guys all know, things were pretty crazy during those last days at the airfield. In the confusion, the maintenance team loaded the extra engine nodes onto Jack Richards' shuttle, the *Galileo2*. Jack had confirmed that he was able to secure only four of the extra engine nodes before we departed. It had gotten too dangerous for them to get to the other two so they left them at the airfield in the fuel depot's underground storage facility. This oversight will probably be what saves our lives."

She could see them relaxing somewhat. Finally allowing themselves to believe that they might have a chance, despite the astronomical odds against them. "I won't mislead you. We are relying on a lot of *ifs*. *If* the airfield is intact, then we can land. *If* the fuel depot has not been destroyed or compromised, then we can refuel and have enough fuel to make it to *Europa*. *If* we can find one of the engine power nodes at the airfield, then we'll have the power to leave the planet."

Max Borden, a machinist from Brooklyn, New York cleared his throat and in a heavy New York accent said, "If things don't work out for us, how much time do we have on Earth? I mean, how long before the planet either breaks apart or gets too hot to live on?" He sat down and looked around, nervously wringing his hands in his lap.

"We're not 100% certain Max, but after comparing my information with the information Kyra and Henry were able to gather, we were able to determine that the planet has anywhere from ten days to a month before there is a chain reaction of earthquakes strong enough to rip the planet apart completely. If that doesn't happen, then about two months from now, the earth's orbit will take it so close to the sun that everything on the planet will burn up."

She looked around at the group. A few were crying or on the verge of it. Tess had the feeling that they were not crying for themselves, but more for humanity itself; for the sheer, overwhelming vastness of it. Over the past several months, she had thought more and more on how things might have been different if the human race were more advanced. *Our selfish and greedy ways have brought us to this point of near extinction,* she thought. In her mind's eye, she saw the millions of starving people around the world. Wars, genocide, racial and religious hatred. The lack of global trust and brotherhood kept us from becoming more than we are. Now we are almost no more.

If our vast global resources were used to better *everyone's* lives, then maybe we could have saved the life of someone who would have made a real difference. How many future Albert Einstein's starved to death as children because their families, their villages, or their countries did not have the necessary resources to support them? How many of them were slaughtered as a result of racial cleansing or religious jingoism? How many of these unknowns carried within them the intuitive spark that could have set humankind on different technological and sociological pathways? Instead of scrambling to get shelters built on the moon, maybe we could have been exploring space and colonizing the stars, with the technology to easily destroy or at least detour the rogue planet that so dismissively smashed into the earth, destroying our only home and condemning over 99% of us to death.

Tess could feel her eyes filling up with hot tears and knew that in a minute, they would be caressing her cheeks. She raised her hands to her face and wiped her eyes, just as Chayton's soft voice came over the intercom. "Tess, we'll be approaching Earth's orbit in ten minutes."

Tess turned away from the group, just as a single tear rolled down her face. As she walked, she looked back over her shoulder and told everyone to buckle up and prepare for landing.

2

Tess strapped herself in and looked at the navigation readouts. Chayton was looking at her worriedly. "Are you alright Tess? I heard what you said back there, and I think everyone agrees with you. Well, almost everyone."

Tess sighed, "Yeah, I know Chayton, but this is so difficult. I'm trying to give them hope when we keep running up against brick walls." She sighed heavily. "Well, we'll do what we can. Let's see how we're..." Her voice broke off as she looked up from the navigation panel and out at the planet before them. "Oh my God Chayton, this is worse than I feared." She clicked on the microphone and leaned forward to speak into it. "Folks, I'm going to lower the window shields and turn on the forward viewer so you can see what I'm seeing. We're all in this together, and I want you to be aware of what's going on. Henry, please join me in the cockpit." She looked over at Chayton and saw him leaning forward in his seat; his eyes bulging and his lips parted. His fingers were nervously twitching against the navigation panel.

She turned to look back out at the planet graveyard in front of her. They were not quite in orbiting distance, but the huge debris field stretched the entire length of their window.

Tess had been observing the earth from the moon for almost two years, so she had an idea what to expect as they got closer, but seeing it from this distance was unnerving. The planet was no longer round or circular, but looked like an old and cracked volleyball or basketball that didn't have enough air in it. Huge cracks and fissures could be seen everywhere on the planet. Some of them glowed brightly, as white-hot lava shot into the air and spilled over the sides. Clouds of steam and vapor issued from these cracks and crevices. The side of the planet facing them was completely dark with the exception of a paltry few points of light, which could have been small, isolated fires.

The debris field orbiting the earth was a nightmarish hodgepodge of broken Earth rock and meteor rock. Tess wasn't certain how much of the debris field came from *Lycos* and how much came from the earth itself.

"Jesus," someone breathed behind her. It was Henry. "Is that what I think it is?" He was pointing left of the center of their window. They strained their eyes towards it. Tess swallowed hard and said, "Yeah, it is." She pointed to the rest of the field. "Look here, there's more."

Henry followed her finger and sharply drew in his breath. His first thought of what he was looking at was one of abstract art. The debris field was littered with vehicles of all types; cars, trucks, busses, and trains. They even saw a few airplanes and boats. Most were battered and crushed, but there were a few that appeared to be completely intact. They could see the bloated outline of *things* in some of the vehicles; things that could only be bloated bodies. Most of the debris field was rubble, but throughout Tess could see huge chunks of Earth slowly rotating within the field. She spied trees and destroyed buildings on one massive section.

"What are those cylindrical shapes out there in the rubble; they're everywhere," Chayton inquired quietly.

Tess, not sure if she could trust herself to speak looked at Chayton and said, "Those are *bodies* Chayton; the bodies of millions of people who were thrown into space when the planet hit." The look in his eyes told her that he already knew the answer to his question, but still needed someone to tell him that he was actually seeing the bloated and frozen bodies of millions of people. He folded his arms across his chest and dropped his head. She looked over at Henry, "Have a seat there, Henry," she pointed to the Navigator's chair behind Chayton, "And please prepare our route to Wright Airfield."

3

The silence was palpable in the passenger seating area as all eyes stared out at the debris field circling the earth. Kyra stared out her own window in total disbelief. As they got closer, she could see things floating in space that should never even *be* in space. *And the bodies,* she thought, *the millions upon millions of bodies! My God...there are so many! How terrible those last days must have been. And here we are...going back.* She looked around and could almost feel the fear and anguish here and it was at that moment that in her deepest heart, she knew that they were not going to survive this. They had escaped the earth the first time, but she would not let them escape a second time. If humanity had any chance of continuing on, it would be with Soren's group, not them.

The ship was now traveling parallel to the debris field. The sight outside her window sickened her, but Kyra was unable to look away. It seemed to stretch on and on. Finally, they turned toward the planet again and thankfully, they were close enough that she could no longer see the bodies and chunks of planet debris orbiting the planet. Once they cleared the debris field, she looked down and could see that they were flying over the planet. She had no idea what part of the world they were flying over, but was grateful that it was dark down there. Unfortunately, her gratitude was short-lived for they were moving towards the other side of the planet, where the sun was shining.

Despite the darkness of the planet, Kyra could still see eerie strips of yellow-orange light coming through huge ragged cracks on the planet. She imagined unquenchable fires raging inside the earth, fed by unending flows of molten lava from long dormant volcanos. As the ship moved closer to the sunlit side of the planet, she could see that things seemed more intact here. Maybe this side of the planet was spared the worst of the impact.

The ship started shaking as they entered Earth's atmosphere, but Kyra barely noticed. She was glued to the window looking out at the landscape. The planet had a hazy look to it, similar to the skyline pictures she used to see of Beijing and Los Angeles. She had always heard that the smog was so terrible in these places, that one could literally see it hanging over the skyline. What she could see now looked similar, only thicker and much dirtier.

They were descending rapidly now, and the ship was shaking badly. She wiped sweat away from her forehead and realized that it was getting warm. She looked out the window again, but the heat shields had been raised. All she could do now was wait it out.

The ship dropped sickeningly and Kyra thought for a quick second that she was going to throw up. Somewhere behind, several people gagged and vomited violently. Kyra closed her eyes and pinched her nose shut. She knew that the minute she smelled someone else's vomit, she would vomit herself.

The ship bucked and rocked in the weakened atmosphere during their descent through the upper layers of the earth's atmosphere. The ship eventually leveled out, and they started flying relatively smoothly. The heat shields covering the windows retracted once more, but Kyra couldn't see clearly through the thick gray clouds. As the ship descended lower, the thickness of the clouds lessened to a certain degree, but not entirely. It was clear enough, however, for Kyra to get a good look at the surrounding landscape.

Her original thought was that this side of the planet was spared the devastating impact of *Lycos*, but she could see that that was only partially true. While this side did not have huge chunks of earth torn out of it, it did show signs of massive earthquake activity. Large tracts of land had been forced up out of the earth creating jagged mountain ranges for miles around.

The devastation was total. Here and there, a few stubborn buildings stood, but there were none with more than two or three stories remaining erect. Their ship's direction changed slightly, and she could see that they were flying over what must have been a huge body of water. She remembered that they were looking for Wright Airfield, so they must be flying close to the Gulf of Mexico. As she looked out, she could see that the water level had decreased significantly. She was looking out at a huge cliff. The destroyed land angled slightly downward as you looked toward the gulf, and then it simply dropped off into an extremely deep chasm. She looked over at the window on the opposite side of the aisle, but couldn't see well enough to determine how far the water had receded.

She realized that she had not seen any people yet, but had she really expected to see anyone in all of this devastation? She had a very difficult time believing that no one survived, but she couldn't imagine anyone surviving *this*. And after seeing how badly damaged the earth was, she couldn't imagine that the airfield would be anything but a jumbled mass of rubble.

"We've located the beacon and are making our approach to the airfield," Tess announced over the intercom, almost as if she had been monitoring Kyra's thoughts. "It looks as if the airfield is still intact, thank God."

Chayton initiated the vertical landing countdown while Henry stared fixedly at the navigation monitor. "You're almost there Tess, do you see it? Just past that line of broken up buildings."

"Yep, I got it Henry. Thanks," Tess replied. Tess felt sick to her stomach as they passed over the northern part of San Antonio. The city was completely devastated. Every building downtown was either leveled or cracked open like a bad egg. Some parts of the city were blackened due to the fires that burned uncontrollably. As she looked around, she could see that not everything was completely destroyed.

The underground prison topside buildings were damaged, but otherwise, the grounds looked intact.

She maneuvered the shuttle over several broken-down buildings until she came to a relatively smooth area of concrete that seemed to be solid and stable. There were a few overturned vehicles in the area, but other than that, it was a pretty decent area. "Alright Chayton, let's do this." The ship's airspeed slowed and then stopped and hovered directly over the concrete patch. At the same time, the powerful vertical landing ports swiveled toward the ground and burst into life. The ship rose slightly, but working the controls, Tess slowly lowered the ship to the ground, blowing the overturned cars and other debris in different directions. About ten feet from the ground, Tess released the landing skids and lowered the ship the final few feet to the ground. She cut the power to the rockets as soon as they landed. Vertical landing took up a lot of fuel and she had a feeling that they would need every bit of it.

4

Tess walked out to the passenger seating area and stood facing the group. A few people clapped and yelled out "Way to go Tess!", but most just sat in their seats with stunned expressions on their faces.

"I know how you all feel," Tess said, waving down the clappers. "I can't believe it myself that we're actually back here where we started a few years ago. But this is where we have to start if we want to make it to *Europa* and live. I'm not going to sugar-coat our situation here because none of you are blind, but we're going to have to work together if we want to have any chance of making it through this. All of you know Julie Dubois, our resident 'doctor'. She's going to give you the run down on conditions outside."

Julie stood up and walked to the front of the group. She moved as if she were either drunk or wearing ankle weights. She also looked tired as if she had slept the entire trip and had just woken up. "The radiation levels are nominal, but not dangerous if we limit our exposure." She rubbed her stomach subconsciously. "Young children should stay inside. The same goes for anyone who is ill. If you're sick, then your immune system will be weak and the radiation, even at low levels, could have an adverse effect on you.

"The air outside is breathable, but the microscopic toxins in the air could damage your lungs if you are breathing it for too long. We have plenty of face masks with portable personal oxygen tanks, good for at least six hours. You won't need to wear them while on the ship because our air filtration systems will be going full blast."

She smiled an innocent smile, "Once you start moving around inside the ship and outside on the ground, you might find yourselves getting tired very quickly and that it's difficult to get around. Before you start thinking that there's something wrong with you, you need to understand that we've been in a light gravity environment for almost two years, and we've adjusted to it. With the loss of gravity here, you won't be as heavy as you used to be on Earth, but you'll be heavier than you were on the moon. I had forgotten that until I had to get up and walk just now." A few people chuckled at this.

Looking grave, Tess added, "We haven't seen *any* people at all during our approach, but I'm certain that they're out there. I can only guess that after two years in this environment, the social customs that we are familiar with no longer exist. Things changed for us during our time on the moon, but not as drastically as they did here. We have to be extremely careful if we encounter any groups here. You can be certain that they know we're here and some could be on their way here now. Don't let your guard down."

"So, what's the plan now?" Someone asked. "And how long will we be here?"

"Henry and I will draw up teams to collect the things we need. I will take two teams with me; one team will come with me to the airfield underground storage facilities to look for the engine node, and the other will stay back and refuel the shuttle. Henry will take a team to the underground shelter in this area. It was their signal that we homed in on."

"Why are we going there for food?" several people asked at the same time. Several folks were talking, but Bobby St. Pier's voice broke through, "I thought everything we needed was here at the airfield? Fuel, food, and the engine node. If everything is here, why don't we just re-fuel, stock up, and get the hell out of here?" Many were nodding their heads in agreement at this.

"I hear you Bobby," Tess said, "but as I said, we're not 100% sure about the food situation here at the airfield. The underground storage facilities were only meant to store airfield supplies and equipment for the shuttles. There might be some food, but not like the underground shelters. I know for a fact that the underground shelters were outfitted with at least three, maybe four years of non-perishable food and water. If we bank on the airfield supplies and find that there are none here or not enough, then we will have lost valuable time waiting around to see if we would find anything here."

She looked at Kyra and continued on, "By now, I'm sure you all have felt the constant rumbling all around us. It's not the ship. It's the earth. The planet is becoming very unstable. Kyra pulled some thermal scans of Earth before we left the moon, and the core is rapidly deteriorating. We think that the destabilization process has already started, and it's only a matter of time before a chain reaction starts that will rip the rest of the planet apart. When that happens, we will have zero-time to do anything else but leave. If Henry's team can find food at the underground shelter, then it will add to our chances of surviving the trip to *Europa*."

5

Less than an hour later, Marla, Della, Billy Li, and Bob were huddled around a built-in wall table in the cargo storage area. They were part of Henry's team. Black and white photographs were spread out on the table. During the approach to the airfield, they had taken lots of wide-angle photos of the area using the *Orion's* thermal imaging equipment. Henry gave copies to each person in his group, and he was now showing them where they were and where they needed to go.

"As you guys can see, we don't have too far to go, but the terrain gets very tricky about right here." He pointed to a large mass of jumbled rubble on the image. "Just looking at the upheaval of terrain here, you can see that there must have been a huge quake here or a large meteorite hit here. All of the rubble that you see comes from the buildings that were here. This is where our signal originated. Hopefully, we can access the shelter from this point here." His finger traced an oblong shape on the image.

"What is that?" Marla asked. "Is that a subway tunnel or something?"

"That's close Marla, but Texas doesn't have any subway tunnels. It is a tunnel though. From what Tess explained to me, the shelters were built with several exits so that the people wouldn't be trapped if they needed to get out. The exit here doesn't look obstructed, but we may have to climb down there to reach it."

"Shouldn't we bring more people Henry? It's probably better to travel in larger numbers just so we can defend ourselves if necessary.

Also, the more people we have, the more food we can carry back, right?"

"This is about as large as I wanted the group to be," Henry replied. "More than that and we might attract too much attention." Henry smiled, "You'll be surprised at how much food you'll be able to carry Marla. Everything that the shelters were stocked with were super-dehydrated, so you'll be able to carry a year's worth of dried meatloaf without even breaking a sweat."

"How far is the walk Henry?" Bob asked.

"Looks to be about two miles, as the crow flies, but there's a lot of debris as you can see here...and here." He pointed to two large, dark areas on the image. "We may have a little climbing to do once we reach this point."

Marla spoke up again, her voice sounding a little shaky. "Henry, I know the terrain will be a little tricky to navigate, but what about the people? Do you think they really pose a threat to us?"

Before Henry could answer, Bob yelled out, "Hell yeah! When our shuttle departed, there were thousands of people trying to get on board. Even though they knew there was only space for a small few, they still fought to get on. I think that same type of craziness will happen again once people know there's a ship here; a ship capable of lifting off and leaving here. We need to be small and mobile and try not to attract too much attention." He fingered his torn jacket, "And Henry, I think it was a great idea to wear these shredded clothes. It helps us to fit in."

Earlier, Henry had suggested that they shred their clothes in an attempt to fit in. He had them soil their clothes and their faces in dirt and oil from the machines in the storage bay area. Some had joked that they felt as if they were preparing for a role in a movie. "They could call it *'Return To Earth'*", Bob had quipped to the others, much to their chagrin.

"I'm certain that we will run into a few people on the way there, but hopefully, they will be isolated groups," Henry said. "Bob's right though; if enough people find out that we have a ship, and if they find out where it is then that could be trouble for us when it comes time to leave." He straightened up and rolled up the map-image. "Unfortunately, we don't have much in the way of weapons. We have two axes and this laser that Andy found at the UN site on the moon." No one asked about the laser because they had all heard the story of what had happened at the UN site. Some had even questioned why he wasn't left behind on the moon for what he tried to do to Henry.

"Alright guys, let's pack up and get out of here. The quicker we get there, the quicker we can get back. I have the only long-range walkie-talkie, to talk to Tess and the ship, but we will be able to communicate amongst ourselves on the short-range talkies, but stay close and never, ever wander off alone. If you get separated, wait for us and we'll come find you. If an hour passes and we haven't found you, then get back to the ship as soon as possible. This is a strange world to us now and we don't know what's waiting for us out there. It's all about survival now, and people will do anything to survive. *Anything*."

Henry looked at his watch. It was almost seven in the morning although you couldn't tell by looking outside. "If Tess is able to find an engine node, then we will be lifting off as soon as we all are back at the ship. I have every intention of being back here before nightfall. The idea of sleeping out there doesn't sit too well with me. Also, from the thermal images that we took as we were flying in, we don't have too much time on the ground here. The core is very unstable, and it's only a matter of time before those constant tremors erupt into full blown earthquakes."

Henry went over to the ramp control grid and pressed the button to lower the cargo bay ramp. As it slowly opened, he and the others adjusted their backpacks underneath their outer garments and pulled their face masks over their mouths and noses. The brightness of the interior cargo bay seemed to diminish as the foggy, grayness of the dying Earth drifted in from the outside.

IV
THE EARTH
OCTOBER 2053

WRIGHT AIRFIELD

1

"Okay...on three again! One...two...three!" The four men strained against the steel pipe they had wedged between two huge slabs of concrete. A smaller slab of concrete lay directly above the trap door that led to one of the ten recessed refueling stations that bordered the length of the broken runway.

When Wright Airfield was re-designed, the idea was that it would enable planes and shuttle craft to quickly refuel directly on the runway, instead of having to go clear across the field to one of the two, large refueling stations. It worked very well, but involved a cadre of people from start to finish. As always though, the weak link was the human link. There were times when ground personnel were forced to wait for hours while the underground Fuel Control Center went through its painstaking process of checking the control center fuel ports before switching on the fuel flow lines.

The men strained even more as the huge slab grudgingly moved upward. Each time it moved up, the others in the group would be ready with smaller slabs to support the bigger chunk of rock, so that they could get the car jacks underneath the sides of the slab of stone. They had found the car jacks after searching a number of the scattered vehicles on the airfield.

Of the ten refueling stations, six of them were completely destroyed. Two more were buried under ten feet of concrete. The ninth one looked promising until they pulled out the tubing and walked toward the ship to connect the ports. The tubing was terribly dry-rotted in several areas. Tess decided that this was not end-of-the-world damage here, but good old-fashioned human neglect. They were now at the last port. If this one was destroyed too, then they would be forced to unearth the two that were completely buried.

The men continued to strain when all of a sudden there was a loud ripping sound. Tess looked up sharply from the Fuel Control Center schematic that she was reviewing. Everyone froze. The men seemed to stop in unison; their heads slowly turning towards one another. A second later, they all burst out laughing. All, that is, except for Lars Nielsen. Lars was a big guy. Large round stomach, but strong as hell. He always surprised people when he told them that he was an entomologist. He looked around at everyone with his face slightly red and said, "Excuse me...I guess I strained too hard."

He wasn't trying to be funny, but they burst out laughing again. Tess laughed too until she saw the slab start sliding back down, closing the space they had created. The men quickly doubled their efforts, and soon they had both sides of the giant rock supported by the car jacks.

With the slab firmly supported, they were able to remove the cover and reach down into the recessed station to unlock the tubing ports. "Alright, this is it," said Max as he pulled out the tubing from its housing cylinder. As the tube lengthened, they each grabbed a side of it to help pull it to the *Orion*, and more importantly, not to drag it along the ground.

While they pulled, Tess inspected the lengthening tube, looking for signs of rot and cracking. *So far, so good,* she thought, as they continued unravelling the tubing, moving closer to the fuel port on the ship. Once they reached the *Orion's* fuel port, she inspected the tubing once more to make sure there were no obvious signs of damage. As she considered this, she realized that despite damage or not, they would have to make this tubing work, or it would be a long and arduous job clearing the other two covered stations.

Her group stood back and looked on anxiously, waiting for the verdict. Tess's flashlight moved back and forth across the tubing as she walked from the refueling station back to the ship. They had brought out several ground lights to see clearly, even though it was ten in the morning. The overhead sky was a dirty gray shroud with a thin ray of sun shining through. Far off, the distant sound of thunder drifted across the flattened landscape towards them.

Tess stood up straight and switched off her flashlight. "It looks good! Let's get it connected! Max, Lars, Sheila, and Albert, you guys come with me." To the remaining three, she said, "If we can get to the Fuel Control Center, then I will try to start the fuel flow to this station." She touched a small circular button on the nozzle connector. "When this light turns green, open up this valve and the fuel will come through. Keep your radios handy, so we can stay in touch." They turned away and started walking towards the main control center off in the distance.

2

Strapped to his seat, Andy gazed out the window as Tess and the others jogged towards a low, crumbling building off in the distance. *She's going to get us all killed on this wild goose chase,* he thought. During her speech earlier, he had listened intently even though he pretended to be asleep. The rest of them may have eaten up all that crap about needing extra fuel and some frigging *node*, but he knew better. He firmly believed that they could still catch up to the other ship. It wasn't too late. But the longer they wasted time here, the further out of reach Soren's ship would be.

He also knew something else; Henry would not allow him to live. *He'll either leave me here, or he'll kill me unless I kill him first.* The thought of bashing in Henry's brains seemed to give him comfort. He needed to get out of here though. He was lucky when he found the laser at the UN compound, but Joe or Henry had the laser now. Henry was gone, but Joe was outside keeping watch. He hadn't come in to check on him yet, but Andy had a feeling that Joe would make his rounds inside the ship soon.

He realized that he would need a weapon, but didn't have the slightest idea where to start looking in this obliterated landscape. As the ship was approaching the airfield, he hadn't seen one standing building. He was certain though, that he would be able to find something that he could use to take over the ship, but he would have to get Joe out of the picture. Joe was still angry about being cut loose in the crater, and Joe wouldn't hesitate to kill him.

A wild thought entered his head. If he could get off the ship and make a run for it, he might be able to round up some of the local populace with the promise of getting rescued. With a sizable force, he could come back and take the ship. Of course, he had no intention of taking any of them with him, but they could at least help him by fighting off the folks on the ground.

He smiled to himself thinking that he just might be able to do it. And the hell with Tess flying the ship; he would just force that youngster to fly it. Chayton-what's his name. *Yeah, this could work,* he thought. He glanced behind him to see who was around. The co-pilot was in the cockpit, and most of the others were on the ground despite Tess's orders to stay in the ship. Just then, he heard the powerful whoosh of the toilet being flushed and turned back around.

He turned around again when he heard the door open and saw that it was Julie, the pregnant woman. This was probably the fourth time she'd gone to the bathroom. She wasn't looking at him as she made her way to the front of the ship, rubbing her stomach. He turned quickly around and started opening and closing his legs, squeezing his eyes shut as he did it.

Julie walked up the aisle and glanced over at him, "Are you alright?" she asked tentatively. Andy noticed that she stayed a prudent distance from him.

He turned sharply at the sound of her voice, feigning surprise. "Oh! Hey Julie! I think I'm okay." He gave her a weak, pathetic smile and then grimaced in pain. *"Oww...owwww!* Not really Julie. I really need to use the can. I've been holding it for quite a while, but I think I've reached my limit. Joe is nowhere to be found, and if I don't get in there very soon, this place is going to smell!"

Julie unconsciously took two steps back. "I'll go get Joe; he can undo those zip ties." She started to turn around, when Andy started crying. "Please Julie. It'll be at least ten minutes before Joe makes it up here, and that will be too late. I don't think I can hold it for another five minutes." He looked up at her, his eyes rapidly filling up with tears. "And you know he hates my guts. He may make me wait just to get back at me."

Julie looked uncertain for a minute, took a tentative step towards Andy's seat, stopped herself and then moved closer to him. Even though she still looked uncertain, she said, "Okay Andy, I'll untie you. You've always been good to me, and I hate to see people suffer." She moved behind him to undo the zip ties holding his wrists to the sides of his seat. His eyes looked at her and showed immense relief and gratitude. He thought to himself that it was a look worthy of an *Oscar*.

MAN'S BEST FRIEND

1

Henry and his team's route to the shelters was nothing short of a meandering walk through a surreal nightmare, filled with burned out vehicles, unstable and crumbling buildings, and half buried skeletons. He checked their location often to make sure they were on track. He still had a strong signal from the shelter beacon, and his locator showed that they were within a mile, maybe half a mile of the shelter.

Apart from the dreary gray of the impenetrable sky covering, the temperature was warm, almost tropical. But he knew that in a matter of weeks or even days, that would change drastically. Kyra had estimated that the temperature would start to rise sharply within the next few weeks, but she conceded that it was only an estimate. Henry hoped that they would be well on their way to *Europa* by then.

He glanced at his watch. They had been walking for almost three hours and had only traversed about a mile. They were constantly detouring around, circling back, retreating, and climbing just to stay on their intended route. Despite their masks and the decreased gravity, they were all tired and wearing down.

The area they were in now looked like the huge parking lot of the Nu-Vista Mall, so named because of its lofty view of the surrounding hills and winding river. Rubble from neighboring buildings all but covered up the parking lanes. Debris was everywhere; in some areas, piled up at least 15 feet high. The buildings that were not destroyed leaned at dangerous angles. Bob insisted on inspecting a few of these buildings for supplies, but Henry advised against it. "This area was hard hit by the quakes Bob, and these tremors are very erratic. It would be just your luck to be in one of those buildings when a tremor hit."

The erratic tremors were an understatement. One minute there would be nothing, and then from deep underground they would feel the rumbling coming, like an oncoming avalanche. The tremors became so commonplace that whenever they stopped, Henry and his team noticed it right away.

They had seen no people, nor even a hint of people in the area. Henry had assumed that he would at least see homemade huts and shanties littered over the landscape, but there was nothing. Once, they came across a body that was a little more substantial than the many skeletons they had passed. The person had been dead for some time, but still looked fresh enough for them to tell that the person had been beaten to death. Upon closer inspection, Henry surmised that maybe the person hadn't been beaten to death, but beaten to submission and then tied to an old rusted street light. The rest of the body looked torn and ragged as if it had been partially eaten.

As they walked towards the dilapidated mall, they heard movement in the back seat of a rusted four-door sedan. They froze, staring intently at the vehicle. A small dog, a Shih Tzu maybe, hopped onto the ground. "Oh, how cute," Marla said and started towards it. Henry put his hand on her arm to stop her. "No Marla. Let's leave him alone. You notice he's not wagging his tail or backing up for that matter. He's not afraid of you. Hell, he's not even skittish."

But Marla had already reached into her jacket pocket to take out a small piece of jerky she had been munching on. She ignored Henry and tried to get the dog to come to her, but he held his ground. The little dog didn't seem afraid, but only watched them stolidly. When the dog made no move to come towards her, she tossed the food to him. It landed lightly, just in front of the two dirty paws. He glanced down at the food, and then looked back at Marla as if to say *surely there's more where that came from*. Surprisingly, the little dog didn't even lean forward to sniff the food or give any indication that something had been thrown at it.

"That's weird," Marla said. "He doesn't seem afraid of us, and he's showing no interest whatsoever."

Henry spoke up, "Yeah, but he certainly smells us. He's been sniffing the air around him the entire time. Come on you guys, let's get going."

Bob reached down and grabbed a baseball-sized rock. He tossed it up in the air a couple of times and then turned it over in his hand. He was tired, irritated, and a little scared of this weirdly rumbling landscape. The appearance of the dog was almost a welcome relief until it acted as if half its brain was out orbiting the planet with the rest of the debris. For no apparent reason that Bob could tell, this last affront to his senses was more than he could stand. Under his breath, he muttered, "Stupid fucking mutt," and hurled the rock straight at the dog.

Bob had never been a star athlete when he was young. As a child growing up, the only sports-related activity he enjoyed was swimming. His oldest brother, Reggie, had made the high school varsity baseball team and was praised as being the first black pitcher the school had ever produced. He tried to follow in his brother's footsteps, but throwing was never his forte. His throwing arm was usually so bad that he almost always lost carnival games if it involved throwing; whether it was darts at balloons, small rings at enlarged soda bottle necks, or rubber balls at furry characters that always seemed wider than they really were.

At any other time during his old life on Earth, probably nine out of ten times, Bob would have missed a throw. But *this* was the tenth throw because he nailed the dog on the hind quarters. It was a dead-on hit and landed with a solid thud. The dog gave a surprised yelp and ran off into the rubble. Before he ran off, he took a half step forward as if he were going to attack, but then turned around and darted between a couple of crushed and burned out cars. He was gone in seconds.

Bob pumped his fist in the air and yelled, "Yeah! I say yeah! That's what I'm talking about! Give me mah prize sistah!"

"Hey!" Henry snapped at Bob, "What the hell's up with you man? Just leave the dog alone. There's no need to antagonize him after all he's probably been through. He was probably already skittish of humans and after that, he might just piss on someone's leg the next time he has an opportunity."

"Henry," Marla said in a low voice. "I think he might do more than just piss on someone's leg. Look". She nodded in the direction the dog had gone, and Henry turned his head. There were three huge dogs standing where the little dog had just disappeared. He looked in the direction they had just come from and his heart sank; there had to be at least 15 to 20 dogs back there lining the trail and climbing over the heaps of rocks and rotted tree trunks. Apparently, the dogs had been tracking them and despite their mangy appearance and apparent malnutrition, most of them were big dogs.

"Oh shit," Billy Li said, barely audible over the eerily silent morning. "Don't make any quick movements!" Henry ordered. "I want everyone to slowly back up to Marla." They did so slowly. The dogs stared at them as if waiting for an order to attack. A huge headed dog muscled its way to the front of the dogs and stood looking at the strangers. To Henry, it looked to be Pit Bull mixed with Hellhound; its facial and body hair barely concealing the ugly scar tissue that marked its rise to the top of the pack.

The dogs appeared to be assessing them. *Maybe gauging our ability to fight,* Henry thought. The mall entrance was about 50 yards away and looked relatively intact. Henry initially had planned to detour around it because he didn't trust it to be structurally sound; but now they would have to run *through* it and trust that it didn't collapse around them. That was the only way they would lose the dogs. He slid his hand slowly into his jacket and wrapped his fingers around the surgical laser tool.

The rest of his group had found other various "weapons" along the way. There was a plethora of sharp and dangerous items to be found; so, it wasn't very difficult for them to find something they each felt that they could wield effectively if need be. Henry had actually uncovered a broadsword. The dull metal on the handle had caught the intermittent light from the sun at the right time, and Henry saw it. The blade itself was starting to rust, but with enough force, it could do the job. He had managed to secure it to his backpack in a way that allowed him to grab it quickly.

Right now, he had the laser, and he knew who its first target would be—*Cujo*, the Hellhound bastard himself. Maybe if he killed the leader, if that was the leader, then maybe it would slow down their attack while they fought over who was in charge. At least that's how it always worked in the movies.

He had been stepping slowly backwards, and he could see that the others were doing the same. When they all came within whispering distance of each other, Henry spoke out of the side of his mouth, "When I shoot that ugly fucker in front of us, you guys run like hell to the mall. I think he's the leader, and maybe it will slow them down until we get inside."

Bob, holding a solid piece of jagged steel at port arms said, "I'll stay here with you. At least we can divert some of the dogs, while the others hustle to the building." Henry considered arguing with this, but realized that Bob was probably right.

"Okay," he said. "We'll regroup at the far end of the building using our clickers to locate one another, but try to find a safe place first. Maybe inside, we'll have a better chance of fighting them off."

To his left, Billy Li said, "We better do something quick Henry; I think they're trying to flank us, if you can believe that shit."

Sure enough, four dogs were sneaking off to their side around a huge pile of debris. *How quickly they learn!* Henry thought. He pulled the laser out of his pocket and aimed it at the drooling Pit Bull. He caught movement out of the corner of his eye, but he kept his full attention on the slowly advancing pack of dogs to his front. Someone on his right, probably Billy Li grunted as he swung his leg back and kicked a lone attacking dog right in the midsection. It was one of the smaller ones and Billy's steel-toed boots connected hard and sure. The dog yelped once as its body flew through the air. It hit some protruding rocks, fell to the ground, and lay there writhing in pain.

They're testing our weaknesses, Henry thought and pressed the button on the laser. He felt that the next attack would be more than just testing their weaknesses. At first, he thought the laser had died because he didn't feel any response. The only indication that it was still working was from the faint heat he felt underneath. In front of him, however, not more than 20 yards away, he saw that he had actually hit the Hellhound in the leg. He barked out in pain and surprise and immediately started limping. It wasn't dead by any stretch, but what Henry saw next told him that in *this* wasteland, apparently being wounded was just as bad.

Five dogs peeled away from the oncoming pack and started attacking the fallen Pit Bull. It barked and looked at them reproachfully, but they kept at it until finally, one of them was able to clamp its yellowed teeth around the Pit Bull's neck. That's when Henry yelled at the top of his lungs, *"Run!"*

INSIDE THE FUEL CONTROL CENTER

1

When they arrived at the main building of the air base fuel control center, Tess's heart sank. The top two floors were demolished. She had hoped they might enter the underground control center from the main entrance, but now she was worried if they would be able to access the area at all.

The Underground Fuel Control Center was at sublevel three, the deepest part of the facility. It was positioned directly underneath the main entrance where a vertical staircase connected it to the sublevels below.

The only other option was an access security door on the other side of the facility, which opened into sublevel one. The area was well protected from the elements because it was built into a small hill, one level below the main entrance; but Tess was worried that they would not be able to gain access through this door because it required an access code.

As it turned out, she didn't need the access code because the exit doors were standing wide open. Although she breathed a sigh of relief, this seemed to bother her more than if the doors were actually closed off to them.

Tess hadn't discounted the fact that someone could have gotten inside. In fact, it could have been personnel who actually lived on the base or worked in the facility, but that still didn't calm her fears that the place had been occupied and that someone may still be inside, living here.

The food supplies that were stored here would have only lasted a few weeks, and there was nothing of real value here, except maybe some flashlights and medical supplies. What they were looking for would have no real value in this wasted world, and only a handful of people would even know what it was. The engine nodes would have been stored on sublevel one, behind a security door. She silently prayed that they were still there.

She looked around and felt encouraged. It was relatively dry in here, so maybe the doors were only recently opened. The fuel center was powered by its own facility generator which would have lost its charge ages ago. They would have to manually open the pumps and use the power from the *Orion* to draw the fuel into the ship.

She turned to the others as they picked their way carefully over the littered hallway, "Stay alert guys. Obviously, others have been here before, and I don't know for certain if they're still here or not. At the end of this hall there is a small room called the *Power Supply Room*. This is where the nodes were kept. God willing, we'll find them there and get them back to the ship."

They nodded at her gravely. She closed the door behind them and activated a chemical glow-stick. Its bright glow illuminated the dark cluttered hallway with yellow light at once. Despite the light from the chemical stick, the place was like a tomb. Tess stopped and listened periodically, but there was nothing. Although they wouldn't have known it, like Henry's group, they all had secured some type of weapon. Albert had found an M-16 military rifle near the entrance, but it was so rusted, no one trusted that it would even fire. A magazine clip was stuck inside and Albert had been fiddling with it to see how many rounds it contained.

They had not encountered any people yet, but it was apparent that someone had been here very recently. They saw muddy footprints everywhere that hadn't quite hardened yet. They checked every office they passed, and Tess found it odd that they had not seen *any* bodies at all. That little string of luck was broken when they forced their way into a room labeled *Server Room*. Someone had locked the door and piled all sorts of miscellaneous office equipment in front of the door. Once they got in, the smell of death hit them like a wave. In the far corner of the server room, behind two huge defunct computer systems, they saw a large mound of tattered clothing with skeletal arms, feet, and heads poking through. Sheila gave a scream and vomited onto a dusty keyboard sitting on a desk. After that, she avoided inspecting any of the remaining offices.

Finally, they made their way to the end of the hall. Three small steps led down to the *Power Supply Room* where the door was slightly ajar. On one hand, Tess was relieved that they would not have to figure out a way to get inside the room, but on the other, she was worried that the engine nodes would be gone. As she got closer to the door, she could see that someone had blown a hole through the locking mechanism to gain access to the room. She and Lars slowly pushed open the door while the others stood ready to stab or jab whatever came out at them.

The supply room was not a large room. It was about as big as a standard two-car garage. Empty shelves lined the walls and several large cabinets sat next to each other at the rear of the room in dark silence. As Tess shined her flashlight across the shelves, she began to despair. Someone had cleaned this place out. The few boxes left on the shelves contained nothing but used and broken computer parts. She ran to the cabinets and started flinging them open. There was nothing in the first two and a couple of empty boxes in the third one. The fourth cabinet contained a box that was half closed. Tess yanked it open and saw the cylindrical shape of an engine power node. She almost collapsed in relief.

"Is that the node?" Sheila asked anxiously.

Tess reached into the box, her hands shaking somewhat and pulled out the node. "Yes, this is it, thank God! It..." The words froze in her throat as she turned the node over in her hands. The underside had a huge chunk ripped out of it. She dropped it to the floor and covered her face. "Oh God, oh God" her muffled voice whispered through her fingers. "It's completely damaged," she said, her voice somewhat unsteady.

Lars picked it up and looked at it closely. "Hmm..." He stuck two of his fingers into the little motor and after a few tries, pulled out a semi-flattened piece of metal. "Looks like it took a bullet. Whoever shot through the door there hit it dead-on." He pulled off his backpack, unzipped it and dropped the node inside. "We might as well bring it with us. You never know, maybe we can fix it."

Tess looked at him, but said nothing. She knew better. These nodes were state of the art equipment with extremely sensitive internal components. About five years ago, she had an opportunity to visit one of the two manufacturing facilities for these components. She had to wear a static free suit just to enter the facility, and the closest she ever came to the components themselves was 25 yards away on the other side of a viewing glass. She would never tell them, but their chances of being able to fix this node were slim to none. "Alright guys, let's get going," she said to them. "We need to get the fuel started. Hopefully, everything down there is still intact."

2

Andy darted behind the hull of a burned-out jet. He knew it wouldn't be long before someone realized that he was missing. He hated ambushing Julie like he did because she was the only one who had ever really been nice to him. He absently rubbed his throbbing hand as he peeked around the edge of the jet. He didn't feel too guilty though. She was still breathing when he put her in the bathroom. She might have a heck of a headache when she comes to, but she'll be fine.

He looked towards the ship where Tess's ground folks were standing around. From this distance, he couldn't tell if the fuel was flowing or not. Since he didn't see Tess, he assumed that she had already headed to the main building to start the fuel pumps. He looked towards the buildings off in the distance and was mildly surprised to see that they were still standing. At that moment, the ground underneath him felt sickeningly like a wave. He could feel it undulating beneath the balls of his feet as he huddled there in the gloominess.

He looked up at the dark gray sky and cursed. He still could not believe that they were actually here. The planet felt ready to tear itself apart and the heaviness in the air made him feel as if he were breathing through a straw, despite the face mask he wore. Very far away, he heard an explosion. It was very faint, but it was there.

He looked back towards the building Tess had gone to and thought he caught movement there. He strained in that direction, but saw nothing else. Feeling confident that he had not been missed at the ship, he turned and headed towards the control center, certain that he would find a weapon that he could use.

NO WHERE TO RUN

1

Henry sprinted through the doors of the building. They had to get someplace that would give them some type of an advantage over the dogs. Fighting in the open would be certain death for them, because there were just too many dogs. If he could find some stairs or something they could jump on, they might have a chance.

As he ran, he caught glimpses of old familiar names in this dreary building. *The Gap, Foot Locker, Victoria's Secret, Pretzel King*, zipped past him as if in a dream. The floor canted at an abnormal angle and broken slabs of marble and concrete marred the normally smooth floor. Everywhere he looked, the windows had been broken out and it was clear that the stores would not offer them a place to hide or fight from. But certainly, there were *stairs* here. If not stairs, then an *escalator*! Directly in front of them stood a frozen escalator rising up to a badly damaged second floor.

"Escalator! Straight ahead!" Henry shouted. He bounded towards the escalator and took the stairs two at a time. He turned to see the first of the dogs pouring through the broken doors and coming in their direction. Marla was the last to hop onto the escalator and three of the dogs were getting very close. As she tried to take two steps, her foot came up short and she hit the escalator hard.

"Marla!" Henry shouted, but it was too late. Two of the dogs leaped onto her back and started tearing at the thick jacket she wore. The third one clamped onto her foot and started pulling her off the escalator. Della, who had been directly in front of Marla fought her way up the escalator and squeezed past Henry, Bob, and Billy Li.

"Come on! Let's get those dogs off her!" Henry yelled, but no one moved. They seemed transfixed by the horror happening before their eyes.

Della screamed back, *"We gotta get the hell out of here! She's gone man! Let's get out of here while we got the chance!"*

Cursing, Henry pulled the laser from his pocket and shot at the huge German Shepherd straddled on Marla's back. He missed because he was too worried about hitting Marla. He shoved the laser back in his pocket and bolted down the escalator, reaching behind him to grab the broadsword attached to his backpack. For one frightening moment it refused to come off, but he yanked at it until the strap finally came loose.

He moved straight toward the dog closest to Marla's head. Her hands were bloody as she tried to protect her face and head. This was a Doberman and Henry could see its ribs poking through its thin skin.

"*Hey!*" Henry roared at it and as it looked up, already ready to pounce, Henry rammed the sword into its mouth until it came out the back of the dog's neck. It grunted once and then went limp, falling on Marla's back. She screamed again and flailed her hands behind her.

The dog that had been dragging her had disappeared, and so had the other dogs. They were still here though because Henry could hear them running amid the debris. After shoving the dead Doberman off Marla's back, Henry said softly, "Hey Marla, they're gone. It's alright, you can turn over now."

She was shivering, but she turned over slowly. Her chin was bleeding where she hit the stairs and there was a nasty purple bruise growing on her lower face. She had only been bitten once, and that was on the hand. Other than her hand, the dogs did not break any skin. Henry attributed this bit of luck to the thick jacket and boots Marla was wearing.

He sat there holding her while she collected herself, trying to calm himself as well. The others would have left her to the dogs. They were standing higher up on the escalator stairs as he turned to face them. "How the fuck could you guys..." his voice froze in his throat. Now he saw where the other dogs had run off to. There were about seven large dogs at the top of the escalator. They hadn't quite started coming down the escalator stairs, but two of them had their front paws on the first step.

Henry said, "Della, come down here slowly. No quick movements. Do it now!" But Della, who had been sitting three steps down from the top, scooted up one more. "No man, we need to stay up here and find a way out of here. I'm not coming back down there." Something in his eyes, however, caused her to turn around and as she did, one of the dogs clamped its huge filthy mouth onto her windpipe.

The loud crunch was sickening as the dog bit down and yanked at Della's neck. Her hands flailed weakly at the head of the dog, while two other dogs, bit viciously into her face. In less than a minute, her hands flopped lifelessly to the stairs. Henry had made a move to go up there, but Bob put a hand on his shoulder. *No*, he mouthed the words and then pointed off to the side. A small army of at least ten dogs were racing around a dried up wishing well. They were coming back to the foot of the escalator.

Henry pulled Marla to her feet, and as he hopped off the escalator, he chanced a glance at Della. The dogs were pulling her limp body by the feet down the escalator. He could hear her head thumping on the stairs as they sprinted down one of the darkened hallways deeper into the mall. They were on the other side of a busted up merry go round, so had a small head start, but Marla would not be able to keep up this pace for long. Already, she was sagging heavily against him. He was thinking they needed to find a place for a last stand, when he heard the first of the dogs coming down the hall.

They were coming to a lighted area in the hallway, flanked by *Banana Republic* on one side and *Hollister* on the other. Bob and Billy Li were out front and suddenly skidded to a halt. Henry stopped too and was about to ask them why they stopped, when he saw the gaping hole in the floor. He looked up and could see the dirty gray sky pouring through the huge opening. He looked in the hole again and could only catch glimpses of concrete and metal. He had no clue how deep it went.

The *Hollister* store was completely demolished. Part of the cave-in had dumped concrete and steel in front of the store. The *Banana Republic* store offered no protection either. There was no door, and Henry could see all the way to the back. He noticed that all of the clothes were gone. He also realized that they would be trapped if they went in there. He turned around. The dogs were getting closer, and there were a lot of them. He spoke in Marla's ear, "Get ready to fight Marla, the dogs are coming."

Bloodied and bruised, Marla surprised him by reaching in her jacket and pulling out her huge knife. She bared her teeth in the direction of the dogs and prepared for their attack. The others did the same. For one brief second, Henry thought how far away things seemed just days ago. They were on the moon last week and here they were, in a busted mall, being chased by ravenous dogs. *Who would have thought it?*

The dogs were coming into view. Henry groaned inwardly at the sight of them. There had to be at least 20 of them. He could see the two who had attacked Della; her blood bright red on their mouths and noses. He would go for those two first. *If I'm going out, then I want to take those two bastards with me.*

The sharp taste of copper filled Henry's mouth as he waited for the charging dogs to attack them. He aimed the laser at one of the bloodied dogs and fired. The shot hit it dead in the chest and it fell hard, causing several dogs behind it to tumble and fall. He was about to fire again when he heard growling coming from his left. He yanked his head in that direction, his face a mask of pure terror and saw a huge German Shepherd emerging from the shadows of the *Banana Republic* store.

Before he even had a chance to decide which dog, he would try to shoot first, he felt something hit him on the left side of the head. He had actually felt something hit him when he first stopped at the huge hole in the ground, but his mind was so focused on the dogs and the oncoming fight, that he totally ignored it. When he looked this time, he saw a little boy and a little girl, standing next to the German Shepherd. They were beckoning wildly at him to come inside.

Henry looked at the dogs rushing at them from the main part of the mall and without thinking, grabbed Marla and shoved her towards the *Banana Republic* store. "*Get inside, now!*" he yelled at her.

For a minute, she was too dumbfounded to respond. Actually, seeing children in this desolate and destroyed place didn't seem to add up for her, but she ran anyway, ducking beneath the dipping doorway frame of the store's entrance.

The dogs were only 20 yards away. He yelled at Billy Li and Bob to get over to the store. They looked at him stupidly and then looked to where he was pointing. This time, there was only one kid waving at them to get inside. Understanding dawned on their faces, and they raced towards the door. Henry jumped through, followed by Bob. Billy Li had been on the far side of the hallway, closest to the *Hollister* store. He had almost made it to the door when one of the dogs jumped an amazing ten feet and hit him right in the chest. The impact of the dog landing on his chest pushed him towards the yawning chasm behind him. Henry had just enough time to see Billy Li and the dog go bowling over the edge of the floor, Billy Li screaming and the dog, incredibly, still trying to bite him as they fell.

He felt someone tugging on his arm. It was the little boy. He pulled back, but the nearest dog was only a few feet away from the entrance. He half turned, attempting to put his body between the boy and the dog, when he saw the boy leap straight up and grab one of the hanging steel girders in the ceiling. With his right hand, he hung from the beam; with his left, he reached into a small pouch hanging around his neck. He deftly pulled out a small cylinder, stuck it in his mouth and blew straight at the dog. Henry heard a soft whistle and then a meaty thud as the small dart imbedded itself into the dog's eye. It yelped loudly, tripped over its front feet and went skidding across the floor. The dog trembled violently for just a second and then was still.

The dog that had been right behind the first one, slowed down just a little when the first dog yelled out, but started turning into the store, when it saw Henry. Before Henry had a chance to settle into a defensive posture, the kid swung down from the beam in a high arch and solidly kicked the dog in the face. He landed smoothly and grabbed the frozen Henry by the shirt as he jumped feet first into a large hole in the floor. Henry jumped into the hole just as the main body of the dogs burst into the store.

And he found himself falling! He realized a second later that he wasn't exactly *falling*, but sliding on a very steep incline. He couldn't see any of the others and thought maybe he was the only one falling. He looked around for something to grab onto, but there was nothing but steel rods poking out at him from both sides. He crossed his arms over his chest and prepared for a hard landing somewhere below. As he slid, he realized that he didn't have his broadsword. At some point, he must have dropped it. He had a fleeting feeling of disappointment that was overshadowed by his rapid descent.

The slide felt interminably long and just when he thought that it would never end, the bottom dropped out and then he really was falling. If he could see where he was falling, it wouldn't have been so bad, but he was falling in darkness. The scant light above only showed him that he was falling in some type of cave. He tensed up, instinctively knowing that he was about to slam into the hard bottom at any minute, and that's when he heard the splashes.

He tensed up again, but this time, he prepared himself for a water landing. It was going to be a hard hit, but water was softer than concrete. Faintly, he heard the sounds of splashes below him and knew that the others were down there too. He just hoped he didn't land on someone's head.

He hit the water hard, as he had expected, and his momentum carried him deep. Immediately, he spread his arms to slow his descent and started kicking furiously towards the surface. He saw lots of fish as he made his way up to the surface.

"There's Henry!" Bob shouted, as he started swimming towards him. Marla and the little girl were holding on to the side of the cave wall. The little boy was nowhere to be seen.

"Henry! Over here man!" Bob half yelled, half coughed as he made his way towards Henry. He swam up to him. "You okay?" he asked.

"Yeah," replied Henry. "Just a little water up my nose. How's Marla? Where is she?"

"She's over there with the little girl. The little boy was here, and then he went under. I tried to find him, but it gets too murky the deeper you go."

"That kid saved our lives! We need to find..." Just then, a small head popped out of the water. The kid smiled hugely and began treading water with his legs only. He lifted both arms out of the water and raised the gleaming broadsword up towards Henry.

Henry was shocked. Maybe he had the sword in his hands the entire time he was falling. Or did he drop it in the store and the kid grabbed it? He didn't know for sure. He was just glad that it hadn't impaled anyone on the way down.

In spite of himself, he smiled back at the kid and reached for the sword. The sword was heavy, which meant that the kid was an incredibly strong swimmer to be able to raise the sword above his head. He waded over to the side of the cave where Marla and the little girl were. The little girl seemed to have taken a liking to Marla immediately.

He steadied himself on the wall, standing on a small outcropping in the water. Bob helped him strap the sword to his back. "You guys saved our lives up there. Thank you!" The boy smiled and pounded on his chest with one fist, "I'm Tarzan!"

Henry laughed and said, "Alright Tarzan! Well thanks for your help." Something occurred to him and his hand shot to his waist band. "Shit! The walkie-talkie's gone!" he said. He wasn't sure when he lost it, but if it was in the water, then it was just as good as gone. Realizing there was nothing he could do about that now, he looked at the kid curiously and asked, "By the way, what happened to the other dog? *Your* dog. Where did he go?"

"That was Buddy. He will meet us at the gate. He does not like to swim." At that, both he and the little girl giggled. Henry turned to the little girl, "And what's your name, honey?"

The little girl drew close to Marla and said, "Yoi". Henry thought for a moment trying to remember where he'd heard her name before and then remembered from his karate days the command to move to the ready position. Yoi. He smiled at her, "Thank you Yoi for helping us. We were in big trouble up there. Is there anywhere we can go to get out of the water?"

The boy, who looked to be about 12, maybe 13, now that Henry had a chance to see him up close, nodded and said, "Yes, over this way. It's not far." He started swimming slowly, moving deeper within the mouth of the cave.

2

"And you're sure she's okay?" Tess asked anxiously through the walkie-talkie. She was leaning against the wall with the walkie-talkie pressed tightly up against her ear. The others were just returning from checking out the rest of the rooms on sublevel three. They hadn't found another node, but they were able to manually release the fuel into the fueling station on the runway. She could hear Chayton in the background issuing refueling instructions to the others at the ship.

Kyra responded immediately, "Yes, she's fine. I can't believe that bastard would hit a pregnant woman!"

"Yeah, I know Kyra. And no one saw which way he went?"

"No, but we think he might be headed your way, so be careful and keep an eye out for him." She could hear the nervousness in Kyra's voice clearly.

"Will do Kyra. The fuel's flowing, and we've found all we can find here. It'll take at least a couple of hours, so I'm leaving Max and Lars here to shut it off when it's done. Unfortunately, we didn't find an engine node, but it's quite possible that whoever broke in here took the other node. Henry will need to find out if our shelter folks have it. Any word from them yet?"

There was silence on the other end and when Kyra finally responded, her voice sounded heavy. "We lost contact with them about an hour ago. We got their last position, and that was it. They never called back at their check-in time." Another pause. "Tess, I'm worried. Henry is very prompt about stuff like that. If he didn't call back, it must be that they're in trouble or worse."

Oh God, Tess thought. "I agree with you Kyra," Tess said. "The planet's becoming more and more unstable, and soon we won't have a choice what we do. The rest of us are coming back to the ship to bring the few supplies we found here. I need to start prepping the ship for takeoff as soon as it's done refueling. We should be back at the ship in about 30 minutes, and we'll figure out what to do next. In the meantime, you guys keep an eye out for Andy, in case he comes back to the ship."

Tess clicked off with Kyra and looked around at the group. "As you guys heard, Andy escaped, and we've lost communications with Henry and his team. Max, Lars...you guys look out for Andy. He may be on his way here now, so be careful. Do whatever it takes to keep safe. He's dangerous and unpredictable and he can stay here and rot on Earth for all I care. It seemed such an inhumane thing to leave him on the moon, but if he keeps this up, he's going to get someone killed."

"If he comes here, we'll be ready for him," Lars replied. He was holding a huge pipe that almost looked like a steel baseball bat.

Tess smiled at him, "I know you will Lars." She walked into the fuel control room. "When this needle stops, that means that Chayton has stopped the draw on the fuel. When that happens, you should close the opening, and then get back to the ship as soon as possible."

3

They headed back up to the first sublevel. They hadn't been at the facility for very long, but it looked as if the sky had darkened while they were inside, despite the scant light coming in through the open door. It was barely after 11am, but the heavy cloud cover seemed to block most of the light.

Tess looked around nervously. She could have sworn that they had closed the door after they came in. She turned to the others and put her fingers to her lips. "Keep it down guys. I'm pretty sure we closed that door after we came in, but now it's open." Her eyes darted around the gloomy interior. "Andy could actually be in here somewhere or just outside that door."

Albert, who had the M-16 rifle strapped to his back, stepped in front of Tess. He unslung the weapon from his shoulder, checked the safety and then walked to the door. The magazine clip that was in it only had two rounds and he wasn't sure if it would even fire, but it would certainly scare someone.

He stepped through the door, pointing the M-16 to his left, as he had no doubt seen from old police shows. He swung the other way in similar fashion, finger hovering near the trigger. He lowered his weapon and looked back at Tess and Sheila, shrugging his shoulders. "All's clear," he began and then he was thrown off his feet as a huge explosion filled the air. Tess had not quite made it to the threshold of the door, but the explosion was powerful enough to throw her back into the room and up against a side wall. She slumped to the floor like a lifeless doll.

The force of the blast knocked Sheila back into the room where the bodies had been piled on top of each other. She flipped over one of the desks in the room and was rammed into the pile of bodies. She could feel the bones breaking and giving way as her momentum pushed her deeper into the pile. She was disgusted and wanted to scream, but her mind felt detached as she felt herself sliding towards unconsciousness. As the musty decay of the bodies intermingled with the acrid smell of explosives, Sheila's last conscious thought was that of running footsteps, yelling voices, and frantic fighting.

THE SHELTER

1

They sat around the small fire close to the water's edge, while the fish sizzled and crackled above the fire. The children had led them about a half a mile deeper into the cave to a small alcove. After a few minutes of scrounging for anything that would burn, they were able to get a fire started. Before Henry could finish dressing Marla's wounds, the kids had caught a few fish and had them sizzling on the fire.

After eating, Bob nudged Henry on the arm. "I'm at a loss here Henry. I know we landed in North San Antonio, but I didn't think that San Antonio had huge bodies of underground caverns like this. And the water's *warm*. Did you notice that?"

"Yeah," Henry replied, "these earthquakes have caused some drastic changes." He thought a moment and then added, "In fact, I actually think we're in the Edward's Aquifer. It should be colder, but somewhere the water's being warmed."

"Or cooked," Bob corrected.

He looked over at the children. The little girl had her head on Marla's lap, while Marla stroked her hair. The boy was sitting against the wall of the cave. He was cleaning the little tube that he used when he shot something in the dog's eye earlier.

Henry walked over to him and sat down. "Thanks again for helping us up there. If you guys hadn't shown up when you did, things would have gone quite badly for us." The boy looked up at him and smiled, but said nothing. Henry looked down at the tube in his hands. "May I see that?" he asked, holding his hands out. The boy upended the tube and shook out a thin, almost translucent sliver into his hand and then handed the tube to Henry.

Henry turned the tube over in his hands. It was a thin steel tube about three inches long and smaller than his little finger. Somehow, the kid had fitted an old smoking mouthpiece onto one end of the tube. To Henry, it looked perfect for blowing darts or needles. "What did you blow through it to stop the dog? Was it a poisonous dart?"

The boy held out his hand to Henry, showing him the thin sliver. "It comes from the fish in here. The fat pointy fish." He opened up his bag and pulled out a small salt and pepper shaker. The holes were all clogged up except the one in the center. Henry could see that the shaker was packed with the needles.

"The Puffer Fish?" Henry asked. He knew that those fish were extremely poisonous, but it was obvious from the needles in the shaker, that the kid knew how to handle them. He handed the tube back to the boy. "Where do you live? Are there any grownups there?"

"We live in the shelter with Miz-T," he answered directly. He turned and pointed up towards the wall of the cave.

Henry's eyes widened. "At the shelter? With Miz-T? Misty? Can you take us there?"

"Yes, two ways though." He considered this for a moment. "Underwater will take one half of the hour. Outside will take three of the hours."

"Whoa!" Bob said, "Wait a minute, *30* minutes to swim underwater? What are you talking about kid? No one can hold their breath for 30 minutes."

Henry turned sharply towards Bob. "Come on man, settle down. Let him finish." He turned back to the boy and said, "What do you mean? Underwater for 30 minutes? We can't hold our breath—no one can hold their breath that long. Can you explain?"

The kid thought a moment and then got down on his knees and started drawing in the dirt. Henry and Bob stood over him and watched as the boy wrote and drew in the dirt. When he finished, Henry smiled and said, "I think we'll take the 30-minute route."

2

Henry was worried about Marla because of her wounded hand, but Yoi had stayed with her the entire way under the water. And it wasn't a long trip after all. Henry estimated that the entire trip under the water to this opening was only about 15 to 20 meters. Any longer might have been questionable, but here they were, standing in another huge cavern. It was drier here, but Henry wondered how long it would be before this area flooded too.

"The shelter is this way," Yoi said, pointing towards the darkest part of the cave. As he started walking, Henry snapped open another light stick and looked down at the ground. He could see a well-worn path heading off in the distance.

They walked in silence until they came to a bend in the trail. They turned onto it and saw movement ahead, maybe 30 feet away. The dark shadow crouched and then sprinted towards them. Henry made a move to grab the little boy by the shoulders, to stop him before it was too late. But it was too late, the shadow, which Henry assumed was an animal had closed the distance quickly. The boy went down to one knee as the animal ran towards him, closing the last five feet by leaping in the air towards him.

Henry opened his mouth to yell, when he recognized the German Shepherd that they had seen in the *Banana Republic* store. It ran towards the kid and they both lay on the ground playing and tussling. Yoi disengaged herself from Marla and joined in the fray. Henry, Marla, and Bob stood there smiling while the dog licked the children in their faces.

They continued walking and within minutes arrived at a huge metallic door set into the stone. Henry wondered what the plan was when they built the shelter with a door here. He looked around. There didn't seem to be an exit out of this cavern except by the way they had come. But then he remembered the massive shifting of the earth and considered that maybe there was an outlet here originally.

Yoi picked up a rock and banged out a pattern of loud and soft knocks, reminding Henry of Morse Code communication. After a few minutes, a series of taps drifted out from the inside. She responded with a few more taps and waited. More taps emerged from inside, to which Yoi responded with one tap. It sounded as if they were having a full- blown conversation. All of sudden, the sound of gears turning and bolts sliding came through the door. Slowly, the big door swung open, the hinges screaming loudly in the silence of the cave.

It opened about two feet and then stopped. Both of the children and the dog stepped through, but before Marla could get close, the bore of a rifle was thrust in her face. "Hold it right there!" a woman said. "These kids trust you, but that don't mean I do. What group are you with?"

Henry answered from behind Marla. "Please ma'am. Would you please put the gun down? We're not here to do you any harm, I promise. Your children saved our lives. If it wasn't for them, we wouldn't have made it from the mall."

The rifle never wavered, "You still didn't answer my question. I said what group are you with?"

"We're not part of any group." Henry responded, "We came from one of the moon bases, and we just landed this morning over at Wright Airfield."

There was a long pause and then the disembodied voice said a little shakily, "I don't believe you. Why in God's name would you come back here? To Earth? To *this*?"

Henry had slowly maneuvered Marla out of the way of the gun and stood in her place. He spoke softly to the woman. "Ma'am, I'm very sorry if this is upsetting for you. Truly I am. We need your help. If you would please lower your weapon and let us come in, we can talk about it."

The woman didn't remove the rifle, but she lowered it so that it was pointing towards the ground. "I swear that if this is a trick, I'll blow you all to kingdom come. My kids are very trusting, but generally they're a good judge of people."

"I think we can help each other, but we first have to start trusting one another," Henry replied.

Another long minute of silence; Henry was about to speak up again when the rifle barrel disappeared inside the door. "Alright, come on inside and let's talk."

3

They stepped inside a semi-dark entryway. The faint musty smell reminded Henry of exercise locker rooms. The ceiling was low and the dim bulbs mounted in the ceiling and encased in metal cages flickered off and on, making the shelter seem even gloomier. Henry looked around and could only see two other adults; a man and a woman. They both had rifles and they were pointed directly at the newcomers. The woman who spoke to them through the doorway, moved from the closed door to the front and led them through the passageway.

Henry felt someone squeeze past him and looked down, only to see Yoi making her way back to Marla, who was the last in line. She grabbed Marla's hand as they walked slowly down the narrow corridor.

The woman leading the way was walking very slowly and appeared to be limping. He hadn't gotten a good luck at her, but she looked to be an older woman, late 50's maybe. When they were speaking through the door, Henry had picked up on the anger in her voice, but there was something else there too. Weariness. "Right this way," she said as she turned into one of the side rooms off the corridor.

They entered a small, indistinct room containing a rectangular table with several chairs pushed underneath. The woman sat down at the table and motioned to the others to sit as well. The man sat down too, while the woman stood guard at the entrance.

From across the table, the woman looked at her visitors and then slowly shook her head. "So, you guys came *back* to Earth from the moon? I don't know what's worse. That you came back here, or that I believe you. So, tell me, what's so important that you had to come back to this Godforsaken place?"

Henry looked at Marla and Bob and then back at the woman. "I know it sounds crazy ma'am, but we had no other choice. My name is Henry. Henry Wilhelm. This is Marla Wilson, and that's Bob St. Pier. Two others in our group didn't make it."

"I'm sorry to hear that, I really am. My name is Thelma. Thelma Branson. You've met the kids; that's Yoi Nguyen, and the young man is Len Robinson. Welcome to North San Antonio Shelter #2."

SHEILA

1

Sheila's head was pounding, and she feared she may have drunk just a bit too much last night at dinner. Most people slid past the imaginary line separating sobriety and drunkenness without as much as a glance but not Sheila. She knew her limit, down to the sip. So, on the mornings when she woke up with a hangover and a pounding headache, she knew exactly which glass it was that did her in.

But she didn't drink last night, did she? She kept her eyes closed tightly, trying to remember what had happened last night. *Maybe I'll stay in bed a little while longer, and then get up and make an appointment to see the doctor,* she thought. But even as that thought was being developed, it seemed utterly alien and untrue. She lay there for a minute with her eyes shut, trying to figure out where she was and why she had such a God-awful taste in her mouth!

Slowly, the memories labored their way to the surface of her awareness. *Planet Earth, refueling, gunfire! Bodies!* With growing disgust, she remembered falling or being pushed into a pile of rotted bodies. She had vomited earlier and realized belatedly, that the sour taste in her mouth was from when she vomited the second time. She opened her eyes and kicked and wriggled herself out of the pile of bodies until she was able to pull herself out and onto the floor. She realized fearfully that if their attackers were still here, they would certainly have heard her by now.

She was about to pull herself completely out of the pile, when something on her shoulder seemed to hold her back. She turned her head and saw bony fingers clasped onto her shoulder, a Timex watch dangling loosely from the wrist. A bone sliver from the cracked wrist had snagged her jacket and caused the hand to hang on her shoulder in a disgustingly familiar way. Repulsed, she yanked the hand from her shoulder, causing it to break at the wrist, and hurled it away from her. It skittered across the floor like a large dry centipede.

She wiped her mouth on her sleeve and started to get up when a sharp pain in her thigh caused her to yell out involuntarily. Keeping her leg still, she shoved the bony bodies away from her, to get a good look at her leg. In the faint light, she could see a large dark spot covering the entire side of her thigh and in the middle of the spot was a three-inch bone sliver protruding from her thigh.

"Oh shit! I can't believe this!" She closed her eyes and tried to calm her breathing with no luck. She knew that she would not be able to walk with that thing in her leg, but she didn't know if she had the strength (*or guts?*) to pull it out. She started thinking of the pros and

cons of pulling it out. *If I start bleeding too much, then I could black out here.* The idea of blacking out in this office mausoleum was a horrible thought, but she had to find the others.

She gritted her teeth and dragged herself out of the pile, trying to keep her leg perfectly still. The room was semi-dark, but the hall outside the door glowed faintly yellow. Probably one of the light sticks that they carried. She dragged herself over to the door and peeked outside the room. The light stick was on the floor near the door. Its normally extreme bright yellow color had dulled to a paler yellow, meaning that it was almost dead. She knew the sticks could last for a good three to four hours, which meant that she must have been out at least an hour, maybe more. She got to a sitting position with her back against the door jam, keeping her eyes glued to the outside door and activated her own light stick. She didn't know what she would do if they came back, but she didn't have time to worry about that now.

Then the thought hit her that Max and Lars had been on the third sublevel below waiting to turn off the fuel pumps once the ship had been refueled. She had to get to them, but the idea of sliding down the stairs and accidentally pushing the sliver in deeper made her feel queasy. No, she would have to remove the sliver first, and then make her way down to the next level. If she was certain that no one was outside, she would have simply yelled for them to come get her, but that was a dangerous option.

She looked around the room wondering what she could use as a bandage around her leg once she removed the sliver, but the room was too dark to see anything that she might be able to use. She thought furiously, but didn't recall seeing a medical kit when they first searched the place.

A fine layer of sweat was just starting to form on her forehead and her thigh burned hotly. Just then, she thought of the t-shirt she wore under her jacket. It was still relatively clean, if not a little sweaty. She slid out of her jacket and shirt and pulled the t-shirt over her head. With a little effort, she got a tear started and tore it into several strips.

With that being done, she steeled herself to the pain she knew was coming and spat on one end of the torn t-shirt. She wiped off as much of the slick blood as she could and then wrapped a clean end around the protruding end of the white sliver. Gritting her teeth, she pulled the sliver up and away from her. She felt white-hot panic when it refused to budge, but an extra effort caused the bone sliver to become unstuck. She continued pulling, grunting, and cursing until the remaining inch of bone slid out of her leg.

She dropped the sliver from shaky fingers and fell back to the floor, her breath coming in huge gasps. She lay there for a full minute before she felt strong enough to sit up without fainting. Her light stick had fallen from her mouth when she fell back to the floor and rolled under the only desk in the room. She sat up grimacing and tied the strips around the wound tightly. Cursing, she lay back down and stretched her arm under the desk for her light stick. She barely touched it with her fingertips and only succeeded in pushing it further under the desk. *"Uggghh...fuck this!"* she cried out in the dark. She almost left it under the desk, but decided to try for it once more. Lying on her stomach and careful not to put any weight on her injured leg, she crawled as far as she could go under the desk. She saw her light stick resting up against something dark underneath. For a minute, she was disgusted, thinking that it was a body part somehow detached from the pile she had dug herself out of earlier. But it wasn't a body part. It looked like a belt or a bag, so she grabbed it before backing out from under the desk.

She stuck the light stick between her teeth and looked closely at the item she had pulled out. It was part of a military uniform, the kind of utility belt that soldiers would wear around their waists. It had two large pouches on both sides. One had three magazine clips that looked to be full and the other had six narrower clips with smaller, fatter gun rounds. As she inspected the belt further, she could see that the other pouch had the same thing. She was surprised to see that the belt had two hand grenades and a holstered hand gun.

Somewhat comforted, she put her shirt and jacket back on and then strapped the military utility belt on. She steeled her nerves and started pulling herself towards the stairs. She realized that the pain was not as bad as it was when the sliver was still in, but her leg was damned tender. She got her good leg under her and using her arms, pulled herself up onto one of the desks that had been pushed into the hallway. She stood up and tested the weight on her good leg and realized that she might be able to limp down to the next level.

She limped over to the handrail of the stairs and slowly, painstakingly, made her way down to the third level. The entire third level was the fuel pump control center, but the actual pump controls were in the first room, luckily for her. She moved as quietly as she could up to the door and peeked in. It was empty. She hobbled in and almost tripped over a backpack lying on the floor. She grimaced, thinking that a spill right now would certainly incapacitate her. She grabbed the backpack and put it on, looking around the room. She began to wonder if Max and Lars were in one of the other rooms, when it dawned on her that they must have heard the gunfire upstairs and ran up there to help.

She could feel cold fingers of terror scratching at her psyche and knew that in a moment, she would be so terrified that she would not be able to function. She looked around the room, anxious to do anything that would keep her mind from getting the best of her. She saw a flashing yellow light on the refueling equipment. She moved up close to the wall unit and using her light stick, peered at the small letters under the pale light - *Flashing Yellow Light Indicates Refueling Is Complete. Stop Pump. Close Fuel line.*

She considered this and realized that Max and Lars never stopped the pumps. This thought brought fresh fear because it meant that something might have happened to them. She went back to the door and peeked out. After a few minutes of looking, she returned and stopped the pump and then closed the fuel line.

She didn't realize the low humming the machinery was making all this time until it finally stopped. Now the place seemed eerily quiet. She looked around and saw another backpack leaning up against the far wall. She limped over to it and picked it up. It was empty. All of a sudden, she was afraid to go back upstairs, suddenly sure that the attackers were still in the place, waiting for her to surface. But she couldn't stay here. She had to get back to the ship and warn them and somehow figure out where Tess and the rest of the group were.

She climbed the stairs carefully, trying to think of a plan, but the only thoughts and images that came back to her were shadows in the dark that slowly moved in on her. She pushed the thoughts out of her head and continued on towards the last flight of stairs that led to the first sublevel. At one point, she had to sit down and use her arms and good leg to get up the flight of stairs. After what seemed an interminably long time, she made her way to the stairway door leading to the first sublevel.

Slowly, she limped across the floor towards the exit door, which hung at an odd angle. She almost screamed as she got closer to the door—it was coated with congealed blood and chunks of bone and gray matter. Her stomach lurched as she moved past it, seeing out of the corner of her eye strands of hair sticking out from the gray matter.

As she inched her way over the threshold, she half remembered that Tess was very close to the door when the explosion happened. She almost cried out loud with the realization that Tess had been blown up and wondered what they would do now without her. Tess had been the driving force for them when Soren abandoned them on the moon. And now she was gone. Sheila almost didn't allow herself to believe it until she stepped over the threshold and saw a sprawled body lying awkwardly on the ground, the head buried in a puddle of muddy water.

She limped over to the body fearfully, not wanting to look at it or touch it, but knowing she couldn't leave her like that. The urge to vomit was overwhelming, but she forced it down as she looked at the bloodied head caked with dried blood and brain bits. Crying, she leaned over and pulled at the tattered sleeve of Tess's shirt to turn her over. She only meant to pull the body out of the mud, but she pulled too hard, and it rolled over onto its back. Sheila screamed and jumped back, almost falling.

"I'm so sorry, Tess..." she began and then stopped. Even though half the face was gone, Sheila could see the unmistakable moustache framing the twisted mouth of Albert. "Oh Albert," She whispered silently. "I'm so sorry this happened to you."

Tess was missing, not dead, she realized. Although she felt bad for Albert, she didn't quite give up hope. Tess was alive, and so was their chance at getting off the planet. She grabbed the M-16 rifle that Albert's body had been lying on top of and slowly hobbled back toward the ship, casting nervous glances behind her.

THE BARBARIANS

1

Tess's head finally cleared. She had floated in and out of consciousness as they rolled and bounced along the rough road. Her hands and feet were bound, and she was lying on her side. She knew that Albert must be dead. The explosion was strong enough to knock her off her feet, and she was at least 15 feet from the door. Albert had actually stepped through the door. She squinted in the gloom and could barely make out Max and Lars. Albert wasn't there, which confirmed that he was probably dead.

She could hear their attackers talking, but she couldn't make out full sentences. She caught the word "moon-folks" a couple of times and "shuttle ship", but the bulk of their conversation eluded her. Once or twice she heard them arguing, and there was probably a scuffle but that was about it. She had no clue where they were going or how far they had gone. She didn't feel her watch on her wrist and assumed that they took it from her. She craned her neck to look behind her and between the boarded up back of the wagon and could see two people walking behind them, each holding a leash to a dog.

Two men wearing vests walked in front of a skinny man leading a skinny horse that pulled the wagon with Tess and her companions. They were both carrying thick shafts of wood, each with a large blade meticulously attached to the end. The larger man's stick had been fashioned with an axe blade on one side and what looked like a sickle on the other. From the middle of his stick jutted a long thick silver shaft that ended in a sharp point. It was stained a dull red.

The smaller man walked a few steps in front of the bigger man as if he was too important to walk with the rest, but he walked with a pronounced limp. He turned to his left to speak to the larger man. "Brutos, let me see the items you retrieved from these intruders." As Brutos handed the bag over, the small man looked into his eyes. "And I trust you checked the dead one thoroughly? No chance of bringing him back?"

Despite his towering height over the smaller man, Brutos answered in a low, very servile manner, "Yes, Lord Vanek. He was full of shrapnel. He died an impure death."

Vanek murmured something and continued rooting in the bag that Brutos had given him. Most of the items appeared worthless at first glance. The woman's watch would be good, as would the walkie-talkie. He would not turn it on just yet, but when the time came, he would use it to lure the moon-folks here, where they would have the advantage. Here, they would be purified before the onset of the *last days*. And their purification would be the final bounty he had promised his followers.

Vanek and his small band turned off onto a road that looked to be in better condition. It led to their home at the base of the high rising hills. He always got a thrill when returning home from what he liked to think of as *the hunt*. He saw himself as Julius Caesar, returning to Rome after conquering some wayward and uncivilized barbarian horde.

The road meandered through a jungle of downed trees as it got steeper and steeper. The skinny horse struggled as the wagon's weight started pulling against him. The two men walking behind the cart moved up close to help, grumbling. After a few hundred yards, the road leveled out and came upon a small guard shack. Surprisingly, the large barbed wire fence showed very little damage, compared to the surrounding area. They leaned-in at awkward angles, but for the most part, still maintained a *keep out* air about them.

The raggedly dressed guards came to attention and saluted Vanek and Brutos as two other men rolled back the gates. The gates were once powered by electricity, but now sat on rusted wheels and rolled back grudgingly. Vanek and Brutos entered a walled off area that housed a large exercise field that was used primarily for exercise back in its pre-*Lycos* days; but now it functioned as a general assembly area for Vanek and his people. He looked at the circular field, with the bleachers on both sides and imagined he was walking into a Roman coliseum.

Vanek had never been to Rome or even out of the US, with the exception being his one and only time on a plane flying from Texas to Chicago to pick up a delicate piece of equipment for the engineering group located at the NASA engineering center in San Antonio. Rough weather that spanned several mid-western states had forced their plane to detour to Toronto. The plane was grounded in Toronto for several hours and although Vanek never left the plane, he bragged to his fellow co-workers back in Houston that he had spent hours touring the city and buying souvenirs for all of them. Unfortunately, according to Vanek, the bag containing the souvenirs was "stolen" out of the overhead storage bins by one of the other passengers.

"Brutos, when we return, I want you to prepare the big guy for purification. The people will need their resolve and energy to meet this crisis from the moon."

"Yes, Lord Vanek," Brutos replied, glancing back at the trailer. As they walked toward *Community Home*, the name that Vanek called the prison, the ground rumbled and off in the distance a muffled explosion drifted across the flattened and irregular landscape.

2

Henry sipped his hot coffee carefully while Thelma recounted the final days and hours before the meteor impact, the terrifying massive earthquakes, and the bleak uncertainty of their lives from day to day. At one point, Henry had suggested that maybe the children should step out of the room, but Thelma dismissed this, advising him that the children were well aware of their situation. "They *live* it every day," she had said.

"These children have adapted much more easily to their new environment than most of the adults here," she continued. "Of course, they were terrified in the beginning, and the shock waves seemed to be endless during those first weeks. Eventually, we simply resigned ourselves to the fact that our deaths could happen at any moment. These shelters were designed to withstand extreme underground stresses, but not of this magnitude. We were lucky. And when I say we, I mean the southern part of Texas. There was minimal flooding, despite our closeness to the Gulf of Mexico. One of our geologists suggested that a fissure opened up deep within the Gulf of Mexico and diverted the waters from us." As Thelma was speaking, Henry recalled the huge chasm he had seen as their ship flew over the Gulf of Mexico. Texas, Louisiana, and a number of other states were indeed lucky in that respect.

"For a while, we were in touch with the other shelter here in North San Antonio, the one in Houston, the one in Dallas, and two in New York, if you can believe that!" Thelma added. "But we lost touch with most of them immediately after the first few hits. We held onto to Dallas for about a month, but they reported to us that the earthquakes had damaged their structural integrity. They were buried alive. Our only contact was the radio operator on duty at the time. He was trapped there by himself and eventually died of thirst and starvation. I think he went crazy in the end."

"What about the other San Antonio shelter?" Henry asked. "How long did you maintain contact with them?"

"They went off the air about three months ago. They reported that their food stores were inaccessible after a series of earthquakes tore through the area and damaged their shelter. It killed most of the people who were housed in that part of the shelter. There were only 15 of them remaining and at least five were children. We voted to send out a rescue party to bring them here, but we lost their signal before the rescue party could leave.

"Since their shelter was only 15 miles away, we decided to go to them anyway. By the time our team made it there, the shelter was empty, and there had been signs of fighting. There were bullet holes, shrapnel, and lots of blood, but no bodies. Our guys gathered what they could and got the hell out of there, but were followed all the way back here and then attacked."

She waved her arms around at the other two adults in the room. "At the time, we were working outside the shelter on the other side, with Yoi. When we returned, everyone was gone, except for Don, the geologist I mentioned earlier. An explosive device must have landed very close to him because his body was shredded with pieces of shrapnel. He told us what had happened before he died. He started crying and told us that Linda, his wife, had been shot in the head before he could get to her. We looked everywhere for her body, but it was nowhere to be found."

She paused for a minute and then added shakily, "They've taken 16 of our kids." She glanced over at Len, who was in the corner sharpening the small blade he kept around his waist. "They captured him too, but he escaped six days later and made it back here. I don't know how he did it, but that boy has a gift for directions in this directionless landscape."

Henry smiled as he looked at Len. "I still can't believe that Tess's son is alive. I wish I could let her know somehow." He lowered his voice and leaned toward Thelma, "And no word from Stan, or the other adults who were kidnapped?"

"No, nothing," Thelma replied. "According to Len, the children had been separated almost immediately after they left here. He said he only saw his father once after that. We considered going after them, but there were only three of us. We stayed inside for at least a week after the incident, expecting them to attack us again, but no one ever came back. After Len returned, we just knew they would come back, but there have been no other attacks. Nothing. Eventually, Yoi and Len started foraging for food and found an entrance to the underground body of water."

"Yeah, the Edward's Aquifer," Henry stated. He looked around at the little group, both saddened and impressed by their toughness and resourcefulness. "Thelma, I'm sorry to hear what happened to your group. I can't imagine the pain and suffering you and your people have endured. Our situation, although not as bad as yours, is still questionable.

"When we landed, the airfield looked to be in pretty good shape, so getting the fuel shouldn't be too difficult. As long as the underground fuel depot is intact, we're still in business. Our biggest challenge will be finding an engine power node. Without that, we may not have enough power to leave Earth's gravity or even make it to *Europa*. And food. We were hoping to find food at this shelter."

Thelma straightened up in her seat, her eyes flashing angrily. "*What?* And what if we said *no*? Would you have attacked us for it?"

Henry could feel the tension increase almost instantaneously in the room. Len looked up from what he was doing in the corner while the two holding weapons shifted uneasily.

"No!" Henry put forth immediately. "We would never do that Thelma. Our goal was to bring all of you with us on the ship. We have plenty of space."

Thelma visibly relaxed, and the angry expression on her face quickly gave way to one of intense sadness. "Oh God! If only you had arrived here three months ago! We all would have gladly gone with you. And the children could escape this hell on Earth." She thought a moment and then said, "Before things went to pot, I remember discussions of a possible Earth-like planet orbiting Jupiter. I don't remember the name of the planet though."

"The planet is called *Europa* and initial reports give it very similar Earth-like qualities. Our history books taught us that *Europa* was an ice planet with frozen water underneath. That may have been how it started out, but the planet as it exists today, is very similar to Earth. I don't know why it was kept such a secret.

"Unfortunately, we don't have specific information on the planet. Only a few individuals on the moon had any real, concrete information on *Europa* and they withheld it from us." He looked from Thelma to the others, almost embarrassed. "They actually abandoned us and took off for *Europa* in one of the other ships, and we haven't heard from them since. Our only hope for survival was to leave, come here for more fuel and food, and then try to make it to *Europa*."

If Thelma was shocked by this revelation, she didn't show it. She simply remarked by saying, "I guess that's human nature for you. As for food, the government was not very thorough with us. We never received all of our dry rations supplies. My guess is that it was diverted by persons unknown. What we started with is gone." She could see Henry almost physically deflate.

"Now, our diet consists primarily of fish. Also, we've been able to cultivate a small patch of dirt on the other side of the shelter, and it has provided us with a few vegetables and fruits. We've even found a few animals that we've been able to raise successfully. If our attackers had searched the shelter and the surrounding area on the other side of the hill valley, they would have discovered us and the animals."

"You have animals here?" Marla asked incredulously and somewhat nervously. "Dogs too?" She was thinking about the dogs that had attacked them earlier. She still hadn't gotten up the nerve to pet Buddy.

"Yes, we do have animals here Marla. And we have our guardian dogs, but they're nothing like those vicious hounds that attacked you earlier. And you've met Buddy already."

"Where do you keep them?" Henry asked. "The animals? This entire area is wasted. And before we dropped into the river, there was nothing but concrete and rubble everywhere."

A thin smile creased the corners of Thelma's lips. "Why don't you guys come with me? You have to see this in order to fully appreciate it. Come on, I'll show you."

3

Chayton looked up at Kyra again; a worried expression crossed his face. Kyra had been pacing back and forth in the cockpit for the last hour. They hadn't heard back from Henry *or* Tess, and that had been hours ago. Someone outside thought they had heard a muffled explosion in the direction of the fuel depot, but they had been hearing distant explosions since they landed.

He went back to his small Navi-Computer. Before she left, Tess had told him to map out the navigation specs for the trip from Earth to *Europa*. She had shared with him that even with a full tank of fuel, they would still have to perform a slingshot maneuver around the earth and then again around the moon in order to reach *Europa*. The problem with performing this move around the earth though was the massive debris field encircling the planet. The maneuver would have to be very precise in order to avoid smashing into the debris orbiting the earth.

Joe Ackerman and Lee Harrison, a former MP, tapped on the outside wall of the cockpit. "Hey Kyra, you wanted to see us?" Lee said. "Yes, thanks guys. Look, we haven't heard back from Tess or Henry in several hours. The fuel tanks are full and the pump was shut down about 20 minutes ago, but there's been no communication or confirmation from any of them. I need you guys to go over to the underground fuel center and see what's going on. It's probably just some electrical interference, and they can't call us to tell us that they're still looking for the engine node or something. Lee, I know you used to work here as a Military Policeman, but do you know how to get to the underground fuel depot?"

"Yep, sure do. The landscape threw me off a little, but I can see the building from here. Once I get closer, I'll be able to get to the entrance. What about Henry? Will you be sending some folks after him too?"

A pained look flashed across Kyra's face. "As much as I want to, I'll have to wait until you guys get back. Their last transmission put them about half a mile away from the shelter, and we knew that they might lose the signal once they entered the shelter. When you guys return with Tess, then we'll figure out what to do about Henry's team, if we still haven't heard back from them that is."

"Sounds good K. We'll get back here *post-haste*," Lee said, as he and Joe headed towards the rear exit.

When the men had left, Kyra resumed her pacing. She was worried about Henry. It was true that they would lose the signal once they entered the shelter, but Henry would have notified them *before* that happened. For more times than she cared to remember, the feeling that if they didn't get off this planet soon, it would never let them leave alive.

4

Tess, Max, and Lars were now sitting up in the open wagon. The convoy had stopped after passing the first set of guards, and they were helped to sitting positions. Tess wondered why they were doing this, but soon heard the voices of many people. There was an odd element of excited chatter in the sound.

Their mouths were still gagged and their hands had been re-tied behind their backs. The zip ties that bound their ankles were cut off. Tess looked around and recognized where they were at once. Although she had never been to the Harlan Penitentiary, named after one of Texas' most celebrated sheriffs, George Harlan, she had read quite a bit about it. There were five levels above ground and four levels underground. The first two above-ground floors consisted of administrative offices, the warden's office, and onsite housing for the on-duty guards. Floors three to five housed criminals convicted of various felonies and misdemeanors, while the four sublevels contained some of the country's most violent criminals.

She stared at the broken building as they approached it, now standing in stark contrast to the sleek state-of-the-art building she remembered seeing pictures of. When it was completed in 2018, she remembered reading that each floor had very high ceilings. The building she saw before her now had been demolished and the ground floors were piled high with tons of brick and steel girders. She wondered idly if the prisoners had been freed or left in their cells to be crushed to death.

They rolled towards an underground tunnel that surprisingly had not been destroyed. In the darkness ahead, Tess could see the flickering light of torches lining both sides of the tunnel that presumably led to the interior of the prison. A number of guards stood transfixed off to the sides of the tunnel entrance as a guard pushed open the gate to the tunnel.

As they made their way through, it was eerily silent, but she could hear soft whispers coming at her from the darkness. She could still hear the noises coming from the inside, but it was muted somehow. As they came out of the tunnel and into the interior of the prison grounds, the noise abruptly stopped. She looked around and felt a wave of surreal unreality wash over her as she stared at hundreds of ragged, gaunt men and women in the bleachers. They could have come straight from the apocalyptic world of *Mad Max*.

Standing in front of them, she saw maybe half as many men and women, but this group all held weapons of the homemade type; knives, spears, axes and various bludgeoning weapons. The only guns she remembered seeing were being carried by two of the group that abducted them at the airfield.

Walking in front of their wagon was a huge giant of a man. He carried some odd homemade spear. Next to him and a few steps in front, was a small, slightly pudgy man. He walked as if he owned the place. Maybe he does, thought Tess.

As they walked towards the center of the field, the short pudgy man raised his arms in the air, and from the bleachers came a thunderous cheering roar. Some rock music was playing somewhere, but Tess couldn't make out who it was because of all the shouting and cheering.

She looked over at Max and Lars. Max stared back at her in disbelief, but Lars was transfixed by the scene. He was staring up at the people in the stands, his eyes wide and his mouth working furiously as if he were grinding his molars. Tess was at a loss. They had encountered no people on their way here and she was beginning to wonder where they could be. Her question was answered here by the cheering voices, but in her gut, it didn't really sound like they were cheering. They sounded desperate, frantic, and maybe a little afraid.

She began to feel dread as they rolled out to the center of the field, towards what she first thought was a podium, but turned out to be another homemade device. A *medieval-looking* device. It wasn't a guillotine she was relieved to see, but it was obviously designed to hold or *hang* something on. There were several large hooks connected to the top beam by thick chains. The dried blood staining the hooks and splashed on the base and sides of the construction obliterated her thin layer of hope, replacing it with a deep, bone chilling fear.

5

Vanek walked away from the wagon, raising his right arm as he did so. The people quieted as quickly as they had started cheering. Brutos stopped the wagon and stood in front of it at military *parade rest*. Vanek began speaking to the crowd, and slowly turned to face each area of the stands. His voice was confident and strong.

"My people...my friends...my family. The time has come again for us to celebrate our survival. Every day, many of our friends perish. Illness takes most of them, and the harshness of our new world takes the rest. But our friends that are sacrificed for the greater good of the community will live in us forever!"

The cheering (*screaming?*) started up so quickly that Tess actually jumped. She looked around at the crazed faces. She looked at the men and women standing in front of the group with the homemade weapons and saw many pierced noses and lips and harshly painted designs on their faces and bodies. Their eyes were red and their hair either matted and tangled in thick dreadlocks or chopped off in uneven chunks. Their clothes were ragged and dirty. Many were missing teeth, but some of the ones who still had teeth had sharpened them down to jagged fangs. The larger number of people behind them cheered too, but not as enthusiastically as the weapon-holders. Tess felt lightheaded and bit down on her tongue as hard as she could with the dirty rag in her mouth. She thought she tasted blood, but she was determined not to pass out.

She glanced at Max again and saw that he had soiled himself. He was shaking violently and looked on the verge of fainting. Lars was still hypnotized. He was a big man, somewhat overweight and was sweating profusely. She could see his foot nervously vibrating against the side of the wagon wall.

"I predicted a long time ago that we would have off-world visitors here and look what we have." Vanek waved his arms theatrically toward Tess and her companions. The crowd booed expectedly. "They left us here to die when they flew off to their *promised land* in space. They left you and your children here to die at the end of all roads. They left you with no shelter, no food, and no hope. What they did leave behind were their minions. They created hundreds of well-stocked protective shelters for their chosen ones. And for what reason you might ask? To stock their new world with our *blood*!"

Tess's heart was beating so hard, she thought it would explode through her chest. The place was writhing with frantic fury...apoplectic with rage. Those with weapons were waving them in the air wildly. Someone bounded out of the bleachers and took off running. For a minute, Tess thought the man was running toward them, maybe to exact revenge on them himself, but he turned toward the tunnel they came in. Before he could even get a quarter of the way there, an arrow whistled deadly through the still air and skewered the man. He fell hard in the dead grass, the burnt tip of the arrow protruding through his throat.

Amazingly, the man was still alive, but by the time he rolled over onto his back, two men armed with axes had jogged up to him. They smiled at him as he lay there gurgling and choking and bleeding profusely. He started to say something when they got close to him, but one of the axes whistled through the air and caught him in the mouth, cleaving the top part of his face from the lower part. When he removed the axe from the man's mouth, the tongue stuck to the blade for a second before plopping to the ground like a dead worm. Next to Tess, Max moaned horribly.

None of this fazed Vanek. He continued his jingoistic monologue in a thunderous and ominous tone. "Many times, we've come across the drained and desiccated bodies of our comrades, discarded like trash on the side of the road. We didn't know what was happening to them until we caught one of *them* and forced him to talk, and boy did he talk. "He told us of their plans. He told us how they needed hundreds, no *thousands* of gallons of blood of different types to keep on hand in case it was needed in this new world. Brothers and sisters, he also told us that very soon, his leaders would be back to collect all of them and take them and their ill-gotten liquids, back to the *new world*. Once they were safely in space, their plan was to set off hundreds of nuclear weapons here on Earth and destroy our world. Our *home. Our precious home!*"

While the crazed people cheered and screamed at the same time, Tess could only stare in disbelief. She couldn't believe the crap he was selling here. He sounded like Soren. The fact that they believed it though was what frightened her the most. She remembered a historical comment from years ago about how history has shown again and again that some of the most dangerous and twisted individuals have manipulated peoples into doing the most horrendous things.

"My people, we will *not* let that happen. We will destroy these invaders and all the other ones who follow. As we speak, their ship sits at our airfield, and they've been mucking around with the nuclear reactor at the base. There are less than 20 men and the rest are women and children. They have no weapons. We will destroy their ship and bring all of them here for purification!" The people who were not already on their feet, jumped up as the crowd started chanting, "Pu-ri-fy! Pu-ri-fy! Pu-ri-fy!"

How could he know that? thought Tess. If they were at the airfield when we landed, then they could have easily estimated how many of us were here, but how could he know that we have no weapons?

Vanek looked around, a small smile creasing his fat face. He turned to Brutos and nodded. Brutos snapped to attention and whirled around toward the wagon. He signaled someone off to the side of the field and made his way to the wagon.

Tess glanced again at her companions and saw that Lars had chewed through his gag. He was dead white and breathing hard. *"YOU CAN'T DO THIS! THIS MAN IS CRAZY! WE'RE NOT HERE TO HURT ANYONE. WE JUST NEEDED FUEL! PLEASE LET US GO! PLEASE!"*

Tess doubted if more than a handful of the crowd heard him. Their ecstatic screams completely drowned out his hoarse and trembling voice. Regardless of whether anyone heard him or not, Brutos walked up to him and hit him square in the nose, breaking it instantly. Tess could hear the sickening crunch and Lars's helpless and feeble grunt. Max put his head down and vomited violently. He was on the verge of faint.

The crowd *oohed* in much the same way they would have if a football cornerback nailed a wide receiver going up for a high catch. Brutos reached into the wagon and yanked Lars out roughly, pulling him to the ground ignominiously.

Tess looked around for a potential escape route. They were backed up to a jumble of bricks and girders from part of the fallen building. The only way out was the tunnel that they came in. The other tunnel that she saw seemed to be connected to the prison itself. From this tunnel, she saw two men half dragging a third between them. The third was gagged and bound like they were. His clothes were bloody, and he had apparently been beaten. They dragged him to the base of the podium.

Vanek nodded to Brutos again and Brutos yanked off the man's gag. Immediately, he started yelling at Vanek. *"You promised Vanek! You promised!"* One of the men dragging him, stopped and punched him hard in the stomach. The man doubled over, wheezing, while they continued dragging him towards the hook contraption. The man's face was bloody, but when he raised his head again, Tess's mouth dropped open in first surprise, then anger. It was *Andy*! That's how they knew about the ship, and the number of people on the ship. That's how they knew there were no weapons on board. They must have captured him trying to sneak up on *us*.

As they got closer to the hook contraption, Andy renewed his efforts by squirming and twisting between the two men. His efforts were futile as they easily pulled him along. Lars was in shock and seemed to have nothing left. Brutos had one arm and two other men were pulling on the other arm. Blood still ran from his shattered nose, but Tess could see from his vacant expression that he was miles from this nightmare. In her heart, Tess hoped that was true. She hadn't realized until now that tears had been streaming down her face.

Vanek made his way over to the contraption and then raised both hands. The crowd silenced itself at once. He looked up to the sky as if praying and said, "My family, please let us have silence for the purification of these heathens and let their screams carry away the impurities of their bodies. When they have become pure, they will serve our needs and we shall not want."

Intuitively, Tess's line of thought had been leading her to this conclusion, but she couldn't bring herself to believe it. "Oh my God," she breathed, "they're going to...execute them." She didn't think Max had heard her, but he yanked his head sharply toward her. "What did you say?" he asked her, knowing full well what she said.

She didn't reply, but stared straight ahead as Andy and then Lars were dragged up the stairs to the platform where the huge hooks were. She looked at the platform and could see that the hooks were not only hooks, but hooks with shackles connected to the same chain. One of the men bounded up the short flight of stairs and lowered the four hook-shackles combination to the floor of the platform.

The men holding Lars and Andy forced them to stand up straight. Andy was still struggling while Lars looked as if he would fall over if they let him go. From inside his vest, Brutos produced a small knife and in a matter of seconds, had cut loose the clothing that the men were wearing. Several old women had joined them on stage and proceeded to rip the remaining clothing from the men until they were completely naked. Andy made a feeble attempt to turn away from the women, but was forcibly held in position by the men.

Vanek now faced the men on the platform. He looked at both of them solemnly and then said, "You will now be purified for our lives." He glanced at Brutos and nodded. Brutos in turn gave an order to the men holding Lars and Andy. "Position for purification!" he ordered.

Tess was feeling quite ill at this point. She perceived all of this in some weird *out of body* fashion. She felt that if she allowed herself to become completely untethered, she would indeed be watching this whole ghastly ordeal from outside of her body, floating high above. She believed deep inside though if she allowed this to happen, she would never be able to get back to herself.

She felt numb, but she pinched herself, hard. She looked on helplessly as Lars and Andy were forced to the ground on their backs. Once the lowered shackles were strapped around their ankles, Brutos motioned for them to be raised. Two men on each side of the raised platform started turning their handles until Lars and Andy were suspended upside down from their ankles, their heads about a foot from the floor.

The women stepped in front of the hanging men and proceeded to brush oil all over their bodies. Tess believed that Lars' mind had cracked. His eyes were rolling in their sockets, and he was babbling. White foamy froth was dribbling out of his mouth into his eyes and onto the floor of the contraption. Andy squirmed and shouted curses at the women each time their brushes touched his body.

At last, the women finished and left the platform. Out of the corner of her eyes, Tess caught sight of a bright glare and moaned inwardly when she saw someone bringing out a torch to Vanek. When Andy saw the torch, he screamed and bucked wildly. *"What the fuck are you doing? This is wrong! I didn't do anything to you, nothing! This is...I helped you! No! You can't do this!"*

Vanek paid no attention to this as he walked up the stairs to the podium. He stood in front of Andy, who continued cursing and screaming until Vanek touched his body with the torch. And then it was only screaming. Vanek had to step back quickly to avoid the rapidly spreading fire on Andy's body. He turned towards Lars, who was still babbling and touched the fire to his chest. For a second, Lars only continued babbling, and then his throat opened up and he howled desperately.

"You dirty son of a bitch! I'll kill you! I'll kill you!" Tess screamed at Vanek's back. She looked over at Andy and Lars again. They were engulfed in flames and black smoke was rising from their bodies in thick plumes. A thick, pungent smell filled the air that made Tess gag. She looked at Max and saw that he had long since passed out. Up on the platform, Andy no longer screamed, but his body jerked spasmodically. Lars was still writhing, but he too had ceased screaming.

Vanek looked off to the side again and raised his arms, "Water!" he yelled and instantly, several men rushed out to the platform pushing a large wagon containing several barrels with tubes inserted on both sides. When they reached the platform, one of them started pumping a handle at the rear of the wagon, while two of them sprayed water onto the burning bodies.

What in God's name are they doing? Tess thought furiously. Andy and Lars would die for certain. Their bodies were too badly burned for them to survive. Why would they put the fire out now, for God's sake?

Once the flames had been completely distinguished, two very large bowls were placed under their heads. Tess pushed down the bile rising to her throat when she heard Andy and Lars gurgling. From inside his tunic, Vanek produced a large knife and then turned to the crowd with his arms upraised. *"For our lives!"* he shouted and quickly slit Andy and Lars' throats. The blood flowed thickly from their necks into the bowls.

Tess lowered her head and began crying again. *At least they're dead now,* she thought, thankful that they did not have to suffer any more than they already had. She had thought the horrors were over until she looked up again and saw that Vanek had replaced the knife with a large goblet. He held the cup under the streaming, steaming blood flowing from Lars' neck for a few seconds, and then turned to the crowd once again. "For our *lives!*" he yelled out, turning the goblet up to his mouth to drink.

Tess could not feel her body at all. In fact, she felt completely disconnected from it. She knew she was on the verge of passing out and welcomed it. She fell to her side. As her sight grew dim, she saw the women rush back to the platform carrying baskets and knives. They crowded around each of the bodies, their arms working up and down. Tess couldn't make out what they were doing, partly because of her blurred vision and partly because the women obscured her view. Before darkness took her, however, she saw one of the women carve a strip of flesh from Lars' body and hand it to Vanek, which he shoved into his mouth greedily. And then she was gone, embracing the darkness that engulfed her as empty laughter trailed behind her.

THELMA'S ANIMALS

1

Henry stared with his mouth half open. He couldn't believe what he was seeing. Thelma had led them through the shelter to another exit, which was totally hidden from the outside. This particular exit led to a manmade tunnel that travelled about a mile away from the shelter. It was designed to link up with a parking garage, but the earthquakes completely destroyed the parking garage and the building above it.

When the earthquakes had weakened, Thelma said they started to explore their surroundings and saw that their original tunnel had been destroyed. An earthquake hit as they were returning, forcing them to find a different way back. They followed an underground stream that led to a huge area that had once been on the surface, but was now some 50 feet underground. Entire neighborhoods had dropped 50 feet below the surface of the earth. The survivors were brought back to the shelter and they retrieved what supplies they could. The biggest find, however, was the petting zoo. Many of the animals were already dead, but they were able to save a number of calves, baby goats, sheep, a few pigs, lots of chickens, and several foals.

Thelma explained that they had success taking care of the animals and breeding them because two of the survivors had actually worked at the zoo. She nodded towards Lisa and Harvey Middleton, the man and woman who had held rifles on them earlier. They nodded back, smiling a little. "We were actually working with the animals when our group was attacked." Thelma added.

"We were worried that they would find out about the animals and come back for them. We felt that way until Len returned and told us differently." She glanced at Len who stared back at her resolutely.

"What did you find out from Len?" Bob asked, looking from Thelma to Len and back again. "What? Did they have their own farm or something?"

"They've resorted to cannibalism," Thelma stated flatly. "Len was there for almost a week and said that at least once every two or three days, they would *purify* someone..."

Bob interrupted her, "*Purify* someone?"

Thelma continued, "Yes, they would hang prisoners from their ankles, oil them up and set fire to them. Len said that they called this the *Purification Ceremony*."

"Oh my God," Marla whispered quietly.

Len spoke up quickly, "Not just prisoners Miss Thelma. They would do this to the desert...the desert..."

Bob helped him out, "*Deserters*?"

"Yes!" he replied. "The people who wouldn't join in or thought it was wrong were put in jail too. They were the first to be pulled out for puri...purification."

Henry turned to face Len, "How many prisoners were there when you left son?"

Len thought for a minute, his brows crinkling with the effort. "All of us, plus a lot more. More than 30 extra people, I think."

Thelma added, "That's close to 60, total. Len told me that there were a lot in the stands too."

"The *stands*?" Henry asked? "Is this some sort of stadium or something?"

Len thought a minute and said, "Yes...and no. It's a field up at the top, and there are jails underground."

Henry considered this and realized that the boy must be talking about the massive Harlan Penitentiary; the underground prison that was built in North San Antonio a number of years back. Henry did some quick math in his head. "Thelma, we have plenty of room on the ship for your people and maybe the other prisoners as well, but we don't have the weapons to get them out safely. In fact, we have no weapons but this laser here. Also, there are only a handful of us who made the trip here. I'll bring this up with the commander of our ship and the others, but I honestly don't know who would volunteer to go there. I'm sorry."

Thelma's face dropped, but she understood. Without the necessary weapons and manpower, it would be a suicide mission. Only one person among them had actually been there, and he was only 12 years old! "I understand Henry and thank you for offering to bring us with you, but what about the animals? You said you would need food to make the trip to this new planet. Is your ship big enough to bring some of the animals?"

Henry's eyes widened at the thought. "That's actually a pretty good idea Thelma. We certainly have the room for it. The *Orion* is a *Generation Ship*. It is completely equipped with a self-sustained biosphere where we can house quite a number of animals and plant life." Just as quickly, the smile left his face, a slow frown appearing at the corners of his mouth. "But then there's the problem of getting the animals from here to there. How could we transport them safely without getting attacked by the dogs?"

"There's a route east of here that we use to travel to the airfield. The dogs avoid that area completely."

"How do you know that?" Marla asked nervously.

Harvey, one of the petting zoo vets answered, "Because there's low level radiation in the area. The dogs can sense this, and they stay away completely."

"Okay, but what about the radiation poison?" Henry asked. "We've all had anti-radiation shots, so we're good for at least a week. What about you folks?"

Harvey said, "Luckily, the folks who built these shelters did not cut any corners regarding medicine. We have enough doses for at least a year, longer if necessary. We'll be fine."

"What about the animals?" Marla asked. "Won't they be sickened by the radiation?"

Harvey smiled, "One of the guys taken prisoner was a biologist and with his help, we were able to synthesize an anti-radiation supplement that we feed to the animals weekly."

"Well," Henry said, "it looks like we almost have a plan. What about transportation? Are we covered there too?"

This time, Lisa spoke up. She had been resting against a large outcropping of rocks. "Yes, that's covered too. We kept several animal transport trucks at the zoo in anticipation of moving to a different location, but *Lycos* shut that option down. All but one of the trucks survived, and we stripped as much from it as possible to discourage thieves. It won't take us long to remount the wheels and we could probably be ready to go in about three hours."

Henry looked out at the animals in their oddly shaped pens. This had been a miracle for them. "Okay, let's do it then Lisa." He looked at her intently, then at her husband Harvey. "I assume you guys have a plan for grass, soil, and whatever else you need for the animals? Even the vegetables?"

They looked at each other and smiled. "Yes, we think so. Just the same, we probably better make that four hours then."

Henry smiled back. "That's good." He turned to Thelma, "Is there any way I can have a look at your antenna controls in the shelter? I need to contact the ship to let them know we're okay and to give them their marching orders on preparing the biosphere for the animals."

"Sure," Thelma replied, "let's head on back. Harvey, will guys be able to get this taken care of?"

"Yes," Lisa replied, "but it would help things go faster if we could get a little help." Henry looked at Bob and Marla, "Bob, Marla, will you guys help Harvey and Lisa with the animals and the sod and whatever else they need help with? I'm going to contact the ship and tell them to get ready."

"No problem Henry," Bob said as he started off after Harvey.

"Good luck Henry," Marla said and she and Yoi walked hand in hand following after Bob.

Henry looked at Len and put his hand on his shoulder. "Maybe you can help me by packing up key supplies from the shelter, huh Len?"

Len smiled, threw a half salute and then ran on ahead of Thelma back towards the shelter, Buddy right on his heels.

IMPRISONED

1

Tess welcomed the darkness. She was completely immersed in it and had no desire to come out of it. There were ugly, dangerous things just on the other side. She was not quite unconscious, but she wasn't conscious either. Some distant, far off memory told her that in situations like this, the key was always to completely relax the body and then ease into wakefulness. Of course, she had never been a situation like this. She had never even had a serious *conversation* about situations like this. This situation came straight from a *Stephen King* story as far as she was concerned.

As she drifted along on the thin membrane separating unconsciousness and wakefulness, a distorted memory slashed its way into her psyche; she saw pigs roasting on an open pit, their legs tied to the rotating sticks. There were two of them and they were held in place by rusty hooks. They both had apples in their mouths. Their eyes bulged hugely and blood bubbled through hundreds of small cuts in their pale, pinkish bodies. Even though she knew pigs didn't wear clothes, she saw them as being naked. She wanted to help them, but her feet were stuck to the ground. Their mouths moved with each rotation as they tried to speak. Slowly, as their pig-talk turned to real words, she struggled fiercely to wake up. In some far-off part of her mind, she knew that she was dreaming all of this, but it was like one of those "waking" dreams where outside sounds seamlessly blended into the dream like ticks burrowing into soft skin.

She struggled to pull herself out of this *no-where* state where her screams were reduced to grunts. Eventually, she began to focus on relaxing each part of her body until she felt herself starting to breathe normally. At just that moment, she felt something brush across her nose. Something *hairy*. This external stimulus was enough to break the hold on her deep sleep. She bolted upright; her nostrils flaring in and out as she slapped at her mouth and face.

"Are you okay?" asked a timid voice in the semi-gloom. Tess swung her head in the direction of the voice, eyes wide and frantic, trying to see who had spoken to her. All she could make out was a vague, slumped form not five feet away from her.

"Who's there?" Tess asked, trying to keep her voice steady and not succeeding. The horror of what she had seen earlier lay fresh and ripe on her psyche. She had to clamp down on the memory or she would be shaking uncontrollably.

"My name is Frieda. Frieda Barnes." The woman hesitated a moment and then words were pouring from her mouth. "Is it true? Are you really from the *moon*? The word is that Vanek and his men captured a group of folks who flew here from the moon. Is it true?"

Tess considered whether she should tell this woman the truth. Maybe there were spies here. The idea seemed ludicrous though. Vanek already knew all about them, so what was there to hide now? "Yes, I'm actually one of the survivors from the moon. My name is Tess Robinson."

"*Oh my God!*" said Frieda. "Did you guys come back to Earth on a rescue mission? Were you planning to take some survivors back to the moon?"

Feeling a little embarrassed, Tess responded, "No, Frieda. We actually had to come back here for fuel. We had some problems on the moon and circumstances forced us to come here for refueling in order to make the trip to *Europa*." She bit her lip. She hadn't meant to mention *Europa* to the woman. Not many people outside of the shelters actually knew about the possibility of living on *Europa*.

"*Europa*...right. That's the Earth-like planet that NASA had been looking at for years. Did they ever confirm whether it could support human life?"

Tess smiled wanly and thought, *that's what I get for underestimating folks.* "You're right, NASA was looking at it, but we never received confirmation that it met the minimum requirements." She thought of Soren and his chosen few leaving them for dead on the moon. "However, based on the actions of another group who was on the moon with us, we have every reason to believe that it *will* support human life." Frieda looked at Tess shrewdly, "I have a feeling there's more to that story, but you can share that with me at another time." She shifted gears, "How did you guys get caught? I heard that they brought in another person with you, but he's not on this level." She hesitated for a second and then added, "I'm sorry for your other two friends Tess."

"Thank you, Frieda. I'm sorry too. What happened here? I mean...what happened to these *people*? How did they resort to cannibalism so quickly? There must be other sources of food out there, right?"

"Before we were captured, our group had these same discussions and the only conclusion that we could come to was that they gave up. They gave up trying to live. To *live* means to adhere to some basic rights and make an attempt to have at least some level of *respect* for life." She looked away disgustedly, "These people don't live...they *exist*. They're like animals.

"Lately, however, it's been getting worse. I've been here for two months, and it has gotten increasingly worse, just like the environment. The earthquakes have been coming more and more frequently and have been increasing in intensity. It's also getting hotter. This time a year ago, we had snow on the ground if you can believe that! Now, it feels hotter than Jamaica in the summer! Many of us think that it's only a matter of time before something really bad happens."

Tess thought about Earth's new orbit and groaned inwardly. Frieda didn't know just how close to the truth she was. This thought brought new panic and a sense of urgency that she needed to do something soon, or she and the rest of her crew would be here to see just how bad things were going to get.

"Not long after *Lycos* hit," Frieda continued, "we had a long-range helicopter crash near our shelter. They said they got lost. Their navigation equipment was totally off, and they had gone too far to turn around so they kept coming, flying line of sight. We caught their mayday when they were only two miles from our shelter. The pilot was the only one to survive the crash, but he had slowly bled to death a few days later. Before he died though, he told us that there were massive areas of the earth that were exposed to the core. He said their scientists believed that more powerful earthquakes were coming and that they would eventually rip the planet apart."

Tess and the others had discussed this as well, but they could only theorize what might happen. Apparently, other scientists had been saying the same thing.

"These monsters here know this too. At least they feel it strongly. One night, one of our guys was begging for his life from Vanek. He told Vanek that the shelter could house everyone here and keep them safe from the earthquakes and the radiation sickness. That wasn't entirely true, but what I heard Vanek tell him is what frightened me the most."

"What did he say?" asked Tess.

"He told him that his people were the chosen ones. That they were chosen to see the end of the world and that he would do everything he possibly could to ensure that nothing stood in the way of their glory. Nothing. And then they dragged him out to the field and killed him." She looked squarely at Tess. "Vanek is crazy Tess, and he'll bring your entire crew here and destroy your ship. His salvation is here, not *Europa*."

Tess remembered how Vanek strutted around the exercise field; a small, self-important monster with visions of grandeur. Frieda was right. From what Tess could see, Vanek was definitely crazy, and she knew it was only a matter of time before his terrible eye fell on her and Max.

"Frieda, how many of your people are here from your shelter?"

"After we were attacked, about 45 of us made the trip here, plus or minus a couple. I don't know how many were killed at the shelter during the fighting, and I'm not really sure how many adults are still alive now."

"What do you mean 'adults'? Are the children from your shelter down here too? Where are they?"

Frieda sighed and nodded. To Tess, it was a heavy, depleted sigh. "They keep the children on the third sublevel. At the time, I had thought that they captured all 18 of them. Later, I found out that two were killed during the fighting. Of the remaining 16, one was never captured, and one actually escaped—if you can believe that! The last time that I saw the children was when we had to send one of the girls up top."

"What do you mean by that?" Tess asked worriedly.

"When we got here, there were at least eight kids from the other prisoners already here, ranging in age from 5 to 11. Our children were about the same age, but we had several teenage boys and girls who were older than 12." She looked at the ground for a second and then added, "I think there were more kids, but no one confirms it."

She paused for a minute as if collecting herself. "In order for Vanek's guards to be completely loyal to him, he offers them 'food' and 'warm bodies'. When the children 'come of age', they send a couple of us down there to find one or two, get them cleaned up, and then send them up top to be concubines for Vanek's people who are 'worthy'. He's done it at least a few times since I've been here. None of them ever come back here, and I haven't seen any of them in the stands."

Tess was horrified. "Oh Jesus," she whispered. "How could our world turn into this?"

Frieda looked at her with sympathy in her eyes. "Things have always been bad here Tess. That's what I used to tell my congregation. We didn't need a meteorite to smash everything to hell to tell us that. Vanek has probably always been like that; if not on top, then definitely under the surface. Given the right set of circumstances, he metamorphosed from a below average working stiff to a power hungry, psychopathic murderous animal. Connect him with someone like Brutos, give him a few weapons, and there you have it, an end of the world psycho camp."

Tess nodded and added, "Given a little motivation, maybe more education, he could have been one of those cult-freaks we always read about, blissfully leading his people over the edge of a cliff towards a 'happy and meaningful' death. I just hope we get a chance to start the world off right if we get to *Europa*." She looked at Frieda thoughtfully, "How did this prison happen Frieda? How was Vanek able to even start something like this?"

Frieda ran her fingers through her tangled red hair. "From what I've heard since I've been here, Vanek was one of the first people to make his way to the prison after the meteorites hit and after *Lycos* pounded us. My guess is that he was pretty close to here and was looking for a place to hide.

"You probably noticed when you were brought here that the top portion of the prison was completely demolished. As the story goes, all of the prisoners were left in their cells. I don't think it was done on purpose, but I think the guards just stopped coming to work. Most of the prisoners who were in the above ground cells were killed. Below ground, in these sublevels, the prisoners were alive, but trapped with no food or water. Some of the prisoners who were here then and had survived have hinted that this is where the cannibalism started. Cellmate against cellmate, a fight to the death, where the winner was able to survive a little bit longer.

"When Vanek and his small band got here, they found the keys and let them out. I had heard that most of the original inmates took off, thinking they would find better places than this. Maybe government shelters or something. Brutos, his second in command, stayed behind and has been loyal to Vanek ever since. I heard that he was on death row for multiple, pre-meditated murders.

"Anyway, when it was clear to the survivors that there were no government shelters, a lot of them made their way here. By then, there were stories of a sanctuary taking care of lost people. They said they had food and water and protection. People began to think that Vanek was some sort of government employee or high ranking official.

"Eventually, they started running out of the food that they had been able to scavenge for, so they started sending out patrols to find smaller groups of people to take their supplies. It still wasn't enough for the number of people who were here.

"Weeks would pass without sufficient food and people started fighting amongst themselves. Then people started to come up missing. It was first thought that they were leaving the stadium, but as it turned out, there was a group kidnapping them, killing them, and then eating them. Vanek and a number of his very loyal guards were behind it the entire time. He sanctioned it and then turned it into some goddamn apocalyptic religion."

Tess thought of Soren and his group. What kind of world will he create, seeing that he started off by condemning them to death? She closed her fists into tight balls and resolved to fix this. Whatever it took, she *had* to fix this.

She stood up and looked around. The jail cell looked like she thought a jail cell *should* look like. There was a bunk bed set up alongside a dirty wall and a rust-stained toilet in the corner. This far down, she didn't expect the cell to have windows, but a dim light glowed through a recessed opening in the high ceiling. Somewhere, a generator was still operational, Tess thought. She walked up to the bars of the cell and tried to look out through the small barred window set in the door. The steel door was separated from the bars by at least two feet. *I guess that's why this was one of the country's most secure prisons for extremely dangerous criminals,* Tess thought sourly. The room directly across from them was dark and she couldn't see any of the other cells. She examined the steel door intently and could see that there was no handle on the door.

"There's no way out unless they let us out," Frieda stated.

"How many people are imprisoned down here in all?" Tess asked, still trying to peer through the small window.

"I'm actually not sure, Tess. Whenever they let us out, it's usually a few people at a time." She grew silent for a moment and then added, "There used to be a lot more of us. When I was first brought here, they had many of us locked up in the cells across the hall. You were unconscious when they brought you in, so you wouldn't have noticed; but each sublevel has a wing of cells on both sides of the staircase. One day, while five of us were out in the yard on some kind of work detail, we were hit by a powerful earthquake. When it was over, the entire side from the first sublevel to the fourth sublevel had caved in on itself. A lot of people were buried alive that day, including my husband." Frieda hung her head and rubbed at her eyes. Tess reached out and took her hand. "I'm very sorry Frieda."

"They locked us up on this side and did nothing to help free the people who were still alive. For days they cried out in pain and anguish until eventually there was nothing but silence. Now, for whatever reason, they keep us separated. The men are on sublevel one, right above us. And as I mentioned, the children are on sublevel three, right below us. Before that last big earthquake, they had some of us on the fourth sublevel on this side, but it had started flooding, so they moved us up. I heard they left a guy down there for helping one of the kids escape. He could be dead now for all I know."

Tess could only stare at Frieda. Her mind was still trying to cope with the fact that Vanek left those poor people buried alive in the rubble. "This place is a nightmare, Frieda. Have you ever tried to escape? It seems to me it's only a matter of time before Vanek sends his goons after *you*."

"Believe me, I've considered it Tess," Frieda responded dolefully. "The guards are everywhere, and if someone is caught trying to escape, they are usually tortured and then killed." She looked down at her feet. "We need to get out of here Tess! I'm sure *my* luck will run out sooner or later, but from what the guards were saying when they brought you here, you might be sacrificed soon."

Tess could feel a deep dread rise in her. The thought that she and Max would be sacrificed too had already occurred to her, but she thought that she would already have a plan to get out of this mess by then. She walked up to the solid prison cell bars that extended from the ceiling to the floor and then at the solid steel door on the other side of the bars and could feel panic, like bile, rising quickly in her throat. *How in God's name are we going to get out of this?* She thought worriedly.

She turned back to Frieda, "From what Vanek said when we were brought here, I could tell that he hates what we stand for. And I'm sure they'll be sacrificing Max and me within a day or two, but I'm not giving up yet." She thought for a minute and then added, "And I don't think Vanek has attacked our ship yet. He plans to, but hasn't done it yet. Maybe that will give my folks enough time to finish refueling. At least then, we will have enough fuel to make it to *Europa*. The only problem is that we need to replace one of our engine power nodes."

"What's that?" Frieda asked.

"It's basically a power node that gives us enough power to operate the ship. Certain functions, such as lifting off from a planet or maintaining the power needed to travel long distances rely on fully functioning power nodes. Our ship requires six power nodes, and one of them is damaged. If it holds out long enough to get us off the planet, then we have to hope that it lasts long enough for us to make it to *Europa*. The chances of this are extremely thin."

Frieda opened her mouth to say something, when all of a sudden, they heard yelling and cheering drifting down through the prison hallway. They couldn't make out what it was at first, but then the words slowly began to make sense. *"PURIFY...PURIFY...PURIFY!"*

Tess looked at Frieda; her eyes were wide with some unspoken fear. "Oh God Frieda, are they about to kill someone?"

Before Frieda could answer, they heard keys rattling in their cell door. A second later, a huge man stood framed in the entranceway. He smiled at them as he unlocked the bars and swung them open. Two other men waited in the hallway behind him. "Okay ladies, let's go! It's time ta pay da piper," one of them shouted as they grabbed Tess and Frieda and hauled them out of their prison cell.

ANIMAL CONVOY

1

Kyra couldn't believe her emotions could swing any further apart. She was elated when Henry contacted the ship, but devastated to hear about Della and Billy Li. To die like they did was unimaginable. And then there was Tess and her group. She explained to him that she hadn't heard back from Tess or the others and was starting to get worried.

He tried to console her as best he could and promised that they would hurry back. They also spoke at great lengths on preparing the animal enclosure of the biosphere in order to support the animals he was bringing. Kyra listened intently and when they were done, she knew immediately which people she could rely on.

She assembled the team designated to work on the biosphere and they converged around the radio and listened to Lisa and Harvey detail the number and types of animals they were bringing. Before they were even done discussing the scenario, the team was already debating on how best to restructure the biosphere to not only support the animals, but to support the vegetation as well.

Henry admitted that it would probably take them three to four hours to get back to the ship, provided they didn't run into any surprises along the way. The biosphere team assured Kyra that they would be ready by the time he arrived. They headed for the biosphere enclosure, chatting excitedly over what needed to be done. No sooner had they left, then Joe showed up...carrying Sheila. She looked very pale; her short curly afro was matted with dirt, and her pants were soaked through with blood.

"She's still alive!" said Joe, as he burst into the ship. He headed straight for the medical module, yelling for Julie.

Kyra got on the intercom and called for Julie to meet them in the medical module. Then she jumped up and ran after Joe, her heart beating in her ears.

2

While Julie cleaned and dressed Sheila's wound, Joe and Lee waited outside the door, talking to Kyra. "We found her about half a mile away," Joe explained. "She was making her way here, but the loss of blood was causing her to hallucinate. She had veered off and at some point, started moving away from the ship. Luckily, she was in an area that wasn't obstructed with debris, and we were able to see her clearly in the distance. When we were sure it was her, we got to her quickly."

"Excellent job you guys," Kyra exclaimed, but she was extremely worried. Tess hadn't returned with them, neither had the other folks that she took with her. "Did you guys look for Tess and the others?"

Lee spoke up, "I did Kyra. I told Joe to get Sheila to the ship as quickly as possible, and I went to the fuel center to look for the rest." He looked down at the ground, fidgeting with his hands. "I found Albert's body, Kyra. Looks like someone threw a hand grenade at him. There was blood on the walls and floor, and there were signs of a struggle inside. But no more bodies. I think the best we can hope for is that Tess, Lars, and Max were taken prisoner."

"Any idea where they may have gone?" asked Kyra tentatively, knowing that Joe and Lee wouldn't know the answer to that, yet hoping just the same.

"No, Kyra, not a clue," answered Joe. "There were lots of tracks, and I have a general sense of which direction they went in, but I would be completely guessing where they took them."

"We *have* to find them Joe," Kyra pleaded. "We have to find Tess. Chayton can't handle this ship by himself." She told them about Henry's ordeal and his plan to bring the animals. "I spoke to him right before you guys got here, so he knows nothing about Tess and the others yet. He'll want to organize a search party for sure when he gets here." She glanced at her watch. "That should be about two hours from now." She thought a moment and then added, "This might be a problem though especially since those folks who took Tess, Lars and Max have grenades. We can only assume that they have rifles too."

Lee smiled and lifted up his shirt. Around his waist, he wore the military small arms ammunition belt. He resembled a *Soldier of Fortune* character. "Sheila was wearing this belt when we found her. She must have found it at the fuel center. There's a 9mm hand gun here, and one of the guys is oiling down the M-16 that she had strapped around her shoulder. We have over a hundred rounds of ammunition for the rifles and about 48 rounds of 9mm ammunition. All we need now are a few more M-16's and a few people who can shoot straight."

"Okay guys, I'm going to check on Sheila. See if you can round up some folks for the search and rescue mission." She looked out the window at the darkening *alien* sky and realized just how truly alien this place had become. *Hurry Henry*, she thought. *Tess's life may depend on it.*

3

Henry and Bob walked ahead of the animal convoy. True to Thelma's word, the dogs refused to follow them, although they paced them from a distance for almost an hour. They barked and fought and growled the entire time they paced the convoy. Marla was a frantic mess. She was certain that their hunger and animal instincts would eventually overcome their reluctance to enter the "radiation field" and that they would come bounding over the rubble and twisted cars that separated them. Eventually, they gave up their pursuit. When they did, she visibly relaxed even though Henry caught her several times throwing nervous glances behind her.

Getting the animals ready for the trip and loading them onto the truck, didn't take long at all. What took an inordinate amount of time was clearing out the shelter. There were lots of potentially usable materials inside, but they only had room enough for essentials. There was stuff everywhere. After two hours of combing through boxes of supplies and records, Henry put a stop to it and got the convoy moving. He was concerned about Tess and her team and didn't want to lose what little light there was by spending too much time in the shelter looking through stuff.

After the dogs peeled off, the convoy was able to travel in relative silence. The animals had been tranquilized to keep them calm during the trip. Periodically, one would sound off, startling everyone, and then go back to sleep.

They crested a small rise and as they reached the top, Henry saw the small glow of green light sticks in the distance. *We made it!* he thought happily. A half mile at most to go! He looked over at Bob, who was smiling also.

"We did it, Henry! We're here! I never thought I'd be so glad to see that ship again!" He grew somber and then added, "Kind of a bummer to leave their people to those cannibals, huh?"

This had been troubling Henry. Here they were, taking Thelma's resources and food, but not offering to help her people escape. He was at a loss, but what could he do? They weren't here to save everyone. They *couldn't* save everyone. So why did he feel so terrible about it?

"Yeah, Bob, it is a bummer and believe me, I've thought long and hard about it. We just don't have the manpower or the fire power to take on these folks. We don't know how well guarded those prisoners are, or if they're even still alive. Also, Kyra hasn't heard back from

Tess, and that's very disconcerting. No, prudence suggests that we get to the ship, get these animals on board, and find out what the hell's going on."

He looked at Bob defiantly, but Bob only nodded sadly. Henry felt strongly that if they made any attempt to rescue these people, a lot of them would not make it back, if any. Then he thought of his conversation with Kyra earlier today. She had told him that she hadn't heard back from Tess and had sent Joe and Lee to find them and see what was taking so long. Why *was* it taking so long to get back to the ship? The fuel wasn't the issue. Kyra had told him that the *Orion* was "topped off" and ready to go. Maybe they were still looking for the engine power node. That would be the only reason Tess would stay out there. He would find out from Kyra the minute they arrived at the shuttle.

A WATERY GRAVE

1

Tess had been terrified when the guards pulled her and Frieda out into the hallway. She prepared herself to fight to the death when one of the guards told them they needed to prepare three girls to "come up".

As Tess followed behind the huge guard who had opened their cell door, she tried to calm her breathing. This would probably be her only chance to make a run for it and with her heart pounding in her ears, she knew she wouldn't be able to focus on how best to get out of here. When she finally got herself under control, she glanced around at her surroundings. Her cell was roughly halfway down the hall. She noticed that some of the cells were dark, but most had faint light shining through the small square windows set in the doors.

There was only one exit from this prison wing, and it was straight ahead. Behind her, there were only more cells and a solid wall at the far end. As they walked towards the wing door, Tess saw a dark-haired woman standing outside in the stairwell with two other men. She and Frieda joined her and waited while the huge guard locked the door.

She was momentarily confused when the guard turned right and headed *down* the stairs, instead of going up. Then she remembered Frieda telling her that the kids were one level below them. One of the guards behind her shoved her hard, and it almost knocked her off balance. "Come on," he snorted, "this ain't no guided tour."

They walked down four flights of stairs until they got to the third sublevel. Everything here pretty much looked the same, but the lights were much dimmer at this level. The head guard, who had to be at least 6'7" and weigh close to 400lbs, bent over and picked up a small steel pipe. He rapped on the door several times and then pulled a ring of keys out of his pocket. The keys were connected to a purple D-Ring and Tess noticed with some satisfaction, that it was the same key ring that he used to open their cell door.

After he had banged on the door a few times, Tess heard scuttling and a few cries as if they had been expecting a monster to come through the door. After what she had witnessed when she first got here, she thought they had every reason to expect that.

The guard found the key he was looking for, jammed it into the lock and in a few quick seconds, had the door standing wide open. Apparently, they didn't see the children as a threat, so none of them were locked in individual cells. Either that or they didn't have the keys for the individual cells down here. Tess had a feeling it was the latter.

Tess estimated that there were anywhere from 15 to 20 kids down here. They were filthy and looked on the verge of malnutrition. Quite a few of them wore bruises on their faces. Their ragged clothing and lost stares reminded her of an old story she had read growing up. If they had been on a deserted beach instead of a dark, dank prison cell, then they could have easily been on the cover of *The Lord of the Flies*.

As she looked down the long hallway, she could see that it was very dark towards to back. And it looked different from the women's wing. For one, the cells at the far end of the wing looked shorter than the rest. In this prison world, she had every reason to believe that each cell would be an exact replica of all the other cells. This difference jumped out at her immediately. Something else stood out and that was the smell. Underneath the normal body odor of the children was another smell, one that smelled of rot or fungus. No one else seemed to notice, not even the other women.

The chief guard walked in a few steps and seem to take satisfaction in the fact that the children backed away from him. "These women heah are gonna fix up three a yous for *'Come Up'*. They gonna clean you up and git you some new clothes to wear. Now won't dat be nice?" "Yes, Mister Gurt," they answered in unison. One of the other guards standing behind Frieda cackled loudly. "I love it when they say it like that at the same time! Makes me feel right special." He patted

Frieda on the butt, and she jerked away from him.

"Shut up Mort and be patient," the third guard said. He had been quiet until now. Tess glanced at him and could see that he was more serious than the other two and probably more dangerous. He saw Tess looking at him, and he only stared back. She read no emotion in his cloudy eyes, but could sense a deep darkness in him that chilled her. She turned away from him hurriedly.

Gurt was unlocking the only locked cell down here, and Tess saw that this was where they kept their supplies. Like the wing she was in, the first two cells were four-person cells and were bigger than the rest. In this cell, the bunk beds had been torn out, and Tess could see all sorts of assorted clothing and footwear, some cooking utensils, and a few small hand tools. The rest of the stuff was hidden in boxes stacked on one side of the cell. One box caught her attention, and she almost gave herself away as she looked at it, but steeled herself at the last minute. She kept all emotion firmly locked down. It was good she did because she had a feeling that Mr. Serious was staring a hole in her.

Gurt turned back to the women, "Alright ladies, get in here and find some nice clothes for our new 'Come Up' gals. Git 'em cleaned up good. We'll back in two hours, so be ready."

The three guards left without waiting for a reply. Tess heard the lock snap firmly shut and then heard the men bounding up the stairs laughing. Tess had a feeling that the serious guard was not laughing. He was making plans.

2

After the guards had gone, Tess ran to the door and looked out through the small barred window. She couldn't see them anymore, but she could hear their deep voices fading out as they walked up to the top level. Behind her, the dark-haired woman whom she had not met yet, rushed fully into the prison wing. *"Bonnie?"* she whispered urgently. "Where are you baby?" She ran from kid to kid looking for her Bonnie.

From the back of the group of frightened children, a slim girl with long mangled black hair emerged. Her olive skin was dirty, and the puffy bags under her eyes seemed out of place on her young face. "Mama!" the little girl cried and ran into her outstretched arms.

"*Mi Bonita!* I was so worried for you! Are you okay?" The woman hugged the girl tightly, desperately, as if she were afraid to let her go.

The other children drifted closer to Frieda and Tess, their initial fear gone or at least depressed for the time being. As they got closer, they reached out and started groping at the two women. For a second, Tess recoiled and started to step back, but then realized that the children were *hugging* them. Or more accurately, they were wanting to be hugged.

Tess was overwhelmed. She took a knee and embraced the three kids that came up to her. Foul smelling hair and body odor filled her nostrils, but she didn't pull back. It hurt her heart to see these children like this, and she wondered how many had died since being locked up down here.

Tess gently disengaged herself from the children and walked over to where the other woman was hugging the little girl fiercely. She placed her hand on the woman's shoulder, "Are you okay? What's your name?"

The woman let go of the girl and straightened up. "I'm Angela. Angela Martinez. This is my daughter, Bonnie. I haven't seen her since they brought us here." She reached for the girl as her eyes began to well up again.

"I'm Tess, and we were brought here several hours ago." She looked back at the door anxiously. "We don't have much time and I need to talk to you and Frieda."

Angela wiped her eyes and nodded her head, "Sure, about what?" "When those men come back, they will be expecting three of the girls here to be cleaned and dressed and ready to become someone's concubine or sex slave." Angela nodded wearily. She knew very well what was going on and she also knew that her 14-year old daughter would be one of the three girls forced to go up.

"Look Angela, this might be our only opportunity to get out of this place, and we have to be ready. I'll be damned if they're going to roast me alive up there. I'd rather die trying to escape than allow that." Frieda was nodding beside her.

"What can we do Tess?" Angela asked. "All of the guards carry some type of weapon. A few of them even have guns."

"I'm not sure, but something occurred to me when we first came in here. Something back there." She pointed towards the back of dark wing where the cells looked oddly off center. "It looks odd back there, but before I check that out, there's something up here that I need to look at." She turned to her right and walked into the modified store room.

With the prison beds removed, the makeshift storage area was quite large, and Vanek's people managed to squeeze in all types of junk. Mostly what she saw were boxes overflowing with dirty clothes and shoes, cleaning supplies, some grocery store boxes filled with dusty canned goods (she hoped this was the food they were feeding the children, while saving the "purified food" for themselves), and surprisingly, a few boxes from *Toys 'R Us*. She could even see a famed *Monopoly* board game sticking out the top of one box.

What had caught her eye when Gurt first opened the door were a few boxes sitting in a Kroger grocery store shopping cart. It was one of the old metal-framed carts, and she could see what was inside it. She had seen the words *"Property of Undergr..."* and the rest was partially covered. She had a strong reason to believe that the box at least, had come from the Underground Fuel Center. She was desperate to see what was in it.

The cart had obviously been there a while because there were quite a number of other boxes stacked on top of the Fuel Center box and then on top of the cart itself. She pushed off the top few and then moved the rest over to the side of the room. She finally uncovered the black and white box with the "Underground Fuel Center" label on it. It was still sealed unbelievingly. Tess yanked at the tape that closed the top and noticed that her hands were trembling. For a second, the tape wouldn't tear, but her repeated pulls eventually loosened it, and it came tearing off. She almost ripped the top flap in the process.

She flipped open the top and looked inside, almost fearfully. To the children and the two women who had crowded around the door, she looked like she was uncovering a rare and expensive treasure. She reached in with both arms and pulled out an unused fuel engine power node. It was still wrapped tightly in its protective, airtight silicone skin. She looked at them with tears in her eyes as she gently laid the node back in the box.

She got up and walked out of the cell, ignoring the streaming tears coursing down her cheeks and the questioning stares from the others. "I'll tell you guys later. Right now, I want to take a look at those cells back there."

Frieda looked at her closely, "What do you see Tess?"

"I'm not sure yet, but if it's what I think it is, then Lady Luck may be smiling on us for a change."

She walked towards the back of the wing, gently making her way between the children. As she walked towards the back, she stared at the odd-looking cells. As she had expected, the cells down here were all the same *originally*, but as Frieda had told her earlier, the recent earthquakes had destroyed the bottom sublevel which caused flooding down there. She felt a twinge of sympathy for the poor man who had been left to starve.

Looking at the slanted cells on this level, she could see that the earthquakes had caused some damage here as well. Apparently, Vanek's people either didn't notice these damages or didn't care.

What captured her attention were two cells on the right. When she had first come into the wing, their oddness immediately jumped out at her. They looked as if they were recessed into the floor. She glanced up at the ceiling and could see long cracks making their way forward from the rear of the wing. Most of the lights had gone out back here, so she couldn't see the remaining three or four cells in the hallway as they were shrouded in darkness.

The smell of rot and mildew seemed to swell all around her, and she noticed that the floor was wet. She had a feeling that the last earthquake Frieda had told her about must have damaged the supports under this part of the floor. She went to the cell closest to her, but the door was still locked shut. She started inching herself towards the next cell, careful not to put a lot of weight on the floor. If she was right about the support here, then her next step could be her last.

She almost jumped when she heard Frieda whisper *"Careful Tess"*. She was right behind her, mimicking her moves. "Frieda, I think this floor is damaged, so stay as close as possible to the cell doors."

Tess made her way to the next cell where the door and the bars were standing wide open. The first few bars were still cemented in tightly, but the next three or four moved freely in her hand like rotted teeth. She grabbed one of the loose bars and worked it back and forth, straining until it finally broke loose of its cement prison.

Once she had it out of the cement block, she was shocked to find that it barely weighed a pound, if that. Then she remembered that ten years ago, NASA had started building the new shuttles with extremely lightweight (and extremely expensive) micro-lattice metals. Looking at the lightweight prison cell bar, she realized that it hadn't taken long for the materials to make their way into civilian construction. Lucky for them it did.

She looked at the jagged edge of the bar and smiled. The curved and serrated edges were rusty and sharp – *a deadly combination,* Tess thought. She handed the pipe to Frieda and started working feverishly on the other loose ones.

3

Tess was still working to loosen the last bar when Angela came up behind her, "A lot of the children are sick. They haven't been eating much as you can imagine. My daughter told me that they used to eat the rats when they caught them, but they haven't been able to catch them lately. She said that one of the older boys here used to catch the rats for them. He would gut and clean them and hang out strips of the meat to dry. She said he's dead now."

Tess had expected that outcome, but hearing it still didn't make the sound of it any less painful. "How did he die?" Tess asked. "Was he purified?" She was speaking directly to the little girl, Bonnie.

Bonnie looked fearfully towards the remaining area of the wing and pointed. "He drowned back there," she said.

Tess looked towards the back end of the prison wing. There were maybe two or three more cells remaining on each side. "He drowned? Back *here*?"

The girl nodded her head; her eyes were still staring at the back of the wing.

Tess looked at the darkened hallway again. She could see that the water had been getting in, but she hadn't thought it was deep enough to drown in, although technically, one could drown in a sink. Now she wondered. The guards had only been gone for 20 minutes, so she decided to see just how deep the water was back there.

She walked slowly down the middle of the hallway until the floor started to drop down. She sat in the dank water and inched her bottom forward, using her feet to tap where the floor was. The floor gently sloped downward and by the time the water made it to her waist, she was at the edge of the floor bordering a huge hole—the rest of the floor had apparently rotted away. She wasn't a hundred percent certain, but had a pretty good feeling that this hole led to a body of underground water. She turned towards Frieda and Angela, *"Grab some of those clothes in the cell and start making me a rope as long as you can!"*

4

It had taken them only a few minutes to shred and tie enough of the clothing for Tess to have at least 15 feet of "rope". She checked all of the knots, redoing a few of them, and then tied it tightly around her waist. She looked up at Frieda, "If I'm not back up in two minutes, pull me in gently. I want to see how deep it might be." On impulse, she splashed the water around and scooped some in her hand. She first took a tentative sip and then a little more. "Hmm...this is fresh water." And then she took three deep breaths and let herself slide into the dark hole in the floor. Frieda and Angela looked at one another and slowly started letting the rope out. Frieda counted out loud, while the children stared on fearfully.

Tess would have given anything at that moment to have a light. It was complete and total darkness as she surveyed the space under the floor with her fingers. She was holding onto the bent steel girders that made up the floor and possibly the ceiling of the fourth sublevel. She moved slowly, not wanting to cut herself on some of the ragged ends. She lowered herself and moved a little further away feeling for the end of the girders when her hands touched something solid. She couldn't be sure, but it felt like rock.

She stopped cold and slowly moved her hands across the rough surface. She was trying to imagine what it could be when she felt something brush across her cheek. At first, she thought it was her hair or part of the clothing rope, but then she felt several more brushes that were actively swimming around her face. It startled her briefly, but she used her hand to wave whatever it was away from her face. She could feel her fingers moving through a school of small fish.

Feeling around the rock, she was able to get a sense that there was an opening or crawl space that opened up into a larger space. Before she had time to reflect on this, she felt the tugging of the rope, not to mention her own burning lungs, and turned around back towards the hole in the floor. It was a little easier going because she could see the faint light from the hallway shimmering just a few feet above her.

They helped her out of the hole and before she could even catch her breath, Frieda was asking her questions, "What's down there Tess? How deep did you go? I was so scared!"

She looked at both of the women and smiled, "I don't think that little boy drowned at all. I think he was able to escape. I believe there's an underground body of water here and maybe the last couple of major earthquakes caused massive fault-shifting down here, affecting this sublevel. Probably the fourth sublevel too."

"How do you know that?" Angela asked.

She pointed to the cracked and slanted walls and ceiling within the wing. "Look around. This entire wing has been compromised by the looks of it." She was looking at them eagerly now. "But that's not the best part. There are fish in the water! A school of them swam past me, which means there must be an entry point somewhere down there. Also, I came up against a solid rock wall...*not* man-made."

Angela looked horrified, "What are you saying? That we can swim out of here? Do you even know how deep it is?"

"I don't know how deep it is," Tess replied, "but I believe that boy swam out of here...or died trying." Her face turned dark, "Besides, we don't have much of a choice here, do we?"

Angela slumped against the wall. "I guess I'm kind of nervous because I don't know how to swim." She looked at the dark water and shivered, "God, that kid had some guts. He didn't even know where it led to or how far it was, but he did it anyway."

Tess swallowed hard. She felt that it was only a matter of time before it might come to this; all of them pulling themselves along under water, groping blindly in the darkness and hoping their air didn't run out. She didn't know how some of the younger kids would make out, but they had to try. They would certainly die if they stayed here, either by starvation or some other horrible end. She wondered how many people would die trying to escape. She turned towards Frieda and Angela and some of the older kids, "Okay, this is what we need to do."

HARLAN PENITENTIARY

1

"Goddammit!" Henry spat out for the second time since Kyra told him about Sheila and Albert, and the fact that Tess, Max, and Lars were missing.

"I can't believe this Kyra. I had a feeling something was wrong when you told me that you hadn't heard from Tess. Based on what Sheila said, it's probably the same group that took Thelma's people."

Bob, Joe, and Lee stood off to the side, listening intently.

"I know Henry," Kyra said. Although she was encouraged by the animals that Henry returned with, she couldn't ignore the sickening feeling in her stomach at their current situation. "We've got to find her Henry! We've got to!"

"I know!" Henry shouted, immediately disgusted with himself for raising his voice. "I'm sorry K. I shouldn't have shouted at you. I'm...I'm at a loss. We don't even know where they may have taken Tess and the others. They could be *anywhere* in this busted city."

"But we *do* know where it is," a voice behind them said. They all whirled around and saw Thelma in the doorway leading out to the bay areas. "Remember what I told you Henry? They took almost our entire group, both adults and children. And the only person to escape and make it back to the shelter was Len. He can not only show you where their camp is, but help you find a way inside."

"Thelma, I can't do that. I can't ask a 12-year old boy to risk his life to take us to a place like that. To go *back* to a place like that! Especially if it's as bad as you say it is. It's extremely dangerous. Maybe he can draw it out for us and show us where the ambushes are. I'm sure then we would..."

"I will go with you!" Len spoke up from behind Thelma. She hadn't heard him come up behind her, and it startled her somewhat. "My mother and father are there, and I want to help save them!"

Henry turned to Len and could see fierce determination in his eyes. "Len, this could be very dangerous for you." He didn't want to mention the fact that his father—and mother for that matter—might be dead, but he could already see that this might be a losing battle. "There's a chance that some of us might not make it back." He hesitated for just a second and then decided there was no use holding back. *"None* of us may come back, to be honest."

Kyra gently laid her hand on Henry's shoulder, "Babe, if we don't get Tess back, then we're stuck here regardless. We have to get there quickly and if Len can do that, then he needs to go with you for Tess's sake and for our own. We can't take the chance that you guys might get lost trying to get there or worse yet, killed along the way."

Henry realized that she was also referring to the constant grumbling of the earth beneath their feet. Since they got back to the ship, the ground seemed to be waking up all around them. Off in the distance, they would hear explosions and then 10 or 15 minutes later, feel the earth lightly rolling beneath their feet.

Right before they landed here, Chayton had run a spectro-analysis of the area, and they were able to see that for miles around, the subsurface of the earth was deteriorating. It was only a matter of time before a chain of events would kick the process into full gear.

He let out a sigh and looked down at the boy. He could see the defiant look in his eyes and realized that the only way he was going to keep Len here at the ship would be to lock him in it. "Okay Len, you can go, but we have to be very careful about this. We can't give them any indication that we're coming, or they will be prepared for us. They might even resort to executing their prisoners if they know we're coming for them. Do you understand me?" Len nodded his head seriously, showing that he understood the gravity of the situation.

He turned to Joe and Lee, "Okay, guys, so thanks to Sheila, we have just over a hundred rounds of army-issue M-16 ammo, two hand grenades, an orange smoke canister and a white one, one M-16 rifle, and a 9mm handgun with 48 rounds of ammo. Is the rifle in good shape?"

"Sure is," said Joe. "Just needed to be stripped down and cleaned up."

"Excellent. Lee, how many rifles do we have from Thelma's group? There were at least the two that Harvey and Lisa had when we first arrived there."

"They had a total of five shotguns, maybe 30 rounds of shotgun ammo, and one 9mm handgun with ammo. There was no M-16 ammunition."

"Thelma, how are we doing on the animal enclosures?"

Thelma straightened up and said, "We're doing great. We've gotten most of the animals situated in the biosphere enclosure. We'll be completely finished in just a few hours."

He turned to Chayton, who had been focusing on preparing their navigations as well as monitoring the fuel intake. "Based on the spectro-analysis of this area, can you ballpark how much time we have before things are so bad that we can't take off?"

"It's hard to say Henry. We are just in one little corner of the earth. Earthquakes, much *stronger* earthquakes, are happening all over the planet. Things could go to hell in the next two hours or the next ten hours. Hell, it might even be months before anything happens. All I know for certain though is that in the last ten hours, the earth's *contractions*, if you will, have been coming closer and closer. We've been quite lucky in our little corner of the world, but the small tremors we've been feeling every couple of hours will eventually speed up and become more violent. At some point, I think they'll start and just won't stop, at least not for hours. We *can't* be here when that happens."

"Okay, thanks Chayton. We'll do our best to get the hell back here before that happens. Kyra, I'm going to leave one of the handguns and one of the shotguns here, in case something happens while we're gone. Since we still don't know where Andy is lurking around, I want to make sure we're protected in case he comes back.

"I'll take one of the 9mm's. Joe, Lee, and Bob, you guys determine who should have the M-16 and the two shotguns. Remember guys, we're traveling light because we may be on the run coming back." He looked out the window at the impenetrable grayness. "Even though the light is gray and dim outside, we will only have one or two hours of it left by the time it starts to get dark." He looked around at their determined faces. "I hope to be on the way back here by then. Let's divvy up this ammo and meet outside in 10 minutes."

2

Tess's clothing was still damp by the time the men returned. They had quickly wiped down three of the older girls, Bonnie included, and had them dress in the remaining clean clothes in the storage-converted cell. There were no bottoms to change into, so the girls just wore clean tops above their dingy pants. Tess was just returning to the front of the prison wing after hiding the engine node in one of the cells at the back, when the lock turned in the door.

The door swung open and the huge mass of Gurt stepped in, holding the pipe in one hand and a huge rusty knife in the other. *"Ready or not, we here!"* his deep voice boomed out. He quickly surveyed the three girls who stood in front of Tess, Frieda, and Angela, but Tess could see that he was only giving them a cursory glance. His attention was focused on the three women.

Mort tromped into the prison wing and closed the door. Tess noticed that the serious one, the one she felt was "making plans", was not here, and she was immensely glad about that. "Where's your partner?" Tess asked curiously.

Big Gurt looked at her distractedly. He had been moving towards Angela. "Who, Baxter? We left his ass behind. I think he's gay and not interested in some of the finer things we got here." He had made his way towards Angela, and his eyes seemed to float dangerously in their sockets. Tess waited. She waited for an opening to try to make her move. Mort stood back greedily watching Gurt advance towards Angela as she involuntarily stepped back.

Just when Tess thought the moment might be right, Gurt reached out quick as a snake and grabbed Angela by the shirt. He spun her around and brought his rusty knife up to her neck. Tess made a step toward them when Mort hit her in the stomach and then shifted behind her with his arm around her neck. Frieda had pushed the girls behind her and now stood frozen in place.

"Guess who goan be pur'fied tonight sweet thang?" Gurt whispered into Angela's ear, but loud enough for all of them to hear. Her eyes went wide, and her mouth dropped open. Obviously pleased with the effect of his statement, he proceeded to unzip his pants. While fumbling in his pants, he turned his head towards Frieda, "You too sweetheart, but not until we have our fill. Guard detail always gits to taste the goods before purif'cation. I'm gonna take this lovely Latin thang here, and Mort and Baxter are gonna do you at the same time. That's if he c'n keep his prick hard long enough." He laughed uproariously while the children stared on in horror.

"We goan save this dark chocolate honey here for last. All three of us goan take care of her." He smiled and in that toothless, gleeful, and dangerous look, a flood of guilt, anger, helplessness, and loss seemed to wash over Tess in wave after turbulent wave.

As if from far away, Tess could hear Frieda telling the children to back up and to turn around, "I don't want any of you to see this," she heard Frieda saying. In the corner of her eye, she could see Frieda on her knees, pretending to console one of the kids, but she was reaching for one of the jagged bars.

Gurt put the knife in his belt strap and shoved Angela towards the storage cell. She stumbled, but caught her balance. When she straightened up, she turned to face him defiantly. He leered at her as he closed the distance. *"A wildcat! Hot damn! This goan be good!"* he said as he continued to fumble inside his pants.

Mort's grip around Tess's neck felt like a vise as he pulled her tight to him. He licked his lips as he watched Gurt advance on Angela. Tess could feel excitement growing in his pants and was disgusted. But the more excited he got, the looser his grip around her neck became.

For the next 30 seconds, Tess felt as if she existed outside of herself and time seemed to stop for everyone but her. Angela and Gurt were frozen in mid-step. The children stood stock still, caught in the process of turning around. Frieda's hand closed around the jagged pipe and remained solidly clenched. She could sense her body slide to the left and as Mort's front became exposed, she raised her closed fist in the air and brought it down hard against the bulge in the man's pants. She crouched down immediately after hitting him, instinctively knowing that he would have doubled over, putting his head directly over hers. When he did this, she skyrocketed herself upward and rammed her head into the man's nose and face.

The groin shot caused him to take in a sharp breath, and for a split second, Tess feared he would start screaming in pain and bring more guards down on them. But after she smashed his face, the only thing that escaped his mouth was a weak exhale of rotten air.

Gurt had turned towards Tess and the now crumpling Mort, when he heard the crunch of Mort's nose. His face contorted into a mask of deadly fury. As he reached down for his knife, Tess sprinted towards him with her arms held out in front of her. From the corner of her eye, she saw Angela dive towards the floor behind him.

Tess hit him in the chest with as much force as she could muster, and it was like hitting a brick wall, but it was just enough to offset his balance and cause him to move one of his feet backward to maintain his footing. If Angela had not dropped behind him, he would have easily caught his balance and jabbed Tess in the stomach with the rusty blade. As it happened, his back foot caused him to trip over Angela, and he fell back like Goliath after being hit by David's stone.

The sound that came a split second later was a loud ripping and snapping sound as Gurt's mass drove him down onto the jagged edges of the steel bar that Frieda had planted into the ground behind him (Tess had an eerie recollection of an old movie called *The Edge*, where Anthony Hopkins' character was able to get a huge bear to impale himself on a sharpened stick). His initial surprise of falling was replaced by the shock of intense pain as his 400lbs sank onto the bar.

The only sound he was able to make before two feet of jagged metal came bursting through his chest like some metal alien, was a wet, gurgling sound.

A sound at the door made her turn around quickly and as she did so, her heart sank. She found herself staring into the dark and unreadable eyes of the third guard, *Baxter*, as they called him. A.K.A., *Mr. Serious*. In his hands he had a sawed-off shotgun. At that moment, another man came bounding down the stairs and pushed his way past Baxter and into the prison wing. *"Holy shit, Baxter! What the fuck happened here?"*

He pointed to Tess and said, "You can ask *her*, but you may have to ask her *real* nice."

The newcomer sneered and reached for a small axe he had cinched in his belt. "Yeah, I'll be glad to." When he took a step forward, Baxter raised the butt of his shotgun in the air and brought it down hard on the man's neck. Tess heard something snap, and the man fell to the floor; his dead eyes stared out accusingly.

Tess's face had been mask of fierce determination, and she had steeled herself to face off to the death with Baxter, and the man now lying on the floor. When Baxter crushed his neck before he went two steps, she felt everything inside go limp.

Baxter dropped back in the stairwell and cocked his head, listening. Satisfied, he came back in and closed the door. He leaned over Gurt and unclipped the keys from his belt loop, being careful not to touch the growing pool of blood soaking Gurt's shirt.

"I'm sorry about that, ladies but I didn't know those two morons were going to come back so soon. When I saw that they had left already, I got down here as fast as I could, but..." he looked around at the two bodies, "you ladies seem to be able to take care of yourselves." "Thank you," was all Tess could mutter. Before she could bring herself to say anything else, a young girl cried out, *"Daddy!"* Baxter ran over to her and hugged her tightly. "Hi baby, are you okay?" The girl nodded; her head buried in her father's chest.

After a minute, he disengaged himself from his daughter and faced Tess, "My name is John Baxter and don't thank me yet," he commented. "We still need to get out of here, or do you ladies have *that* figured out too?"

Tess, finally coming around, smiled uncertainly, "Actually, we just might."

3

In less than ten minutes, they had unlocked all the cells holding the men and women on sublevels one and two. Tess counted just over 40 gaunt men and women. Although she was encouraged by this, she was saddened beyond measure. Max was nowhere to be found. Apparently, he had been taken up to the field and was being sacrificed at that very moment. *Goodbye, Max*, she thought to herself sadly. By the time she got back down to the third sublevel, her sadness had been replaced by red hot anger. She went into the wing and saw Baxter talking to two women and three men who weren't there when she left. "Who are *they*?" she asked suspiciously.

He pointed to the two women, "This is Becky Florence, and that's Hana Fumiko. Becky was a cop here in San Antonio, and Hana was part of the army reserves before things went to hell. These guys are Curt and Donovan Dixon, and that's Steven Tremont. Steve was a Los Angeles paramedic and Curt and Donovan owned an indoor/outdoor sporting shop in Canada. Calgary to be exact."

Tess wondered how the two brothers ended up in San Antonio, Texas, but left that question for another time.

"These are good people Tess. In fact, there are a lot of good people up there, but Vanek and Brutos run this place like a goddamn Nazi camp. There are probably 15 more people up there who have been trying to get out of here, but Vanek has this place locked down tighter than a drum. His loyal guards have *all* the exits blocked."

"Well, I'm certain that he doesn't have *this* exit blocked."

As Frieda and Angela guided the men and women deeper into the wing, Tess described the apparent escape of the boy and how she entered the hole at the sloping end of the prison wing and found herself in a body of fresh water. She recounted how she felt fish swimming near her face.

Curt and Donovan were looking at each other curiously. "Before things went belly up, we were actually thinking of opening up a store here in Texas, so we made a few trips down here," Curt told them. "Don, remember when we looked at this area north of old San Antonio?"

Don, his dark hair just starting to turn gray, crossed his arms and hung his head for a second, thinking. After a short pause, he brightened and looked at them. "Yeah! I remember that. In addition to selling sporting goods, we also sell outdoor activity packages. Stuff like hiking, mountain climbing, orienteering, that sort of stuff. However, each local store only offers activity packages that are local and in their own backyards, so to speak."

Tess was nodding, but she wondered what he was getting at. She looked towards the prison wing door that Frieda had locked after everyone had come into the wing. "Donovan...Don, we don't have a lot of time. What's your point?"

Unperturbed, Donovan continued, "Yeah...right...sorry about that, eh? Well, we inquired into a lease of the area on the other side of this range of hills. The plan was to build zip-line stations in the hills that ended at the edge of the water, but it was denied because a building permit had already been issued for this prison."

He paused for a second, and his eyes became bright with understanding. "I would be willing to bet that that last earthquake, and all the other mothers before that one, created a massive underground fault that shifted, bringing a portion of the underground body of water into contact with the sublevels. The weakened floors eventually gave way, and the water slowly flooded in. I imagine that this level will be underwater two months from now."

Tess smiled, "My thoughts exactly."

"What I think this means," Baxter finished for him, "is that if that boy was able to escape, then we could be only minutes from getting the hell out of here."

Tess could see the concern on Becky's face, "What's wrong Becky? What are you thinking?"

Becky stared at the dark hole in the floor and then added quietly, "How do we know that he escaped? He could have drowned down there, hundreds of feet away from any exit point."

"I was actually thinking about that," Hana intervened. "Someone needs to go down there with a rope attached to them. Find the exit, tie off the rope and then come back for the rest of us."

Even though Tess didn't know the girl, she liked her immediately. "Excellent idea, Hana!" She looked around their small group. It would have to be one of them; the other adults looked too weak to volunteer for this. Before she had a chance to ask the question, Hana spoke up again, "I'll go. I'm a strong swimmer and a licensed scuba instructor, so I'm very comfortable underwater."

"I'll go too!" Steve Tremont added. "There needs to be at least two people on this first run and as a paramedic, I can be on the other side to help with any problems." He thought about what he said and corrected himself, "Not the *other side*, but on the other side of the *river*...oh forget it!"

They laughed at him for only a second before growing somber again. Tess laid a hand on Steve's shoulder, "Thanks Steve, but I'll go. If you don't mind, I'd like for you to check out the kids and some of the adults and find out if there are any medical issues we need to be worried about. Then you should come on the next trip back, what do you say?"

He nodded, fully understanding Tess's concern. A few of the adults looked badly shaken, and there were a couple that were bleeding from recent injuries.

Baxter turned quickly and went to the storage cell. Tess could hear him rooting around and throwing stuff out through the door. A minute later, he backed up into the hallway; his arms were loaded with rope, flashlights, and chemical light sticks.

Tess's jaw dropped when she saw the items. *Maybe I should have looked closer! Duh!* she thought to herself. From far away, she could hear the muted noises of the sacrificial frenzy going on above.

4

Under the water, Tess silently prayed that it wouldn't be a far trip because the stitch in her side had grown progressively worse from the hand grenade explosion at the fuel center. Each time she tried her deep breathing exercises, she found that she just couldn't get enough air without grimacing in pain.

Hana led the way and Tess followed carefully. It was a little tricky avoiding the rope tied around Hana's waist at first, but she soon got the hang of swimming next to it, and she watched out closely for any potential snags. They had both activated their light sticks right before they slipped into the dark water. As Tess looked around, she was amazed at the difference the light sticks made under the water. She could easily see how the walls and the floor had been compromised by too many earthquakes and how the incredible shifting of the earth had pushed a wall of granite rock in the hillside up against the underground portion of the prison. The underground body of water here combined with the river on the other side of the hillside had completely flooded the area.

She also saw that where the water went, so did the fish and other small aquatic animals. She saw small schools of fish swimming lazily near the sides of the granite rock. A few swam past her quickly. She turned around and glanced up. She could see the dim light coming through the hole in the third sublevel floor, but she also saw something else: She could see the outline of the fourth sublevel. A huge slab of rock rested up against it at an odd angle and although it had been damaged, it didn't look completely compromised.

She turned and followed closely behind Hana, but not so close as to get kicked in the face. Hana was breaststroke-kicking strongly, using the rock outcroppings to keep herself from sinking. Tess glanced down. Although she could see the rocky bottom, there were dangerous-looking crevices here and there that seemed to camouflage even deeper depths.

Although she tried not to think about it, Tess could feel her lungs starting to burn with the need to expel the carbon dioxide slowly building up inside of her. She looked past Hana and could see no dim light or tell-tale sign that they were getting anywhere close to the surface. She wasn't sure how long they had been under, but she knew that on a good day, she could hold her breath for at least two and half minutes, maybe even three. She felt that she was getting very close to that time.

Her heart sank when their forward progress slowed as the route forced them to descend deeper. The fault seemed to have closed, and Tess realized languidly that the fault had originated deeper, and the effect here was minimal. As they descended to go under a rocky arch, she tried unsuccessfully to *not* think about the deceptive crevices.

Where the hell is the exit? She thought wildly. She wasn't in trouble yet, but if they didn't find this exit soon, she would be. She tried to calm her body down, but as they continued through the narrowing passageway after swimming under the arch, she started having thoughts about turning around. *How in the hell did that kid make it this far?* her mind screamed at her, as if from another world.

Hana had turned to her as if to signal something, but Tess was on her last reserves. Her lungs burned and her side ached. She had to turn around. She could see Hana waving her arms around, but her oxygen-deprived brain couldn't translate what Hana was doing or trying to say. She turned to go back, but Hana grabbed her foot before she could take one stroke.

Tess whirled violently, her survival instincts flaring at the surface of her senses, and tried to hit at Hana. But Hana was strong and apparently still had enough air in her system to give her a slight advantage. She grabbed Tess's resisting arm and pulled her first to herself and then pushed her up.

Up into an air pocket! Their heads popped above the surface like ballast tanks. The enclosed rocky ceiling above their heads was about five feet high, but there was air here. Tess coughed and sputtered, trying to take in huge lungsful of air. After what seemed like an hour, instead of minutes, both ladies looked at each other and laughed.

"Jesus Hana! I thought you were trying to kill me! Why didn't you just *say* there was an air pocket here?" They both laughed again.

Hana wiped her eyes, coughed some more and grew somber. "I was starting to get worried myself. It seemed like it was just getting darker and darker, and I was starting to run out of air. I don't really know why I looked up, but when I did, I saw the air pocket." She felt a tug on the rope and responded back with three easy tugs, their signal to the others that things were okay. "I'm sorry I yanked you Tess..."

"Are you kidding me? Hana...you saved my life!" Tess exclaimed. "We were too far to go back. If I had tried to make it back, I would have drowned. You did the right thing...thank you."

Hana smiled, "Well, at least we have a mid-point. I'll mark it for the others." She took a light stick from her pocket and activated it. She submerged and wedged the light stick tightly into part of the rocky arch. "You ready?" She said to Tess after she secured the light stick and resurfaced. Tess nodded, and they both checked the ropes about their waists. Hana took several deep breaths and then submerged again. Tess took her handicapped breaths and followed suit.

The second half of their journey lasted only a minute and a half. As soon as they swam past the arch, the narrow corridor expanded and almost at once, Tess could see dim light filtering down through the water. She and Hana swam towards the surface and emerged in a water-filled alcove, just a little bigger than their air pocket. Once they reached the surface, however, they simply had to wade over to the rocky edge and pull themselves out. An easy climb over the edge, and they were on lying on the grassy hillside once again breathing in huge lungsful of air.

Tess rolled over and stood up, "Let's get this thing tied off Hana, and I'll go back and explain the air pocket and get the others moving."

"Are you okay to make it back Tess? I have no problem going back."
"I know Hana," Tess replied, "My main reason for going back is that

I want to bring the engine power node myself, but the fact that you've been in the military is a significant plus, and we might need your skills out here until we get more folks out." She looked around at the growing darkness. "I'm good to go, especially with our air pocket. I'll get Steve out here on the next train." She smiled and helped Hana tie off the rope to a nearby tree. Two minutes later, she was back in the water, following the rope back to the third sublevel.

5

Henry and Len half-crawled, half-crouched back over to the others. Thus far, they had been lucky. They hadn't seen a single guard or sentry. Their small group had stopped on the north side of the prison grounds where Len had escaped. Even though the shadows of the trees kept them hidden, they stayed well away from the tall concertina wire-topped fence.

"They're having some type of ceremony," Henry whispered to the small group. "We couldn't get close enough to see, but I don't think I really want to. Len pointed out where he emerged out of the hills, and it's up there near the river's edge."

They crept around a huge jutting slab of rock that seemed completely incongruous to the gentle slope of the hillside. Henry looked around as they made their way past the huge chunk of rock. The entire area bowed and dipped with uneven plots of dirt, grass and rock. When they passed the jumbled mass of steel and concrete that made up the top floors of the prison, Henry assumed that the earthquakes did the damage as opposed to the meteorites. But looking at the way the ground heaved upward in some places confirmed that the earthquakes were the real culprits here.

Soon, they were sloshing in wet, swampy water that rose quickly past their ankles. Not too far away, Henry could hear the sound of running water and knew that they must be getting closer to the river where Len escaped.

Len had told them that he escaped underwater, but at the time, Henry had no idea how that could have happened. After seeing the results of the earthquake activity and the closeness of the prison to the river, he thought he might see how but was doubtful.

Len led them along the edge of the narrow river as they paralleled the gently rising hills to their left. Soon, the distance between the river's edge and the slope of the hills began to shrink, and Henry found himself trying to maintain his balance as the hill's slope grew steeper and steeper.

They finally came to a sharp break in the hillside where the hill looked as if it were pulled apart violently. Where it had separated, the river had poured in quickly, filling the void. The gap was only ten feet across, but the drop was easily 15 feet to the water. Thick, gnarled roots poked through the ragged walls of the hill. This made a clean jump almost impossible. Henry turned around and whispered to the others, "I think this is where he came out, but we need to climb up a little and then come down on the other side. There might be an easier—"

Len touched Henry's arm and pointed towards the other side of the ripped hillside. He followed the direction of Len's arm and saw several people bunched together and in the dying light, he thought he saw one of them holding a weapon.

"*Damn!*" he cursed. "I see several guards down there. Maybe they figured out how Len escaped and are standing guard in case anyone else comes out this way."

Lee inched up to him and stared out at the guards. "This doesn't change anything Henry. We need to get in there and get Tess and the others. There are only three of them, and I think we can take them. It'll have to be knife work and we'll need a diversion, but we can do it."

Despite the waning light, Henry could see the determination in Lee's eyes. He knew Lee was right, but he had hoped that they would have found Tess and the others first before encountering any opposition. He nodded to Lee, and they moved closer to the others and worked up their diversion.

6

They were moving quickly, but Tess still thought it was too slow. She was still a little shaken from her earlier experience, but she was able to help Frieda and Curt get the next group in the water. Hana, Steve, and Tess assumed by now that Baxter and his daughter were on the other side now. They had just put Angela and her daughter Bonnie in the water while Donovan agreed to take one of the smaller kids.

Nathan, Angela's husband, had talked his wife into going first with Bonnie. "Bonnie's more comfortable with you in these situations, so you take her with you. I'll be right behind you." But as soon as they left, he turned to Tess abruptly, "Are you *sure* the fourth sublevel looked intact, Tess?"

"Yeah, I'm certain of it." She looked at him curiously, "What's bothering you, Nathan?"

"They sent my friend down there and left him there to rot. I know we need to get out of here, but we just can't leave him down there to die. He saved a lot of us when we were first attacked. A few days ago, we overheard the guards saying that the entire fourth sublevel had flooded and that Brutos told them to stop feeding him. I want to see with my own eyes if he's dead or not. I couldn't leave here in good conscience if I didn't at least check. If it's not completely flooded, then maybe he survived. You don't need to go with me Tess; I can do it alone." Behind them, another couple submerged in the dark water and were gone.

Tess looked the man up and down. He was very thin and could barely move when he walked. She knew he would never be able to help someone on his own. She would have to go with him.

She sighed heavily and called out to Frieda. "We're going to quickly check on the man they locked up on sublevel four. If he's alive, then we'll get him and get back here as soon as possible."

"Tess, you might not have time!" She cocked her head up at the noise coming from outside, three levels up. "I'm only guessing, but you may only have 10 minutes, 15 at the most."

"I'm going to lock you guys in here in case they're here when we return. Just keep getting them in the water Frieda. We'll be back in five minutes or less. You can count on it!"

Before she left, she looked at the remaining folks. There were still quite a number of children and adults left. They had at least 12 more trips, maybe 14. *That could be another five minutes, ten at the most,* she thought. She could still hear cheering and thought she smelled something burning. The smell may have only been in her mind, but since they didn't find Max in any of the cells, if he wasn't burning now then he would be soon.

"Okay Nathan, let's take a quick look downstairs. We have to move quickly though. I have a feeling that they're going to come looking for me real soon and when they can't find their guards, all hell will break loose."

She started to unlock the prison wing door, but stopped in mid-turn. She reached down and grabbed one of the shorter jagged bars and continued to unlock the door. "Just in case," she said to Nathan and they headed out, locking the door behind them.

7

Hana had been moving everyone over to a more secluded area as they came out of the water, but she didn't know how they would be able to hide from the guards she could hear coming their way. They were 12 now as Baxter and Steve helped pair after pair climb out of the water. Curt walked them over to the area where everyone else sat in the grass.

Hana had found a solid piece of tree which fortunately, had a natural hand-hold while you jabbed someone with it like a bayonet. Most likely, the guards probably had guns and if that was the case, then they would be slaughtered. Hana had no intention of being cooked like a piece of rotisserie chicken and vowed (as did quite a few others), that they would fight to the death if it came to that. Maybe they would be able to give the children a running head start away—

A snapping branch behind her interrupted her thoughts, *"Don't move motherfuckers or I will kill you! All of you!"* Hana's heart fell, they had been outflanked somehow. A scowl stole across her face and her hands tightened on her weapon.

8

Nathan and Tess crept down to sublevel four. The frenzy on the field had reached fever pitch. Even from down here, Tess could hear someone shrieking in pain. The high-pitched scream could have come from a man or a woman, but she knew who it was coming from. Max Borden. She blamed herself that she was not able to save him. Soon, they would come for her; *the grand finale*. She had a feeling that Vanek would make an example of her because she threatened his empire. She was keenly aware of this.

By the time they reached the fourth sublevel landing, the water had reached their waists. It wasn't completely flooded, but it was getting close. Nathan waded over to the door and looked in through the small window, but it had been covered with some dirty cloth. Tess could make out a faint light behind the cloth. Nathan looked at her and nodded. She made her way to the door, slid the key in the lock and opened the fourth sublevel prison wing door.

It was very dark down here, despite the two ceiling lights that still burned stubbornly. It was too dark for Tess to see the back wall of the wing, but she could see how the walls closest to her were bowed in and cracked. Thin streams of water issued from several cracks and coursed down the wall. *Lucky for him those cracks are small,* Tess thought, *otherwise, this place would have completely flooded weeks ago.*

"Hey bro?" Nathan whispered. *"It's me man. Are you...here?"*

Tess considered this an odd question since the man had only two options for getting out of here; one was through the locked door that they came in and the other was the rising dark water at the back of the wing, provided there was even an opening back there.

Tess was becoming more and more accustomed to the drastic changes in human behavior when put in these types of situations, so even though she wasn't sure what to expect, she did not let her guard down. For all she knew, this man down here might drop out of one of the unlocked cells to give his *"bro"* a hug or he might come bolting out from his hiding place with a sharpened bedpost, ready to skewer him on the spot. To let your guard slip, even a little, could mean death. In her heart, however, she had written the man off as dead and half expected to find his rotting corpse curled up in the corner of one of the cells.

Nathan glanced into the first two dimly lit cells and saw nothing. The next cell was open, but there was no light. He looked in and called out, but got no response. He was just starting to move forward when a loud, almost inhuman scream emerged from the cell behind Tess. The hairs on her forearm stood on end, and her heart started jackhammering almost immediately as she turned around. She knew already that she was much too late to do anything.

The man, although thin, looked far from weak. Tess could see wiry muscles working beneath his dark brown skin as he raised a basketball size block of concrete over his head, preparing to smash her head in. But Tess could only stare. The pipe she had been carrying dropped from her hand. Her mouth started working, but no words came from her lips. In a distant part of her mind, she felt her feet moving forward even as she tried to formulate the words that her overloaded mind tried to force out.

The man took a tentative half-step forward and stopped. Recognition slowly dawned in his eyes. His lips trembled as he dropped the concrete block. It splashed loudly in the silence. He walked towards Tess, eyes filling with tears, *"Surely, I'm dead. How can this be?"*

Tess couldn't move. She wanted to, but it seemed her body was refusing all commands from her brain. Standing in front of her, his body a little thinner, his eyes a little more deep-set and troubled was her dead husband Stan. She had convinced herself so utterly that he was dead, that she would have believed he was a ghost before believing he could have survived the astronomical odds against him.

She reached out a tentative hand and touched his face gently as if it were a live wire. "Oh my God...Stan, I can't believe you're alive."

He grabbed her in his arms, and they both fell on their knees in the deep water, holding each other tightly and weeping. Eventually, their lips found one another, and they kissed passionately, desperately. Tess would never have believed in a million years that she would be in an underground prison, kissing her long-feared dead husband, while maniacal cannibals sacrificed innocent people...and still feel sexual heat kindling in her loins.

She pushed back from him and stared intently into his troubled brown eyes, "Stan...what about..." she started, but found that she couldn't finish it.

As if he were reading her mind, Stan only shook his head, "I'm sorry baby. Your mom's dead, and I'm not sure about Len. They were bringing him and several other kids up to be purified or violated, and I snapped. I don't remember how, but I broke loose and killed one of the guards. Len got loose and ran, but I was knocked unconscious and woke up here. I guess the intent was that I suffer slowly."

Tess hung her head and could feel a deep sadness begin to sweep over her when Nathan walked up to them, understanding now dawning on his face. "Oh shit bro! This is your *wife*? The shuttle pilot? Wow!" He looked at Tess shrewdly, "I thought you guys were on the moon? What are you doing here?" Before Tess could answer, muffled cheering floated down to them from the prison outdoor grounds. Tess and Stan jumped to their feet and pushed over to the door. When they entered the stairwell, they could hear yelling, but Tess couldn't tell what they were saying. She looked up just as a dirty face looked over the railing.

"Hey! Gurt? Is that you? Get yo fat ass up heah. Brutos wants that nigger pilot up heah now!"

Tess jerked her head back before the man could see who he was talking to. *"We need to get upstairs now!"*

As soon as the caller moved away from the railing, they started inching their way up the stairs. Tess was starting to feel the pressure now. It was only a matter of minutes before Brutos sent someone down here to see what was keeping Gurt and the others.

Higher up on the first sublevel, they could hear a bunch of laughing, talking, and a bunch of grab-assing. They were no doubt getting ready for the main attraction, Tess thought. They slipped around the corner of the third stairwell and froze in their tracks. A man stood at the door peering into the small square window in the door. His hands were cupped to the sides of his face and his head moved from side to side, trying to get a better view through the dirty glass.

As Tess thought about what to do, she realized sickeningly, that she left her pipe down on the fourth sublevel. She looked around, and there was nothing on the floor big enough to do any damage to the man. Just then, Nathan tapped her on the elbow, *how about this?* he mouthed to her and handed her the piece of pipe she had dropped on the floor when she first saw Stan.

She smiled briefly at him as she curled her fingers around the pipe. She motioned for them to stay where they were and slowly headed for the man. She raised the pipe, intending to hit him on the back of the head when someone yelled from higher up. The man turned around just as Tess approached him.

His eyes went wide when he saw her and his mouth dropped open. Tess had just a second to register that he was starting to reach for the huge knife stuck in his belt loop. Instead of swinging the pipe like she had intended, she pointed the ragged end of the pipe towards the man's face and jammed the pipe into his mouth.

She felt little resistance as the pipe shredded the man's lips and corners of his mouth, but after breaking all of his front teeth, she felt it wedge tight against his gums and the roof of his mouth. His hands immediately forgot the knife in his pocket and groped at the pipe jutting from his mouth.

Stan jumped up and grabbed at the man's knife, trying to yank it free. It sliced through the man's belt, and his pants immediately sagged down to his knees. Oddly enough, the man reached for his pants while the pipe still hung from his bleeding mouth. In the back of his throat, he was screaming and choking at the same time.

Stan wasted no time and rammed the knife into the man's stomach. Bright red blood spurted out onto his hands, but he kept stabbing at the man. The man slipped in his own blood and came down hard on his bottom, staring at Stan in disbelief. Stan pulled out the knife once more and whispered in the man's ear, "This is more humane than you deserve," and slit the man's throat.

Sound seemed to erupt all around them and Tess could hear many pairs of feet running down the stairs, voices yelling and cursing. She grabbed the key out of her pocket and rammed it into the lock, praying that it didn't get stuck going in. It went in smoothly and they hustled through the door just as two men rounded the last set of stairs. She slammed it in their faces and locked it before they had a chance to grab the door handle.

She turned towards the far end of the prison wing and what she saw there caused her knees to buckle. She would have fallen flat on her face if Nathan and Stan hadn't been there to catch her.

9

Dammit Lee! Henry thought to himself when he heard Lee shout at the guards. The plan had been for Lee and Joe to sneak down towards the water's edge and hide behind several large trees, not far from the small group of guards huddled in a clearing close to where the water emerged from the opening in the hills. They would create a diversion and then Henry and Bob would attack the guards from the high ground. Lee went too far and approached the guards head on, totally exposing himself.

When Lee had yelled out, Henry and Bob weren't even close enough to help. Luckily, the guards stood up and raised their hands to the sky. One of them dropped the rifle or club they were holding. When Henry saw this, he motioned to Bob to go over there, in case there were more guards about. He turned to Len to tell him to stay where he was, but didn't see him anywhere. *"Len? Where are you?"* he whispered furiously. For the third time that evening, he wished they could have left him back at the ship. He couldn't be concerned about him now, because just then, he could see several figures rushing out from behind a huge slab of rock and broken trees jutting out of the side of the hill.

10

Tess leaned heavily on Stan and Nathan. Dimly, she could hear pounding on the prison wing door behind her, but the noise could have been coming from another world as far as she was concerned. Standing in front of her, like an apparition from the past, was a tall, lanky kid; dark brown complexion (like his father) and thick curly hair, evolving into dreadlocks. She stared, her mouth moving, but nothing came out.

"*Mom!*" Len yelled and ran towards his mother, his arms outstretched, his eyes bright. Tess's arms seem to have a mind of their own as she raised them to embrace the son that she knew was dead. Stan reached around and hugged them both. He was just as speechless as Tess was. Nathan and the last few folks in the wing stared at them in silence, until the sound of breaking glass seemed to dominate everything in the room.

THE FINAL PURIFICATION

1

Brutos looked towards the entrance leading down to the sublevels. He could feel his anger rising in him like a river ready to overspill its dam. That imbecile Gurt and his cronies had been gone far too long. He understood that they were probably sexing up some of the prisoners—it was what he allowed, but he had told them to be ready once the other guy from the moon had been sacrificed. They had finished the ceremony at least 15 minutes ago. Now, they were taking the smoking body off the platform and still Gurt had not brought the pilot woman up yet. He had experience in dealing with people who failed him and Gurt and his boys would know soon enough what it meant to fail. What it meant to fail him.

Before things went to hell, Barney "Brutos" Clekman worked as the head prison guard at Harlan Penitentiary, and the inmates were terrified of him. Truth be told, even the warden was afraid of him. The fact that Brutos secretly videotaped the "happily" married warden in a number of uncompromising (and unflattering in Brutos' mind) positions with some of the inmates went a long way in giving him leverage over the warden.

As such, he had lots of leeway when it came to prisoner treatment. He was a coolly cruel man whose moral barometer on "cruel and unusual punishment" had broken well past the red mark. He used his blackmail card to hire his own guards and turn the prison into his very own mafia kingdom. Prostitution, drugs, and goods trafficking became the norm within the walls of Harlan Penitentiary and those who sought to enlighten the public on what was happening at the prison, found themselves the recipients of many late-night visits.

But like most despot kingdoms, Brutos' crooked and dangerous world was bound to crumble. His rule was undermined by an unassuming undercover FBI agent, who put up with almost a year of hard prison life, just to gather enough strong evidence to convict Brutos and his key people. They were sent to different prisons, but Brutos remained behind and was placed in the worst place of Harlan Penitentiary—solitary confinement on sublevel four. The next time Brutos saw the light was when Vanek released him after Lycos hit.

Brutos was a hard man whose level of compassion was as thin as the mildew wetness that seemed to coat everything in the fourth sublevel, but he was a loyal man. He was almost on the verge of starvation when Vanek found him and let him out. Right then and there, he became Vanek's loyal henchman and bodyguard.

He glanced at Vanek who gave him an impatient look. He waved and quickly turned towards the entrance leading down to the sublevels. In his mind, he already knew when and how Gurt and his ignorant cohorts were going to leave this earth. If they had stolen from him or lied to him, then he would have only taken a hand or a tongue, but their lateness annoyed Vanek and that annoyed him. They would die of course, but they would die very badly.

As he walked through the doorway leading to the sublevels, he grabbed three of his other "soldiers" and headed down into the dimness to mete out justice and to bring that shuttle-flying bitch to her destiny.

2

Hana Fumiko wasn't prepared for this. When she heard the guards coming towards them, she motioned to Steve to crouch down, which he did immediately, but there were more people coming out of the water. She tried to get them to stop and hide, but it was too late; she had been seen and heard, but maybe the others had not been seen. She dropped her stick and stood up, raising her hands in the air. "Don't shoot! It's just me. I'm coming out."

"Bullshit!" one of the men yelled. "We saw at least four or five crouched behind that chunk of rock there." He raised his voice a little louder, "The rest of you, get your asses out here or I'm gonna put a bullet in each of your heads!"

Hana's heart sank. All of their efforts were in vain. When they found the exit out of the prison, she had allowed herself to hope, even just a little, and was surprised at how much strength it gave her. Now, it was all lost again and the worst part was that the children would surely pay the price for this, just as she would.

She heard a noise coming towards her from higher up the hillside and her heart sank even further. She had been mentally calculating if she could get close enough to the two men to maybe distract or better yet, disarm one of them. She thought it might give the others a fighting chance. But when she heard the noises traveling down the hillside towards her, she knew that she would have been killed before she ever got close enough to do anything.

As she stared at the man closest to her, he leveled the shotgun at her as if he meant to shoot her anyway. She closed her eyes tightly, praying she wouldn't feel much pain when she heard someone yelling.

Her nerves were so wound up, that she thought she would jump right out of her own skin. *"Stop! For the love of God, stop Lee!"*

Henry was sliding down the hillside, trying to get to Lee and Joe as quickly as he could. He saw him level the shotgun at the young girl, right before he saw a group of children huddled behind the ragged and broken landscape of the hillside. He realized seconds before Lee raised the shotgun that these people weren't guards. They were prisoners.

"Lee! These are prisoners! There are kids over here!" He kept running; his eyes focused on the dark specter of Lee pointing the shotgun. It would occur to him later that he could have easily broken his neck or leg sprinting down the uneven and rocky hillside.

Lee looked up at Henry. Did he hear him right? *Children?* But from where Lee stood, he didn't see any children. Only this woman and another man coming towards them with his arms raised. He had seen shadows darting amongst the thin trees and had assumed there were others here. But he hadn't seen any children.

Henry slid to a rocky and unstable stop just in front of Lee. He was breathing hard, but he was able to get his words out. "Lee...I believe...these are escapees." He looked at the woman as if for confirmation. She nodded, her eyes still wide. She seemed to recover herself quickly as she turned towards the tree line on the hillside, "Come on out guys! These are not guards. They've escaped too."

Henry looked around. They now seemed to be coming out of the woodwork. It was starting to get too dark to see well, but there was a hell of a lot of kids and probably twice as many adults. Apparently, they had been hiding quite well, Henry thought amusingly. "How many more of you are there?" he asked urgently.

Frieda walked up, dripping wet. "I was the last one to leave and just before I left, Tess, Angela's husband, and another man had just come back into the prison wing."

"Tess is alive?" Henry asked, trying unsuccessfully to keep the shrill emotion out of his voice.

"Yes, she is, but I hope she's behind us now, because I heard glass breaking just as I submerged. I think the prison guards are trying to break into the prison wing."

Henry turned to Bob, "Do you think you can get back to the ship on your own? We need to get these people out of here. Lee, Joe and I will go back for Tess and the others."

Steve looked at them curiously, "A *ship*? What are you talking about? This river is going nowhere and there are many areas where a ship might run aground." He stared out at the body of water in front of them, trying to see something that wasn't there.

Henry smiled at him, "The ship we have doesn't float on water. You'll see when you get to the airfield." He turned again to Bob, "Circle around the prison as wide as possible and get going!"

Bob nodded and then turned to Steve and Hana, "Gather up your people now. I want the kids in front, people who need help after them, and the strongest folks in the rear. Keep together and carry a child if you have to. *Now let's get the hell out of here!*"

"But my husband hasn't come out yet!" Angela cried, pushing her way through the group. "I can't leave him here. I'm staying put."

Henry glanced at the girl clinging to Angela. "Is that your daughter ma'am?" he said, pointing to Bonnie. She hugged the girl tighter and nodded. "You really should get your little girl out of here as quickly as possible. Things might get ugly around here, and you don't want to take a chance on her or you getting hurt or killed. That's probably what your husband...what's his name?"

"His name is Nathan," she whispered.

"That's probably what your husband Nathan would want you to do. He'd want the both of you safe." He laid his hand on her shoulder, "I'll do my best to get your husband out of here, I promise."

Angela looked uncertain for a minute and Henry thought she might put up a fight and stay here anyway, when she nodded her head slowly. As the group started moving out, Angela turned to Henry and grabbed his hands, "Thank you and *vaya con Dios*." She released them and merged in with the departing group, her daughter still clinging to her sides.

Frieda, along with several other men and women made up the rear. When Frieda got close to Henry, she stopped in front of him. "I also wanted to tell you that when I was underwater making my way to the surface, I saw one of your guys swimming back towards the prison. He looked like a kid though."

Henry smirked and just shook his head. "The young man that you saw is Tess's son." Frieda's eyes went wide and she clapped her hand over her mouth. "We'll get him too, so don't worry about him. Be careful and be alert." She nodded and caught up with the others, leaving Henry, Joe and Lee behind.

"Alright guys, let's go get them!" Henry said, his smile long gone.

3

"*Come on!*" Tess yelled at Nathan, Stan and Len. They sprinted towards the dark end of the wing. She grabbed Len's arms, surprised at the strength she felt in them. "Lenny, help your father through here. He's weak, and you'll need to pull him along with you."

"It's Len, Mom," he said to her, his voice was calm, but his eyes were bright, ready.

"*What?* Oh...I'm sorry honey. Len it is! Now let's get moving son." She could hear noises behind her coming through the broken window in the door and was afraid to turn around, lest she see a horde of them barreling down upon them with homemade tools of death.

She grabbed the engine power node and slid it around her shoulders. Len and Stan splashed into the water. As soon as they were gone, she turned to Nathan, "Okay, let's go."

"Ladies first," Nathan said, and held out his hand over the water.

Tess looked at him in wonder and a little shock. "We can worry about that type of stuff when we don't have wild cannibals breathing down our necks! Let's go together!" They both slid in the water after a few deep breaths and started pulling themselves along.

Tess didn't think she and Nathan had started too far behind Stan and Lenny, (no...*Len*), but she didn't see them anywhere. Although it was dark down here, she saw no light from them at all. Soon, she did see a dim light, but it was the air pocket light. She was amazed. She thought that she would at least have seen their light leaving the air pocket, but they must have stayed here briefly and got going again. They were probably pretty close to getting out.

They hit the air pocket and took a few deep breaths. When Tess had caught her breath, she looked over at Nathan, "Only about 90 seconds left Nathan...almost ther..."

What hit her next felt like the concussion of a powerful earthquake. She could feel her body being lifted and pushed up into the air pocket. She and Nathan barely had time to take another breath and hold it before the water below them rushed up to fill the air pocket. She looked at Nathan and pointed towards the direction where Stan and Len had gone, but he shook his head at her.

At first, she didn't know what to make of this gesture and then she turned her head and saw rocks moving in slow motion from underwater cliffs high above their heads. Tess watched in horror as large and small boulders filled in the narrow opening. Nathan pointed back and she nodded at him, anger and frustration filling her eyes.

She glanced once more behind her, toward the exit where Len and Stan had just gone. The once taut rope drifted in the dim light like a dead fish. Tess assumed that the rope must have snapped due to the loose rocks and falling boulders. They swam back towards the pale light of the third sublevel and before Tess could even register what was happening, rough hands had snatched them out of the water.

"Well, well...lookit what we got here Brutos!" a disembodied voice yelled down to her. She lay on the floor, surrounded by a wide variety of dirty shoes. She got to her knees, and the first thing she saw was the prison wing door hanging on its hinges. There were black burn marks on the walls of the prison wing. *They must have tossed a hand grenade through the window*, Tess thought wearily. She half-turned toward Nathan when someone hit her hard and solid in the back of the head, and she fell back to the floor.

She was dazed, but not out as one of the guards leaned down to tie her hands. When he was close enough, she quickly shifted onto her side and kicked up viciously at his face, connecting with his jaw. He stood bolt upright and then spat out blood and a couple of teeth. Brutos laughed uproariously at this, which caused the man to turn and laugh too, sticky gobs of blood and saliva dripping from his mouth.

Two other men turned her over, careful to stay away from her feet and began tying her arms behind her. She could see that Nathan had already been subdued. In his weakened state, there was nothing he could do. He was lying on his stomach like a spent fish while someone tied his hands behind his back.

Tess felt renewed strength flow into her body, and she bucked her head back into the nose of one of the men trying to tie her arms behind her. He yelled and started cursing, his nose already swelling. Brutos laughed again at this, but stopped immediately. "Roy, put this bitch out. She's making me tired."

Tess was about to scream out a string of curse words that would have made her blush if she heard someone else saying them, but she never got the chance. She felt a bright flare of pain and then nothing. She fought with all her will to stay conscious, but it seemed the harder she tried, the more elusive it became. In her mind, she saw a bright pinpoint of light and tried to focus on it, but it drifted further and further away until there was nothing but darkness.

4

Lee had been staring down into the dark water when the powerful underwater explosion hit them. At first, Henry feared it was the onset of another earthquake. He glanced up sharply at the sloping hillside, half expecting boulders, rocks and uprooted trees to come tumbling towards them, but there was nothing.

"What the hell was that?" Lee asked. "Another earthquake?"

Henry stood still at the edge of the water waiting. He could still feel vibrations, but they weren't getting stronger. He was thinking it was some sort of underwater explosion when all of a sudden, the rope, which a moment before had been lying on the ground, stretched tautly as if yanked on by a giant far below the surface of the water.

Lee looked at it warily, "Is that them, pulling themselves up?"

Before Henry could answer, the rope snapped with a loud popping sound and the frayed end went zipping past his face like a bullet. He watched it disappear into the water, thinking that he could have easily lost an eye if it had hit him in the face.

"What the fuck just happened?" Joe yelled.

Still a little bit shaken by the near-miss of the rope, Henry said, "I'm not sure if it was an earthquake or not, but I'm willing to bet that something huge down there fell on the rope and yanked it in." He was thinking that they might have to go in without a rope when two heads popped out of the water.

"Len! You made it!" Henry exclaimed.

Len didn't smile, but helped his coughing father to the edge of the grassy banks. Joe came over and all three of them helped Stan and Len out of the water. As soon as they got Stan out of the water, Len turned around and went back under.

"Len, wait!" Henry yelled, but it was too late, he had already gone back under.

Stan yanked his head around. "Dammit! He's probably gone back for his mother. I heard something underwater that sounded like an explosion, and all of a sudden, we were being pushed by the water. The next thing I know, the rope was zipping past us. I think something huge fell on it and yanked it loose." He looked down at his hands, "I think Tess and Nathan may have been forced to go back."

Just then, Len popped up to the surface like a *Jack in the Box*. *"I can't find them!"* he wailed. *"There's a big rock blocking the way!"*

"Don't worry son, we're going back for her." He looked at Henry, who simply nodded in the affirmative. Henry returned the stare and then asked, "Are you Stan? Tess's husband?"

Stan looked up at him, a half smile on his face, "Yep, you got it. Guilty as charged." Henry helped Stan to his feet and then shook his hand vigorously once he was standing. *"It's great to finally meet you Stan!* It really hit Tess hard when she thought you guys were dead. I'm Henry by the way. That's Lee, and that's Joe."

Stan put his arm around Len. The boy was almost as tall as his father. "Nice to meet you guys. I can only imagine how hard it's been on her. We've got to get her out of there. We've killed at least four of their guys, so I'm sure by now, they're dragging her up to be sacrificed."

"Absolutely Stan. Are you okay to walk?" Stan nodded and Henry continued on, "Unless you know another way in, we're going to have to go in through the main entrance, since this route is blocked now."

Stan thought a moment and an idea occurred to him. "When I was brought here, there was another prisoner who told me that some people escaped through the gaps in the rubble. With all the earthquakes, those gaps may be gone by now, but it's worth a shot."

"Alright, it sounds better than a frontal assault. Let's get going guys." Earlier, he had handed Joe his broadsword, so he wouldn't have to swim with it. Now, he took back. "Stan, you can use my handgun, I'll keep this baby here. There are about 20 rounds of 9mm ammo left; hopefully, that's enough."

"It's better than a kick in the teeth, that's for sure!" Stan replied. Henry chuckled at this and the four men and one man-child, set off around the side of the hillside, hoping they weren't too late to help Tess. He turned to look at his son, but Len had started loping agilely down the side of the mountain. "Len!" Stan shouted, "Wait for us!"

Henry turned to Joe and Lee, "Catch up with him. Stan and I will be right behind you." They took off after the boy, barely spotting him as he slipped into a small grove of trees towards the bottom of the hill.

"Stan, your son has grown up tough in this world. I'd like to say that we'll take care of him, but my gut tells me that he's more capable of taking care of *us*, than the other way around." They hustled carefully down the side of the mountain, careful of the huge ruts and toppled trees. "He saved our asses when a pack of dogs were after us." He chuckled at this and then grew somber, "Don't worry Stan, we're gonna get your wife and we'll get the hell off this rock too."

They caught up with Joe and Lee minutes later where they had stopped behind a partially destroyed portion of the brick wall. It was as far as they could go without being seen. "Where the hell is Len?" he whispered to them as he settled himself against the wall.

"He slipped through this space here and disappeared," Lee said. Henry looked down at the hole frowning, "He went through *that*?

Jesus, how did he fit through there? Are you sure?" "Yeah," said Joe. "I saw him."

"Okay...well, we can't do anything about that now. Spot me you guys."

Joe and Lee lifted him up so that he could peek over the stone wall. They were very close, but there were men posted everywhere on the other side of the wall. He didn't see Tess, but he saw the other guy that they had caught. He was being strapped up on their execution rack. He saw a way for them to get out there on the field when he caught a faint movement just to left of the rack. *It was Len!* His first thought was that the kid had gotten down there pretty damn quick. His second thought, more urgent, was that the kid was going to get himself killed! He motioned for the guys to let him down. *"We need to get in there quick! I found a way...let's go!"*

5

Tess could hear disconnected voices coming at her from many directions. She wasn't completely unconscious, but she wasn't awake either. It felt as if her existence floated on a knife edge, trying to decide which way to go.

There was a sense of urgency that overshadowed everything in her mind. As much as she enjoyed the relative safety of the darkness that surrounded her, she knew that she needed to be awake. She would not allow herself the comfort of oblivion.

Her eyes fluttered open, struggled briefly to stay open and then thudded closed. During the few seconds they were open, dream-like images floated past her and a dull, consistent pain, a million miles away it felt, throbbed steadily. Slowly, she kicked ferociously up towards the light, towards the surface of her consciousness. It seemed the closer she got to consciousness, the more real her pain became.

The last thing she remembered was being underwater with Nathan. Something had happened that forced them to turnaround. When she got back to the prison wing, she had been captured and knocked out. And with that thought, her eyes popped open.

She could feel herself being dragged across the ground. She could also feel cooler air on her wet skin and knew that she had to be outside. She sensed that not much time had passed since they pulled her out of the water, and she could hear cheering. From the corner of her eye, she could see people waving their arms and yelling crazily. The thought that they were probably dragging her to the sacrifice stand made her stomach lurch.

The two men yanked her roughly to her feet as Vanek sauntered towards her. Now that she was standing, she saw that he was shorter than her by at least three inches. "I see that you are awake...*thief*," Vanek spat at her. He now stood directly in front of her. His rotten-smelling breath wafted across her nose and she almost gagged. It smelled of rotten eggs and bad meat. Vanek turned to his people and looked at them defiantly. "I told you my friends. I told you that they would come and take from us. They broke in here and took our children. Our *precious* children! They killed dozens of our own. And they stole this...thing!" He pointed to Brutos who held the engine node high in the air for all to see. The people started booing and screaming out curses.

Tess looked around. Although her head was still hurting, she was starting to come out of her semi-conscious fog. Vanek was using this charade to tighten his control over these people. She knew that he could kill her and Nathan anytime, but his power lay in the belief that he had their best interests at heart. *Us* versus *Them* always seems to work in mob-psychology. This thought almost made her laugh.

"Oh? You think this is funny, spaceship woman?" He moved in closer to her and belted her hard in the stomach. Tess grunted and her legs gave out. If the two men hadn't been holding her up, she would have dropped to the ground. A few people laughed. Behind her, Nathan struggled as he was being chained up on the stand. "Come on guys," he wheezed. "This is not what Americans do. This is not what *humans* do..." his voice trailed off.

"Shut it," said one of them binding his feet. He stood up and punched him solidly in the mouth. Nathan grunted at the blow, coughing and spitting out blood.

Tess summoned her strength and yelled out to the crowd. "He's using you! Can't you see that? Don't do this! We can get you out of here! I'm a pilot, and we have a ship at the airfield. We need that power node he's holding to get off the planet." She looked around at the crowd. There must have been 40, maybe 50 people here. "We can take *all* of you—it's not too late. *Listen!* The earth is falling apart. These earthquakes that you feel are coming from the core of the earth. It's been damaged and has been trying to fix itself, but the planet's too far gone. But worst of all, Earth's orbit will put us too close to the sun. In two months, maybe less, the sun will scorch *everything* on the planet! We have to leave now! We're running out of time!"

Although it didn't have the desired effect that she was hoping for, she did notice that the jeering and cursing had dropped by almost half. Vanek smiled and stepped back up to her. She cringed, more from the thought of his rank breath in her face again, than from any sucker punches he might throw.

He spoke low, so that only she could hear him. "I *know* what's going on here. I'm an electrical engineer, and I had a seat on one of your precious shuttles. I was part of the team that had to fix a faulty relay on one of the booster rockets for that shuttle that blew up. Yeah, I can see from your face that you know the one I'm talking about. Well, that fuck of a commander left me, and the rest of the team on the outside of the ship. Jack 'fucking' Richards! He took off with us still on the outside of the fucking ship!" His voice started to break, but he clamped down on it.

"I cut one of the booster rocket wires just before we jumped off, hoping that they would have to abort the takeoff. That would have given us time to fix it and get back on board." His eyes bored into Tess, two dark marbles of anger and hate. "You see, my family was still on board that ship. I had to get back on board with my family."

The destruction of the ship brought back painful memories for Tess. She thought she had lost her entire family in that explosion, but her husband and son had survived through some weird twist of fate, although now, she wasn't sure if they made it out of the water.

She stared back at Vanek, not willing to drop her gaze, "But there was a gunman on board. He fired a shot and that's what decompressed the ship and destroyed it." Tess said this confidently, but now that he'd admitted to what he did, she knew in her heart that it probably was not the gunshot that ultimately blew up Jack's shuttle. The damage to the booster rocket would have become more and more unstable as the fuel pressure increased. She had no doubt, that this man's direct actions played a part in the destruction of the *Galileo2*. This man killed almost a hundred people, his family included.

She looked at him coldly and with contempt, "Are you so heartless and insecure that you would kill your own family and a hundred other innocent people? You don't need to answer me; I can see the guilt in your eyes, no matter how much you try to hide it." And as she stared at him, a new understanding blossomed in her mind; *he's crazy, and he knows it!*

Vanek had looked off into the distance during Tess's recriminations of him. At first, he appeared to be seriously considering what she had said to him, but it was clear to Tess that his mind was somewhere else. "My family was on board and I killed them by trying to sabotage the booster rocket. A man would have..." his voice trailed off. "A man would have let his family live. A man would have *sacrificed* himself to let his family live." He looked back at Tess, a vacant, but somehow dangerous look in his eyes. "Oh yes, I know what's going to happen, and I welcome it!

"When Earth goes, we all go and maybe, just maybe, I'll see my family again. None of us are going anywhere. Not them..." he waved his arms around at the people in the stands, "not your people from the ship and certainly not *you*." He turned to Brutos on his bad leg and grimaced, "Strap her up, and then send out a search party to round up the others."

Brutos nodded to the two men holding Tess and they obligingly pulled her back to the stand and strapped her in. She looked at Nathan. He was silently praying to himself. Tess closed her eyes too and thought of Stan and Len during their last Christmas together. It was a happy memory; one she came back to again and again when she was on the moon. It had helped to alleviate the pain of loss that she felt so intensely back then. She only wished that she could have saved the others back at the ship. They were doomed one way or the other. If Vanek and his people don't enslave them, then it'll be the massive earthquake that will jumpstart the final destruction of the planet. If they're lucky enough to survive all that, then they'll die when the sun cooks the planet. A single tear dropped from her eye and rolled slowly down her cheek.

Vanek walked over to the huge container filled with oil. He picked up the short-handled mop hooked to the outside of the drum, dipped it wholly into the drum and then raised his face to the crowd. "For their crimes against us, I will do the honor of preparing them for sacrifice!" He turned and slathered Nathan with it. Nathan tried to ignore it and kept praying, but slowly, he broke down and started crying. His mind was whirling. They would light him on fire, and he would die an agonizing death. He volunteered a few months a year as a volunteer fire-fighter, and he knew first-hand just how intense the pain would be.

"Stop Vanek!" Tess yelled. "Don't do this! For God's sake, don't do this!"

Vanek halted in mid-stride and looked at her. A smirk crossed his lips and he turned towards her and splattered her with the little bit of oil remaining on the mop head. "I think, my dear, that God left this accursed place years ago. He may have left on the eighth day, after seeing what He created here, eh?" He moved closer to her, "Since you want me to stop with him, why don't we start with *you* first?"

He reached into his pocket, pulled out a grimy lighter and lit it. He raised the lighter in the air as he walked towards her, his angry grin getting wider as he got closer to the stand. Tess looked at him defiantly. *"You can go to hell, motherfucker!"* she spat at him.

Vanek laughed and cocked his arm when someone in the stands yelled, "No Vanek! Don't do it! She can save us! I want to live!"

He froze in his tracks, his eyes widening. No one had ever resisted him or spoke out against him like this. This will not do. "Brutos! Find whoever said that and bring his ass down here to die with these two!"

Brutos and one of his men started towards the group, when someone else shouted out, "If they have a ship, we should go with them! I don't want to die here either!"

There was a chorus of shouts in agreement. Tess looked out at the people. She could see that a small group of them were speaking out, but none of them had weapons. If Brutos' guards started attacking them, they would be massacred. Fights were starting to break out among them as Brutos and his men started yanking people out of the crowd.

Vanek turned back to Tess. "You've done nothing here, but buy yourself a few extra minutes." He lit the head of the mop and cocked his arm to throw it onto to the stand. In the stands, people were yelling, but she couldn't tell if it was out of fear or sacrificial excitement.

Looking at the fire, Tess braced herself for the white-hot pain that she knew would come soon, when all of a sudden, a small dart or needle imbedded itself deeply into Vanek's exposed forearm. He grimaced and looked at his arm. "What the *fuck*?" he said as he scratched at the spot where the needle went in.

He stopped scratching when he felt something bite him in the neck. He slapped his hands to his neck to crush whatever was biting him, but all he did was push the needle deeper into his neck. "Ouch...*shit!*" was all he could say. He looked back at Tess, but his neck muscles seemed to be moving in slow motion. *I'll burn this bitch yet*, he thought, but he no longer held the fire in his hands. He looked down slowly and saw it smoldering at his feet. At some point, he had dropped it, but hadn't realized that he had dropped it.

"Ah'll bur you yet...bith," was all he could say. His mouth was not working right, and it was getting very difficult for him to breath. He slowly looked around for Brutos, but he was up in the stands fighting. "Brut...Bru" he wheezed through his tightening throat. His lungs were starting to burn and his vision was closing in on him. He felt a sharp pain in his legs and felt himself being knocked to his knees.

He had no energy to get back up. All he could do was look up as someone approached him. His watering eyes looked up into the eyes of some skinny black kid. He blinked, and the kid was behind him. All of a sudden, the kid grabbed him by the hair and yanked his head back strongly. He stared up at the kid, unable to do anything. His throat was clamped shut and he was barely breathing as it was. The kid looked back at him and started to speak. As if in a dream, the kid's words floated from his mouth to Vanek's ears, "I will not let you hurt my mother!" And with that, Len sliced open Vanek's neck.

6

Tess stared open-mouthed at the boy. "Oh my God, Len. I didn't know what happened to you. Are you okay? Is your father okay?"

"Yes, mom...I'm okay. Dad is too." Len replied, his voice cracking.

Tess looked around the field. All hell had broken loose, and she heard gunfire. "Untie me honey. Quickly. We need to get out of here." Her eyes were filling up with tears.

"Don't forget me!" Nathan shouted and then laughed shrilly. He kept thinking just how close he had come to being burned alive.

Len jumped up on the stand and quickly untied his mother. She rubbed her arms as they moved over to untie Nathan. He looked at Len with admiration in his eyes, "My boy, you are one tough *hombre!*"

They crouched down behind the stand, out of sight of the melee behind them. She grabbed Len tightly and hugged him close to her chest. She couldn't believe she was actually holding her son again. She thought she had lost him again during the underwater explosion. She didn't know if they would make it off the planet, but her husband and her son had survived. She got to see them at least once more. She knew they couldn't stay here long, so she reluctantly disengaged herself from him.

"Stay down!" she said to Len and Nathan as she crept to the side of the stand. It was chaos. Suddenly, someone was coming towards them. It was one of the guards. He must have seen them before they got behind the stand.

"I know y'all are back there, so just come out...now!" the guard screamed at them. He continued towards them.

She looked around for something to hit him with and found nothing. "Get behind me!" she whispered to Len. She waited for the guard to come. She had nothing to fight with, but maybe she could surprise him enough for Len and Nathan to escape.

The guard had almost come all the way around the stand when she heard a hideous crunch. The guard fell to the ground, blood pouring out of the huge dent in his head. She lifted her head and saw Lee smiling at her. Joe stood at his back watching the crowd.

"You ready to get the hell out of here lady?" he said to her. Lee glanced at Len and winked. "Good job, kid."

She looked at him and couldn't help but smile, "Hell yeah! Let's go!" She looked around, "Where's Stan? Is Henry with you?"

Lee nodded and smiled, "They're covering our asses. You guys ready?"

She nodded, stood up, and immediately felt wobbly. She thought maybe she had suffered some head trauma from being knocked out at least twice in less than 24 hours, but she noticed everyone else having trouble standing. "Oh no," she whispered. "It's starting."

"We need to get the others and get the hell out of here now!" Joe yelled.

"I think it's much too late for that now, don't you think? I wouldn't do that if I were you." Brutos said to Joe, who was trying to reach for his rifle.

Tess looked up and saw several men standing around the stand with rifles in their hands. Brutos was standing there with a grenade in one hand and the engine node in the other. She pulled Len close to her.

Despite the weirdly undulating ground, Brutos seemed to hold his balance well. "Get up! All of you!" He looked over at Vanek's crumpled body and then looked at Tess and Len. "Thank you for doing my dirty work. Vanek was a charlatan, a faker. He was never a believer; never truly one of us. And he wanted to *die* here! Fuck that! When I first saw your ship land, I knew at that moment what needed to be done. Vanek wanted to attack you as soon as you landed. He wanted us to destroy the ship, but I delayed him.

"When we caught your spy earlier today, he was more than willing to tell us what we wanted to know. I think it was his intention to be part of our group; maybe even to lead us." Brutos barked a sharp, humorless laugh.

Tess knew he was talking about Andy. Poor sap. He sold his soul to the devil and got burned at the stake for his reward. It was very fitting. He pointed his pistol at Tess, "*You* are going to fly that shuttle for me...or you'll watch me put a bullet through each of their heads, starting with him." He pointed his gun at Len. "Now get off your asses, and let's be quick about this. I don't want any more surprises."

At that moment, a huge burst of static electricity seemed to fill the air and Tess heard the unmistakable sound of the *Orion* coming in for a landing.

INTO THE LION'S DEN

1

Chayton was having a helluva of time controlling the *Orion*. Kyra was sitting in the co-pilot's seat trying her best to follow his directions. *"Pull back hard Kyra! We need to get our nose up!"* he shouted at her.

Kyra was bathed in sweat as she wrestled with the controls in front of her. "I'm trying dammit! This thing just won't move!"

Chayton realized that their angle of descent was too steep when they were coming in, but he knew it would be like this, especially being one power node short. The prison wasn't too difficult to find in the waning light. It was the only thing they could see on the landscape within miles, once they got airborne.

Right before they decided to leave, the airfield had gotten dangerously unstable. The last earthquake had compromised the underground fuel dumps, and the people outside had said they smelled oil or gas coming from underground. At that point, Kyra made the decision to get everyone on board and was just locking her shoulder straps in the co-pilot's seat when Chayton suddenly yelled out, causing her to jump in her seat.

"Holy shit! Who the hell are *they*?" He said, as the shuttle slowly rocked on the weakening airfield.

Kyra stared out the window and could see men, women, and children running towards them. If she had to guess, she figured it was close to 50 people, maybe more. A man in front of the group was waving his arms wildly at them. He held a faded green light stick.

As they got closer, Kyra laughed and told Chayton to let down the rear ramp. He was about to tell her she was crazy when she shouted in his face, "Open it now Chayton! That's Bob out there!"

2

Ten minutes later, they were airborne. The passenger area was alive with laughing, talking, crying men, women, and children. Apparently, there were quite a few of them who knew Thelma, screaming out their hellos as they ran up the ramp. Thelma could only wave as she held her head in her hands and cried.

Chayton brought the ship around in a wide arc, circling once over the airfield when one of the underground fuel pumps exploded underneath the runway. It caused a chain reaction that didn't stop until all of the runway pumps had exploded. He stared at the huge ball of fire. It was only a matter of time before the entire underground fuel depot went up in flames.

Now here they were, trying to land on the short and narrow field of the prison. Chayton had to trust that Kyra would do as he had instructed her because right now, he couldn't be worried about her. He had to concentrate on landing the huge ship. His intended landing area was the large open field that looked two sizes too small for the *Orion*. The people running back and forth across the field made it even smaller. Sparks of light flashed here and there; *Gunfire*, he thought grimly. He could see a large fire at the end of the field closest to his approach where a group of people were clustered. At his approach, they seemed to scatter like roaches.

"Thelma!" he yelled over the loudspeaker. "Get them ready…we're landing in ten seconds! And hold on!"

"They're ready!" Thelma yelled back to him from the bay doors. She nodded to the two men who had the guns Henry left behind. "No one gets on this ship but our people, got it?"

They both nodded, and held onto their harnesses tightly. They waited tensely for the ship to land and the bay doors to open.

3

As soon as Tess saw the *Orion* coming in for a landing, she nodded at Joe and Lee and darted her eyes towards where the ship might be. She hoped they understood that that was where they should make a run for it, but she couldn't be sure. She could only hope. They nodded back, their heads barely moving. A huge bolt of static electricity surged from the ground up towards the ship as it neared the ground. When Brutos and his men looked up, Tess yelled *"RUN!"* and they all bolted.

Tess grabbed Len by the arm, and they ran hard to where she guessed the rear of the shuttle would be. She heard a crack and a split second later, something whizzed by her ear. She heard more guns going off and half expected a bullet to slam into her back. She turned to get a better grip on Len and saw that Brutos and his men were no longer shooting at them. Their attention had been drawn to a low brick wall where she saw sparks of light flashing. *Stan*, she thought.

The *Orion* had touched down about 50 yards ahead of them as they sprinted towards it. Len looked up in awe at the huge ship, his mouth hanging open. Nathan was having a difficult time keeping up. He was very weak and was barely able to stand on his feet, let alone run. She pushed Len toward the ramp and grabbed Nathan, "Come on, Nathan! Get your ass in gear!" He was so out of it that all he could do was grunt, but his eyes registered a huge thanks to Tess. "Don't get too happy yet! We still need to get out of here!"

They reached the ramp just as Joe and Lee came up alongside them. The ground was trembling, and she felt as if she were on a huge treadmill. The fence that surrounded the field seemed to be vibrating furiously.

"Come on!" A man up on the ramp yelled as he held out his hand towards them. Tess didn't know who the man was, but she reached up and let herself be pulled onto the ramp. Len came up after her. She saw two other men with guns pointing out into the field where people and guns were screaming left and right.

Tess helped Nathan up the ramp, turned, and saw Kyra coming in through the bay doors. Kyra hugged her tightly, "I'm so glad you made it!"

Tess hugged her back, just as tightly, "I didn't know if I was going to make it Kyra," she admitted. "This is my son, Len".

"Oh my God, Tess! That's wonderful!" She hugged Len, who just stood there awkwardly.

Tess smiled and then frowned just as quickly. She remembered the engine power node that Brutos had slung around his shoulder. "*Shit!*" she screamed. "The power node is still out there!"

"*What?*" Kyra said. "You found one?"

"Yes, but it was taken from me. I need to get that Kyra. It's the only way we'll make it off the planet."

"Tess, you can't go back out there, it's dangerous!" Kyra said. "There's gunfire everywhere!"

As if on cue, there was a huge explosion that rocked the ship and almost knocked them off their feet. "What the hell was *that*?" Kyra said.

Tess got to her feet slowly. "I don't know, but it felt like something just blew up."

Somebody screamed, and she looked up sharply. It was Frieda. "Oh God, Tess! I didn't know what happened to you guys. Bob said that you might have gotten trapped underwater." She hugged Tess, almost as tightly as Kyra did.

"It was close Frieda, but we made it. Is everyone here? Steve, Hana, the children?"

"Yes! We're all here. Bob got us here safe and sound."

Just then, Angela came through the bay door with her daughter Bonnie. She spied Nathan sitting on the floor and ran up to him.

Dropping to the floor, she hugged and kissed him. "Nathan! You're here! Thank God!"

Tess smiled, but she was starting to get worried as she looked around for Stan. She moved Kyra away from the group of people in the bay, "Kyra, I've got to get back outside. We *need* that engine power node."

"What do you mean, you need to go back outside?" a voice behind her said.

She whirled around, and there was Stan. Somehow, he must have slipped in without her seeing him. She hugged him and then said to him gently, "Babe, we won't be able to leave the earth's gravity, let alone make it to *Europa* without the engine power node. They took it from me when they caught me, and I saw the big guy carrying it when I was at the fire stand. Somebody's gotta go get it."

"Send one of the guys out there to get it. You can't fight this guy honey; he outweighs you by 200lbs easily."

"I'll go," said Henry. He had just jumped up onto the ramp. "Besides, you need to get the ship ready to go Tess. In fact, you and Chayton need to get this thing off the ground now. These earthquakes are coming closer and closer together. And you heard Brutos. He wants this ship. We can't allow him to get on board. I think he still has a couple of hand grenades. If he gets on board, he could threaten to blow up the ship."

Tess opened her mouth to protest, but she realized that Henry was right. To the rest of these people, she was indispensable. Chayton was good, but he couldn't handle the ship by himself if something happened to her. It needed two pilots to get it into orbit. Hell, without the other engine power node, their chances of making it into orbit were slim to none.

"We need to hit them now, while we got 'em on the run!" Joe said. "They ran out of ammo before we did."

"Did anybody see where Brutos went?" asked Tess. "He's the one we need to find and unfortunately, he knows the importance of the power node. Andy told them everything. And then they burned him alive."

"Serves the bastard right," said Joe.

Ignoring Joe's comment, Henry said, "He went down into the prison. I saw him and two of his men run down there when their ammo ran out. The rest just scattered like rats." He turned to Joe, "Let's collect up what ammo is left and go get those fuckers!"

Tess grabbed Henry by the arm, "Listen Henry, I won't be able to keep her up long. Hovering burns up a lot of power, and the uneven draw on the power nodes will drain them that much faster. You'll have about 15 minutes, 20 at the most. Longer than that, and we'll be staying on Earth. Do you understand?"

Henry nodded and hugged her. "We'll get that power node Tess." Tess turned and headed towards the cockpit. Henry headed back towards the ramp and saw Kyra looking at him. As he got closer, he could see that her eyes were puffy and red from crying.

He was about to speak when she put her finger to his lips. "Don't say anything, but *'I'll be back Kyra, I promise'*."

He grabbed her hand and kissed it, "I'll be back Kyra, I promise. I love you." He ran down the ramp where Joe was waiting for him. As soon as he was down, Kyra raised the ramp. He could hear the hiss of air as the ship sealed itself.

"Come on Henry," Joe said, tapping him on the shoulder. They trotted over to a partial wall on one side of the field. Lee was already there waiting for them.

"I guess you're coming too, huh?" Henry said to Lee.

"Yep, that's right," Lee said. "Let's finish this and get the hell outta here."

Henry clapped him on the shoulder and turned towards the tunnel leading down into the underground prison cell blocks. He could still feel the earth trembling from the last round of earthquakes. The field was no longer smooth, and Henry had a bad feeling that the next earthquake would be more than just a tremor. He glanced back at the *Orion* as the engines roared into life, and wondered if he would ever see it again.

4

Tess slowly engaged the vertical takeoff engines. After the recent earthquake, they had no room to taxi for a normal runway takeoff. She glanced at the power grid for the engine power nodes. So far, they were holding steady, but she knew the longer they stayed in the low Earth gravity, the more the strain would be on the power nodes. "Chayton, punch in 20 minutes on the clock. If they're not back by then, we might as well find a safer place on the planet to land because that will be our only option."

Chayton looked at her; his disappointment was barely concealed on his face and punched in the time. "Couldn't we just *try* to make to make orbit Tess? I mean, anything is better than dying here."

"Chayton, without that last engine power node, our engines would strain too hard, too unevenly. The ship would explode long before we reached escape velocity. If it didn't explode, it would never leave Earth's orbit or the gravitational pull of the sun. Our ship would join the asteroid field now circling the earth, and there we would stay until Earth's orbit moves closer to the sun. Then we would burn up just like the planet."

Chayton seemed to visibly deflate as Tess explained their fate. He looked at the clock now showing 19 minutes and 18 seconds. He sighed.

"By the way, Chayton," Tess added. "That was a hell of a thing you did today. You saved a lot of people, me and my son included."

At that, he seemed to perk up a bit and even tried to smile. "Thanks Tess. What'll we do if they can't get that power node?"

"Let's just hope they get it, huh?" she said. "Now keep your eyes on that power readout, and let me know the minute it changes."

5

Henry, Joe, and Lee headed toward the entrance leading down into the sublevels of the prison. There were bodies all over the place. Some had been shot during the melee, but most were still smoldering from the explosion of the fuel tank in the yard. Henry thought maybe a stray bullet hit the tanker and caused the explosion. Henry had seen a group of these people—probably the ones who spoke out—trying to run to the ship. In the end, they were gunned down by Brutos' people. The few who remained scattered to the winds.

But Brutos was still here, and he was hiding with two of his men. Henry did a quick time check and saw that they had just under 15 minutes to find Brutos and get that power node. He groaned inwardly at what he had to say next.

"Hey guys," he whispered, "we need to split up. There are four sublevels, and we barely have 15 minutes to search them and find Brutos. He could be anywhere down there."

Lee added, "And don't forget, there are two other guys with him. At least two that we know of."

"I'll take sublevels three and four," Joe announced and then took off.

"I'll take two," Lee said. "Be careful Henry."

"You too," he said as he pushed open the bent gate door leading down to the prison wing on sublevel one. When he got there, he looked around at the walls and could see cracks spider-webbing from cell to cell. *The next tremor that hits us will do more than crack the walls,* he thought, as he moved from cell to cell. Luckily, he could just look through the gate to see if anyone was inside. As he walked towards the back, it occurred to him that no one would try to hide here because there were no places *to* hide. The bars made that impossible.

As he walked along, peeking into each cell, he remembered reading that the deeper sublevels were more like solitary confinement with steel doors and small barred windows to look in on the prisoners. If anything, they would offer the most places to hide, not here. He was starting to have a bad feeling in his gut that Brutos and his men would be waiting for them further below. He was also beginning to think that separating was a very bad idea. He turned quickly and jogged back towards the entrance of the wing and headed down to sublevel two as quickly as he could.

6

Henry slid through the half-opened entrance to sublevel two. He could see clear to the end of the hallway. On his left and his right were rows of solitary confinement cells. They all had doors, but only three were closed. He felt a slight draft coming from somewhere and thought about the cracks in the walls on sublevel one. It was only a matter of time before this place caved in.

The silence weighed on him like a physical presence, and his nerves were jumping like live wires. He felt, no, knew that at any minute, Brutos and men would pop out of one or more of the cells like misfit *Jacks in Prison Boxes.* But there was nothing. Only a rotten smell, the skittering of rats, and a disturbing rumble coming from deep underground.

He opened up the last closed door and almost jumped out of his skin. He saw Lee propped up on one of the dirty cots. His eyes were open, but Henry could see that his throat had been cut open. The front of his shirt was dark red with his blood.

Cursing, Henry backed out of the cell and headed towards the door leading out of the sublevel. He looked around the dank hallway, his eyes wide. *They're down there somewhere, waiting for me,* he thought and crept down the stairs to the sublevel three entrance, his hand automatically tightening on the 9MM handgun.

The door was bent at an odd angle, and the hinges looked as if they had been blasted off. Henry looked through the small, dirty window set in the leaning door. The hallway inside was empty, but all of the doors were closed. Brutos and his guys could be hiding anywhere in there. He slid through the opening, trying to be as quiet as he could.

It was dark down here, and the only light came from a dim ceiling bulb towards the back of the wing, and it was flickering. The thought of being down here in near pitch-black conditions was unnerving. As much as he didn't want to use his flashlight, he was forced to turn it on. He had a flashlight with a red filter, so it wasn't glaringly bright; but in darkness like this, it felt like a search beam.

The first two doors he tried were locked, and he moved on without looking in. The third door he tried was unlocked. He opened it slowly and standing in the middle of the room was one of Brutos' guys. He had his hands up. "Don't shoot! I want to go with you guys. Brutos forced me to come down here!"

"Get on the floor!" Henry yelled at him. "Where's Brutos?"

"Right behind you," said a voice and before Henry could turn around, something hit him in the back of the head. He felt his knees unbuckle as he crumpled to the floor. His gun and flashlight dropped from his hands as he struggled to remain conscious. Lights seem to dance in front of his eyes as he lost consciousness.

7

"I said 'drop it'", said a voice very close to Henry's right. He was standing up, but the last thing he remembered was collapsing to the floor. He was having trouble breathing because something tight was around his neck. He attempted to reach up towards his neck and found that his arms were bound behind him. He opened his eyes and saw Joe in front of him, and he was pointing his rifle directly at him. He glanced down at the floor and saw two men, both dead by the look of them.

"Drop your gun, or I'll put a bullet in his skull," Brutos said to him. "And if you want that power node, you don't dare shoot me, or you'll never find it." He laughed at this. "Or you won't find it in time." A small smirk played across his lips as he tightened his grip around Henry's neck.

"No...Joe," Henry wheezed out. "Don't do it...don't...trust him."
"What else can we do Henry? We need that power node." He started lowering his rifle and stopped. "Okay...but look, I need to be able to trust you. I need to—"

The loud gunshot rang out loudly in the empty hallway. One minute, Joe was standing there, pointing his rifle at Brutos and the next, he was spun around and knocked violently off his feet by the force of the bullet tearing into him.

"No!" Henry yelled. "You didn't have to do that!"

Brutos laughed, "Sure I did. He would have shot me the first chance he got."

The ground started heaving, slowly at first and then stronger and stronger. *This is it,* Henry thought as dust started drifting down from the ceiling. "C'mon," Brutos said as he yanked on Henry's arm. "Let's go find your friends, huh?"

8

They had to land. The engine power nodes were straining. Tess feared that if they didn't land now, the cells would burn themselves out, and they would be stuck here for certain. The field was completely empty with the exception of dead bodies. Tess looked out at the landscape. Steam was shooting up through large fissures in the ground.

She was able to find a relatively flat area to land, but the minute she landed, she could feel just how unstable the ground was. "Chayton, we need to be ready to take off vertically very quickly. These earthquakes are causing sinkholes everywhere."

"Okay, I'll be ready Tess," he replied.

The intercom buzzed and Chayton flipped the switch to talk. "Yeah, what's up?"

"Somebody's coming, we need to lower the ramp." "Who's that?" asked Tess.

"It was one of the guys in back. They said they see someone coming out of the prison."

"Well, who is it?" Tess shot back impatiently. "Is it Henry and his guys? Do they have the power node?"

Before Chayton could ask, a voice shouted through the intercom. "It's Henry! Henry and the big guy. The big guy has his arm around Henry's neck, and he's got a gun to his head! Tess...they took all the ammo with them. We've got nothing left!"

Tess flipped on the exterior intercom, "Brutos, we don't have much time. The ground has been rumbling the entire time we've been on the ground. This place is ready to sink into the earth. I don't trust you, but if allowing you on this ship will save Henry and the rest of us, then I'm willing to let you in, but you can't bring that gun."

"No deal, Tess!" Brutos shouted back at the ship. "Can I call you 'Tess'?" he asked mockingly. "No. This gun is my ticket. Let us in now, or he gets shot. You need this engine power node. If you keep dickin' around with me, I'll shoot this fucker, and then you'll still let me on."

Tess flipped off the intercom. *"Fuck!"* she cried. "I can't let him on with a gun! He'll hold us hostage or God-forbid, shoot a fucking hole through the hull. Shit!" She slammed her fist on the console.

Chayton looked at her nervously. "Tess, I don't know if we have a choice. He's got the power node, and we need it. We'll have to deal with him later, once we're in space." He considered his next words then plunged forward. "Maybe he'll change. Become a better person. It could happen."

Tess looked at Chayton, a look of disbelief on her face. Just as quickly, her features softened, and she smiled wanly. "Maybe you're right Chayton. He's a murderer and a psychopath, but right now, we need to get off this planet, and he's the one holding all the cards. Let the ramp down and thanks for having a cool head."

Tess flipped the intercom back on. "Okay Brutos, come aboard. What about our other people?"

"Well...what about them?" he said snidely. "They won't be joining us. Open the ramp, it's starting to get nasty out here!"

She gave Chayton a nod, and he hit the ramp control switch to let down the ramp. He spoke into the internal intercom on his side, "Julie, please head to the cargo bay. Henry looks injured and may need some help."

Tess looked out her window again. Henry's arms were tied behind his back, but otherwise he looked fine. Brutos had the engine power node strapped across his back, and he had his gun pressed tightly up against Henry's head. They walked slowly towards the ship.

A loud explosion buffeted the ship and beneath them, Tess felt a sickening drop. She looked over at Chayton. "As soon as they get on board, we need to get this bucket off the ground!"

"Got it!" Chayton said without looking at her. He fastened his seat harness and waited for confirmation that they were on board.

"Everyone, prepare for takeoff," Tess spoke into the intercom. "It might be a rough, jerky one, so be ready."

She looked out the window again to see if Brutos and Henry had made it to the ship yet. She didn't see them, but what she *did* see caused her to lean heavily against the window. "Oh my God," was all she could whisper.

9

Henry didn't trust Brutos either, but he knew that Tess was not in a position to argue. They needed that power node and from the way the ground was roiling under his feet, they needed to get out of here quickly. He continued working his wrists back and forth. He had to get loose. He had no illusions that Brutos would allow him to walk on that ship. *He could shoot me right now, and they would still have to let him on the ship. And once he gets on that ship, he'll use the threat of shooting a hole in it to control everyone.*

The ramp was opening up, and he was running out of time. He could feel the pressure of the gun being pressed tightly into his skull. As stealthily as he could, he worked his wrists back and forth. The knot had loosened, but not enough, not yet. Brutos leaned close to Henry's ear, "Hey...who's Kyra? You called her name when you were out. Maybe I'll pay her a visit for you since you're not going to be there."

Henry turned his head to look at the ship just as Brutos pulled the trigger. The last thing he saw before searing pain filled his world was Kyra at one of the windows screaming in horror. Brutos let Henry fall to the ground and aimed for a second shot when he was brutally knocked to the ground.

The gun flew from his hands, and he fell painfully on top of the engine power node. He turned his head to see who had jumped him when a black blur slammed into his face. He kicked out hard and knocked his assailant to the ground.

Joe hit the ground with a thud and rolled quickly away. He climbed to his feet painfully; his shoulder bleeding profusely where he had been shot. He staggered backward as he stood up.

Brutos got to his feet and looked around for the gun. Joe saw it first and sprinted for it. He knew he would never be able to pick it up and use it in time, so he focused on just kicking it out of Brutos' reach. Brutos ran towards it like a linebacker running for a fumble. Joe reached it first and swung his foot at the gun as hard as he could. To his surprise, he connected with it and sent it sailing in the air toward one of the open fissures. It bounced just short, but its momentum sent it tumbling over the edge.

Brutos watched it sail into the chasm and then turned angrily back to Joe. He had lost his balance when he kicked at the gun and now lay on his back on the ground. Brutos reached behind him and yanked the engine power node off his back and raised it above his head. "The next time you get shot, you should stay dead," he said, barely moving his lips.

Joe was transfixed in space and time. He could see what was about to happen; he could see his impending death. But all he could do was stare at the tendons standing out in Brutos' neck as his hands clamped down on the power node.

As Brutos started his downward swing, Joe regained enough control of himself to close his eyes as he prepared himself for the pain and then...nothingness. But there was something. Just when he thought his face was about to get caved in, there was the sound of a thud. He opened his eyes slowly and saw that Brutos was no longer standing over him. He turned his head to the left and saw Stan and Brutos wrestling and rolling on the ground.

Their struggling moved them dangerously close to the edge of the fissure where he had kicked the gun a minute earlier. Stan had lost weight, but he was holding his own, at least for now.

Joe struggled to his feet. He had lost a lot of blood and was starting to feel lightheaded. He stumbled towards Stan and Brutos and realized in horror that the power node had been knocked to the ground and as they fought, it got kicked around closer and closer to the cliff edge. Joe sprinted towards it and dove on it just as Brutos laid a hard uppercut punch into Stan's midsection. Stan crumpled to the ground like a rag doll, gasping and heaving for air.

Joe was able to snatch up the power node, but Brutos was quick and kicked him in the back before he regained his balance. With a surprised yelp, Joe tumbled over into the darkness of the fissure, still holding tightly to the engine power node.

Cursing, Brutos went to the edge and looked over and to his surprise, saw Joe hanging there from one of the straps on the power node. The other end of the strap had miraculously wedged itself between an outcropping of rock.

Laughing, he reached down to get a hand hold on the strap, "Looks like you're staying here after all." He raised his other hand, meaning to smack Joe in the face, when he heard something behind him and turned around sharply.

Stan was standing there, blood dripping down his face. In his hands, he held a small length of pipe he found buried in the dirt. "Maybe you're the one staying here," he said quietly and swung the pipe as hard as he could at Brutos' face.

Brutos made an attempt to move his face out of the path of the pipe, but he wasn't fast enough. The pipe cracked across his cheekbone and through the pipe, Stan could feel the sickening crunch of Brutos' jawbone. The other end of the pipe, jagged and twisted, tore into his cheek and ripped it completely open.

The force of the blow knocked him off balance, and he stumbled backwards towards the edge of the fissure. When he caught his balance, he looked at Stan with pure hate, "You're going to die now motherf…" he started saying when there was a tremendous explosion that seemed to come from everywhere, and the ground heaved upward all around them. One minute, Brutos was standing there and the next, he was gone.

Stan saw the shocked look on Brutos' face just before he himself fell to the ground. He quickly rolled back from the edge. The entire area was starting to collapse into a giant sinkhole. He lay on his stomach while the seemingly liquid ground gyrated beneath him. "Joe!" he called out. "Joe! Are you there?" Nothing.

He was beginning to fear for the worst when Joe called out weakly from inside the crevice. "I'm here! Help! Quick…the buckle's coming loose!"

Stan scooted forward on his stomach, afraid that if he stood up, he might be tossed over the edge like Brutos. He reached the edge and peered over carefully. He could see Joe hanging from the engine power node strap, barely three feet away, holding tightly with both hands. He leaned over the edge as much as he dared, straining to reach the strap.

He slid out just a bit further and stopped. Anymore, and he would be dangerously off balance with no counterweight to prevent him from flipping over the edge. He stretched his arms as far as they could stretch without overextending himself and found that he was able to grab the strap. He was careful not to pull it for fear of it coming loose.

No sooner had his left hand joined his right hand on the strap, then another hard tremor pulled the strap completely out of its tenuous hold in the wedge of rock. Stan was now completely bearing the weight of Joe and could feel himself sliding across the ground, closer to his body's tipping point.

"Oh shit!" he yelled out as he tried fruitlessly to dig his feet into the ground. "Joe! It's...pulling...me! I can't hold it!" Stan knew that he would not be able to hold Joe's weight for long; he just didn't have the strength or the leverage to pull him up. Either he would get unceremoniously yanked over the edge or the strap would go slipping through his hands. He was slowly losing his connection to the ground, yet he held on, his hands and arms trembling. He felt his fingers going numb and knew that he would let go of the strap whether he wanted to or not.

Joe looked up into Stan's face, understanding now dawning in his eyes. "Stan, I know you can't hold my weight and you're being pulled over. I'm going to let go now. It's not your fault. I wish I could have had a chance to know you."

"No!" Stan yelled. "Don't do it! Don't let go!" But in his heart, he knew that was the only way. He could feel his body sliding to the point of no return. He saw Joe close his eyes, mentally preparing himself to let go when he felt a huge weight on his back and legs. *It was Henry!* And it was enough to halt his forward slide. "I can't hold the rope much longer!" he yelled out, but then he saw Len and Bob leaning over the edge, their arms outstretched.

In a few short minutes, they had pulled Joe up and over the edge of the fissure, while Henry helped Stan with the power node. Henry had dried blood on his face from where the bullet grazed him. He saw Stan looking at him in wonder. "This actually doesn't hurt much," he said, touching the side of his head where the bullet had nicked him. "It's the damn rock I banged my head on when I fell, that hurts like a son of a bitch."

They were lying on the ground panting when Tess's voice boomed over the external loudspeaker. "Hey guys, I know you're having a men's pow-wow session out there, but get your asses in gear! This whole area is gonna go!"

They jumped up and sprinted towards the ship. To the folks looking out the windows, they all appeared to be drunk, weaving back and forth, almost falling because of the weirdly undulating ground.

They hopped onto the ramp of the *Orion*, helped up by several folks who were waiting for them. Kyra slammed her fist into the intercom button and yelled, "Okay Tess, they're on!" At the same time, she hit the button to close the ramp. "And we're calibrating the engine power node now!"

THE DYING PLANET

1

Tess heard Kyra, but couldn't take the time to answer her. She was completely focused on getting the ship off the ground and then gaining some altitude. Wherever the earthquakes ripped open the ground, steam and gas columns erupted through the air, some going as high as 100 feet. She didn't want the ship to be right above one of those steam columns when they let go.

The *Orion* continued to climb slowly, picking up more and more altitude. The ground seemed to disintegrate as fissures and cracks opened up all over the field. The top part of the prison crumbled inward as a huge hole opened up directly beneath it. Tess wasn't sure how it could happen, but she could see bright orange liquid flowing deep within the hole.

Looking out in the distance, she could see similar steam vents opening up and shooting steam columns into the air. It reminded her of those old pictures showing Jurassic-era dinosaurs grazing in the foreground of some prehistoric volcano, while steam vents pumped out hot steam.

The core of the earth had been damaged when *Lycos* hit, and in the areas where it was exposed, huge streams of boiling hot steam issued forth. Even now, Tess wasn't 100% sure that the earth would explode, but what did she know? And she wasn't staying to find out. She looked over at Chayton. He was staring fixedly ahead, concentrating so hard, she could see a blood vessel pulsing in his temple.

"Steady Chayton," she said to him. He nodded curtly, still staring straight ahead. She looked at the power node grid and could see that the new engine power node was still calibrating. She cursed silently. She was certain that it would have calibrated by now, but the fact that they were actually drawing power from it at the same time caused the calibration to be slower.

They would have to remain at this altitude until it completely calibrated, but atmospheric conditions had gotten steadily worse. Strong winds buffeted the ship, threatening to flip them end over end. Even though the cockpit door was closed, Tess could hear the people in back screaming each time the wind slapped at the sides of the ship.

They flew across the busted landscape. It seemed every crevice or open hole they crossed over had filled in with steaming lava. The bright orange liquid fire was spewing out of some areas as if the earth had finally decided to vomit up its insides. Tess could see huge chunks of land slowly sinking into the earth as the weak rock continued to open up.

In the distance, she could see that the color of the landscape was changing. According to the ship's clock, the time was close to four in the morning, but the sun was slowing rising as they tracked east. The scarred Earth slowly transitioned to a winter wonderland. She estimated that they were somewhere over Ohio or West Virginia, but she could no longer tell for certain. Wherever they were, huge melting snowdrifts covered the cities they were traveling over. They could have been flying over Siberia for all the snow and ice she saw.

She saw no people here. Those who had survived the impact would have left long ago before the temperatures dropped. She looked at the outside air temperature gauge and was not shocked to see that it was almost minus 15 degrees Fahrenheit, and their altitude was only 4,000 feet.

"70% Tess," Chayton announced from his seat. "The calibration is at 70%."

"Thanks Chayton," she said without looking at him. Her eyes were still fixed ahead. They continued in their north-easterly direction towards New York. Chayton's navigations had them traveling out over the Atlantic Ocean. Tess hoped that they would be at their escape velocity by then and would be headed for space, but at the rate the engine power node was calibrating, she wasn't quite sure anymore. She had no desire to be over the Atlantic, but this direction would enable them to negotiate the "asteroid" field, not to mention their direction towards the moon after their slingshot maneuver.

By the time they reached what Tess assumed should be Western Pennsylvania, the frozen tundra was gone, replaced by large bodies of land-bound water. Tess banked due east towards New York, where the melting snowdrifts were quickly turning into white water rapids, rushing across the bruised earth.

Tess looked out at the surrounding landscape. The entire area had been violently forced upward creating a smaller, uglier range of *Rocky Mountains* that extended for miles in both directions. Huge fissures had opened up and swallowed entire towns. As the ship continued its eastward course, they entered into what Tess estimated was New York airspace. Strong winds blew incessantly, while trees, broken slabs of buildings, and what seemed like hundreds of vehicles tossed and turned in the angry, rushing water.

They flew on in silence, and as they neared what should have been the mid-Atlantic Seaboard, Tess's mouth dropped open. It was as if the entire area had been violently ripped apart from as far north and south as she could see. As they flew over the chasm, the only thing she could see was a small thin line of fiery orange deep in the darkness.

"Oh my God, Tess. What do you think happened here?" Chayton asked her quietly.

"I don't know Chayton. Could be shifting faults or maybe the tectonic plates are being wrenched apart."

As they neared the other side, Tess could see the frothy, turbulent waters of the Atlantic Ocean racing over the new cliff and pouring ceaselessly into the chasm. She felt as if she were looking at a massive Niagara Falls. As they flew over the black water, she knew this image would be burned into her consciousness forever.

"We're at 100%!" cried Chayton. He was actually crying. Seeing the destruction of the earth up close like this was completely overwhelming. "Tess...we're seeing things that only dead people see."

"I know Chayton, I know," was all she could utter. "Let's punch in our slingshot orbit and get the hell out of here."

He nodded to her and then punched in the numbers. As their countdown reached zero, Chayton chanced a glance again at the dark waters rushing into oblivion and shuttered involuntarily. He faced ahead as they rushed headlong into their own oblivion.

V
SPACE
JANUARY 2054

THE CASSIOPEIA

1

"And what's this for?" Len asked his mom as he sat in the Navigator's chair behind her.

"That helps us to determine our exact location in space. Since we know the relative positions of other planets and stars, we are able to map our location based on that information," Tess replied.

She looked over at the entrance and saw Bonnie standing there quietly. "Okay...that's enough for today," she told her son. "You two stay out of trouble, okay?"

"Okay mom," he said and kissed her on the cheek. He grabbed Bonnie's hand, and they ran off towards the back of the ship, almost bumping into Chayton in their haste.

"Wow...looks like they're in a rush to be somewhere fast." Chayton said as he seated himself in the co-pilot's chair.

"Yeah...I think Betsy is giving birth soon. They want to be there when it happens."

Chayton laughed, "It's not every day you get to see a sheep give birth...while traveling in a space ship!"

Tess chuckled, "Yeah, well, you're right about that." She stood up and stretched. "Alright, I'm off to bed. Wake me if you need anything." She headed out the cockpit entrance towards her quarters but didn't get very far before Henry caught up to her.

"Hey Tess...how are you?" he said as he walked with her to her compartment.

"A little tired, but doing okay. How about you? I see your wound is healing up nicely."

Henry touched the smooth line that streaked across the side of his scalp. Although he refused to admit it, he got the chills each time he thought about how close Brutos' bullet came to ending his life. "Yeah...it is, but even after a month, the area is still tender when I comb my hair."

Tess smiled. "By the way, have you had any luck linking up with the satellite?"

"That's actually what I wanted to talk to you about. The signal is very faint, and I'm not sure if it's still orbiting *Europa* or not. It might still be on the far side of Jupiter, but it should have broken that orbit weeks ago. I think either one of two things could have happened to it: either Jupiter's gravity has pulled it into a wider orbit, or it's floating out towards the edge of the galaxy. I probably won't know anything until we're almost knocking on *Europa's* front door."

"I guess the least negative option is that it's orbiting Jupiter," Tess said, "but that still leaves us in a tight position. If we can get *something* from the satellite that shows us several possible landing areas, then we can at least set our approach vector in that direction—we'll be riding on fumes as it is. If we have to go searching for a suitable place to land, then we're going to be in big trouble."

"And that brings me to my other point," Henry replied quietly. "I expanded the search parameters for the satellite in case its orbit changed, and I caught a faint signal of the *Cassiopeia*."

Tess's eyes widened, "*What?* Have they landed on *Europa*? What's their position?"

"They haven't landed yet," Henry replied, "but it would appear that their situation is tenuous. I first caught their signal a couple of hours ago and have been trying to pinpoint their exact location. Once I found it, I plotted their position at that time, but when I checked again later, their location had changed only slightly."

Tess considered this and said, "Maybe they've taken up orbit above the planet and are waiting for the satellite images to confirm a landing location. That's what I would do, provided I had the fuel and resources necessary to do that." She grew somber for a few minutes and then added, "It *is* odd though that they would still be orbiting the planet after all this time. I'm sure their fuel situation can't be good."

"I thought they were trying to confirm a landing location also," Henry added, "but I've triangulated their position, and it looks like they're moving *away* from *Europa*...not purposefully, but *helplessly*. I think they've had a problem and are now adrift."

Despite the fact that Soren had abandoned them to their deaths on the moon, Tess felt a twinge of concern for them. There were a lot of good people on that shuttle. She could be angry at Soren and Rey and some of the others who were behind this, but she could not be angry at the innocent ones.

"Unfortunately, there's nothing we can do for them now, but pray," said Tess. "I guess we'll have more answers in the next few weeks as we get closer to *Europa*."

2

All of the children (and most of the adults) had their faces plastered to the below deck view windows. They were still two weeks away from *Europa*, yet the huge planet Jupiter completely dominated their outside views.

Tess had requested a ship-wide meeting to discuss what was going to happen in the next couple of weeks, and she thought it was very important that everyone know their part, even the children.

"Okay, everyone, let's get started," Henry announced to the children and adults present. Chayton was in the cockpit, but he could hear everything over the intercom. Henry motioned for everyone to move in closer so they could hear Tess. The children, and a few adults, reluctantly tore themselves away from the view windows as Tess stood up to address the group.

"I've been in space many times," Tess began, "but I've never seen a view like that before. Not this close." She waved her arms towards the windows as the huge black and orange storm on Jupiter looked back at them indifferently. "You know, it's funny, but during the past few weeks as we've gotten closer and closer to Jupiter, the amount of data that we've collected on the planet would put many of our old experts to shame. Stuff that we assumed we knew about this planet and its moons, only amounted to less than ten percent of what we've been able to gather just during our approach here."

She looked at them; she felt very close to them. A rainbow of faces looked back at her. Their numbers had increased significantly since they left the moon some three months ago—they now numbered close to 120 people. There were more women than men, and the number of children had doubled to close to 40. Tess reflected sadly that most of the children only had one parent.

A lot of them were thin and some of them were ill. They had lost a few people during the first few weeks of the trip all due to advanced radiation poisoning and various other ailments that had progressed too far for Julie and Steve to do anything about. There had been a few scuffles, but they were few and far between. They functioned by routine and lived for *Europa*. It was hard at first, when Jupiter was nothing more than a distant bright light; but as they closed the distance, the light became more substantial and concrete, as did their hope.

"In six to eight days, we will be entering Jupiter's planetary system, but we won't be able to see *Europa* up close because its orbit will have taken it to the far side of Jupiter. About two days after we enter Jupiter's system, we should have an excellent visual of *Europa*."

Unexpectedly, the group clapped and cheered. Most of the children whooped and hollered too, but the smaller kids only did so after observing what the older kids were doing.

Tess couldn't help from smiling. Their excitement was infectious. When it quieted down, she continued. "I can't wait myself, but that's one of the things we need to discuss today."

Although she didn't want to sound too grave, it must have been evident in her voice because the group grew quiet quickly.

"We have not been able to successfully link up with the *Pegasus1* satellite that's been orbiting *Europa* collecting data." She glanced at Henry and Kyra briefly and continued on. "Our original group from the moon actually collected the data from the satellite, but it was withheld from most of us, so we don't know for certain what to expect on the planet. We can assume that since they departed for the planet, they must have received reliable data or at least *survivable* data. They would have also received information on major fresh water sources, potential landing sites, and so on. We don't have that data yet, and we won't know if we can even retrieve it from the satellite until we get closer to the planet."

"Well, the way I see it Tess," Bob said, "is that we don't really have a choice, do we?" It was spoken in that matter-of-fact way most Louisianans had a knack for, with no malice intended.

"You're absolutely right Bob," Tess replied. "This has been a one-way trip for us, and we're headed down to the planet regardless. I just wanted everyone to be aware of that fact." As she looked at the crowd, she could see that no one was really expecting anything different. They all knew the risks.

She forged ahead, "The other important thing that we need to discuss is the other ship, the *Cassiopeia*."

They started murmuring and looking at each other. "What about it, Tess?" Frieda asked, looking much older than her 30 years.

"We've confirmed their signal and found out that they are in the Jupiter planetary system. After tracking their signal, we've also confirmed that they may be having or have had some problems of unknown origins."

"What do you mean, 'unknown origins'?" Thelma asked.

"We just don't know why they've stopped, at least not yet. In a few days, we'll know a lot more because we will be within 10,000 km of their ship." Tess looked at Stan, and he nodded back at her. "The reason I'm bringing this up is because we need to make a decision. I feel that it's a decision we all need to make together because it involves all of us.

"If we come upon the *Cassiopeia* and find it incapacitated, then we need to determine if we should stop to help them. There are about 50 people on that ship and probably 5 to 10 of them are very dangerous. We believe that the rest were either tricked into boarding or were coerced. If we decide to help them, there shouldn't be a problem with space or food, since we are so close to *Europa*." She stopped and looked at them levelly and saw that everyone was listening intently.

"Not as important as the people," she continued, "but critically important to us and our possible survival on *Europa* are the Starter Kits. There are six Starter Kits in the *Cassiopeia*. Each Starter Kit has solar powered generators, heating and cooling units, pre-fab four-person dwelling units, encyclopedia units, and a lot more. We can use them to jump start our...village."

Before she could continue, they all started talking at once. Questions arose and were answered before she could add any input. *Can we trust the dangerous ones? Who knows, but we can handle them if we have to! Do we really need those Starter Kits? Hell yeah! We don't know what the planet will be like when we land! We need some type of backup support. How are we going to get that stuff? Well...I'm not too sure about that.*

Stan stepped up next to Tess and spoke up loudly, "These Starter Kits are stored in the Cargo Cabin connected to the top of their ship. If the ship *is* incapacitated and we decide to retrieve the Cargo Cabin, then once we get close to the *Cassiopeia*, we'll have to determine their power situation and how best to secure the Cargo Cabin.

"Both the *Orion* and the *Cassiopeia* are capable of carrying one Cargo Cabin, which can be mounted on the top or bottom of the ship. Right now, the Cargo Cabin is connected to the top of the *Cassiopeia*. When we grab it, we will connect it to the *bottom* of our ship. The challenge, however, is making the connection. As I mentioned earlier, if the *Cassiopeia* still has power, or more specifically, *cockpit docking control*, then they can release the clamps once we've docked onto the Cabin. If they don't have docking control, then the only way to release the clamp is from a spacewalk where the clamps are manually released from the outside."

"So," Joe said doubtfully, "the person doing the spacewalk has to stay on the outside of the busted ship while the docking ship lands on top? Damn! That's a little close for comfort!" A couple of people laughed nervously and turned to face Tess.

"Stan's right," Tess said. "This is about the only way we can do it. Getting the people out won't be too difficult because we have an umbilicus connection at the top of the shuttle and on the bottom." She breathed deeply, "I realize this is a tough decision, but it's one that we need to make in the next few days, because we will need to intercept their location and match our speed to theirs. Whatever happened on their ship has caused them to drift further from *Europa*. Eventually, Jupiter's massive gravity will pull the ship into a tight orbit until it eventually crashes on the planet. For all we know, it's slowly happening now."

Bonnie, standing next to Len raised her hand and asked shyly, "How will the ship land with all of that stuff on the bottom?" A few folks turned and stared at her, and then their mouths fell open. A few of them were murmuring, *hell of a question kid*.

"Excellent question, Bonnie!" Stan said. "A ship cannot enter a planet's atmosphere with a Cargo Cabin in place, simply because the connection is not strong enough to withstand re-entry. Because of this, the Cabin must be deployed from low orbit, or very close to the planet."

Len smiled at Bonnie, and they walked back over to the windows to stare out at Jupiter while the discussion on how to handle the *Cassiopeia* and the Cargo Cabin grew in intensity behind them.

3

"Engaging magnetic boots now," Stan said into the microphone set in his helmet and flipped the green switch on his handheld controller. He could feel the comforting pull of the magnetic pads in his boots as they connected to the hull of the *Cassiopeia*. "Okay Chayton, let's go."

The decision to attempt retrieval of the Cargo Cabin had been a no-brainer. They all knew the risks, but knew they needed the supplies and Starter Kits in the Cabin. What worried everyone all the way up to this moment was the total lack of communication with the *Cassiopeia*.

Tess had hoped that by the time they reached the *Cassiopeia*, they would at least have made contact with the cockpit crew, but there was nothing but static. They had been hailing them unsuccessfully for hours since their rendezvous earlier that day. *"This is bullshit!"* Tess said. "I don't know what happened to them and right now, we don't have time to speculate." She looked at Stan and Chayton, "Other than me, you guys are the only ones qualified to do this spacewalk and get that Cargo Cabin connected. We don't have much time. Do you think you can get it connected and get the people out in time?"

Stan had looked at Chayton and then back at Tess, "Yeah, I think so. We'll both work on getting the Cabin connected, and then I'll get inside to get the people ready to go." The look in his face showed what he was thinking in his heart; *if there are any people alive that is.*

Outside the shuttle, he remembered why he liked being in space. The immense vastness always humbled him. He glanced over at Jupiter and simply stared at the incredibly huge, glowing sphere that seemed to dwarf everything else near it. He looked at the eye and could see massive, terrible swirling storms even though they were still thousands of miles away.

"My God, you just don't know how large these things are until you're directly underneath one." Chayton's voice cut through his reverie. They were both standing on the hull of the *Cassiopeia* and Chayton was standing to the front of the Cargo Cabin, pulling up the slack of his tether. His head was craned upward the entire time.

They had come through the umbilicus connection at the bottom of the *Orion* once it had gotten into position above the Cargo Cabin attached to the *Cassiopeia*. Using their backpack jet thrusters, they maneuvered themselves down to the *Cassiopeia* and over to the Cargo Cabin. At the moment, Chayton was staring up at the massive undercarriage of the *Orion*. The scarred, heat-battered black heat shields loomed above him like a foot poised to step on an insect. He stood there motionless until Stan's voice boomed in his ear. "Chayton! Let's move. No time for daydreaming."

Chayton snapped out of it with a jerk. "Sorry man...I was lost there for a minute. Okay...moving towards the Cargo Cabin."

Tess positioned the *Orion* about 200 feet above the *Cassiopeia* and matched its drift speed. Using the onboard spatial positioning system, she was able to position the ship directly over the Cargo Cabin hook up connections. Darkness blanketed Stan and Chayton as the wide shadow of the *Orion* descended upon them. "Tess, we could use a little light down here," Stan chuckled into the mike.

"Ask and you shall receive." Tess flipped a switch that bathed the two men and the entire top of the *Cassiopeia* in bright light.

Stan and Chayton continued their slow walk towards the Cargo Cabin. Once there, they would verify the connections on the Cabin, as well as the locking calipers. If they were still functional, she would be able to lower the shuttle until she connected with the Cabin.

The Cabin stood about 20 feet high, but it rested 10 feet deep in the huge recessed compartment at the top of the *Cassiopeia*. Stan and Chayton climbed the easy 10 feet to the top and headed straight for the huge connectors in the center of the Cabin. "Tess, we're at the connectors," Stan said. "They look intact and we should be able to configure the receiving end in just a few minutes."

"Roger, Stan," Tess replied. "Standing by."

Henry sat at the radio controls in the Navigator's seat behind Tess, trying to contact the *Cassiopeia*, but static continued to pour through the speakers. If the sun shields on the other ship were open, they would have been able to at least see through the windows; maybe catch a glimpse of someone looking out, but only dark portals stared back at them.

After about five minutes, Stan spoke into his mouthpiece, "Tess, we've configured the receiving end. We're headed back down to check the release clamps."

Tess's voice came back much quicker than he expected. "Look guys, I'm reading a slight increase in *Cassiopeia's* drift speed, which means we must be in Jupiter's gravity pull. We need to speed it up out there. Any suggestions?"

Stan thought it over and replied, "Chayton and I will need to split up then. Chayton, you'll have to complete the Cabin undocking procedures, while I go inside and prepare the umbilicus. Tess...how much time do we have?"

"You have about 80 minutes, Stan. Any longer and we'll burn up our fuel trying to pull free of Jupiter's gravity."

Crap! He thought to himself, but he said "Okay...thanks Tess. Chayton...you know what to do here. I'm going to get inside the ship and get the umbilicus opened. If they're still alive in there, I'll get them moving."

"Be careful Stan," Tess spoke up in his ear. "Some of them are very dangerous, although I imagine in this situation, they're less likely to be confrontational. Still, watch yourself."

"I will babe," he responded and slowly made his way towards the aft umbilicus entrance on the portside of the ship. The generation ships had been designed with a number of umbilicus entrances; one on each side and one at the top and bottom of each section of the ship. Only the top and bottom portals could be used for personnel transport in cases of emergencies. In fact, all of NASA's newer shuttle models, regardless of size, had the same configuration. Stan smiled to himself, thinking that for once, NASA's effort at standardization was a blessing and not a curse.

Stan was closest to the portal entrance near the biosphere and cargo section towards the rear of the ship. He wasn't sure where the people might be, but regardless of where they were, they would have to travel through the cargo section's umbilicus portal—the current position of the *Orion* above the Cargo Cabin prohibited the umbilicus connector to make it past the cargo section.

If the cargo area was compromised, then they would need space suits to move from the living quarters through the cargo section and out the top portal, or wait until Tess had connected the Cargo Cabin and moved the *Orion* forward. Stan was worried that they might not have time for that.

Regardless of what he needed to do, he would not go inside without knowing what he was up against. Not after what Tess had told him about Soren and Rey and some of their goons. In some weird way, he figured all the folks left on Earth, him included, should be grateful to them. If they had not abandoned Tess and her people, then Tess would never have had to come to Earth. He didn't think too hard on that thought though. The present right now was what he had, and he would hold onto to that as hard as he could.

He reached the portside umbilicus portal in good time. After a minute of looking, he found the protective sleeve covering the portal access button. Once he activated the opening, the interior door leading inside would lock automatically to avoid the accidental decompression of the ship. If someone was in there, they would have 30 seconds to vacate it before the doors locked.

He pressed the button and waited. He was totally blind to what was happening within the ship. He couldn't hear the automated voice in the airlock booming out its warning and there was a heat shield covering the small window. All he could hear was Chayton giving the 'all clear' to Tess to maneuver the shuttle into docking position. Stan dropped his eyes to the green LED lights on the bottom right panel of his facemask. He had set the timer to 80:00 minutes and the last 5 minutes would countdown in red. Right now, the timer read 65 minutes.

The light on the door panel changed from red to green and then slid open. He was just about to step in when two people rushed out at him, their arms reaching for him. His reactions betrayed him before his mind could interpret the situation and a scream bolted from his mouth, while he flailed his arms towards his face to fend them off. Their hands and feet slapped and bumped him as they rushed out past him and into space. They were both naked and Stan could see cuts and bruises all over their bodies. The face of one of them had a frozen look of pain and incomprehension.

"Stan! Are you alright?" Tess and Chayton were asking, almost at the same time. "What happened?"

"I'm okay," he said, slightly shaken. He took a deep breath and continued, "There were two bodies in the portside umbilicus portal. A man and a woman, I think. They were naked, and they looked as if they had been tortured and placed in the umbilicus where they died. Okay...no more bodies in here, so I'm heading in."

"Oh my God," Chayton said in his ear. Stan looked over and saw Chayton looking at the bodies floating out into space. They seemed to be doing a weird three-dimensional dance in space as they hurtled towards Jupiter.

"I'm telling you Stan, be careful. Don't take any chances. Once we dock with the Cabin, we'll be done. If they resist or if there's a problem, then we'll have to leave them or we'll all die here."

"I hear you honey. I brought Henry's surgical laser tool, but I hope I don't have to use it. I don't know about its killing potential, but I'm sure it'll give out a nasty burn with the added benefit of not blasting a hole in the ship," he replied, giving out a small chuckle.

"Not funny. I'm serious...watch them," Tess said.

"I know, and I will. Alright, I'm inside and my tether is connected to the external tether-link. I'm about to close the outer portal door. Once inside, I should be able to communicate with them on their internal ship communicator inside the umbilicus. I'll keep the airways open." Stan pressed the release button, and the external door closed quietly behind him.

Once inside, he didn't feel so vulnerable. As a Mission Specialist, he had made twice as many spacewalks as Tess and Chayton put together, but he could never shake the feeling that he was standing, no, *leaning* over a cliff or building hundreds of feet tall. In a way, that's what he was doing, but the distance was immeasurable.

And yet on every mission, he continued to volunteer to go outside. He likened it to the same feeling of combined fear and excitement that he used to feel when he got in line to ride rollercoasters when he was young. Before each spacewalk, he could sense his eagerness building, but the minute he stepped outside, his nervousness would come rushing back like an old friend. It never affected his work, or at least he liked to think that it never affected his work and he was always able to function effectively; but that unsettling feeling of leaning over the abyss hung around his psyche like a bad luck charm.

And Stan could pinpoint the exact time when this bad luck charm fell out of the sky and into his lap. Ten years ago, he and Tess went rock climbing in Central New Mexico with Tess's good friend Lillian Reynolds and her husband Braddock. The first day was great. They had perfect weather, and their guide took them up flawlessly. On the second day, however, Braddock tried showboating and either didn't pay attention or ignored the guide's direction. He attempted to negotiate a difficult and rather dangerous maneuver and missed.

In his fall, he yanked his wife off the side of the cliff and they both plummeted to the earth together, but as Braddock fell, kicking and screaming, his foot kicked Stan in the head, knocking him off balance and causing him to slip and fall. The next thing Stan knew, he was tumbling and spinning, periodically slamming up against the side of the cliff. By the time he opened his eyes, Braddock and Lillian lay broken some 200 feet below him and he found himself hanging helpless from Tess's rope, too far from the cliff to do anything. It was this thought that came to mind as he stood in the airlock and the feeling that he was hanging helpless from someone else's rope.

He had pressed the button to close the door, but decided not to vent the air in the umbilicus just yet. He still wasn't sure what had happened on this ship, and he knew that there were some dangerous people on board. He would try to find out what the situation was before clearing the umbilicus area.

He turned towards the interior door and was startled to see faces staring at him from the inside. It was a small window, so there were only two faces looking in at him; two men from the looks of their scruffy beards. They wouldn't open the door until he cleared the area, and the bright red light above the door made sure of that.

"Oh my God," one of the men's voices said through the intercom. "Who are you? Where did you come from?"

Stan pressed his exterior mike on his helmet. I'm from the *Orion*. What's your situation in there?"

"Oh God!" the man said again. "Are you here to help us? These fuckers are crazy! Soren has gone crazy!"

To Stan, the man looked a little off himself, but it could have been the stress of the situation. "What's going on in there, sir? Before I open these doors, I need to know exactly what's happened. I'm familiar with the name Soren, and I need to know the situation in there before I come in."

The man started babbling again, when someone shoved him over. "Get out of the way Walt! Let me talk to him."

Walt looked reluctant, but he moved over to let the other man speak. An older black man, slightly balding with a black and gray scruffy beard, put his head in the window. Like Walt, his face was thin, bordering on gaunt. "Hi, my name is Burt. Burt Stone. I'm a doctor. We've got a lot of sick people here, and we're all suffering from malnutrition. We lost gravity a couple of weeks ago. We need help badly."

Stan could see the sincerity in his face, but he needed a little more reassurance. "Burt, I wasn't with your original group on the moon, but Tess and Henry and others have told me—"

"You're with Tess?" Burt asked incredulously. "Yes...she's piloting the *Orion*." Stan replied.

"And the others? The others from the moon. Are they here too?"

Stan wasn't sure if everyone from the moon made it or not, but at the moment, that wasn't important. "I'm not sure Burt, but yeah...I believe most everyone is here."

"Oh God," Burt said. "We didn't know. Most of us didn't know what Soren was planning. By the time we realized it, we were on the shuttle with his armed thugs, and we were trapped. It was so wrong for him to leave them like that."

He stopped for a minute to rub at his thin face. When he looked back up at Stan, his eyes were wet. "Tess was like a daughter to me. When he abandoned her and the others, it was like leaving my own child behind." He lowered his head again.

Stan could feel Burt's pain and as gently as he could, asked him again, "What *happened* here Burt? Where are Soren and his men?"

Burt collected himself and seemed to grow more resolute. "We're locked in the biosphere cargo hold by our own doing. Soren's half-assed pilot, Rey, didn't know what the hell he was doing and burned out three of our power nodes just getting here. The remaining fuel and power nodes are the only things keeping us from freezing to death out here."

"Why are you locked in the cargo hold?" Stan asked.

"Soren and his people started fighting over the women and then they started fighting over the food." He looked behind him and then faced forward again. "They started raping the women, so I moved everyone back here and we locked ourselves in. The bulkhead doors are strong and we were able to destroy the bulkhead opening mechanism. We couldn't get out now even if our lives depended on it, but it kept *them* out at least. Unfortunately, we left a number of good people in there because we just couldn't get to them in time." He looked down at the floor.

Stan had heard enough and felt that he could trust this man. "Okay Burt, I'm clearing the umbilicus, so we can talk face to face." He pressed the control button and hidden compressors hissed and pumped in air from the ship. In less than a minute, the light above the door turned green, and the door latch slid to the side.

He stepped into the room and undid his helmet latch. His magnetic boots kept him grounded as he moved into the section. He noticed immediately that the air was not as fresh as the air on the *Orion*, and the smell of body odors were keen. He looked around the room and at first glance, estimated about 30 people here, give or take a few. They were all so emaciated, that at first, he thought the split between men and women was about even, but a closer look revealed that there were significantly more women than men. A few were floating in the weightlessness, but most were either tied down or holding on to something to keep from drifting. The area looked like a refugee camp.

"Nice to meet you," Burt said, holding out his hand, while his left held onto a metal support on the wall.

"Likewise," Stan said. "Look Burt, we don't have a lot of time here." And then to everyone, he said, "Look everyone, the *Cassiopeia* is slowly drifting towards Jupiter." He glanced at his watch. "In about an hour, we won't have enough fuel to pull away from Jupiter's gravity and still make our approach to *Europa*."

They started murmuring. A few folks stood up and walked towards Stan. "What do we need to do?" they asked, almost in unison.

Stan spoke into his mike, "Tess, what's the status of the Cabin hook-up? As soon as you're latched on, we can deploy the umbilicus and get everyone off this ship."

At the mention of Tess's name, the folks in the cargo bay looked around wide-eyed at each other. It was clear that they were shocked to hear that she was still alive. Shocked and saddened by their unwilling participation in the abandonment of her and the others.

"We're almost there Stan. Tell everyone to hold onto something...there could be a little bump."

Before Stan had a chance to open his mouth and tell the others to hold on, he felt a slight jarring and that was it. He smiled. He didn't think this because Tess was his wife, but he always thought she was the best pilot he'd ever flown with and he had flown with many.

"Connected," her voice breathed into his ear. "Chayton, prepare to guide the umbilicus to the *Cassiopeia*. Stan, you might want to get those people ready. As soon as the connection is made, we'll flood the tubes with oxygen, but tell them to be prepared for gravity over here."

4

On the topside of the *Cassiopeia*, Chayton watched the umbilicus tube extend from the bottom of the *Orion*. It looked like a giant flexible telescope opening from the large end to the small end. It came slowly down towards the receiving umbilicus on the top side of the *Cassiopeia*. It was stiff, but not completely rigid and allowed for some flexibility in the angle. In fact, the last 10 feet of the tube was very flexible and allowed for unsteady conditions to avoid damaging the tube and more importantly the receiving ship.

When the tube was five feet from the top of the *Cassiopeia*, Chayton was able to guide it the rest of the way using the manual extender connected at the end of the tube. He positioned the large, circular tube over the top portal connector on the ship. Once on, he clamped it down and the automated, self-sealing mechanism kicked in, totally securing it over the entire circumference of the opening. Chayton watched the indicator on the tube change from red to yellow to green, indicating that the apparatus had connected securely. A second light indicator changed from red to yellow to green as the umbilicus was pressurized and filled with oxygen. When the light turned green and remained that way, Chayton spoke up, "Okay Stan, the umbilicus tube is ready. The ball's in your court now."

Stan had already rallied the people inside, and they were ready to go. A few carried personal belongings in backpacks, but most had nothing to bring. "Alright people, let's get out of here." He pointed to two tall young men standing off to the side. "Hey guys, give me a hand with this ladder." They pulled themselves over to him to help with the ladder. He glanced down at his watch; 40 minutes. They were running out of time fast.

"Okay...let's get up here! We don't have a lot of time. Remember people, you'll have to pull yourselves along by using the hand rails inside. There's no gravity in the tube, but we have gravity on the ship. Our people will help you out once you get there."

Chayton's voice crackled in his ear, "Stan, I'm having a problem here. I can't activate all of the release clamps on the Cargo Cabin. I was only able to get one released; the manual releases for the other three are damaged."

"What?" Stan replied. *"Son of a bitch!* Are you sure Chayton?"
"Yeah...I'm sure Stan. Sorry to give you the bad news."

"Okay...why don't you come on in here and help get these folks ready to exit through the umbilicus. The cargo section in here is cut off from the rest of the ship. I'll have to come out and make my way to the passenger umbilicus portal, because the only way to blow those release catches is from the cockpit."

"That's ridiculous Stan! I'm already out here. I'll head to the other airlock and take care of it myself. We don't have much time, and we'll easily lose ten minutes while you make your way out here and then to the other portal. No. Get those people in the tube. I'll take care of this."

"He's right," Tess interjected. "You're already there, so continue getting those people up here."

"Alright! Alright. Okay...good luck Chayton and hustle up man!" As an afterthought, he added, "And watch your back in there!"

"Hey, you read my mind," he replied heartily. In fact, he had already started towards the other umbilicus portal. There was no way Stan could have made it there in time. He glanced at his watch. Provided there were no problems, he thought he would have plenty of time to get inside, blow the releases and then get back to the ship before time ran out. It would be close, but he could do it.

He reached the passenger airlock quickly, opened it and slid inside. Once safely inside, he undid his tether and clamped it to the exterior of the ship. He pushed the button closing the airlock door and waited a quick 20 seconds, while the airlock re-pressurized itself. The wall panel assured him that it was safe to take his helmet off, but he decided that he would leave it on in case he needed to make a hasty exit. He opened the interior door and walked inside.

There were no lights on here in the sleeping quarters so he flipped his helmet switch and the light built into the top of the helmet came on, illuminating the entire bay. As he turned around to survey the room, his breath caught in his throat.

The room was a mess. Things were floating everywhere. A few boots, some books, bedding, clothing and blood drops. Lots of blood drops. He was glad that he'd decided to keep his helmet on because the slow-moving blood drops bumped against his helmet and exploded into smaller droplets, each of them bouncing off in different directions. A severed, shoeless foot drifted lazily across his field of vision, red toenail polish standing out on the expertly manicured toes. It bumped a paperback book, and they both bounded off in opposite directions. He made his way over to the light panel. Despite the fact that the ship was out of fuel, he thought the power nodes may still have enough energy remaining for the lights to work. He tapped on the switch pads and at first nothing happened, but then slowly, the overhead panels begin to flicker on.

As the room brightened and he could see his surroundings better, he felt that maybe he should have left them off. Blood seemed to be everywhere; on the walls, on the floor, on the furniture. *But where were the bodies?* Other than the woman's severed foot and a few odds and ends, there was nothing else to be seen. He walked along the corridor connecting the sleeping quarters with the passenger seating.

After that would be the cockpit, where he could release the Cargo Cabin clamps and get the hell out of here.

He started towards the hall leading to the cockpit, when he glanced over and saw a lump under a blood-stained sheet. He was sure it was probably a body, but morbid curiosity forced his legs to move in that direction. He had to check it out at least. *What if it was someone still alive?*

He walked slowly towards the blood-stained lump; his own lump rising in his throat. As he got closer, he could see some words written in dried blood on the wall above the lump. It was hard to make out, because it was written at an angle and was badly smeared, but he thought he read *"Not a was hereee..."* He looked closer. No...the "t" was an "l". *"Nola was hereee..."* He swallowed hard and reached a gloved hand up to pull back the sheet.

The sheet was stuck, so he pulled harder to un-stick it, but it wouldn't give. He grabbed a handful of the sheet and gave a hard tug. The sheet flew off the bloody lump and drifted across the room. He yelled involuntarily as he looked down at the mutilated body of a woman. Thick red hair (or bloodied?) was tied off in two large braids. One blue eye stared up at him sightlessly, while the other hid behind a bruised and puffy eyelid. The woman's tongue was swollen and protruded halfway out of her mouth. Both of her feet were amputated and her arms were tied down severely. Chayton felt his gourd rising when he saw the deep bite marks over her entire naked body. Bloody handprints covered her breasts and legs.

"Chayton!" Stan yelled. "What happened? Are you all right?"

"I, uh...I thought maybe there was a survivor here, but no. Whoever she was, she's dead now. I'm okay guys, sorry."

"Where are you Chayton," Tess said in his ear. "What's your status?"

"I'm making my way through the passenger seating area. I haven't seen any other people and..." He trailed off.

"And what?" Tess repeated.

"And there's blood. There's fucking blood everywhere!"

Stan was listening too and could hear the edge of panic in Chayton's voice. He very calmly reassured him, "Chayton, keep your head on dude. Don't let this get to you. Remember...we don't have a lot of time here. Blow those releases and get your ass back here. Okay? Don't worry about what happened there or where the bodies—"

A bolt of noise sliced through Stan's head as Chayton screamed piercingly. Tess was on the line immediately, "Stan! Chayton! What happened? Who was that?"

"Chayton! What's going on?" Stan shouted into his mouthpiece. He had sent the last passenger up the umbilicus and was preparing to go in himself when Chayton screamed. He couldn't help him just yet, because he had to close the umbilicus from inside the tube. Once the people were all the way through, he could go back out, but that wouldn't leave much time. He glanced at his watch. *Seventeen minutes.* "Tess, I'm getting no response from Chayton. Have the releases been blown yet?"

"No...they haven't been blown yet and I'm getting nothing from Chayton. You need to get him out Stan and forget about blowing the releases. We just don't have that much time. If we have to, we could always force the disconnection by pulling away from the ship. That option has its pros and cons though."

"Yeah, but that's a last resort. Plus, if the releases don't let go, then we could damage our own ship, maybe even compromise the undercarriage. No. I'm going in there. The umbilicus is almost totally retracted. Once I find out what happened to Chayton, then I'll make my way to the bridge and blow the releases."

"No, Stan," Tess said weakly, knowing that it would do no good. Stan was right. If she tried to force the disconnection, they could damage the Cargo Cabin and possibly endanger their ship.

"I have to Tess," Stan said. He turned his attention to Joe, who was helping the passengers enter the *Orion* from the umbilicus. "Joe, are they all through yet?"

"Just got the last one Stan. I'm sealing the umbilicus airlock...now. Alright, you can disconnect the umbilicus now."

Stan put on his helmet and climbed up through the topside portal of the *Cassiopeia*. He disconnected the umbilicus and watched for a second as it retracted back towards the *Orion*. He went back the way he came and exited from the portal after turning on his magnetic boots. Once outside, he unhooked his tether from the side of the ship and reconnected it to his belt.

As he made his way towards the passenger umbilicus portal, he could see Chayton's tether connected to the outside of the ship. He opened up the door and stepped into the airlock. Once he was safely inside, he connected his tether to the tether-link below Chayton's. Tess spoke in his ear as he was closing the airlock door, "Be careful Stan. Be very careful."

Stan could detect just a hint of fear in her voice, "Don't worry, I'll be back...that's a promise."

"You'd better be." Tess said shakily. "I can't lose you again."

5

After depressurizing the portal entrance, Stan checked the oxygen levels here. They were good, but like Chayton only a few minutes earlier, he decided to leave his helmet on. He didn't bother searching the sleeping quarters. When Chayton yelled out, he had been in the passenger seating area or in the corridor leading to the cockpit.

Although he had the small laser surgical tool clamped onto his belt, he brought a pipe with him that one of the passengers had in the cargo area. He may not be able to swing the pipe in zero gravity, but he could at least keep someone at bay with it; if it became necessary to do so.

He quickly crossed into the passenger area and his breath caught in his throat. The place looked like something out of a horror show. There was blood everywhere. He walked towards the corridor leading to the cockpit, being careful to look in each row once he passed the high-backed chairs. A bloody sheet seemed to hang in mid-air towards the back of the section. Globules of blood and pieces of other floating stuff drifted by indifferently and he was immediately glad that he decided to leave his helmet on.

He had just checked the second row when something flickered in his peripheral vision. Before waiting to see what it was, he brought the pipe up to port arms. His lips unknowingly pulled back in a savage grimace.

He turned back towards the cockpit corridor, and his heart seemed to leap out of his chest. An apparition floated towards him faster than he thought possible in zero gravity. It was a man, but Stan would have believed it was anything but. He was naked, and his body was covered in red and black, greasy stuff. Chunks of hair flowed out from him like tentacles, and it made him look like some weird cross between a man and a hairy octopus.

He had been coming towards Stan in spread eagle fashion, so the pipe hit him square in the chest. He didn't have enough momentum for the pipe to puncture his chest, but it stopped him cold. He grimaced and floated to the floor, swinging his right arm at Stan as he drifted down. He had a bloody knife in his hand. No...not *in* his hand, but taped to his hand and wrist.

Stan stepped on the man's wrist once he landed on the floor and slammed the pipe down on his hand. The man howled like an animal, but Stan continued driving the pipe into the man's hand until he was able to work the knife out of the taped contraption on the man's wrist. He finally worked the knife loose as bits of bloody tape and flesh drifted away. Stan kicked at the floating knife, and it sailed across the room, barely a foot above the floor.

The man was glaring up at him, still squirming. Stan jammed the pipe into his throat. *"Who the fuck are you, and where's the other guy in the space suit?"*

The man only rolled his eyes. Despite all of the reddish black goo all over his body, the whites of his eyes seemed too white. The hair *"growing"* from his body wasn't all his own hair, Stan was able to clearly see. From the looks of it, he had sown or pinned the hair to his body, oddly resembling some hairy animal with mange. Each patch of hair flowed dreamily from the scalp attached to him. There were probably eight, maybe nine scalps attached to him. Dried and caked black blood crusted his body from head to foot.

Stan could feel this morning's meager breakfast lurch in his stomach. He forced it down and thought of something else. The thought of taking off his helmet to vomit in this tomb turned his stomach even more. He could only guess what the smell was like.

"Stan," Tess said, "you've got less than ten minutes. You've got to hurry. Forget who he is and let's—"

"I am Rey, and I am in charge!" he first giggled and then laughed. "You want to take my woman too?" he asked, almost innocently. Stan felt his skin crawl.

Tess, hearing Rey announce himself, felt a surge of anger and revulsion ripple through her. *"Stan, don't trust him! He's one of Soren's inner men."*

Stan stared down at the man who was clearly crazy. He had a feeling that the man surprised Chayton and maybe stabbed him. He didn't know this for sure, but he *did* know that he had to get to the cockpit to blow the Cargo Cabin releases. And that meant taking care of this crazy fuck.

Stan forced Rey to stand up. Yes, he knew this man, if not by face, then by reputation. Tess had told him that he was her lover. She told him how he had manipulated her and the others before they abandoned them. Yes...he knew this man and was using every ounce of his willpower not to smash the pipe into the back of his filthy, matted skull.

As he looked at Rey, he noticed that he was not as gaunt as the others in the cargo bay area. In fact, this man actually had a paunch. At first Stan thought that maybe they had all the food in the forward sections, but he remembered that Doctor Stone said they had all the food in the cargo section of the ship. Now standing here looking at all the blood, it wasn't hard for him to make the connection on what had happened here. Here, it was survival, and this man was the last survivor.

Stan glanced at his watch. He had about five minutes left. He looked up at Rey and saw that the man had turned toward him, just that quickly. On reflex, Stan rammed the pipe into his grinning, bloody face. Rey's body moved back with each blow and Stan followed, each time smashing the pipe into his face until he had pushed Rey up against the wall.

Blood spurted from Rey's busted nose and drifted off in a hundred different directions. Out of the corner of Stan's eyes, he saw a flash of silver as a small knife fell from Rey's other hand. Somehow, he had gotten another knife from somewhere, or he had it concealed on his goo-crusted body.

Stan continued ramming the pipe into his face. At one point, the pipe end jabbed him in the eye and stuck there for just a second. Repulsed, Stan tried to yank it out of Rey's face, but it didn't come out. He started to brace himself to pull it out, but Rey reached out and snatched at his air hose, attempting to pull it out. Stan reversed his direction and pushed with all his weight. Rey screamed and grabbed at the pipe, but Stan's magnetic boots made him unmovable as he leaned all of his weight into the pipe. He felt the pipe break through the last resistance of bone and sink deeply into Rey's brain.

Rey gyrated and trembled wildly for a minute, and then his arms dropped limply to his side. Stan pushed him to the floor and yanked the pipe out of his eye, using his foot to hold Rey's body down. More blood squirted out of Rey's face as Stan pulled the pipe out.

It slowly dawned on him that he was hearing other voices. Tess, Joe, and Henry were all talking at once. Tess's voice broke through, *"Stan! Stan! What's happening! Speak to me!"*

"I'm here," he said, his voice a little shaky and hoarse. "I had a small problem with Rey, but he won't bother anyone anymore." He looked at Rey's body hovering slightly above the floor. Urine started seeping out of him, like some poisonous yellow mist. "I'm headed to the cockpit now. I still haven't found Chayton."

"Thank God you're alright!" she cried, *"but you're out of time Stan. You need to get out of there now!"*

He looked at the digital readout in the bottom right corner of his helmet. *It was in the red at just over three minutes!*

Whether he or Chayton got out was secondary, he knew that now. Tess and the others would need every advantage possible to survive on *Europa*, which meant that they would absolutely need the Cargo Cabin. He would release those hatches first, and then try to find Chayton (if he wasn't dead, that was), and then he would try to make it back.

He continued on down the corridor towards the cockpit. Since no one had come to Rey's rescue, he assumed that there was no one else, so he moved quickly, but not recklessly. He just didn't want to take that chance.

He walked into the cockpit. The high-backed pilot and co-pilot seats were facing towards the front. He looked out and all he could see was the huge stormy planet of Jupiter, seeming to draw them ever closer. He looked at his watch. He was almost to the two-minute warning. He turned towards the cargo release panel near the Navigator's console.

"Tess, I'm here! Prepare for Cabin release!" he yelled into his mike. "Hit the release and get the hell out, *please!*"

He lifted up the clear protective panel and pressed the release button. For a second, he didn't think anything had happened, but he felt a slight vibration coming from deep within the ship.

"We're loose! We have full control of the Cabin Stan, now get out, NOW!"

"Alright, I'm coming, but don't wait Tess. If you get pulled into Jupiter's gravity well, then you won't have enough fuel to land on *Europa*. You cut those tethers loose if you have to. Promise me you won't wait."

"Just get a move on Stan! *Go!*"

He headed towards the corridor, but he heard noises coming from one of the seats. He turned around, thinking Chayton had somehow been tied to the seat and walked around to the front of the pilot's seat. He spun it so that it faced him and almost fell back in horror. In the pilot's seat was a fat man, grotesquely disfigured. His face bled from scores of wounds. He was naked also, and his chest had been scraped and clawed at. But it wasn't the man's face or his chest that bothered Stan. Nor was it the wildly blinking, knowing eyes in the man's face that bothered him. The man's limbs had been removed and four bloody tourniquets were tied so tightly around the ends that they were lost in the meat of his arms and legs. Blood crusted around the man's mouth where he had presumably chewed off his tongue.

Stan stared at the man. "*Soren*," he said and the man's eyes opened wider at the sound of his name. "You deserved this Soren for what you did. And just so you know, Tess, my wife, and the others that you abandoned on the moon are in the *Orion* right now. *She'll* live. The *others* will live. And so will *you*, Soren. You'll live on this ship until it crashes into Jupiter."

Soren blinked his eyes wildly and thrashed helplessly in the seat. Stan turned the seat back towards the planet and headed out of the cockpit. As he started down the corridor, he noticed a dim light coming from the two cockpit latrines. He hadn't noticed it when he first came through from the passenger area.

He lifted his pipe up, ready to smash it into someone's face if necessary and pressed the door button; an avalanche of bloody bones and skulls tumbled out. Stan yelled and flailed at the body parts floating out of the latrine. Bones, arms, legs, and heads floated by with strips of rotted skin and flesh drifting behind them. He slammed his fist down on the red button to close the door, before more could drift out.

He almost decided not to open the other latrine door but made himself anyway. He lifted his pipe again and pressed the button. He prepared himself to jump back, but when the door opened, he saw Chayton, slumped over the seat of the toilet. There was a huge blood stain on the side of his suit. He lifted Chayton's helmeted head up. His face was pale. He was about to take his gloves off to check Chayton's pulse, when Chayton's eyes opened and then slowly closed. It was brief, but it was enough for Stan. "*I found Chayton! We are leaving!*"

Even as he said this, he noticed a perceptible change in the ship's speed and orientation. It had been drifting along with no real speed that he could discern, but now, he felt that it was actually accelerating. "Stan, the *Cassiopeia* is caught in Jupiter's gravity well!" Tess yelled into his ear. "We've disconnected already, but the *Cassiopeia* is starting to pick up speed. The tethers have snapped off and in about three minutes, you'll be out of our range."

"Out of range for what?" Stan puffed into his mike. He was pulling Chayton by one of the straps on his suit. It wasn't too difficult to pull him because of the zero gravity, but it was difficult maneuvering around the seats and through the corridors without Chayton actually helping.

"Stan, you won't be able to use your jet packs to fly to us now because where you are, Jupiter's pull is too strong. But if you could make it out the top portal in time, you might be able to blow your tanks. First Chayton's and then yours. This might give you enough initial speed to make it to us. It's your only option."

"Alright," he said, "I'm on it!" He stopped only once and that was to initiate Chayton's self-sealing mechanism inside his suit. He couldn't help him with the knife wound, but at least he would be able to bring him out into space safely.

They had arrived at the passenger hatch portal, and he used his buddy hook to connect himself to Chayton's limp body. He got himself in the portal and started pulling Chayton up through it. For one frightening moment, Chayton's foot hooked onto the ladder rung. Stan almost panicked, but slowly lowered Chayton's body and then pulled him up again. This time, his body slid up smoothly.

6

Earlier, when he was standing on the hull of the ship, he had no sensation of movement. Now, Stan could feel the ship slowly accelerating. He knew it was his imagination generating this movement, but he swore he could sense Jupiter getting larger and larger.

He kept his magnetic boots turned to high to compensate for Chayton's boots being off. He could see the *Orion* drifting nearby. It looked impossibly far away. He faced towards Chayton and clamped his front clamp to Chayton's front clamp. He didn't think he would have the time to blow the tanks separately, so he planned to do them at the same time. With them facing one another, he should be able to force their direction in a relatively straight line towards the ship.

"Alright Tess, I see the tethers drifting from the bottom of the *Orion*...and I see you've released the others as well." He tried to sound light hearted, but his voice trembled slightly.

"Yeah," Tess answered, "I know how your sense of direction is." After a pause she said, "Just make sure you grab at least one of them."

Stan aimed his body and Chayton's body towards the five tethers drifting from the bottom of the *Orion* and then turned off his magnetic boots. As their bodies drifted from the top of the ship, the feeling of movement was more apparent than ever as the *Cassiopeia* slowly slid beneath them; its much heavier mass causing it to move more quickly towards Jupiter than Stan and Chayton. Stan wasn't fooled though; their bodies were headed in the same direction.

He craned his neck up and saw the stiffly drifting tethers and pressed the fuel jettison buttons for both jet packs at the same time. Stan could feel his body violently pushed as the explosive decompression of the tanks propelled him and Chayton towards the shuttle and the drifting tethers. Their initial velocity would be enough to push them towards the *Orion*, but Jupiter's gravity would eat up that speed until eventually they would be pulled back into her hold.

Stan glared at the drifting tethers. He knew that their speed was diminishing with every second, but he was powerless to do anything. As they moved slowly towards the last two tethers, Stan reached his hands above his head, fingers outstretched. He only had one chance to grab one of the tethers. They were getting closer, but their speed was dropping quickly.

He could see the closest tether very clearly now. Could see the fine materials that made up the strong braid of the tether, but as they got closer to it, he could also see that it was out of his reach, by mere *inches*. He strained towards it like a dying man straining for his last breath. He couldn't reach it. He saw it drift past his outstretched fingers, almost mockingly.

"*No!*" He yelled. Knowing it would do no good, he stretched out as far as he could go. He thought he felt something in his shoulder tear, but he couldn't reach it. He was about to make one more futile herculean attempt to reach the tether when Chayton's arm shot out and grabbed at it. Miraculously, it hit his open palm and he closed his hand around it. He looked at Chayton unbelievingly. His eyes were barely opened, and he smiled. Stan reached up and grabbed the tether right before Chayton passed out again and his fingers relaxed and floated limply above his head.

Stan used both hands to connect the tether to his suit. When he had it connected, he yelled into his mike, "Tess! Pull us in! We're hooked on!" Almost immediately, he could feel the slight tug of the tether pulling them up into the well of the undercarriage portal entrance. Just before they were pulled into the shuttle, he caught sight of the *Cassiopeia* moving steadily towards Jupiter. It was very small now.

VI
EUROPA
FEBRUARY 2054

1

Henry stood up in front of the group. He smiled at everyone, but he shifted from foot to foot and looked around at the group nervously. "As most of you already know, we released the Cargo Cabin this morning based on the last set of coordinates that we received from the *Pegasus1* satellite before Jupiter's gravity asserted its pull on it. My best guess is that the orbital controls of the satellite failed just enough for Jupiter to disrupt its delicate *Jupiter-Europa* orbit. It'll probably crash into Jupiter later this evening."

"Did we get the information we needed for landing?" someone at the back of the room asked.

Tess walked up next to Henry, "Yes and no," she said. "We were able to identify a large landmass on the planet and that was where we sent the Cargo Cabin, but we couldn't verify that this was the best area to land. We could tell that there were several large bodies of water nearby, but that was about it.

"The Cabin's current location is on a heading due west of us, about 1500 miles away. We won't know until we're within a few hundred miles, what kind of area this is. Right now, we're flying over a part of the planet where there's a huge snowstorm, and the cloud cover completely blocks our efforts at visual confirmation of ground conditions."

Dr. Stone was standing near the front of the group and asked quietly, "What does that mean Tess? That we might land in an area similar to Siberia?"

"Anything's possible Doc, but I'm just not sure. We can't read anything through this thick storm cover. We're still reading the Cargo Cabin's signal, which is a good sign, but we won't know for sure what the terrain looks like there until we have some visual confirmation." She looked around at the group and then added, "And now that we've reduced our speed, and are moving in an extremely low orbit, we're burning fuel that much faster. We won't be able to make another orbit of the planet."

2

Everyone was glued to windows, trying to get a close-up view of the new planet. Even though the storm had stopped and the cloud cover gradually cleared up, the landscape was still bleak. As far as they could see, ice and snow blanketed the ground. Off in the distance, they could see majestic ice-covered mountain peaks.

Kyra was sitting next to Thelma staring out the large window when her stomach dropped. The ship had been flying over a huge mountain range of snow and ice when all of a sudden, the ground dropped several thousand feet. Kyra stared in awe at the immense chasm. "This is incredible," whispered Thelma. "This makes the Grand Canyon look like a baby."

Kyra looked over at Thelma. "You're right about that, but God I hope we don't have to live in this. We're getting close to the Cargo Cabin, and the terrain is still..." Before she could finish her sentence, she noticed a break in the scenery. Patches of dark were cropping up in the white landscape. She was about to share this with Thelma, when Tess's voice came over the intercom.

"I've got great news everyone! If you're looking out the windows, you probably can see that the landscape is starting to change. Stan, Henry, and I have the added benefit of being able to see what's coming up. Keep watching outside, you won't be disappointed!"

As the ship moved over the land, Thelma and Kyra and just about everyone on the ship could see the terrain slowly giving way to first rock outcroppings, then large patches of dirty ground. Soon, they were able to see sporadic trees that looked very similar to pine trees. Within minutes, they were soaring over large fields of grass and trees.

They passed over several small bodies of water and then a much larger one that snaked many miles to the south of them. After ten minutes of flying, all signs of snow and ice had disappeared. They passed several waterfalls of very blue water and a forest of trees whose fiery reds and blinding yellows seemed almost surreal.

Thelma could feel the ship decelerating and began to get nervous. She had been specifically looking for animals, any kind of animal, but there were none to be seen. She rationalized that they could be hiding from the noise of the huge ship's engines, but that didn't console her. She was beginning to have doubts about the atmosphere.

The question of atmosphere had come up before, and they were told that it was similar to Earth's; however, they were never able to confirm its chemical makeup. Unfortunately, Thelma knew, as did most of them, that it didn't matter at this point. They had no other place to go. This was home, and their fate was in God's hands now.

3

The ship sailed over another body of bright blue water, before slowly circling a wide area. Everyone stared out of their portal windows, eager to catch a close-up glimpse of their new home. Although no one consciously thought about it, they all knew that this could be their death sentence. Like Thelma, they knew that the air could be as poisonous to them as breathing in methane gas, yet they were excited and had hope in their hearts. They all wanted to believe that they did not make it through a living hell just to die millions of miles away.

Holding Len's hand tightly, Bonnie had her face plastered to the portal window. *"Look!"* she cried out. *"I see an animal!"* Everyone on her side strained to see what she was looking at, but all they could see were thick groups of trees slightly swaying in the breeze. A frown crossed her pretty face, but she kept her eyes glued to the window.

Joe was seated on the other side of the ship, looking out. He could see the flashing beacon of the Cabin on his side. He thought how lucky they were that the Cabin didn't drop into the water, but Tess had assured them that it was built to remain afloat for weeks, if not months, just for that eventuality.

Doctor Stone was sitting across from him and asked him if he was okay. He smiled and said, "Never better Doc. Never better."

In the cockpit, Tess, Stan, and Henry looked out at their new home. "I'm sure Chayton is going to be pretty upset that he missed this view," said Tess, smiling. "This is probably the last time any of us will ever have a bird's eye view like this again." She thought for a moment and then added, "At least for a long, long time."

Stan grabbed her hand and kissed it. "Hey, there's our landing up ahead. You ready for this?"

"Yep, let's do it," she replied smiling.

4

Many of the adults sat white-knuckled as the ship came to a halt on the grassy field, while the children screamed giddily. Tess, Stan and Henry came out of the cockpit and headed back towards the passenger area. Stan looked at Tess and then at Henry, "Okay guys, let's go check it out!" he said excitedly.

Everyone unbuckled and followed Tess and the others to the rear cargo bay area. Most of the adults looked nervous, but Tess could still see a hint of excitement, lurking just underneath the nervous stares. She smiled (despite her own nervousness) and said calmly, "Okay folks, here we go," and pressed the ramp button.

As soon as the ramp opened, she could feel warm air rushing in. Instinctively, she held her breath, but slowly released it and took a deep breath. Stan walked beside her, holding her hand. Len and Bonnie scooted past them with Buddy right on their heels. Yoi and Marla walked hand in hand down the ramp as dozens of kids ran past them. Stan looked at Tess and laughed and ran down the ramp behind the kids. They all ran out onto the grassy yellow field out from under the huge wings of the *Orion*.

Tess looked behind her and could see the rest of them pouring out of the shuttle; some more eager than others. They were all smiling though. She waved at Chayton as he was being helped down. Hana was on one side and Steve was on the other. Curt Dixon tapped Nathan on the shoulder, "Do you think this would be a good spot for our new outdoor fitness center?" Donovan smacked the back of Curt's head good-naturedly as Nathan and Angela laughed. Some of the children giggled as they ran past Sheila and Bob kissing at the bottom of the ramp.

Julie walked carefully down the ramp holding her new baby girl. John Baxter and his daughter walked beside her, his hand around her waist to keep her steady. Tess was looking up at her smiling as her own hand made its way to her lower stomach.

As everyone made their way down the ramp, she looked over and saw Henry, Kyra and Joe talking excitedly as they examined the waist-high yellow grass. She was starting to wonder if this field was grass or maybe some type of grain.

She turned towards Stan and saw that he was staring at her. She smiled back and hugged him tightly. He put his lips up against her ear and whispered, "How are you feeling?"

She stepped back and looked at him. "I'm feeling much better. Last night was the first time I slept without dreaming about how lucky we were to make it here. So many times, we could have been lost. So many times, we skirted impossible situations. I lost you and Len and then I found you, only to almost lose you again." Her eyes filled with tears, and her voice began to crack.

Stan hugged her for a minute and then disengaged himself gently. "We're here now and that's what counts. We're all that's left of Earth, and we need to live for all the good people who died. We need to make this new world a better place than the one we left. Better for everyone; our friends, our son, and that new baby of ours." He rubbed her stomach gently.

Tess looked into Stan's earnest face and felt a tear course down her cheek. She moved in close to him and pressed her cheek up against his chest. As she stood there, feeling the beat of his heart, her eyes looked out at the huge snow-capped mountains in the distance. A warm breeze blew in and warmed her skin as they stood there beneath the huge Jupiter-dominated sky.

THE END

Made in the USA
Monee, IL
29 September 2024